Books by Robert L Skidmore

The Satterfield Saga
If Genes Could Talk
Yankee Doodles in Black Hats
Green Eyes, Red Skies, Pale Ales, White Sails
Point of Rocks
The Drums, the Fog, the Terrible Shadows of War
The Sorry World
Did You Lose Your Elephant
The Ballbreaker

The Inspector Richard Thatcher Series
The City of Lost Dreams
Cluster of Spies
The Hollow Men of Capitol Hill
The Distracting Splat at the Eiffel

The Conor Gifford Series
The Day the Mountain Cried
Circles within Circles
Keep a Happy Ghost, or None
The Gods Are Talking
The Jealous Mistress with a Hubris Problem
The Accidental President

Other
The Silicon Wizard
Which Way from Here? (Editor)

The Accidental President

Robert L Skidmore

iUniverse, Inc.
New York Bloomington

iUniverse books may be ordered through booksellers or by contacting:

iUniverse
1663 Liberty Drive
Bloomington, IN 47403
www.iuniverse.com
1-800-Authors (1-800-288-4677)

ISBN: 978-1-4401-8963-0 (sc)
ISBN: 978-1-4401-8961-6 (hc)
ISBN: 978-1-4401-8962-3 (ebook)

Printed in the United States of America

iUniverse rev. date: 12/07/2009

"For Ms. Margaret as always and for George and Eileen, friends from the murky past who are responsible for the old house on the cover."

Chapter 1

Harrison Standish Tate, the President of the United States of America, sprawled on one of the two slightly faded beige sofas that flanked his grandiose desk and stared at the ceiling of the Oval Office with unseeing eyes. Completely oblivious to the luxurious trappings of the nation's power center, his mind was focused inwardly. After two years in office, he was no longer intimidated by his surroundings. Not only was he unimpressed with what he had accomplished in rising to this pinnacle of power, he regretted the fact that fate had contrived to lift him so high. Indeed, he considered himself a coincidental president. He now believed that the two decades he had spent as Sheriff of Loudoun County Virginia were the happiest and most rewarding of his life. If he had known then what he knew now, he would have resisted the seductive call of political ambition and not have pursued the offices that formed his staircase to the presidency.

"Mr. President, the cabinet is assembled and waiting for you," Grace Hanson called to him from the doorway. Grace, his loyal secretary, had accompanied him on his fateful journey from sheriff to chairman of the Loudoun County Board of Supervisors to lieutenant governor to governor of Virginia.

The interruption brought Tate back to the present. He turned. "Thank you, Grace. I'll be along shortly."

Grace nodded obediently but made no effort to hide the concern etched on her face.

"Their lordships will benefit from spending a few congenial minutes with their peers," Tate called after her as she closed the door softly behind her.

Tate briefly considered the members of his cabinet, not one of whom did he consider a trusted friend or ally. He had appointed them to their current exalted positions, and each had been selected out of political expediency. Several had been competitors for the office that Tate now held, and not one of the rivals considered him qualified for the office. Tate did not disagree with them on this point, at least. Tate had served as governor of Virginia for four years, a job with a one-term limit, and he had been considering a dubious run for the senate when a deadlocked convention had turned to him as a compromise candidate, a man from a no longer influential state. A full two centuries had passed since Virginia had earned its reputation as the birthplace of presidents.

The convention had viewed Tate as a man with a limited electoral track record and no known political vices, an appraisal that amused Tate, particularly the emphasis on no known. The delegates had selected him because they considered him unflawed, something that could not be said about the other candidates. Standing a mere five foot six inches high and weighing less than a hundred and forty-five pounds, Tate, the genial son of an old and distinguished Virginia family, did not threaten anyone. At most, he had a diminutive presence.

"I should fire the whole damned bunch of them," Tate declared as he rose from the couch.

In his opinion, the individual members of the cabinet had so compromised themselves and their principles to reach their current positions that they were all empty shells. To a man, they were now devoted to one thing, attaining the office that Tate now held. Self-interest constituted their only motivating force. He despised all politicians, including himself.

As he exited through Grace Hanson's office, he paused. "I really don't want to do this."

Grace smiled encouragement to her boss who she worshipped.

"Is the pompous asshole in there?" Tate asked, using the language of the streets that he had acquired as sheriff. Tate referred to Alexander Hamilton Sperry, his secretary of the treasury.

"Waiting for his fifteen minutes of glory," Grace, who knew firsthand how cops talked, recognized that Tate was just venting.

"It might come sooner than he thinks," Tate grumbled.

Grace laughed. "I think you need some time off."

"Me too," Tate agreed, surprising Grace. "Cancel everything on my schedule for this afternoon."

"Do you want me to alert the Secret Service?"

"That's the last thing I want. They would ruin everything."

"Yes sir," Grace called after Tate as he started for the door where he paused again.

"Find out where Gif is." Tate referred to Colin Gifford, an old friend currently working as chief of the Office of Special Investigations of the Virginia State Police.

"Should I give him a heads up?"

"Of course not," Tate laughed. "We don't want him to go into hiding. Just find out where he is without letting him know that we are looking for him."

"Good morning, Mr. President," the Secret Service agent standing watch outside the door to the Cabinet Room greeted Tate.

"Good morning, Charles," Tate responded amiably.

He waited for the agent to open the door and then entered to confront a room of chattering, self-important men and women, all sitting around the highly polished elliptical mahogany table. At Tate's direction, this meeting included only the fifteen secretaries plus the vice president and Tate's chief of staff. The usual assortment of aides, assistants, and note takers had been excluded. This promised to be an acrimonious meeting, and Tate anticipated that the principals would prove to be more than adept in leaking details to the media in a self-serving and self-promoting manner, thus rendering the spear-carriers superfluous.

"Good morning, ladies and gentlemen," Tate smiled as he made his way to his chair in the center of the table where he sat facing John F. Walker, the vice president.

Following precedent, Tate had personally chosen John F. Walker for the job. Walker had been the junior senator from Alabama, a position he had held for only two years when selected to compete as Tate's running mate. A John Edwards lookalike, Walker's public persona was everything that the diminutive Tate privately envied. Assuming that the voters would share that feeling, Tate made the same mistake that the first George Bush made when selecting Dan Quayle. Tate's enemies reacted just as Bush's had. They recognized a political threat when they saw one and focused on Walker as a primary target, hoping to destroy the man before he had the chance to realize his potential.

"Good morning, Mr. Vice President," Tate smiled at Walker as he lowered himself into the presidential chair.

Tate hated the damned chair. An engraved brass plate saying "The President," reserved it for Tate. The grandness of it all did not bother Tate; it was the high back that did. A small man, Tate was sensitive to the fact that the chair was simply too big for him. He suspected that the others felt that he was too small to be president and that they privately ridiculed him for how he looked out of place when he sat in the ostentatious thing.

"Good morning, Mr. President," Walker smiled back. Walker had country club manners and always paid Tate the courtesy his position demanded, unlike some of the others who spoke quite critically when out of his presence. All too often, the words reached Tate.

Tate took a deep breath and deliberately frowned at each member of his cabinet before speaking, letting them in turn know that he was unhappy. Finally, he spoke: "We all know why we are here. However, just to be sure we understand each other, I will set the ground rules. Nothing we say here today will be repeated outside this room. I understand this impinges on your constitutional right to leak to the media, but nonetheless I want all present free to speak frankly today without fear of retribution."

Tate paused to give any who dared the opportunity to register an objection. None did.

Tate continued: "No decisions will be made at this meeting. I want information and views. I will consider what you have to say and will subsequently and privately consult with those of you who will be involved in the implementation of my decisions. I am confident that I will surprise no one when I say our nation is facing an economic crisis of catastrophic proportions. Nothing is to be gained by rushing to the media and fanning the flames of economic fear in our citizens by discussing what is said here today in confidence. Our country will be best served by us if we mitigate the panic by producing a unified and reasonable national response that contains at least some hope of containing the economic forces now working against us. Finger pointing at each other or blaming constituent elements of our society will not be helpful. Does everyone here understand what I am saying?"

"Of course, sir," Vice President Walker responded eagerly.

Tate nodded acknowledgement but again coolly surveyed the participants one by one. He established eye contact with each of the principals who were seated in order of precedence beginning with the secretaries of state and defense who sat on his immediate right and left. Each replied curtly using identical words: "Yes, Mr. President." Then, Tate glared at the primary target of his enmity, the secretary of the treasury who sat across the table from him on the right of the vice president.

Alexander Hamilton Sperry reacted with a predictable, arrogant nod. Sperry was the former governor of the state of New York, former mayor of New York City, and former CEO and chairman of the board of the Harbor Trust Company that had been founded by his great grandfather. Sperry, whose parents had presciently named him after the country's first secretary of the treasury, Alexander Hamilton, did not conceal his resentment of the fact that Tate sat in the chair he believed rightfully belonged to him and would one day in the not so distant future.

Tate ignored the condescending Sperry's rude silence and continued his survey. Before this meeting was over, Tate knew he and Sperry would clash and that Sperry would inevitably lose. Their respective positions made this inevitable. After encountering no spoken objections, Tate smiled wryly. "Very well gentlemen and ladies, let us begin."

Tate paused to see if one of them would dare to preempt his privilege of speaking first. Not one made a sound until the dour secretary of the treasury cleared his throat.

"I..."Sperry began.

"Very well, let me handle the introduction," Tate said, pretending he had not interrupted Sperry before he could begin his pompous, self-serving harangue.

Several of the silent participants smiled.

"I'm no economist," Tate declared. "That admission should not come as a surprise to anyone present," Tate smiled to indicate he was making a small joke. "But I have ears and eyes that I use to hear what is being said and see what is written on the papers that I am handed. The consensus seems to be that our current recession has its roots deep in the housing market and can be traced to something called derivatives."

Those words obviously caused the secretary of treasury considerable discomfort because he shifted abruptly in his chair and sat up straight preparing to defend himself. Although now an aspirant politician, Sperry's background stretched deep into the nation's banking community.

"Over the past ten years taking advantage of relaxed oversight, many if not most of our profit seeking bankers granted loans and lines of credit to virtually anyone desiring to purchase a house, a business or whatever. Their only requirement seemed to have been that the borrower was breathing. Few if any questions were asked about income or whether the applicant even had a job."

"Mr. President," Sperry interrupted, unable to restrain himself.

"Yes, Mr. Secretary," Tate responded coldly.

"I must protest that you are greatly over-simplifying the situation," Sperry said.

"I'm not surprised that you feel that way, Mr. Secretary," Tate smiled thinly. "I'm almost finished. Please kindly restrain yourself for a few more minutes."

Sperry's frown conveyed his irritation, but he did not speak.

"I'll take your silence as acquiescence," Tate said. "Whether the economists are correct in their conclusions or not, I can't say with certainty. The breed does not speak with one voice. In any case, some of our more objective analysts accept the derivative finger pointing. One thing is clear to me. Our financial markets are in a state of crisis. This country operates on credit, and very little is now available. It is up to us to do something about that situation. The question I want to focus on today is this. What are we going to do about it?"

Tate abruptly addressed a cherry faced Sperry. "Mr. Secretary, would you please share your informed views with us today."

Inspector Conor Gifford, Chief of the Office of Special Investigations, a small unit that previously reported to the governor of the Commonwealth of Virginia but now operated under the authority of Colonel Harris Townsend, Commander of the Virginia State Police, turned abruptly and glared at his ringing cell phone.

"Shit," Gifford complained.

Although based in Richmond, Gifford was halfway through the second day of a planned two weeks of leave that he was determined to devote exclusively to cleaning and repairing his old settlers home located on the eastern slopes of the Blue Ridge Mountains in western Loudoun County. Gifford had acquired the retreat, an expanded log cabin, during his previous service with the Loudoun County Sheriff's Department. Following ten years of training and service with the Federal Bureau of Investigation, Gifford, dissatisfied with the federal agency's extensive bureaucracy, had joined Harrison Tate's Loudoun Sheriff's Department. After Tate had graduated into a political career, Gifford had replaced him as sheriff. Gifford's one and only campaign for sheriff, an elective office, taught him that politics were not for him. After extensive soul searching, he had moved to Richmond to take over the Office of Special Investigations where he had latitude to handle the sensitive and challenging cases that the governor placed on his desk.

Gifford thought about ignoring the cell phone. Only Colonel Townsend and OSI knew the number, and the landline in Gif's mountain refuge was disconnected. In the past, he had impulsively ignored such summons and had lived to regret his actions. He surrendered, but not graciously.

"What?" Gifford demanded.

"Inspector Gifford?" A cordial female voice asked.

"Unfortunately."

"This is the White House, sir. Please standby."

"For how long?" Gif asked, irritably.

"Gif," Grace Hanson, President Harrison Tate's long time secretary came on line.

"Grace," Gif responded. "Tell your boss or anyone else who might be interested in that asylum where you work that I am not available."

"Are you enjoying your vacation?" Grace, accustomed to Gifford's feigned surliness from their days together in Loudoun County and Richmond, laughed.

"It's a working vacation," Gif persisted. He genuinely liked Grace and Harrison, and he owed them both much, but he was tired of fending off Tate's insistence that Gif come to work for the White House.

"Do you have time for a simple cup of coffee?" Before Gif could answer, Grace continued: "Just heat the pot. Your friend will be there sometime around two, probably. Don't tell him I warned you. He wants the visit to be a surprise."

"Tell him I won't be here," Gif spoke into the empty phone. Grace had hung up on him.

After Alexander Hamilton Sperry, the secretary of the treasury, bored the assembled group with his now familiar list of recommendations–this was the third time he had given the same harangue—President Tate offered the others a final opportunity to agree and/or disagree. First to speak after Sperry was Secretary of State Harriet Pope, another political rival who had served in the Senate for one term before launching her almost successful presidential campaign. A former college professor, Pope tended to talk down to her audiences, lecturing rather than discussing. Tate personally found her rather shallow but tended to defer to her views on foreign affairs, a subject in which he had little interest beyond the level of national security. When it came to discussing the subject of the failing economy, Pope seldom got past the point of admonishing the president and her peers that no decisions could be taken in a vacuum. "Our economic problems today are global issues," she always declared smacking the table with the flat of her hand to emphasize the seriousness of her point.

After Sperry and Pope had performed, the others made their less than significant contributions until finally Tate, having exhausted his waning patience, abruptly ended the meeting.

"Thank you everybody. I will take your views under advisement and get back to you."

Sperry, who had chafed under the barrage of counterviews offered by his peers, flushed, angered at the abrupt way Tate had terminated the meeting before Sperry could challenge those who had questioned his vital recommendations.

"Mr. President, if I may?" Sperry blurted.

"Thank you, Mr. Secretary. I will be in touch," Tate dismissed the appeal as he rose to his feet. He glanced at the vice president. "John, if you could join me in my office for a few minutes," Tate invited, closing the door to any attempt by Sperry to follow him into the Oval Office for a follow-up harangue.

"Yes sir," Walker said as he rushed to follow the departing president from the room.

Tate winked at Grace as he passed her desk with the vice president in tow. Grace greeted him with a raised thumb to indicate she had contacted Gif.

"He's in Loudoun," Graced called to the presidential backside.

"I'll need a few minutes in private with the vice president," Tate said.

He paused at the door, noted that Sperry was trailing a few feet behind, allowed Walker to enter and shut the door before the secretary of the treasury could push his way into the inner sanctum.

The Secret Service agent who guarded access to the Oval Office accurately read the president's gesture and stepped in front of the door. "Good afternoon Mr. Secretary," he smiled at the pursuing dignitary.

Sperry hesitated as he considered pushing his way into the Oval Office. The sheer bulk and casual determination of the agent led him to decide otherwise, and Sperry withdrew.

Grace waited until the outer door closed behind Sperry before smiling sweetly at the Secret Service Agent.

"Thank you Jerry."

"My pleasure," Grace," the bemused agent smiled back.

The secretary of the treasury was not the most popular cabinet member among the White House staff.

Back in his office sanctuary, Tate sat down on a couch and waved a hand to indicate that Walker should seat himself opposite.

"God, I hate these interminable cabinet meetings."

"Sperry is a genuine asshole," the vice president laughed.

"I won't argue with that," Tate said. "What did you think of his presentation?"

"Like you, sir, I'm no economist," Walker shrugged. "Despite his pomposity he makes more sense than some of the others."

"We've got a real problem, John. Do you think his proposals will work?"

"Do you, sir?"

Tate sighed, again frustrated by the ambiance that surrounded him. It was impossible to get a straight answer to a simple question; the Oval Office intimidated every visitor, even his vice president.

"I guess we're going to have to give them a try. No one else seems to have a better idea. Do you by chance have any pressing plans for later today?"

"Nothing I can't break."

"Good," Tate ignored the slight ambiguity in his vice president's response. "I think I'll take the afternoon off, get away for a while, and do some private musing."

"Good for you, sir."

"I don't expect anything to come up, but one of us should be available to answer the phone in case the country starts to sink."

"If I have to call you…"

"Grace will be able to handle it," Tate equivocated, determined to make sure that he really had some much needed down time."

After Walker departed, Harrison spent a few seconds pondering the possibility, not for the first time, whether he had made a major mistake in selecting the eager, young man as his vice president and potential successor. Before he could reach the obvious conclusion that he really wanted to avoid, the door opened and Grace joined him.

"Gif is at his place in Loudoun. I spoke briefly with him," Grace admitted, pausing to give Harrison the opportunity to complain. When he did not, she continued. "He claims to be on a working vacation," she smiled.

Harrison chuckled.

"I told him to heat the coffee. I hope you don't mind, but I wanted to be sure he was available. He can be perverse."

"As usual, Grace, you handled it just right. If there is nothing pressing, I'll sneak out now."

"Sure you don't want me to alert the Secret Service?"

"No, we have to surprise them. Otherwise, they'll have time to come up with a dozen bureaucratic reasons why I can't do what I want to do."

"They're just doing their job."

"And I'm just doing mine," Harrison said.

Grace retreated. "Aren't we all? Where will you be?"

"I'll stop by and chat with Gif, and then I'm goin' fishin', as the locals say."

"On the river?"

Grace referred to the Potomac River west of Point of Rocks where Tate still owned the acreage that his great, great, great grandfather had first settled. Once a prosperous farm that supplied milk and produce to generations of D.C. families, the land had laid fallow for the better part of the past century. Harrison Tate now used the old farmhouse high on a bluff overlooking the Potomac as a sanctuary and stored his leaky boat in a shed on the river. His occasional fishing outings always gave his protective detail severe heartburn.

"Will you spend the night there?"

"No just a couple of hours on the water, and then I'll join Martha in Leesburg.

Harrison and Martha, like several preceding Tate generations, called the massive Leesburg Victorian home. They had spent all of their married life there in comfortably isolated bliss until Tate's political ambitions had uprooted them, much to Martha's displeasure.

"That will please your Praetorian Guards," Grace laughed.

The Secret Service considered the Tate Victorian a security nightmare because the Tates had vigorously resisted the many security upgrades that the protective detail thought imperative.

"I'll check in later today," Tate said as he rose to his feet. "Don't tell anybody where I am."

"Walker will hold the fort?"

"Our loyal vice president and you. If Walker has to contact me, you handle it without telling him or anybody else how to find me."

"The Secret Service will know," Grace said.

"And I'll fire the lot of them if they don't live up to their name."

All too often, in Tate's opinion, the Secret Service wasn't secret enough.

"You have fun but stay safe. There are a lot of crazies out there."

"You aren't referring to our loyal supporters are you?"

"They voted for you, didn't they? That has to tell you something about their sanity."

"What happens, happens," Tate said softly, acknowledging his fatalistic streak.

Chapter 2

Gif heard the roar of the heavy motors and the crunch of the reinforced tires grinding the gravel of his driveway and went to the front door in time to see the lead car of the small caravan skid to a halt on his lawn. He stepped outside, frowned severely for show, and waited until the rear door of the limousine popped open and the President of the United States stepped out. Tate was dressed most inappropriately, given his high office, in faded blue jeans and sports shirt.

"Hi neighbor," Harrison Tate smiled at Gif's frown. "Was just passing through and decided to pay my respects."

Gif shook his head, feigning irritation. "Coffee or beer?" Gif said as he opened the screen door and held it for his visitor.

The two nearest Secret Service agents shook their heads in disapproval of Gifford's casual treatment of the president. Tate waved a hand to indicate they should deploy outside.

"Budweiser, cold, if you have it," Tate spoke to Gifford's back before taking a seat in his host's preferred recliner in front of the television. "Seen any good games lately?" Tate asked as Gifford returned carrying two frosty bottles.

Gif handed one to his guest, shook his head negatively in response to Harrison's question, and sat down in an older version of the chair Tate now occupied. "Keeping busy?" Gif asked as Harrison took his first sip from the bottle.

"There's always this and that," Harrison replied. "What about you?"

"There's always the occasional murder," Gif replied. "Nothing out of the ordinary."

"Sorry to hear that," Harrison chuckled. "Run of the mill serial killers can get to be tedious," Harrison referred to a recent Norfolk case that had hit the national media and occupied Gif almost full time for three months.

"Like you, I have to take what the public gives me," Gif said. "I note in the media that you are having a bit of a problem with the stock market and unemployment. It seems to have the rich folk worried."

"Thank God that doesn't trouble the likes of you and me," Tate played the understatement game, something he and Gif had made into an art form during their long chats in Tate's old sheriff's office. "The fact that a handful of our major companies have gone belly-up and some of our citizens are having difficulty paying for their mortgages is bothersome."

"Home owners should blame their bankers, not you," Gif said, getting into the swing of the conversation.

"The problem seems to be that some are having difficulty finding their bankers to so inform them."

"Bank failures tend to have that impact," Gif chuckled. "From what I read, the mortgagees are not completely blameless."

"Don't quote me, but I agree with you. There's the little matter of some borrowers overstating their ability to make payments."

"Particularly those taking out million dollar loans without a job to their name."

"But not to worry, Gif," Harrison laughed. "Your federal government is working hard to resolve the problem."

"That's exactly what troubles me," Gif said. "Someone is going to have to come up with the money to pay off all those trillions you are printing and passing out willy-nilly."

"There is that problem," Harrison nodded. "But the national economy is not what I dropped by to discuss with you." Harrison held up his empty Budweiser bottle.

"I was hoping you might not get around to that other little thing," Gif said as he took the bottle and headed towards the kitchen. "After I tell you no way, we can talk about the good old days in the sheriff's office."

"Don't go negative on me, Gif, before you hear what I have to say," Harrison said as Gif handed him a fresh Budweiser.

"Do your minders allow you to imbibe like this during working hours?" Gif asked, nodding towards the front of the house.

"I'm taking the day off," Harrison said seriously. "So, I am free to do what I want."

"I hope you have someone watching the world for you while you are indulging yourself," Gif laughed.

"Don't worry. I left things in good hands. The secretary of the treasury is working on the economy, and the vice president is minding the world."

"I hope so. I've heard rumors to the effect that you and your economic guru are not the best of friends."

"And where did you hear that?"

Gif nodded in the direction of the television set.

"Don't believe everything you see and hear on that little marvel."

"You don't think our polished pundits with the blow-dried hair and pancake makeup understand what they are reading?"

"Gif you are being difficult."

"Me? You ought to hear what I hear about your vice president, the guy you have watching the world for you."

"And that is?"

"That he is an amorous little rascal."

"As I said, don't believe everything you hear. Don't you want to know why I am visiting you today?"

"I assume you are on the way to the Tate shack where you intend to mount a personal campaign designed to intimidate some innocent Potomac fish."

"As a seer, Gif, you're a bust. You're half-right, again. The whole purpose of this trip is to consult with you on the economy, and the fishing expedition is only a cover."

"A cover," Gif laughed. "You've been spending too much time with the spooks from Langley."

"I need your help, Gif," Harrison said.

"Not mine. I hate fishing."

"I'm serious, now. I have a job for you."

'No you don't. You just think you do, Harrison. If you are lonely, hire a court jester."

"I have a serious job, tailor-made for you."

"If I'm not mistaken, we've been through this before, but if you insist I'll refresh your memory."

"So refresh it. I am getting along in years," Tate smiled.

"Some even call you senile," Gif said. "Seriously, Harrison, I refuse to be your political hatchet man no matter what kind of title you hang on me. We had this conversation in Richmond before you appointed me to my current job. My views haven't changed."

Gif referred to his accepting a position as a special investigator concentrating on serial killers and difficult cases. At the time, Tate had been newly installed as governor with a campaign promise to reduce crime in his portfolio, and Gif had insisted that his small office be transferred from the governor's office to a sheltered position under the authority of the commander of the Virginia State Police where he would be free of political pressures, even Tate's.

"I need you in the White House," Tate persisted.

"Harrison, old friend, that would not work for either one of us. You know I've never mastered the art of smiling and chatting while stabbing a colleague in the back."

"Sometimes...."

"Sorry," Gif said. "Can we change the subject?"

Gif was tempted to ask what problem concerned his friend but did not do so, knowing this would open the door for even more pressure.

"I've got many enemies," Tate said.

"That comes with the job," Gif responded bluntly.

"I know," Tate frowned. "Even the greatest job in the world has its downside."

"Are you still enjoying it? Was it worth the effort?"

"The high always comes on the first day. From that point things go downhill."

Gif did not allow his friend to elaborate. "If anyone can handle it, Harrison, you can."

"I hope so."

They sat in silence with each waiting for the other to change the subject. Tate seemed so depressed that Gif, worried about his friend's state of mind, almost capitulated by asking for details. Finally, Tate stood up, shrugged his shoulders, and smiled weakly. "Are you sure you won't join me on the river? I promise I won't pressure you further."

"I'm sorry, Harrison," Gif said, standing up. "I have much to do here and like you have little time to do it. I expect to be summoned back to Richmond at any moment."

Gif's words were not true. He had a full two weeks of leave ahead of him, and he was determined to enjoy it.

"Thanks for the beer and conversation," Tate started for the door. "We'll keep in touch."

Gif silently followed the President of the United States to the door and watched as the palace guard leaped into action.

As soon as the caravan had crunched away, Gif returned inside, shutting the door firmly behind him. He regretted responding so negatively to his friend's appeal, but he knew it would be a major mistake for both Harrison and himself if he took up the offer of a position in the White House.

Gif turned off his cell phone isolating himself from the outside world and returned to his janitorial chores.

As soon as he left the Oval Office, Vice President John F Walker hurried down the corridor to his own office. He hadn't been completely truthful when the president had asked if he had anything pressing on his plate for the afternoon. Walker had replied "Nothing I can't break." Walker had his regularly scheduled discreet rendezvous pending, and he had no intention of calling it off. While the junior Senator from Alabama, Walker had more control over his calendar than he did as vice president. He had, however, with the assistance of Beatrice, his secretary, successfully blocked out three afternoon hours once every two weeks, and he stubbornly allowed nothing to interfere, not even the opportunity to play acting president on those rare occasions like today when Tate would arbitrarily grab some free time of his own. Walker reasoned that the loyal and matronly Beatrice could manage the world in his absence and was reliable enough to know when she should interrupt Walker if circumstances demanded it.

"Beatrice," Walker announced as he entered his office.

"Sir?" His loyal co-conspirator reacted with a smile.

"Our master has decided to take the afternoon off and is leaving us in charge," Walker said.

"How nice," Beatrice said before she remembered that today was her master's sacrosanct afternoon. "But…"

"I know," Walker interrupted before she could speak the thought they shared. "I will continue as planned. You know how to contact me, discreetly of course. Are you free to man the office? Or should I say woman the office?"

"Whatever. Yes sir, I'm available." Beatrice smiled at the innuendo in her response. She, of course, would not admit she was ready however Walker might interpret her answer.

Walker missed the ostensible humor in the response. He was too focused on his afternoon appointment. Beatrice always reacted as Walker anticipated, honoring his every request.

"We don't expect any major problems, and if anything untoward should come up, I'll be a ten minute ride away," Walker said.

Actually, District of Columbia tourist and commuter traffic made the ride between Crystal City in Arlington and the White House a little more difficult than that, but that was a problem for others to worry about. Walker, who had secure communications in the high-rise apartment, reasoned that he would always be available whenever a need arose.

"Please summon Dexter forthwith," Walker referred to his chief of staff as he headed towards the office.

"Yes sir," Beatrice reacted immediately by turning to the phone.

"And have your confidential sources let us know as soon as Tate departs the building," Walker referred to the secretarial grapevine.

He entered his private office and shut the door softly behind him. He went to his desk, opened the top drawer, took out his cell phone, and dialed a familiar number from memory.

"Hello," a seductive, feminine voice responded.

"Hi, it's me," Walker said.

"Imagine that," the voice answered.

"You can stop holding your breath. We're still on," Walker declared.

The person on the other end breathed deeply, feigning a response to Walker's trite comment.

"Meet me in one hour. I have something important to share," Walker said.

The person on the other end demonstrated independence by hanging up without replying. Before Walker could decide how to react to that possible slight, the outer door to his office opened and his chief of staff entered.

"Have you heard? Walker demanded.

Dexter was not the typical vice presidential chief of staff. An ambitious but inexperienced thirty year old, he had served on Walker's senatorial staff as a gofer and had moved along in the same capacity to Walker's campaign staff where Walker had grown comfortable with him over the intense electoral battle. Since Walker followed the average vice presidential norm, he needed a gofer more than he did a managerial assistant. Walker involved himself seldom in policy and administration, and he spent his days burnishing his media image much as he had as a first term senator from Alabama. Walker contentedly left the heavy lifting to his master. He doubted that he would ever take the last step up to the presidency and deep down really didn't want all that responsibility. As a consequence, he had disappointed others in his entourage when he had selected Dexter as his chief of staff. Walker really didn't want a manager; what he needed was someone to cater to his every need, personal as well as professional.

"No sir," Dexter responded eagerly.

"The president is taking the day off, and we are now running the world," Walker smiled.

"Really?"

"What do you think about that?"

A worried expression flashed across Dexter's countenance.

"Relax," Walker laughed. "We're not going to drop the bomb on anyone."

"Will the football be following you around?" Dexter referred to the little gray man who carried the suitcase with the atomic triggers.

"No, no. The president isn't taking that kind of leave. He's going fishing again at the family homestead on the Potomac. We'll just be manning the ship here for the day."

"Very good sir," Dexter relaxed. Then, he frowned, remembering his master's scheduled afternoon appointment. "Does that mean you will not ..." Dexter hesitated.

"Don't get carried away, Dexter. Of course it doesn't change my appointment. Is everything ready at the apartment?"

"Yes sir."

"Good. As soon as I hear the president has left the building, I'm going to need your car."

"Yes sir, no problem. But who will handle things here?"

"You and Beatrice. Give me your keys."

"What if something happens?"

"Don't you worry about it. Let Beatrice take care of the important things."

Dexter exhaled.

"She knows how to contact me if she has to. You just stand by as usual and do anything she asks."

"Yes sir. Will you be coming back to the office after…after your meeting?"

"Of course."

"And I should not tell the Secret Service where you are?"

"Of course not. Don't be an idiot."

The outer door opened, and a smiling Beatrice poked her head in. "Good news, boss. The old man just left."

"Good!"

Walker leaped to his feet and tossed Dexter's keys into the air. Now, all he had to do was evade the Secret Service, drive Dexter's car across the bridge to Crystal City, and park in the lot underneath the high-rise building that contained the apartment which was paid for and furnished with discreetly raised campaign funds. The apartment, located a convenient fifteen minutes from the White House, served as Walker's private hideaway.

As soon as Walker had left the office, Dexter hurried down the hall on an errand of his own, leaving a frowning Beatrice looking after him. It was just like Dexter to take off and leave her with all the responsibility of covering for Walker. In Beatrice's opinion, Dexter and Walker were adolescent brothers.

Twenty minutes later a whistling John F. Walker, Vice President of the United States, exited the elevator in an ebullient mood and hurried across the hall to apartment 1102 without having encountered a single resident, apt confirmation of his choice of discreet hideaways. He unlocked the door and entered without knocking.

"Bubbles, I'm here," Walker announced his presence.

As a matter of discretion, Walker insisted that his paramour never use his true name as he did not identify hers. One never knew when operating on his level who might be listening, a friend, an enemy, the media, or worst of all, his spouse and her manifold sources. Bubbles was Walker's uninspired choice of names for his companion who went by the name Nan Starbright. Nan, of course was a working girl, and Starbright undoubtedly was an alias, probably one among many. Walker did not mind that he did not know Nan/Bubbles's real identity because he considered their interlude a transitory event. After four months, he doubted that he would keep her employed much longer. She understood. An attractive, early thirties, peroxide blonde, Nan for her part realized that change was a circumstance of her profession. The money made all the uncertainty worthwhile.

"I'm in here, your majesty," Bubbles answered from the bedroom.

Walker entered to find a nude Nan Starbright reclining on the opened bed.

"What kept you, lover. Age slowing you down?"

Walker shook his head in feigned disgust.

"And I wish you would call me something other than Bubbles. That makes me feel like a dumb blonde."

"What would you prefer?" Walker asked as he poured himself a drink from the bottle on the dresser.

"Do you really need that?" Nan asked as he tossed two ice cubes in the nearly full water glass.

"Christ, you're beginning to sound like a wife," Walker complained, this time seriously. "I get enough of that crap at home."

"And you undoubtedly deserve it," Nan did not back off.

Walker downed almost half of the whiskey before he set the glass on the bedside table and sat on the bed where he began to unlace his shoes.

Before taking off his socks, Walker stood up and entered the bathroom where he opened the medicine cabinet and took out a bottle filled with blue pills. He removed the cap and dropped two into the palm of his hand before taking them in one gulp with a swallow of tap water.

"I suggest you go carefully with those things," Nan called from the bedroom.

Walker, who was returning the small bottle back to the medicine cabinet, defiantly drew his hand back, reopened the bottle and took several more pills.

That will teach her a lesson, Walker thought, recalling the advertisement that cautioned that if he suffered an erection lasting longer than four hours he should immediately consult his doctor.

Nan, who had been watching Walker's image in the mirror on the far wall, shrugged and slid to the center of the bed prepared for the coming ordeal. Walker returned to the bedroom, continued to undress, dropping his clothing carelessly on the floor. He paused to finish off the whiskey, poured another glassful, and joined Nan in the bed. He was already feeling a little giddy from the pills and whiskey.

"You really ought to go easy on that stuff," Nan cautioned.

Defiantly, Walker grabbed the glass and emptied it before turning to face Nan. "OK, baby, let's romp," Walker said as he reached for her.

A smiling and relaxed President Harrison Tate sat in the bow of the sun punished family skiff facing the single Secret Service agent who was operating the undersized and aged outboard motor. When Harrison had started taking his occasional free afternoons on the Potomac, his detail leader had insisted that the president allow him to provide a modern, more water-worthy boat with room on board for at least three additional protective agents, but Tate had steadfastly refused. After Tate's two years in office, the Secret Service still complained about the boat and the detail's restricted ability to protect the president while on the river, but Tate continued to ignore the protestations. The area west of the Route 15 Bridge which connected Virginia and Maryland shores was Tate's home territory, and he refused to accept the contention that any serious threat to his well being existed there. The land along the Virginia shoreline was largely undeveloped, and Tate who owned a sizeable portion of it was determined to keep it in its natural state at least during his lifetime. He could do nothing about the Maryland side which was also au naturel. The B & O Canal once disfigured the Maryland shore, but it had long since overgrown, and no longer posed as an eyesore to the lovely river.

In the interest of security–Tate was not a foolish man–he had compromised. He had allowed his protective detail to station agents in two boats that were to remain a minimum of two hundred yards in front of and behind the president's craft. They were to hug the shores and keep as far out of his line of vision as possible. He refused permission for the construction of watchtowers or any kind of physical improvement along the shoreline, but he acquiesced to foot patrols as long as they kept out of his view. The detail leader had argued that if his men could not see the president they could not protect him.

"I'll chance it," Tate had ended the discussion.

Overtime, an uneasy working compromise had been attained. The detail could do its job as long as the agents did not intrude on Tate's sense of solitude. Tate really was not interested in catching fish. He just wanted, needed, time alone during which he could reflect in peace about his many problems.

This afternoon the president and his companion, Special Agent Isaac Ward, drifted with the current in silence. Ward understood the president well enough to know that he should speak only when spoken to. This admonition applied even to cautions dealing with security. Although Ward's slumped demeanor signaled a relaxed attitude similar to the president's, Ward's eyes constantly searched the river ahead and worked from shoreline to shoreline. He knew that if anything untoward happened while they were on the river, his ass would be on the firing line.

Ward worried that the current was keeping them close to the Virginia shoreline. That was good and bad. It minimized the risk from Maryland while it enhanced the threat from Virginia. Ward relied on the detail members in the two accompanying boats to watch the river in front and behind them. He just hoped that the deployed agents along the two shorelines were alert. This was an almost impossible task. The skiff drifted with the current because the president insisted that the outboard motor be left in idle. Sometimes at night Ward had nightmares about this detail on the isolated river. In his dreams, the president always had a large round bull's-eye stenciled on the back of his shirt. Ward even failed to derive peace of mind from the Secret Service's unilateral decision to position Copter One with its backup security team and medical personnel at Leesburg Airport, a short ten-minute panic flight from the river.

"Shall I turn back now, sir?" Ward asked the president who did not immediately respond.

Ward waited, not wanting to repeat himself. Finally, Tate blinked his eyes as if he were waking from a deep sleep, and shook his head negatively. "Wait until the bridge comes into view before coming about."

"Yes sir," Ward replied dutifully.

Ward decided to turn as soon as they approached the bend that led to the bridge. That would mean they had outreached their shore protection, and it would be his prerogative, his obligation, to protect the president from that public thoroughfare. Something about this afternoon, maybe it was the president's moody demeanor, had Ward very, very worried.

"I've caught some mighty fine catfish under that bridge," Tate took some of the sting out of his selfish order. He derived no enjoyment from being arbitrary and demanding with his security detail. He recognized they were there for only one purpose, to protect him, not to cater to his private whims.

Unfortunately, neither the president nor a single member of his protective detail on shore or on the river caught a glimpse of the man dressed in camouflage fatigues lying prone beside a large log on the rise overlooking the bend in the river just before the bridge. The man peered at the president through a high-powered sight attached to his Remington Model 710. He squinted as the skiff began to slowly rotate towards the Virginia shore making the Secret Service mandated turn just as he knew it would. He lowered the rifle and patiently waited, snuggling as close to the ground and the log as possible. He had the president's two escort boats in view, and they did not worry him. He was more concerned about the land patrols. He glanced to his left and right but discerned no movement. His time of maximum exposure was approaching. The fact he would have an opportunity for only one shot didn't bother him, for he was an expert marksman who constantly honed his skills on the firing range. His weapon was zeroed in for three hundred yards, a long shot, but one he was confident would hit its mark. He planned to fire after the president's skiff turned from the shore and started back up river. He would wait until the rear escort boat had passed and the protective detail had their backs to him. At the same time, the shore patrol would be rushing ahead of the president's boat, moving away from the shooter, more relaxed as they crossed already cleared land heading for home.

The moment he had been waiting and planning for was at hand. He regretted having to kill Tate, who had always treated him correctly, but the money was too good to pass up. This would be his historical moment as a paid assassin and his most profitable one too. One million dollars. One seldom had the opportunity to make that kind of money for performing what for him was a simple task. Of course, he would have a brief few minutes of exposure once he fired. The Secret Service presidential protection detail ranked with the best. He had planned accordingly. Surprise would provide his cover. The attack point had been carefully chosen. A ravine cut through the hillside behind him. He planned to withdraw quietly but quickly up the ravine to his parked car. Once there, he was confident he could handle any untoward contact with a panicked security detail.

"I hate for this to end," Harrison Tate smiled at his companion as the agent increased the power and the bow of the boat began its westward run. "It is so peaceful and relaxing…"

Those were the last words that President Harrison Tate spoke. A tremendous blow struck him in the back and knocked him forward. He turned as he fell half over the side of the old boat.

The loud crack of a powerful weapon shocked the agent at the tiller at the very same moment the president groaned and fell.

"Oh shit," the agent shouted as he released the tiller and leaped to shield the stricken president with his body.

The agents in the accompanying boats reacted professionally. They grasped their weapons and scanned the two shorelines searching for the source of the shot. The agents at the tillers revved the motors and raced towards the president's floundering old boat, which was turning with the current.

"Shot fired, shot fired, Pioneer is down, Pioneer is down," one agent shouted into his radio."

Those alarming words flashed through the Virginia airspace with a velocity and force that shocked dozing monitors into action.

Twenty detail agents deployed in two man teams on each side of the Potomac River immediately dropped to their knees and began to scan the countryside.

The detail leader and four assistants who had been calmly monitoring the radio from the front porch of the Tate ancestral home instinctively leaped to their feet. The team leader grabbed the microphone.

"We've lost him," the frantic agent in the president's boat shouted into the team circuit before the detail leader could demand a report.

"One shot. I think it came from Virginia, but I'm not sure," one of the agents on an accompanying boat reported. "It could have come from either side. With the echo…" He did not finish his sentence.

"Anyone see anything?" The team leader interrupted.

Silence greeted the question.

At the Leesburg Airport, the pilot of Copter One started his engine and shouted into his radio: "Copter One en route to Pioneer's site." Behind him, members of the quick response team checked their weapons while the on duty doctor nervously gripped his satchel. The thought "why me, why me" kept running through his mind as he tried to review first procedures for treating gunshot wounds.

"Base is alerting the Smokies in Virginia and Maryland and the Loudoun and Frederick County sheriffs to establish roadblocks in the area," the Secret Service duty officer at the White House reported. "Dark Day Procedure One being implemented."

"One, negative, two, negative, three…" the individual search teams belatedly responded to the team leader's query.

"We're putting Pioneer on Escort One and heading back to your position," the radioman on the lead escort boat reported to the team leader.

⁂

"I'm going good, good, good," Vice President John F. Walker shouted in Nan's ear.

He had been thumping away at Nan's body for at least forty-five minutes, and she was gritting her teeth fighting the urge to ask him to stop.

Despite the air-conditioning, both participants were now breathing heavily, and thick beads of perspiration streamed from their bodies. Walker gasped from the exertion, but he was committed to teaching his bedmate a lesson. He had decided this was going to be her last outing with him, and he wanted her to leave with first-hand knowledge of what a real man was like. He was determined to make her regret having gotten so familiar and glib with him, presumptuously acting like a damned wife.

"Are you almost finished?" Nan groaned. The incessant pounding hurt, and her body was beginning to buckle under the pain.

"Hang in there honey," Walker ordered just seconds before a giant hand seized his heart and began squeezing it unmercifully. Walker groaned and collapsed heavily on top of Nan.

"You bastard!" Nan shouted. "Get off of me."

When the vice president, the acting chief of the free world, did not react, Nan pushed him and with difficulty slid up and out from under him. She hit him roughly on the shoulder with the palm of her hand, turning him over on his back. Walker's eyes were shut, a grimace froze his face, and he did not appear to be breathing. To Nan's surprise, his enormous erection still pointed towards the ceiling. Shocked, she slid off the bed and stared.

"Honey?" Nan spoke softly. "Are you all right?"

Walker did not respond.

Reluctantly, Nan touched his neck as she had seen actors do on television. She could feel no pulse. When Walker did not react, she pushed him several times on the shoulder. The only thing that reacted was his waving flagpole.

"Oh Christ," Nan swore to herself. She had sensed that Walker had been getting ready to dump her and that she was prepared to live with. She had lost any interest in Walker as a man anyway and had let the relationship continue because the money was good, but she hadn't wanted it to end this way.

Unsure what to do next, Nan was pondering her options when the secure phone that Walker had had installed in the bedroom began to buzz. She didn't dare answer it. She decided her only option was to get out of the apartment as quickly as she could.

As planned, the shooter hurried up the ravine to his little red car where he stripped off the camouflaged fatigues and the latex gloves and tossed them and his weapon into the trunk. Moving with controlled haste, he climbed behind the wheel, backed out on to the Lovettsville Road, and drove west away from Route 15 and the bridge. He turned on the car radio, which was set to 103.5 and smiled as he listened to the weather report. He kept the speedometer needle locked on a careful thirty-five miles an hour. He covered an easy three miles before he encountered the first school bus.

Chapter 3

Grace Hanson, President Tate's secretary, was sitting at her desk enjoying the quiet respite caused by her lord and master's absence when the door burst open and two excited Secret Service agents from the protective detail entered without knocking.

"Have you heard the terrible news?" the older of the two asked, his voice cracking.

Alarmed, Grace shook her head negatively.

"It hasn't hit the media yet, but the president has been shot," the wan faced detail member said.

"The president?" Grace said softly, as tears filled her eyes. She waited, but the Secret Service agent did not elaborate. Grace, afraid to ask the obvious question, sat with her trembling hands in her lap.

The agent shook his head negatively.

"Did the president survive?" Grace insisted, her voice breaking with emotion.

"He is being airlifted to Loudoun County Hospital as we speak," the agent avoided saying the terrible words.

In the vice president's nearby office, Beatrice and James Dexter, the young chief of staff, were sipping coffee, chatting, enjoying their brief minutes as the key associates of the acting chief of the free world when the outer door flew open and four members of John F Walker's protective detail entered with weapons drawn. Silently they rushed past Beatrice and Dexter and without knocking or permission entered the vice president's inner office.

"Shit," the detail leader swore before pushing past the others and returning to the outer office.

"Beatrice, where in the hell is he?" The team leader demanded.

"Calm down," Beatrice laughed, amused by the detail's chagrin at having their charge escape once again from their suffocating clutches. "He's slipped out for a few minutes of down time away from all of this nonsense."

"Nonsense, my ass," the detail leader, normally a polite and deferential man, erupted. "Tell me where he is right now."

"If the vice president wanted you to know that, he would have told you," Beatrice replied, irritated by the man's rudeness.

"We have a crisis situation. We must contact the vice president immediately."

"Tell me what the crisis is, and I will consult the vice president. We'll let him decide whether you need to speak with him or not."

The agent took a deep breath before replying. "All right, damn it. Tell him the president has been shot. We don't know what's going on. We have to get him under protection."

The color drained from Beatrice's face, and her hands began to shake, but she did not move. She glanced at Dexter who had collapsed into his usual chair. "This is the truth?" Beatrice stammered.

"Do you think we would joke about something like this? Is he in the building?"

Beatrice shook her head. "I can get him on a secure line."

"Get the SOB on the phone," the agent ordered from his position directly in front of Beatrice's desk.

Beatrice stared at the angry detail man, decided he was deadly serious, then turned and picked up the green phone on the credenza behind her. She waited for the secure phone to activate and then punched the buttons. The phone rang on the other end. Beatrice waited anxiously, thoroughly aware that her boss was undoubtedly heavily engaged. She anticipated that after a delay he would answer, angry at being disturbed. The phone continued to ring, but Walker did not pick up. Finally, Beatrice looked at the agent. "He's not answering."

"Where the hell is he?" The agent demanded.

"I'm not sure that the vice president would want me to answer that question," Beatrice answered softly, aware that her response would not be sufficient under the circumstances.

Dexter picked up a remote from the coffee table in front of him and turned on the television. It was tuned to CNN, which was on a commercial.

"You don't have a choice," the angry Secret Service agent declared. "His life could be in danger."

Beatrice hung up the phone. "He must be on his way back. He knows I would not call unless there was an emergency."

CNN returned from a commercial and the heavily made up newsreader began discussing the economy.

"The media does not have the news yet," the agent declared needlessly. "Damn it Beatrice, tell us where he is."

Beatrice stubbornly shook her head. She was more afraid of her boss than she was of the Secret Service detail.

"He's at an apartment in Crystal City," Dexter spoke for the first time.

"What's the address?" The agent demanded.

"I told you he must be on his way back here," Beatrice defended herself, relieved that Dexter had taken the pressure off her. He could take the brunt of Walker's ire. The last thing he would want would be for the Secret Service to learn the whereabouts of his trysting site.

"Then we have to pick him up on the way," the agent said as he waited for Dexter to give him the address.

When Dexter did not immediately speak, the agent grabbed Dexter by the arm and pulled him towards the door.

Twenty minutes later a panting Dexter and six Secret Service agents were standing in the hall outside of the vice president's Crystal City hideaway.

"Whose apartment is this?" The lead agent demanded as he banged on the door.

"The vice president's," Dexter answered as they waited for a response from inside.

"Why didn't we know about this place?" The agent glared at Dexter.

"Because the vice president didn't want you to know," Dexter answered. "Holler at him, not me."

When no one responded to the repeated knocks, the lead agent turned to the two men standing behind him. "Break it down," he ordered.

"You'll b…be sorry," Dexter stammered.

The agent shoved Dexter to the side, giving his companions room to batter the door. After repeated kicks, the wood around the lock shattered, and the door burst open. The six agents crowded into the apartment with their guns drawn, leaving a shaken Dexter standing in the hall.

"Mr. Vice President?" The lead agent called.

He got no response. The lead agent motioned for his companions to screen the apartment while he waited near the door studying the room which was well furnished but sterile, completely devoid of the small things that reflected an occupant's tastes, no books or magazines, family pictures, antiques, or cheap souvenirs.

"No one lives here," he spoke to Dexter who had joined him.

"No," Dexter responded. "He just uses it as a refuge from the pressures of his office.

"Refuge my ass," the agent laughed mirthlessly.

"Chief, you better get in here," an agent called from the bedroom.

"You stay here," the lead agent ordered Dexter who hadn't moved from a spot near the door.

Dexter, who wanted to stay out of the vice president's line of anger, was perfectly willing to let the Secret Service get out in front and take the heat.

The lead agent entered the bedroom and found his companion standing beside the bed, an odd expression on his face, his weapon lowered to his side.

"Christ, it's him," the agent said without turning to look at his superior.

The lead agent rushed to the bed where he found Vice President John F Walker lying flat on his back, an odd expression on his face, a sheet pulled up to his neck.

"Mr. Vice President?" the lead agent spoke softly, hoping the man would wake up and curse him, fearful that he would not.

The vice president did not move. The lead agent leaned over, felt for a pulse but found none. He glanced at his companion who nodded once and stepped back from the bed.

"The son of a bitch is dead," the lead agent declared, his voice shaky with the concern that he felt. Whatever had happened to the vice president, the fault would fall on his shoulders.

"Christ, look at that," the agent pointed at the sheet covering the vice president's midsection.

For the first time, the lead agent who had been staring at the vice president's puffy face with the open unseeing eyes and odd grimace on the lips noticed that the sheet in the middle was raised almost a foot in the air.

The lead agent grabbed the sheet and pulled it back, worried that he would find the vice president's body riddled with bullet wounds or torn and ripped by a knife. Instead, the vice presidential penis stood at attention, stiff as a tent pole. It was so engorged with blood that the lead agent imagined he could see it throbbing.

"Holy shit," the lead agent exclaimed.

"I don't see any wounds on the body," the second agent declared.

By this time, the other four agents had entered the room and joined their companions in standing by the bed and staring.

"What a way to go," one of the agents whispered.

"Oh shit, why on our watch?" Another asked.

"We're dead meat," the fourth said.

"This doesn't look like the work of terrorists or an assassin," the fifth agent, more intellectually inclined than his companions, observed. "I'll bet it's another one of those Rockefeller things," he referred to a previous vice president's suffering a heart attack while engaging in a little extramarital recreation.

"Christ," the fourth agent said. "They're not going to be able to have an open casket service with that thing sticking up like that."

"No one's going to believe this was an accident or caused by stress," the lead agent said. "Not with the attack on the president at the same time."

He hesitated while images of the inevitable media onslaught that would follow coursed through his mind. He wasn't sure who would take more heat, the associate commanding the president's protection detail or himself. He feared he would because his team hadn't even known where their man was when whatever happened to him happened.

"We've got to lock this place down," the lead agent declared. "Don't touch a damn thing because no one is going to believe a word that we say. I've got to get back and give everybody a heads up."

"The shit's going to hit the fan," one of the agents declared.

"It already has," the lead agent declared.

Chapter 4

Hiram Alphonse Adams, Speaker of the House of Representatives, sat in his hideaway office passing the dull afternoon by chatting with a constituent while sipping liberal doses of Wild Turkey Bourbon, 100 proof strong.

"Damn, Hiram, this is really good whiskey," Jeffrey Goodenough, a long time supporter from Jefferson City, leaned back in his chair and smiled.

"Nothing but the best for old friends," Hiram Adams agreed.

At age eighty the Speaker, who years ago had retired in place, was serving his last tour as a member of the House of Representatives and was determined to enjoy every second of it. He treated his current eminence as an office perk. After forty years of government service, he felt he had earned it. He had lost his wife of fifty years almost a decade ago and fearing boredom had kept chugging along alone. A conservative Democrat in politics, he had long ago exhausted any political agenda that he had carried as baggage into office.

"You're going to miss all this," Goodenough waved a hand to indicate the Speaker's luxurious surroundings.

"After a while the burden becomes mighty tiresome," the Speaker smiled.

Hiram could carry conversations such as this in his sleep, and truth be told he tended to dose off frequently during the course of his long afternoons. Fortunately, visitors such as Jeffrey Goodenough were too polite to mention it and usually continued with a monologue until their host and benefactor rejoined them. The free Wild Turkey was just too good to jeopardize with idle gossip.

"Surely you are going to run again," Goodenough politely continued to earn his bourbon. "The people of Jackson City would not know what to do if they didn't have you here looking out for them."

Before Hiram could reply with his usual response, someone tapped on the door to his inner office.

"Yo," Hiram called.

The door opened and Jake Tyrone, the Speaker's chief of staff entered. Jake, who was sixty-three years old, had served Hiram for over forty years. After starting as an office boy at age twenty, Jake had performed just about every task in every official position that a congressman has to offer, and in his opinion he had seen everything. Nothing about congressmen and their peculiar idiosyncrasies and malfeasances could now surprise him. Like his mentor, Jake Tyrone was also marching in place waiting for the day he too could retire to his extensive real estate holdings in rural Missouri, all acquired on his bureaucrat's salary with a substantial assist from a judicious and discreet investment of the income from a minor portion of the congressman's political war chest.

"Pardon me, Mr. Speaker," Jake used the subservient tone he always used with Hiram when others were present.

Before Hiram could respond, four conservatively dressed young men pushed into the room.

"Sir, I'm Terrence Wattles," one of the men waved a credential case at the Speaker.

"They're all from the Secret Service," Jake called over Wattle's shoulder. "They insisted …"

"Sir, we have some very distressing news for you," Wattles declared.

Hiram, who doubted that the distraught young man could have anything to tell him that he hadn't heard many times before, reacted naturally.

"Please, gentlemen, have a seat. Jake, kindly fetch us four more glasses, and one more for yourself. This is mighty fine Wild Turkey, so we might as well relax and enjoy it while we consider what to do with this distressing news."

Hiram smiled at Jeffrey Goodenough, wondering if his constituent from Missouri was enjoying the flummery.

"Sir, the president has been shot," the Secret Service agent blurted.

Hiram, who had been through even this distressing routine before, knew exactly how to react. He realized that at least two of those present in the room would relay their observation of the Speaker's reaction to this painful news to the media. Hiram placed his glass carefully on the table, sat up straight in his chair—at least as straight as his arthritic spine permitted—and adopted his most grave expression. Hiram, of course, pretended to be intimate with Harrison Standish Tate, but they were not close. They represented different political parties, and Tate at best could only be described as an accidental president. A small time ex-Virginia sheriff, Tate had done nothing, in Hiram's opinion, to earn the right to serve as the nation's leader. This of course was no time to belittle the man. Hiram wisely waited for the Secret Serviceman to continue.

"I'm afraid the president did not survive, sir. He was fishing on the Potomac, out near Point of Rocks, and a person or persons unknown shot him."

Hiram still did not comment. He sat with the false concern freezing his features and waited while thinking that being shot while doing something as frivolous as fishing on the Potomac was only fitting.

"They have taken the president to the Loudoun County Hospital."

"I pray for the country," Hiram spoke softly. He knew he had to respond and that gratuity was the best he could come up with at the moment. He was confident that Jake would be able to devise a more insightful response and make sure that it was substituted for Hiram's inadequate reaction when presented to the media.

"There's more sir," the Secret Service agent surprised Hiram by continuing. "We are part of your protective detail."

"Protective detail," Hiram Adams repeated.

Adams recognized the ominous tone and waited for what he feared might come. When the agent hesitated, Hiram asked: "Was the vice president with the president when he was shot?"

"No sir," the agent responded. "The vice president suffered an accident himself."

"An accident?"

"We are still waiting for the details of what happened. It is my duty, sir, to inform you that both the president and vice president are dead. You are the acting president, sir, and we are your protective detail."

Hiram Alphonse Adams stared at the agent in disbelief.

"Jesus H Christ, Hiram," Jeffrey Goodenough, the Speaker's friend from Jefferson City, appeared flabbergasted.

For the first time in his life suffering a complete loss of words, Hiram stared at his friend. He knew the Constitution, the 20th and 25th Amendments, and the Presidential Succession Act of 1947 better than anyone else in the room. Many years previous when he had first been elected Speaker he had been tantalized by the fact that he stood third in line to the presidency. Then, he had been rather disappointed that no Speaker had ever succeeded to the presidency, not ever. Now, however, the brutal facts of the situation frightened him. He was too old to take on that monumental responsibility, particularly not in times of a crisis. His once brilliant mind had atrophied, largely from age, the ravages of alcohol, and disuse. He could perform the ceremonial duties of the office of Speaker, but this was something else. Besides the Presidential Succession Act clearly states that anyone who takes office under its provisions will only act as president. Having never been implemented under these circumstances, no one knew how long an acting president could or should serve. It was clear, however, that only a vice president could rise to the title President of the United States.

"I'm too God damned old," Hiram Alphonse Adams blurted.

"Congratulations, sir," the Secret Service agent declared.

Unsure whether the damned fool was referring to his age or his dramatic ascension to higher office, Hiram declared: "I'm eighty years old."

"May we escort you to the White House, sir?" The agent persisted. "Only there can we guarantee your safety while we sort out what is going on." The agent did not point out that the leaderless staff there was clucking about waiting for someone to take charge and tell them exactly what to do.

As the Secret Service detail led the confused and compliant acting president from the room, he turned and shouted over his shoulder. "Jake, get Miss Mary and come with us. I'm surrounded by madmen and need someone I can trust." Hiram referred to seventy-five year old

Miss Mary Murphy who had been with him longer than his chief of staff.

"Yes sir," a pale faced Jake Tyrone called after the departing Speaker.

A worried Jake stood in place like a statue after the acting president and his entourage left the room. Jake knew better than most that his friend, mentor and boss was not up to the challenge that had been thrust upon him, not mentally and certainly not physically, and he also knew that neither he nor Mary were either.

"May God bless and save the United States of America," Jeffrey Goodenough declared.

The words shocked Jake from his stunned trance. "We're all going to need someone's help," Jake spoke to no one in particular before he hurried from the room.

Chapter 5

Conor Gifford, the vacationing Chief of Virginia's Office of Special Investigations, was sitting under the roof of his back patio comfortably sipping from a frosty bottle of Budweiser and watching a thick rib eye steak reaching perfection on the grill when he heard the sound of crunching gravel emanate from the front of his rural refuge.

"Shit," Gif declared.

He had been enjoying the peace and quiet at the end of a near perfect day and had been looking forward to topping it off with a quiet, solitary meal. He knew, however, that the sound he heard heralded the arrival of an unwanted visitor, no matter who it was. Stubbornly, he remained seated, hoping the intruder would assume no one was home and go away.

Unfortunately, it did not work out that way. Gif was standing in front of the grill turning his steak over one last time when a uniformed Virginia trooper came around the back of the house.

"There you are," the trooper said, relief etching his face.

"Hi," Gif replied inadequately. He recognized the traffic officer from the local state police barracks but did not remember his name.

"That looks good," the officer stopped next to Gif and studied the grill.

"Your timing is impeccable," Gif said, wondering what the man wanted. He knew it wasn't a social call.

The officer studied Gif's expression giving Gif the impression that he was not finding what he had expected. Gif waited for him to explain.

"I guess you haven't heard the terrible news," the officer said hesitantly.

"I've been rather out of touch with news, deliberately," Gif replied, letting the man know that he wasn't pleased with the interruption. As soon as the word "deliberately" was out of his mouth, Gif regretted his reaction. It wasn't the officer's fault that he had been sent to interrupt Gif's solitude.

"Richmond has been trying to reach you, but your phone is down." The officer did not elaborate on what was terrible about the news, and Gif stubbornly did not ask.

"I know," Gif said. "This is my first day of leave, and I tried to shut out the world."

"Until I showed up," the officer said, not sounding apologetic. "Please call Colonel Townsend. His office is most anxious to get in touch with you."

"I will. Thank you," Gif said, not moving towards the house. Gif took his steak off the grill giving the officer a not very polite hint about his intentions. Assuming that Townsend had an assignment for him that he did not want to hear about, Gif was in no hurry to respond to his summons.

"And I have to get back on the highway. We've got roadblocks set up everywhere."

Gif interpreted that piece of information as indicating that local bank robbers had been at work again. He knew that Loudoun had suffered a series of branch stickups during the past two months.

"I could share a piece of my steak," Gif said, not meaning it.

"No thank you, sir," the officer said. "I really do have to get back on the road. Everything is in an uproar."

Gif assumed the comment was intended to politely put him in his place. The officer probably hated being diverted to the task of message carrier because of Gif's indifference to his professional responsibilities as much as Gif disliked having him interrupt his quiet dinner.

"Good luck officer. I hope you catch the miscreants," Gif said, a casual swipe at making amends.

The officer looked at Gif curiously, shrugged, waved one hand and hurried back the way he had come.

"I'll let Richmond know I delivered the message and ruined your dinner," the officer called as he rounded the corner.

Gif shrugged, picked up the steak, and carried it to the small table facing his chair. He sat down, took another deep drink of Budweiser, and went to work on his meal.

Secretary of the Treasury Alexander Hamilton Sperry was seated at his desk in his luxurious office in the Main Treasury Building, a historical landmark that Sperry privately and appropriately treasured. Tradition has it that President Andrew Johnson, whose relations with Congress were so bad that they impeached him, deliberately had Main Treasury situated so that it blocked the view between the Capitol and the White House. The reality of the situation was that Johnson used Main Treasury as his temporary office during the period immediately following Abraham Lincoln's assassination. The Andrew Johnson Suite on the third floor paid tribute to this event. Alexander Hamilton Sperry took immense pride in the fact that a statue of his namesake, Alexander Hamilton, the first Secretary of the Treasury, stood on the south side of Main Treasury, and he often visited the statue hoping that the action would inspire others to assume that Sperry was a descendant of that great man.

A tap on the door disturbed Sperry's ruminations, and he irritably shouted.

"Go away."

The door opened, and Clete Clapp, Sperry's executive assistant entered. Clapp, despite the subservient implication of his title, was the one man working in the building who was not always intimidated by the irascible and arrogant secretary of the treasury. A product of the New York City political machine, Clapp was arrogant in his own right, at least when dealing with subordinates, and he liked to pretend when Sperry was not present that he was the power behind the throne. Clapp closed the door behind him and casually seated himself in the chair facing Sperry's desk. Turning sidewise, he draped one leg over the arm of the chair and smiled subserviently at his boss.

"It's happened."

Sperry stared at his assistant.

"Everything that we've been waiting for has happened.'

Sperry pointed a long finger at Clapp and then at the walls, silently reminding his assistant that walls have ears.

"Some bad guy shot the president this afternoon while he was teasing the fish on the Potomac near his little Point of Rocks hideaway," Clapp said evenly, deliberately masking any sign of emotion in his voice.

"Really," Sperry grinned as he tossed the memorandum he had been reading unceremoniously on to his desk. "What did the fish think about that?"

"I don't know about the fish," Clapp smiled back. "But Harrison Tate certainly didn't like it one little bit. He's dead."

"Are you sure?"

"I didn't feel his pulse," Clapp said. "But the Secret Service thinks he's dead. They're in a state of panic next door," he referred to the West Wing of the White House.

"How is that idiot Walker taking it?" Sperry watched his aide closely.

"The idiot is not taking anything. At least, not now. I can't speak for earlier in the day."

Sperry, now relaxed in his chair, reached across his desk, opened a cigar box, took out one without inviting Clapp to share his celebratory gesture with him, and made a show of lighting it while he waited for his assistant to continue. Undaunted, Clapp took a cigar from the box and mimicked Sperry's casual gamesmanship with the cigar.

"What does that mean?" Sperry finally demanded after his initial puff of self-congratulatory smoke, which he aimed in Clapp's direction.

"It means the idiot is dead also," Clapp replied. Clapp did not light his cigar. He didn't like the damned things, and Sperry knew it.

"Dead." Sperry sat up straight and stared at Clapp.

"Dead," Clapp repeated. "He's not breathing. And he didn't get a chance to put his name in the history books as a president."

"What happened to him?"

"He was in the sack with somebody, a broad or a queer or something in between, and expired in the act. At least he was found in a hideaway apartment without a stitch on and still sporting a giant erection."

"You're positive?" Sperry said as he turned his chair to face the window, his proactive mind racing.

"I didn't personally take a picture of the damned thing."

"I'm not talking about the damned erection."

"I know. Guess who that makes our next president?" Clapp addressed the back of Sperry's head.

Sperry chuckled without turning to acknowledge Clapp's question or continued presence. As the occupant of the fifth position on the presidential succession list, Sperry certainly knew who would be the next president. He still had the Speaker of the House, the President pro tempore of the Senate, and the Secretary of State ahead of him. That meant he didn't have a chance to move to the front of the line, but there were now two slots vacant.

"We've got an eighty year old Speaker of the House, a member of the opposing party, as our president as soon as he takes the oath. What do you think his life expectancy has become?" Clapp asked.

"I wouldn't sell him life insurance," Sperry turned back to face Clapp. "We're facing a time of constitutional uncertainty. Neither the Constitution nor the Secession Act has provision for anyone but the vice president to be sworn in as president. Everyone else can only serve as acting president."

"For how long?"

"No one knows. Until the next election, I guess."

"Only an acting president," Clapp smiled. "Our Speaker can only be acting president."

Sperry did not bother to comment on that. He stood up, still carrying his cigar. "Think I'll drop in next door and see if I can be of any neighborly help in this time of national tragedy," he smiled.

"Want me to come with you?" Clapp asked.

"No," Sperry answered firmly. "You stay right here and make sure no one raids the vaults in my absence," Sperry laughed, really enjoying the situation. "I'll give you a call if I need you."

At the White House, Speaker Hiram Alphonse Adams was sitting in the Situation Room waiting for someone to tell him what to do. The door opened and Secretary of the Treasury Alexander Hamilton Sperry entered. He nodded to acknowledge Secretary of State Harriet

Pope and Attorney General Claude Pinkerton, one of Tate's buddies from the University of Virginia and a key member of the Virginia mafia who controlled the White House, and sat down in the chair opposite Adams.

"I'm sorry I am late but I just got the terrible word," Sperry nodded at the doddering old Speaker while struggling to keep from smiling at the irony of the situation.

"Thank you for coming, Mr. Secretary," Adams replied politely. "We were just trying to decide what to do next. The Director of the Secret Service has briefed us on the situation."

Sperry turned and looked directly at the Director of the Secret Service, a man who he considered to be just another functionary.

Nobody spoke. Finally, the Director of the Secret Service broke the silence. "We have both crime scenes under control and are investigating."

"Who did this?" Sperry demanded as if he not the Speaker were in command.

The Director of the Secret Service hesitated, reacted with an angry glare in Sperry's direction, and then turned to face the Speaker.

"Nobody can answer that question, Mr. Secretary," the Speaker smiled disarmingly at Sperry. "The investigation is still in the early stages." The Speaker turned to the attorney general. "Please continue, sir."

"As I was saying, sir," the attorney general said. "I believe you should take the oath as acting president immediately. We must reassure the country and the world that the government is still in control."

Sperry chuckled at the last comment.

"Very well, sir," the Speaker decided. "Please tell me how we should proceed."

"I suggest that we summon the chief justice to administer the oath," the attorney general said.

"Would you please handle that for me," the Speaker asked politely.

"Mr. Speaker," the secretary of state interrupted. "I suggest that we discuss the foreign policy implications of our situation. I'm not quite sure…"

"I'm sure all of these details can be discussed in due course," Sperry interrupted. "As all are aware the major problem the country is facing at the moment is the economic situation."

All present stared in disbelief, first at the secretary of state, and then at Sperry.

"After, of course, determining who is responsible for the terrible calamity that has befallen us," Sperry punted.

"If you will excuse me, sir," the attorney general said as he stood up.

"And I will take my leave to confer with my investigators," the Director of the Secret Service said.

"Of course," the Speaker smiled. He then turned to the secretary of state. "And if you will excuse us Secretary Pope. We must discuss the foreign policy implications of our situation at our earliest opportunity."

Those words appeared to shock the secretary of state who reluctantly but dutifully rose to her feet. She glanced at the still seated Sperry.

"And if you Mr. Secretary would kindly do me the favor of staying behind for just a brief minute," the Speaker turned to Sperry who nodded.

After the door to the Situation Room closed and the Speaker and Sperry were left alone, the Speaker spoke first. "I think we are the two grownups in the room, Mr. Sperry. How do you suggest we handle this very abnormal situation?"

"I don't understand, Mr. Speaker," Sperry stalled.

"Here we sit," Hiram Alphonse Adams spoke bluntly, "representatives of two opposing parties. I am a senior Democratic official, and you are the most formidable Republican of President Tate's administration still standing."

"The secretary of state ranks ahead of me in seniority," Sperry feinted.

"Please, let's speak bluntly, and honestly, you and I," Adams said. "We both know that the secretary of state is in over her head. We are the ones who have to cope with this national tragedy."

Sperry nodded. The Speaker at age eighty was not as senile as many thought.

"We both know that I am too old to handle the burden of the presidency," Adams declared. "And I have no interest in the job.

As president, I would simply be a historical phenomenon, and the constitutional situation is unclear. I can take the oath as acting president but what happens after that?"

"Don't ask me," Sperry shrugged. "I'm not a constitutional lawyer." Sperry had difficulty reading the old man.

"I am going to take the oath as acting president," the Speaker spoke more forcefully. "What should I focus on first?"

"I suggest that you leave the investigation to the law authorities, the FBI and the Secret Service. You could even appoint a task force to supervise the investigation," Sperry said before deciding to see how far he could push the old man. "And after reassuring the nation that life as we know it will persevere, you should address the major problem facing us."

"And that is?"

"The economic situation that our departed president was not wise enough to confront."

"And you think I am?" Sperry chuckled.

"No, frankly, I do not. But maybe the two of us are."

"And you are willing to continue working for me, a member of the opposing party?"

"I have no choice. I frankly don't care about your political views. I worry about our nation, our economy." Sperry hoped that the last two sentences did not sound too hypocritical.

"How lucky we are to have you in your current situation," Adams said.

Sperry looked at Adams sharply, not sure if Adams was speaking sincerely or sarcastically. The northerner in Sperry had difficulty reading southern politicians with their exaggerated manners and excessive charm.

Neither spoke. Finally, Adams broke the silence. "Maybe you and I should work out a compromise here and now."

"A compromise?"

"Yes. Why don't we set aside past differences and work together for the good of the country. That might be a unique situation, don't you think?"

Sperry smiled. Maybe the old man was as senile as he had originally thought. If so, he would certainly be in over his head as acting president and would need someone to guide and control him.

"If we were to work out an arrangement, the country might be supportive of an administration with the two parties actually working together. How should we begin?"

"Would you consider joining me as the acting vice president?"

The suggestion surprised Sperry almost as much as it appealed to him. If he were to move in as acting vice president with only this old man ahead of him, it would advance his private timetable by at least two years, and if something untoward happened to Adams...he did not even dare complete the thought.

"For how long?" Sperry asked.

"Who knows? Until the courts or the people decide we should be replaced."

That thought puzzled Sperry. "The question of how long an acting president should serve has never been resolved."

"Then let's work on it together."

"Do you think we can trust each other?" Sperry asked without revealing he was confident he could outmaneuver the old man if he didn't succumb in the process.

"We can give it a try," Adams said. "What do you suggest we do first?"

"After you announce that you plan to make me your acting vice president?"

"Of course."

"Where do you want to start?"

"Where do you suggest that I establish an interim office? I certainly can't push the grieving widow out into the street and fire his loyal staff, not immediately."

Again Sperry laughed. The old man was more devious that he thought. Suddenly, an idea struck him. "If we are going to work together as a team…" he began.

"Don't get ahead of me," the Speaker interrupted. "Let me make one thing perfectly clear. I'm not about to try to cope with all the problems facing this beloved country. I love and respect it too much. I'm willing to be the figurehead. I'll take the oath, pose for pictures, and make a few speeches. You can run the world, behind the scenes of course."

"Like a Mitterrand?"

"Exactly, just as long as you remember who is number one."

"I've got a suggestion that might appeal to you. Have you decided where to set up your office?"

"Of course I haven't," Adams reacted sharply. "That's why I asked for your opinion."

The old man's tone irritated Sperry, but he controlled his temper. "As you noted you are going to have to give time to the widow and our departed president's colleagues to clear out of the place," Sperry forced himself to sound reasonable.

"Yes," Adams agreed. "We must give Mrs. Tate time to cope with her sorrow and to decide what to do next. Haste on our part would not be appreciated. Not by the American people…" he let his voice trail off.

"And advisers who have no one to advise, or executive assistants with nothing to execute…" Sperry let his words die.

"Can occupy their grand offices as long as they wish. Just as long as the power resides elsewhere," Adam's smile broadened.

"Exactly," Sperry agreed. "You know the Treasury Department has a grand history and a perfect location…"

"Between the Congress and the White House," Adams contributed.

"…with a tradition filled past," Sperry continued. "The Andrew Johnson Suite that a president occupied after the assassination of a beloved president," Sperry smiled.

"While he jousted with a group of radical Republicans," Adams added.

"I suggest that you would find the office accommodating," Sperry declared.

"And my new acting vice president would be located just across the hall," Adams said. "I accept. Look how well we complement each other. And of course we can let the Tate appointed staff do whatever it wants in their current quarters just as long as they remain outside of the chain of command."

"They will tire of the boredom in due course," Sperry said.

"Exactly," Adams agreed.

"And move on as they must. I think we see eye to eye, Mr. President," Sperry offered his hand.

Adams took it with an odd twinkle in his eye that Sperry assumed was relief.

Chapter 6

After finishing off his steak, Gif collected his cooking utensils, his dirty plate, silverware, garlic salt, and empty Budweiser bottle and retreated to the kitchen where he cleaned up the mess. After helping himself to a second frosty bottle of Budweiser, he sat down in his recliner, glanced at the silent television, thought about watching a tape, but let a guilty conscience direct his hand to his sleeping cell phone. He turned it on and to his surprise it buzzed immediately.

"Gifford," he answered.

"Inspector? This is the duty officer. Please stand by and I will patch you through to the colonel."

This response surprised Gif. He had expected at this time of day that Colonel Harris Townsend, the commander of the Virginia State Police, would be home where he refused to take any calls except those that could be classified as true emergencies.

"Gif," Townsend came on the line. "What can I say? There are no adequate words to fully express our loss."

"I'm sorry, Harris, but I have been out of touch. I don't know what you are talking about," Gif said.

A deep silence greeted that comment. Gif waited.

"God, I hate being the one to have to tell you this," Townsend finally spoke. "You were closer to him than anyone but his wife."

Gif immediately assumed that Townsend had to be talking about Harrison Tate. "Oh, shit," Gif exclaimed as a cold shiver ran up his spine. "What happened?"

"Some nut shot the president while he was fishing at his place on the Potomac."

"Did he survive?" Gif asked coldly, remembering that Harrison had practically begged him to go fishing with him, and Gif had selfishly declined.

"No."

"Did they catch the bastard?"

"My information is still scanty. The Secret Service and the Feds are sitting tight on the details. He was heading back up the river to call it a day when one shot took him down. The hit struck him in the heart, and he died instantly."

Suddenly, Gif realized that the trooper from the local barracks who had brought him the message to call the colonel had referred to roadblocks. That made it twice today that he had let his old friend and mentor down. While he had been calmly enjoying his steak, the killer had made his escape.

"And that's not all," Townsend added. "The vice president died at approximately the same time. We lost both of them."

"Another shooting? Were they together?"

"I don't know for sure. The Secret Service isn't talking, and the media is in a frenzy reporting mainly rumors. What we hear is that the vice president was enjoying a little hanky panky in a Crystal City hideaway and died from the exertion."

"What does his companion say?"

"I don't know. I was hoping that you would have inside information. The boys from the barracks can't get anything."

"But you think the two…events are related?"

"You will have to find that out for me. Both events took place in Virginia, so we have a stake in the investigation. I hate to ask this of you, given your closeness to the president, but…"

"I understand, Harris. Thank you. Not even the army will keep me from finding out what happened. Do they think terrorists might have been behind the attacks?"

"A good question. I don't know. I imagine the White House is in shock and whoever is in charge right now is frantically trying to find out what happened and to figure out what to do about it."

"Do you know where they took Harrison…" Gif hesitated, trying to keep his voice from breaking with emotion "…or where Martha might be?" Gif referred to Tate's wife.

"I heard they took the president to Loudoun Hospital. I don't know if he is still there or not, and I don't know where Martha is. Now, you know everything I do. Again, I'm sorry, Gif. I know how you must feel."

"I know. I'll get on this right now and will get back to you when I learn something," Gif said and hung up.

Twenty-five minutes later Gif while driving well in excess of the speed limit approached Loudoun Hospital, which was, located about eight miles from Leesburg off Route 7. Expecting to find a media circus and an army of official cars barricading the approach, he was surprised to discover the access road virtually devoid of traffic. He skidded to a stop directly in front of the emergency room entrance, tossed his Official Police Business card on the dashboard, and rushed inside where he confronted the first white clad orderly that he met.

"Where is the president?" He demanded, flashing his credentials.

"You're too late, man," the orderly shrugged.

"Where do you have him?" Gif insisted, tempted to grab the wiseacre by the lapels.

"We don't have him. They didn't even unload him here."

"What does that mean?"

"The copter landed, our emergency room doctors checked the body, and the feds took off for Walter Reed."

"The president was dead?"

The orderly nodded and turned away from the disturbed lawman.

"Walter Reed Hospital?" Gif was not sure the orderly was telling him the truth.

The orderly pointed at a passing doctor. "Ask him. He was one of those who checked the body."

Gif turned to find a white coated man with a stethoscope draped around his neck staring at him. Gif again waved his credentials and demanded: "Where is the president?"

"In heaven if he's lucky," the doctor answered, his tone making clear that he did not appreciate Gif's attitude.

"Then he's dead," Gif said.

"Unfortunately, yes. You are running behind if this is an official investigation. The Secret Service chose not to keep the president here. They climbed back into their copter and took off for Walter Reed." The doctor frowned. "I assume they didn't trust us to handle the autopsy."

Gif watched as the doctor and the orderly turned away and continued down the hallway. He paused for a few seconds before deciding to continue on to Walter Reed where he hoped he would be able to find Martha and share the misery with her.

One hour later Gif finally found the chaotic scene he had expected to confront at Loudoun Hospital. The residential streets leading into the U.S. Army's premier medical center were jammed with curiosity seekers, media satellite trucks and police vehicles representing Maryland and D.C. departments. Unable to force his way through, Gif parked his Prius near a hydrant and spent a good half hour waving his credentials and forcing his way through the throngs. At the entrance to the Walter Reed compound, he with difficulty persuaded the harassed military police to let him approach the main building where he encountered a barrier of stern Secret Service agents blocking access.

"I command the Office of Special Investigations of the Virginia State Police, and I represent the governor," Gif declared as he again waved his credentials.

"Tough shit," one of the Secret Service agents guarding the door declared. "My orders are to let no one through and believe me you are no one to me."

Gif thought about punching the smart ass in the nose but resisted the impulse, doubting that would earn him access. He hesitated, trying to decide just what to do, when he saw a familiar face crossing the lobby behind the unrelenting and obviously harassed agent.

"That's Tom Harrington, right there," Gif pointed over the man's shoulder.

The agent turned to look, and Gif shoved past him. He was pushing the door to enter when the agent grabbed his shoulder from behind. Gif turned sideways and shoved the door wide enough to shout:

"Tom!"

A second agent grabbed his other arm and was roughly pulling him away from the door when a voice from inside called:

"Stop. Let him through."

The unequivocal order caused the two agents to hesitate, and Gif seized the moment. He jerked free and ran toward Tom Harrington, the Director of the Federal Bureau of Investigation.

"It's OK. The inspector is with me," Harrington said to the Secret Service agents just as they grabbed Gif from behind.

The expressions on their faces indicated that they did not appreciate Harrington's intervention. They hesitated, and Gif pulled free.

"Fuck off," Gif growled, clenching his fists and daring his pursuers to touch him again.

The two agents exchanged angry looks, uncertain how to handle the confrontation.

"Come with me, Gif," Harrington took charge.

"The responsibility is yours," one of the agents called after them.

"Glad you came along," Gif said.

Under other circumstances, he might have smiled at Harrington, a close friend dating from the time when Harrington had been the Special Agent in Charge of the bureau's Richmond office and Gif had been new in the Office of Special Investigations. They had collaborated on several high profile cases, the most recent being two years previous when Gif had headed up a joint federal task force investigating a series of Capitol Hill murders, and Harrington had represented the bureau's Metropolitan Washington field office.

"I wish we were meeting under other circumstances," Harrington said.

"Harrison?" Gif asked about the man both considered a personal friend.

Harrington shook his head, indicating that the president did not survive.

"Is Martha here?" Gif asked about Tate's wife.

"She's upstairs."

"I want to see her," Gif said.

"Certainly." Harrington turned towards the elevators.

"First, is there someplace where we can talk?"

Harrington silently turned and led Gif along the corridor to an empty office. Once inside, Harrington went to the window, looked out, and Gif waited. Since his legs felt weak, he sat down. Finally, Harrington turned. "It's a shitty night."

"Did they catch the shooter?" Gif asked.

Harrington sat down, looked at Gif, and shook his head. "No. The bastard got clean away."

"What can you tell me?"

"Everything, but it's not much. The president was on the river in his family boat with only one guard on board with him. The Secret Service had two boats, one up river and one down, about a hundred yards from the president–that's the way he insisted it be handled–and protective squads were in the woods on each bank. After an hour or so, the president called it a day and was upriver from the bridge when he turned towards the Virginia shore and was heading back when one shot was fired catching him square in the heart. I'm told he died instantly."

"Just one shot?"

"Yes, a high powered rifle from some distance."

"None of the detail saw anything."

"No. They immediately radioed an alert. Local police on both sides of the river responded and set up road blocks."

"If the killer fired from the Virginia side, and he wasn't a local resident, he had to make his escape via the Lovettsville Road."

Harrington nodded.

"He could drive west to Lovettsville or east to Route 15," Gif continued. "A roadblock in Lovettsville or one at Route 15 should have picked him up."

"Maybe."

"Maybe, hell. I know the area."

"I know, Gif. The killer moved fast and a good ten or fifteen minutes passed before the cops got roadblocks set up at either intersection. It had to be close, but the bastard got clean away."

"Shit," Gif swore. "If the killer got to 15, all he had to do was turn left, cross the bridge, and take one of a number of highways in and around Frederick going in any direction."

"We fear that's what happened. Now, the area is gridlocked with rush hour traffic. We've got unhappy motorists backed up for miles in all directions, particularly on 15."

"Where in the hell was the sheriff's department?" Gif demanded. "Harrison Tate was one of their own, and they should have had people in the area anytime he visited the county."

"We can't put the burden on them. They had patrols deployed, but they weren't in position to help, not immediately."

Gif, who like Harrison Tate had once been sheriff in Loudoun, shook his head doubtfully but changed the subject. "The killer would not have taken a chance of taking his weapon with him. He disposed of it somewhere before he got to his car."

"We agree. The weapon would have been too big an incriminating risk to have in his possession if he encountered a roadblock. We have a task force in the river area searching for clues now. Nothing has turned up yet."

"It will," Gif spoke with more assurance than he felt. "If he tossed the weapon in the river, it might be difficult to find. The Potomac current could have carried it down river."

"We've got frog men in the water now. We have a better chance of finding the weapon than the slug."

"You don't have the slug either?"

"No, it went completely through the president's body. It could be in the water or might have ricocheted to the Maryland shore. We probably will never recover it."

"And since the shooter has already departed the area, we won't find him either."

"Not unless a resident or passerby saw something."

Following a brief silence, Harrington said:

"Gif, you know they'll be appointing a task force to handle the investigation."

"Not on your life," Gif immediately reacted, sensing where Harrington was heading.

"It wouldn't be your first presidential task force," Harrington referred to the Capitol Hill serial killer investigation."

"I let your predecessor and a president con me into serving as a figurehead while you handled the investigation," Gif said coldly. "You can use me as a fool once, but not twice."

"Don't you want to see our friend's killer brought to justice?"

"You know damned well I do, but you don't need me. I'm too close to the case, to Harrison, to be objective. If I found the killer, he wouldn't live to face justice."

"You don't mean that."

"Don't try me," Gif muttered.

"Let's agree to disagree and leave this discussion to another time," Harrington tried to calm his friend.

"Fine. Discuss it with whoever you like just as long as it doesn't involve me," Gif said coldly. "Can I see Martha now?" Gif changed the subject.

"We can try."

Gif was tempted to ask why his friend was letting the Secret Service push him around. Certainly, the FBI would take over the lead in the investigation, and Harrington was Director of the FBI, but Gif had to acknowledge that the Secret Service marched to its own drummer. With the authority of the president behind them, the Secret Service usually had the muscle to have its own way. Since neither Gif nor Harrington was in a position to know who would be sworn in as president within the hour, neither could predict how much bureaucratic support the Secret Service could muster. Gif despite his anger and grief let the moment pass.

Harrington escorted Gif past the frowning Secret Service agents who filled the lobby, guarded the elevators, and controlled the corridors. They were not stopped until they reached a suite of rooms on the fourth floor where a burly member of the First Lady's Protective Detail blocked the door.

"We want to speak with Mrs. Tate," Harrington said.

"Sorry director," the agent refused to move.

"This is Inspector Gifford, a close personal friend," Harrington persisted. "The first lady will want to see him."

"No," the agent declared. "The first lady said "no visitors."

"Agent," Harrington said forcefully. "Tell Mrs. Tate that Inspector

Gifford is here or you are going to have much more on your hands than you can handle."

Those words coming from the Director of the FBI had their effect. The agent glanced in the direction of his three companions who were standing nearby. None spoke. Finally, the agent relented. "Wait here," he ordered.

He turned tapped on the door and entered, closing it softly behind him. It had barely shut when it reopened and the agent stepped to one side. "The first lady will see Inspector Gifford," he spoke in a low growl.

Gif nodded at Harrington. "I'll see you later, Tom. Thank you."

Ignoring the scowling agent, Gif entered the room and found Martha Tate sitting alone on a settee with crossed legs, hands folded on her lap, red-rimmed eyes, and an extremely sad expression on her face. Gif closed the door behind him and hesitated, suddenly concerned that he had made the wrong decision in forcing his way into the room and intruding on her grief.

"Gif, I am so glad that you came," Martha greeted him as she rose to her feet.

Gif hurried across the room and embraced his friend's widow. He felt her shudder as she pulled back and retreated to the settee.

"Martha, I'm so sorry…" Gif said, stopping, not knowing what to say next.

"I know," Martha said. "Please sit down. Harrison would not want us to grieve."

"How can we not?" Gif spoke softly, shaking his head, still standing.

"It comes with the job," Martha seemed to be comforting Gif. "Harrison was quite fatalistic about the risks. As a lawman, he had learned to live with them, as I am sure you have."

"But…"

"Please do sit down Gif."

"I don't want to intrude," Gif said. "I just…"

"I need the company of an old friend," Martha said. "Someone I can talk honestly with. That's not something that one can do in this damned place."

Gif assumed she meant the nation's capitol and not Walter Reed Medical Center specifically.

"Harrison stopped by to see me on his way to the river," Gif tried to change the subject.

"I know. He told me he would."

"He asked me to join him on the river," Gif said. "If only I had."

"Stop!" Martha ordered firmly. "Don't blame yourself for anything. There's nothing you could have done. Whatever is going to happen, will happen. This was all ordained."

"Martha, there is no such thing as inevitability. If..."

"Please Gif. Don't torture either of us with your what ifs. And stop pacing the room and sit down. You're getting on my nerves."

"Sorry," Gif said contritely and sat down in a chair facing Martha and the settee. "Is there anything I can do for you?"

"Have you talked with Tom Harrington? I thought I heard his voice at the door."

"Yes."

"Has the bureau taken over the investigation?" Martha, the former sheriff's wife who had lived with law enforcement most of her adult life, asked.

"They are in the process."

"And?"

"They don't know who the shooter was. I wish I could tell you more."

"Is there some kind of conspiracy? You've heard what happened to poor John Walker?"

This was not a conversation Gif wanted to have. He had no information to share that would help the grieving Martha. "I've heard but no one seems to know exactly what happened, yet. The deaths..." Gif hesitated.

"Tell me, Gif. No one else will speak honestly," Martha ordered.

"The murder of a president and the death of a vice president at virtually the same time strike me as too much to be a coincidence, but the bureau does not have any evidence at this time to publicly suggest otherwise. Tom Harrington will ensure that every possibility, every lead will be pursued."

"Will you lead the investigation? Harrison would have wanted that."

"I haven't been offered it. I don't even know who will become pres…be in a position to consider it," Gif said.

"That senile old man, the Speaker," Martha spoke harshly.

"Then he wouldn't consider me," Gif said.

"I could insist on it," Martha said.

"Please don't. Harrison and I were too close for me to be involved. Critics would say I'm too subjective to lead the investigation, and they would be right. I would have to decline."

"But you could work with the bureau. You have before. And both…took place in Virginia, your jurisdiction."

"It is a federal investigation, Martha. The bureau is competent, and the media will be all over them. I can't cope with the media, now."

"Yes you can," Martha persisted.

Gif simply shook his head negatively. This was no time for him to be debating with his friend's grieving widow.

"I want revenge," Martha declared.

That thought gave Gif pause.

Before either could continue, someone tapped on the door.

"I beg your pardon, ma'am," the harassed agent who guarded the door announced.

Before he could finish, a hand shoved the agent rudely to one side and the Speaker of the United States Congress, Hiram Alphonse Adams pushed his way into the room.

"Please excuse my intrusion, Mrs. Tate," Adams said, ignoring Gifford.

A small entourage trailed behind Adams.

Martha glanced at the Speaker, did not immediately reply, and turned towards Gifford.

"Martha, if there is anything I can do to be of assistance, please have your staff phone me," Gif said as he pushed out of his chair. "I plan to stay in Loudoun for the immediate future."

"As will I Gif. I'll call you because I want to continue our discussion," Martha said before taking a deep breath and turning back to Speaker Adams.

As Gif retreated towards the door, he heard Adams say: "Mrs. Tate, speaking for the entire nation, I want to convey our sincere ..."

Chapter 7

After one phone call to Richmond to brief Colonel Townsend on what he had learned, Gif avoided contact with everyone involved in the investigation. The media in turn highlighted the Tate assassination for two days until the public grew sated with the repetitious coverage of the slowly developing and tightly guarded investigation and began to focus on the more sensationally salacious Walker demise. Gif got so tired of viewing pictures of Walker's body with its elevated penis being wheeled in a body bag from the Crystal City apartment to a waiting emergency vehicle to the accompaniment of repetitive, off color speculation and commentary he quit watching television news and followed the story in the *Washington Post*, a newspaper he normally avoided.

Although he kept his cell phone muted, Gif's concern and natural curiosity finally got the better of him, and he drove to the Loudoun County Sheriff's Office to consult with his old friend and protégé, Dick Simmons, who had served under Gif as chief investigator and with Gif's sponsorship had replaced him as sheriff. After parking his Prius in the lot behind the former bowling alley that still served as headquarters for the sheriff's department, Gif entered by the back door expecting to find himself in familiar setting. To his surprise, he did not recognize a single one of the deputies he passed in the hallway on his way to his old office. They all were so young that they looked to Gif like high school kids. The real shock came when he opened the door to the sheriff's outer office expecting to find his old secretary Kitty managing everything as she had for Gif and Tate before him.

"Yes sir, may I help you?" A pert young brunette greeted him.

Suddenly, Gif remembered that Kitty had retired six months previously. At the time, he had wondered how the old department was going to function without Kitty's efficiency and encyclopedic memory, but the sense of loss he had felt at the time had been immediately covered over with word that Gizzie Kane, the young investigator he had personally trained and whose career he had nurtured until she took over as chief investigator, another of Gif's old posts, had abruptly retired on the day she had completed her twenty years. He had called Gizzie, and she assured him that the decision had been hers. She alleged she had grown tired of the constant pressure and wanted to devote time to her maturing family. Knowing Gizzie, those words had struck Gif as hollow, but he had not pursued the matter.

"Hi, my name's Gifford, and I would like to see Sheriff Simmons if I may," Gif smiled at the interloper. She struck him as being almost too attractive and too young for the responsibility she now held.

"Do you have an appointment?" She glanced at an appointment book open in front of her.

Although Gif got the message--no appointment no access--he smiled. "I think Dick will see me. I used to work here."

"Gif, is that you?" Simmons deep voice called from the inner office.

"You may go in, sir," the young lady smiled.

Before Gif could move, Simmons appeared in the doorway. "Gloria, this is Sheriff Gifford. Gif, Gloria." While Gif and Gloria shook hands, Simmons continued. "I can't believe so much time has passed since your last visit, Gif. How long have you been here, Gloria?"

"Six months, now, sir," Gloria said.

"Welcome, Gloria," Gif smiled. "You must forgive me. It was quite a shock not finding Kitty behind that desk. She was a local institution."

"I know, sir," Gloria said pertly. "Trying to replace someone like Kitty is impossible."

"Gloria is doing an excellent job, Gif. Don't let that pretty exterior mislead you."

"I'm sure," Gif said, tired of the polite chatter. He preceded Simmons into his old office. Gif hardly recognized the place. The scarred desk that he had inherited from Harrison Tate had been replaced with a shiny, pretentious, mahogany edifice. A leather couch and two oversized leather chairs stood in the place of the old metal chairs with the torn seat covers that had lined the walls.

"Looks like the Loudoun Sheriff's Department has come into some money," Gif said, recalling how he and Tate had had to fight for every penny in the budget.

Simmons laughed. "This is nothing. Our new building is projected in next year's budget. One of these days you'll drop in for a visit, and we won't be here."

Simmons closed the door behind him, waited for Gif to try one of the leather chairs, and seated himself in the padded executive chair behind his huge desk.

"I don't feel at home here anymore," Gif shook his head.

"Things haven't changed that much. All this growth has brought prosperity to the county."

"I am not sure that it's all for the good," Gif said. "Listen to me. I sound like one of the old families speaking."

"No, you're right. Money isn't the only thing the new population has brought with them. Have you checked our crime statistics lately?"

Gif shook his head. "I can see that you've had to hire a lot of new deputies. I didn't spot a single familiar face on my way in."

"And they all looked young, too," Simmons laughed.

"Who replaced Gizzie?" Gif asked, not sure he wanted to hear the answer.

Simmons hesitated. "I know Billie Williams wanted the job," Simmons referred to another of Gif's protégés. "But I decided we needed some new blood. I brought in a young man, Brian Sadler, who had a remarkable career in the Military Police."

"It's your department, now, Dick," Gif said, his tone conveying his disapproval. "How did Billie take it?"

"Oh, he was disappointed, but we kept him on as deputy chief investigator."

Gif did not comment, letting his silence convey his attitude. One thing he did not like was change, particularly on what he considered to be his home turf. "What can you tell me about the investigation?" Gif changed the subject abruptly.

"I was hoping you could share with me," Dick said.

"I'm not involved," Gif said honestly.

""I'm sorry to hear that," Simmons said. "The Feds use us for the grunt work but share nothing."

"You haven't been involved in the search out at Harrison's place?" Gif had played this game, but this was the first time his former subordinate negotiated with him.

"Oh, they called us in to set up road blocks which produced nothing. The shooter was long gone by the time we got there. I was in the area myself."

"Really?" Gif noted that Simmons had not answered his question.

"Yes. As soon as the Secret Service alerted us that Harrison was heading for his river place for a few hours of relaxation, I checked things out for myself."

"Only you?"

"No. Even though they didn't ask for support, I had four cars running a routine lookout. We always did for Harrison."

"Did he do this often? The solitary fishing thing?"

"Only every couple of months."

"And your men did not set up road blocks?"

"Not until the Secret Service alerted us that…that something had happened. We got deployed too late."

"Really?"

"What are you implying, Gif? That we did something wrong?"

"No, Dick, of course not. I'm just trying to visualize how the damned thing went down."

"Well, the Secret Service screwed up. If we had deployed protection as we could have, Harrison would still be alive, or at least we would have the bastard in custody. As it stands, nobody has anything."

"The subsequent search produced nothing?" Gif tried again, a little surprised at his former protégé's defensive attitude.

"Not a God damned thing. They have had frogmen in the river for a week and found nothing, and we have had men searching every inch of the countryside with the same result. This damned guy knew what he was doing."

"They didn't find the weapon?" Gif pressed.

"If we had, or they had, I would have told you. The perp must have taken it with him. It is all so bloody frustrating. I'm not even sure that the feds want to find anything."

Surprised, Gif reacted. "I don't believe that, Dick. Harrington is a damned good investigator, and he wouldn't try to cover up anything. He feels about Harrison the same way we do."

"I know, Gif. It's all just terribly sad and tragic. Sheriff Tate was a great man."

"And a good friend," Gif said. He thought about venting his own sense of failure, of having let his friend down in a time of need. "I wish I could have been there to help him."

Gif did not admit that he could have been if he had not been so self-centered.

"I know," Dick said. "We all share that reaction. If there is anything that we here in Loudoun can do, we're ready to help."

"I find it difficult to believe that the killer took his weapon with him. That's the one thing he couldn't explain away if stopped." Gif returned to one of things that troubled him.

"I know," Simmons agreed. "But a thorough search of the area produced nothing."

"Have there been any credible claims of responsibility by foreign terrorists?" Gif asked. "A terrorist wouldn't leave his weapon, his most treasured possession behind."

Simmons shook his head negatively. "Not that I'm aware of. You'll have to ask your federal friends that question. I know nothing that hasn't appeared in the media."

Simmons referred to the fact that the media had reported that Abu Nidal, Ansar Al-Islam and a number of lesser terrorist organizations had issued releases claiming credit for the Tate assassination. On the other hand, the Department of Homeland Security had subsequently issued a statement that flatly declared that no agency of the United States Government had developed any credible information that linked any foreign terrorist organization to the shooting.

"It could have been rooted in something domestic," Gif opined.

"I have the impression that the Secret Service thinks it might have been a single crazy acting on his own," Simmons said.

"Nothing to indicate some kind of grand conspiracy?" Gif asked.

"Nothing."

Simmons' response surprised Gif. It was too quick, too absolute, too certain, so unlike an experienced investigator. Gif knew that he had taught Simmons to think better than that.

"So we have a dead president, a dead vice president, no suspects, and a senile acting president," Gif said bitterly.

Simmons did not react.

They sat in silence until Simmons broke it with a question. "Are you going to get involved with this task force they are setting up?"

"What task force?" Gif asked.

"We all assumed they would ask you to take over the investigation," Simmons avoided a direct answer.

"I'm too close to it all," Gif said. "What task force?"

"I'm told that Acting President Adams has asked Tracey to head up a task force to take charge of the investigation."

Simmons referred to Tracey Schultz, the former Director of the Federal Bureau of Investigation, who thirty years previously had shared an apartment with Gifford when he and Tracey had been bureau trainees. Gif's decision to quit the bureau and join the Loudoun County Sheriff's Department had been responsible for breaking up their intimate relationship. Over the years, they had clashed and cooperated on numerous investigations as each had independently advanced in their respective careers.

"I hadn't heard that, but I'm not surprised," Gif said. "If true, Adams just went up in my estimation. Tracey is a good choice."

"I know, but I was rather hoping that it would be you heading up the investigation," Simmons said.

"The bureau will continue to handle the investigation. Tracey will just take the political heat. Believe me, I know how that works."

"Still, since both Schultz and Harrington are good friends of yours, you might be able to help them out."

"They don't need my help," Gif said firmly as he stood up.

"If you do get involved, don't hesitate to call on your old friends here," Simmons said.

"Those that still remain," Gif said sourly. As soon as the words were out of his mouth, he regretted them. Dick was a former protégé, and time not Simmons had wreaked the changes that Gif regretted.

Simmons raised his hands in surrender. "Just remember that Harrison Tate has a lot of old friends, Gif, and we all will do what we can to assist."

"I know, Dick," Gif said as he stood up. "Sometimes things happen that are just too much for some of us to bear."

Chapter 8

Nan Starbright, aka"Bubbles," true name Maria Fernandez, took a direct flight from Dulles to Miami on American Airlines using her working name. On arrival, she went by taxi to her sister Benita Fernandez's apartment in Miami Beach where she plied the same trade as Maria. Because Benita was five years older and not half as attractive, she serviced a much lower class hotel clientele than her sister. As a consequence, Benita's profile, while known to the local police, was much lower than Maria's whose specialty was the power brokers of Washington.

Although sisters, the two were not really close. They had a brood of siblings and had been more competitors than sharing pals. When Benita opened the door and found Maria standing there with four suitcases at her feet, Benita frowned and asked:

"What the shit do you want?"

Maria smiled, ignored her sister's unfriendly welcome, and asked: "Would a bed for the night be too much to ask for?"

"I'm broke. Try Eduardo," Benita started to close the door. Benita referred to their brother who lived in a Mexico City slum.

"I've got money, Benita, don't be mean," Maria said.

"It's pay as you go," Benita said, appraising her sister's clothes and baggage. Four years previously, Maria had bailed out leaving her with an empty fridge and owing two month's rent. "In advance."

"Agreed," Maria said as she shoved a suitcase into the doorway.

Benita stepped back and watched as her sister struggled to get her luggage inside the apartment. "Looks like you had a good run. What's wrong, got the law on your back?"

"Give me a drink, and I'll tell you all about it," Maria lied.

Benita laughed. "Help yourself," she nodded at the open rum bottle on the kitchen table.

As the two sisters sat at the table and shared the rum, straight up, Maria entertained Benita with a tale of a broken romance thwarted by a jealous wife and a lying lover.

"Bullshit," Benita chuckled, not believing a word of her sister's story. "You were always a lousy liar."

Maria smiled, opened her purse, and placed two hundred dollar bills on the table. She watched closely as her sister greedily eyed the money, more than she usually earned in a full night of steady groping and slurping.

"You owe me a lot more than that," Benita declared.

"Like hell I do," Maria answered, reaching for the two bills.

"Let's negotiate," Benita said, grabbing the money.

The Fernandez truce lasted for ten long days, boring ones for Maria, a period of constant irritation for Benita who spent her nights working and days trying to sleep with a restless Maria rattling around the small apartment. Maria at first tried to respect her sister's need for rest but worry about what was happening in Washington made her restless. She paced the floor, walked the streets, read the newspapers, tracked the investigation on CNN, but nothing really helped. Concern that the frantic focus on Walker's ludicrous death would lead the investigators or the media hounds to her innocent involvement gradually lessened as the newsreaders and commentators edged toward a common conclusion: There was no discernible link between the deaths of the president and vice president. In Maria's mind, she was just a simple working girl and Walker was the one who had insisted on taking all those damned pills.

When it became apparent that the only person--James Dexter--who could point in her direction was keeping his mouth shut, probably trying to conceal his own involvement, Maria began to consider the possibility of returning to Washington. She hated living with Benita, and she missed her own lovely apartment. In her haste to escape, she had simply locked the door and left all her lovely expensive things behind, more concerned about the possible embarrassing exposure that being involved in such a scandal would bring than she was about simple material luxuries. As the threat subsided, particularly after Walker was crated up and shipped home to be buried in rural Alabama, the media began to focus on the investigation into the president's assassination, leaving the Walker death as an amusing, sensational, but probably irrelevant side issue. The marginalization of Walker's bedroom escapades gave Maria hope.

She had enjoyed her career as a top line call girl, and she particularly had learned to take all of its rewards for granted. She began to contemplate returning to Washington where the supply of randy and rich power brokers was so plentiful. She acknowledged that she had to act discreetly. She had rather liked her working nom de plume, Nan Starbright, but that could be reluctantly but easily changed. She had used her working name when she had sublet the apartment from a Foreign Service bachelor currently stationed in Paris. Moving out would not pose a problem. All she would have to do is hire a couple of guys with a truck, tip the building super generously, and slip away one weekday afternoon. With a new name, a change in hair color, and an apartment in D.C. or Maryland, Nan Starbright could vanish into the anonymity that all such fictional characters deserve.

The more that Maria thought about resuming her old career, the more attractive and potentially possible it became in her mind. After a particularly abusive exchange with Benita, Maria purchased a new cell phone and retreated to the lobby of a Miami Beach seafront hotel to phone the one person in her old apartment building that she felt she could trust. Terry Caldwell was a fifty-five year old spinster who had a one room utility apartment in Nan's Dupont Circle building. Terry, who labored as a secretary for the Department of Agriculture, had been flattered by the attention of her glamorous, much younger neighbor. Neither of the two women considered their casual relationship a friendship, but it was useful. Since they lived on the same floor and both were single, they occasionally gave each other chance assists, a grocery store purchase, the retention of a spare key in case of need, mail pickups when one or the other was out of town, nothing more intimate, just neighborly help.

"Terry, Nan," Maria said when Terry answered on the second ring.

"Oh, Nan, I'm so glad that you called," Terry responded immediately.

"Why? Is something wrong?" Maria reacted, worried that she had made a mistake in calling Terry.

"I was worried about you."

"Oh," Maria recovered. "I'm sorry I wasn't able to give you a heads up, but my sister Benita, I think I've mentioned her, had an accident."

"I hope it wasn't anything serious."

"No. as it turned out, she was involved in a bad accident and ended up with a broken leg. When the silly hospital called me, she was unconscious, so I just packed up and hurried down here."

"Is she recovering?"

"Now, she is. I've got her home, and I'm holding her hand. I'm ready to come home now, but I'm not sure when I will be able to get away. Is everything OK up there?"

"I'm sure you've been following all the news," Terry said.

"Yes, about the president. That was awful." Maria was hopeful that Terry would elaborate.

"Oh yes, and that silly Walker. Men!"

"I guess he was just a playboy. Did they ever figure out what happened?"

"All I know is what I read in the papers and see on television. I guess he was one of those self-indulgent men who couldn't be happy with what he had at home."

"Have they found out who he was with?" Maria held her breath.

"Oh, I don't know anything about that."

"How are things at the apartment?"

"The same."

"Have you had a chance to check out my place?"

"I wasn't sure if you wanted me to. I've got your mail collected. Nothing but catalogues. Do you want me to look at your apartment?"

"When you get a chance. I left in a panic and when you do that you're always worried that you didn't get all the lights turned off. That kind of thing."

"OK. I'll go over as soon as we get off the phone," Terry said. "When will you be coming home?"

Wishing that she could answer that question, Maria answered: "I'll let you know as soon as I know. If anything should happen at the apartment, just give me a call. I have a new cell phone." She gave Terry her new number.

Gif, assuming that there was nothing he could do to assist the investigation of his friend's murder, occupied himself at home with his phone off. Certainly, the federal authorities with whatever local manpower they needed could handle the woodland search and resident checks along the river. Gif doubted that they would find many clues. Their best chance at apprehending the killer had evaporated with the fifteen minutes after the shooting. After that, the killer would have cleared the site, and the roadblocks would have been rendered futile by the passing minutes. The shooter clearly knew what he had been doing. Also, if the searchers had found the discarded weapon, he would have heard of it from Thomas Harrington or Dick Simmons. Gif paid little attention to the frantic media reports claiming knowledge of developments because he knew firsthand what they were worth.

He did not attend the public viewing at the White House. That would have been too painful. He also avoided the official service for the slain president. He knew Harrison Tate would not expect him to listen to a pompous cleric utter gratuitous words about a man he had not personally known. Gif firmly believed that his friend Harrison, his warmth, good humor, loyalty, intelligence, and ambition had already departed the cold body. Gif was not sure where Harrison's spirit had gone, and he doubted that some performing cleric knew either. In fact, Gif doubted that it had gone anywhere; it had simply evaporated and no longer existed outside the memories of friends like Gif.

Gif did, however, phone Grace Hanson, Harrison's secretary, who was cleaning up the loose ends in the Oval Office getting ready for her return to Richmond. After exchanging regrets, Grace informed Gif of Martha's plan to hold a private service for family and close friends at their Leesburg home, the last act of a too brief presidential career. Grace insisted that Gif attend for Martha's sake if not for his own.

Ten days after the assassination, Gif parked the Prius in front of a hydrant and walked two blocks to the old Victorian residence. When challenged by an alert Secret Service agent at the entrance to the long driveway, Gif used his credentials to identify himself. The agent checked a short list, found Gif's name, and stepped back allowing Gif to enter. Another agent again cleared Gif at the front door, and he entered the front hall and found himself at the end of a relatively short line. Harrison's two sons, both businessmen now approaching middle age, greeted each new arrival at the door to the spacious formal room that in the distant past had been used by Harrison's patrician Virginia ancestors to host formal balls marking significant family occasions. In those days family members would travel considerable distances on horseback and in wagons and buggies and remain as guests for up to a week at a time.

"Thank you for coming, sir," Harrison's older son greeted Gif at the door. "Mother would like a word with you when you get a chance."

Gif nodded but said nothing else. Both men knew that Gif had been one of Harrison Tate's intimates for almost thirty years, and neither felt that pious words were necessary. Gif followed the line to the open casket and reluctantly stared at Harrison Tate's body one last time. Although the funeral home had obviously done a first class job on the highest-ranking patron of their Loudoun establishment, Gif glanced briefly at the lifeless, waxen face, patted the back of a cold, exposed hand, and moved on.

"Gif, over here, please," Martha Tate spoke from the settee strategically placed some distance from the coffin.

Gif hesitantly approached the widow who was appropriately dressed in black. He noted that her face was still pale, as it had been that night at Walter Reed Hospital, but her eyes were now clear.

"Martha." Gif took her extended hand and leaned over and kissed her on the cheek.

"That bastard," Martha whispered, the anger still in her inflection.

"I know," Gif agreed.

"Please sit down, Gif," she indicated the one chair that had been strategically placed in front of the settee.

"I don't want to block the line," Gif said.

"But I want you to," Martha said. "This isn't a social occasion, and I'm not interested in exchanging pieties with those of the Washington establishment who were neither friends nor supporters. They had to be included because of their rank in the hierarchy."

Gif glanced behind him, identified the acting president and several members of Tate's cabinet who were being held at bay by the two sons who had deserted their post at the door. Acting President Hiram Alphonse Adams stood about fifteen feet away chatting with Tate's Secretary of the Treasury Alexander Hamilton Sperry who Adams to everyone's surprise had named the acting vice president, an unprecedented appointment to a historically nonexistent office. Even more astonishing was the fact that Adams and Sperry shared adjoining offices in the Treasury Department, an act that left the White House and Executive Offices virtually intact, still occupied by their incumbents who had been selected by Tate. Even the entire Tate Cabinet still served in place, anxiously of course, and Adams appeared to be in no hurry to bring in his own henchmen.

"I know Martha," Gif said. "Are you still living in the White House?"

"Hell, no. I'm living right here. I don't plan to visit that cold, unfriendly place ever again."

Gif did not know what to say to that. He was, however, glad he had come. Martha obviously still needed the support of an old friend.

"I hope you know that if you ever need anything, I'm here," Gif said.

"Of course. Please understand that I need only one thing. You must catch and kill that bastard who shot a wonderful man for no reason that a decent person can comprehend."

"Martha, I know why and how you feel. I share the same emotion," Gif said. "But I am not an assassin, and I'm not involved in the investigation."

"Why aren't you?" Martha was bitterly unyielding.

Gif did not know how to respond to that question. He stood up, silently regretting his inability to pacify his friend's widow.

"Why don't you talk to her and explain how you feel?" The unrelenting Martha nodded at someone behind him.

Gif turned and was surprised to find Tracey Schultz standing alone about twenty feet away, coolly watching him and Martha. Tracey, Tom Harrington's predecessor as FBI chief and Gif's intimate friend and roommate some thirty years previously when both had been bureau trainees, did not react when Gif turned. Tracey and Gif had parted, not amiably, when Gif resigned from the bureau and joined the Loudoun Sheriff's Department and Sheriff Harrison Tate. Tracey made no secret of her belief that Gif had sacrificed a promising career for a bucolic, pressure free life. Over the years, their paths had crossed as Tracey had risen in the FBI's bureaucracy, and she had repeatedly let Gif feel the sting of her disappointment in him. He had expected Tom Harrington to recommend that the acting president appoint Tracey, his mentor, to head the Tate Task Force after Gif had firmly declined the offer that night at Walter Reed, but Tracey's acceptance had surprised him. He immediately assumed his waspish former roommate missed the limelight.

Gif looked at Martha, not sure how to respond. "Honestly, Martha, we don't have anything left to say to each other."

"Just tell her you want to help catch the murderer who killed your best friend," Martha ordered.

Gif looked at Martha, glanced at Tracey, and suddenly realized he did not know what to say to either one of them. Several seconds passed before Gif made the inevitable decision. "Martha, I will do what I can."

"Nobody's holding you back, Gif," Martha dismissed him.

Gif took a deep breath and turned. Chatting with Tracey was no longer a pastime that he treasured, particularly since she had not called when she left Washington over a year previously, an oversight that Gif had not appreciated. Tracey liked to turn on the charm when she needed him and to ignore his existence in the long intervals in between.

"Hi lover," Tracey greeted him, a familiar glint sparkled in her eyes, warning Gif that she was about to enjoy herself at his expense despite the solemnity of the occasion.

"That greeting is trite and embarrassing," Gif frowned, "coming as it does from a retired, elderly person."

"I agree," Tracey replied. "I retract it. Hi, old man."

"I'm surprised that they let you in," Gif said. "I thought this occasion was for close friends and family."

Tracey hesitated, giving Gif the impression that he had scored with the truth. Harrison Tate had confirmed Tracey's appointment as Director of the FBI, but he had delayed for over a month causing her considerable anguish.

"Congratulations on your recent selection," Gif referred to the acting president's announcement naming Tracey to head the Tate investigation.

"Thank you," Tracey said sourly. "I understand you had no interest in finding the killer of your best friend."

"It was never offered," Gif said defensively, ignoring the conversation he had had with Tom Harrington.

"Really? Tom has a different story."

"How is the investigation progressing?" Gif asked, tired of fencing with his old apartment mate.

"Not very well. Are you still on the public payroll or are you now preoccupied with tormenting the Blue Ridge wild life?"

"I'm still employed," Gif said.

"Good," Tracey said. "Are you interested in joining our task force?"

"We've already shared a similar experience, and I didn't like it, not one little bit," Gif replied quickly, ignoring his conversation with Martha and his promise to see what he could do to assist.

"But it turned out so well," Tracey said sweetly.

They both referred to the fact that Tracey as FBI Director had persuaded the president to appoint Gif to head a task force investigating a congressional serial killer. Gif felt he had been used as a figurehead whose sole function was to divert public scrutiny while the bureau under Tracey's command pursued the killer. Gif had conducted an independent investigation and coordinating with Tom Harrington had caught two murderers operating under the same rubric.

"Any leads?" Gif asked.

"The Secret Service believes the killer was a singleton with a real or perceived slight. You know how many demented creatures that hold the government responsible for their problems exist out there."

"I didn't ask 'what does the Secret Service believe?'" Gif was not about to let Tracey divert him. "If you don't have any leads, what do you think?"

"I don't think much. I don't buy this coincidence crap. Too many strange things are happening in Washington these days. What do you think?"

"What I think is not pertinent," Gif said.

"I know that," Tracey snapped. "I didn't mean to imply that it was."

"What do you make of that Walker thing?" Gif ignored Tracey's slight.

"Gifford, this is a lousy venue for this conversation. Will you agree to meet with me and discuss the situation rationally? The shooting occurred in your backyard."

"I'm not interested in playing your games, Tracey," Gif replied with less certainty than he should have.

"Frankly, we need all the help we can get."

Tracey had him on two key points. Harrison had been his friend, and he owed him, and the shooting had occurred in Virginia where he was Chief of the Office of Special Investigations responsible for investigating crimes that required more than normal police procedures.

"Where can we meet?" Gif relented.

"A neutral site?"

"I'm sure that Dick Simmons can accommodate us." Gif referred to the Loudoun County Sheriff.

"That would hardly be a neutral site. Are you free now?"

"After the service?"

"Yes. I'll meet you at your little shack," Tracey said.

Gif agreed despite Tracey's final insult and turned away catching Martha Tate watching them from across the room. She nodded her approval before averting her eyes.

Gif was sitting on a chair in his front yard when Tracey Schultz, driving an official black government sedan, arrived. He immediately noted that she had company, Tom Harrington, and frowned, realizing he was going to be double-teamed. Tom was a friend, but at the same time he was the FBI Director, Tracey's protégé, with a sensational investigation on his back.

Gif greeted the two as they climbed out of the sedan. "How

wonderful it is to have government transportation in this day of high gas prices." He smiled to take some of the sting out of his sarcasm.

Harrington laughed, but Tracey, as was her wont, took up the challenge. "Am I to assume that the Virginia State Police no longer can afford to provide vehicles to its officers?"

"No, but some of us do not take advantage of the taxpayers' diminishing largess," Gif replied, nodding in the direction of his Prius.

Tracey glanced at the odd little car and dismissed it. "Some people have no taste."

"A frenemy," Gif frowned at Tracey. "And a friend," Gif smiled at Harrington, unable to conceal his delight with his spontaneous choice of words.

Harrington glanced at Tracey. "I'm not sure what a frenemy is, but I'm glad it's you and not me our host is describing."

"I'm sure it's something he learned from his educated girl friend, the bone crusher," Tracey shrugged, not admitting her own ignorance.

"Please come into my humble abode," Gif said as he held the door open.

"I know what humble is," Harrington said. "But I am not sure there is much of that around here."

"At least not walking around," Tracey said as she pretended to assess the furnishings.

"Some things are definitely humble," she said as she sat down in Gif's favorite recliner.

Tracey carefully posed with her straight back not touching the chair. She held her elbows against her sides and folded her hands in her lap, all an act intended to convey disapproval. Harrington ignored the second recliner, also facing the television and fieldstone fireplace, and sat in the leather couch with the book-lined wall at his back.

Without asking, Gif continued to the kitchen where he took three frosted bottles of Budweiser from the fridge, opened them, and returned to hand one to each visitor. Gif joined Harrington on the couch, making it necessary for Tracey to turn in their direction.

"Nothing has changed," Tracey said as she dismissively glanced around the room. Having spent an occasional night in Gif's prized refuge during periods when their relationship was enjoying a rare truce in their continuous conflict, the kind that inevitably followed a deep intimate relationship gone sour with each participant blaming the other for its demise, Tracey took pleasure in belittling Gif's pride in his old settler's home.

"During our brief discussion at Martha's, you referred to strange things happening," Gif spoke directly to Tracey, assuming she would be the one to explain her need for Gif's participation in the investigation.

"Maybe I made the wrong choice of words," Tracey set her beer on the table beside the recliner.

"It wouldn't be the first time," Gif said as he leaned over, wiped the damp ring from the table, and placed a coaster under Tracey's bottle.

"Please, children, spare me," Tom Harrington intervened. "Can we please defer the swordplay until later."

Gif, not offended by his friend's intervention, glanced at him and wondered about his choice of words. "swordplay." He assumed Harrington was playing his own word games.

"Speaking only for the edification of our humble host," Tracey continued. "I was referring to the odd political situation now facing this country of ours."

Harrington nodded agreement. "An acting president and an acting vice president, representing opposing political parties, occupy offices in the Treasury Department and not the White House."

"With neither indicating an interest in moving to where they belong," Tracey said.

The two working in harmony made Gif wonder if they had rehearsed this approach. He knew both well enough to realize that they would have discussed how they would handle him if they were serious in wanting him involved in the investigation. This suspicion made Gif keep his mouth shut. He waited for the dog and pony show to continue.

"And no changes have been made in either the cabinet or the White House staff." Harrington did not disappoint Gif when he continued to serve as Tracey's straight man feeding her lines.

"Just one," Tracey said. "Correct me if I'm mistaken, but I notice that Acting President Hiram Alphonse Adams, our current benefactor and master, moved his entire public relations staff into the White House

Office of Communications. His media man is now handling all press conferences and releases."

"Speaker Adams may play the good old boy role, but he is a very astute politician," Harrington said.

"You think he has an agenda?" Gif asked, keeping the conversation moving because he was as interested in what wasn't being said as much as what was. He assumed Tracey might be hinting at some kind of political conspiracy, and if she were, he had to know if it was just speculation on her part or based on something she had yet to reveal. The all too coincidental deaths of a president and vice president on the same day and the simultaneous elevation to power of a very odd political pairing certainly smacked of political intrigue at the very least.

"Of course he has an agenda," Tracey spoke sharply. "Name me a politician who doesn't."

"Well, Adams is not acting like a man with extreme political ambitions," Harrington said, still feeding Tracey easy curve balls.

"He could be the semi-senile old man that he pretends," Tracey smiled, acknowledging Harrington's lead-in. "Or he could be a dangerous and devious eighty year old still at the height of his game."

Harrington and Gif waited for Tracey to continue.

"Adams and Alexander Hamilton Sperry uniting to lead the country sounds too good to be the result of simple coincidence," Tracey said, pausing to give the others a chance to offer views.

"I'm not a constitutional scholar," Gif took the bait.

"You won't get an argument from us on that, Gifford," Tracey laughed, unable to resist the opportunity to needle Gif.

"But maybe one of you intellectuals can enlighten me," Gif fired back.

"The 25th Amendment," Tracey said. "Provides that the vice president shall become president under certain circumstances."

"But," Harrington, a lawyer, added. "The 25th Amendment does not state that any officer in the line of succession other than the vice president can become president. The Presidential Succession Act of 1947 stipulates that officers other than the vice president shall only act as president."

"You're kidding," Gif blurted. "That means that Adams can only be acting president, not president."

"If you read the newspapers, you would know that. Adams can exercise the powers of president but can drop the 'acting' from his title only if he contests and wins the next election," Tracey said.

"But that is two years away," Gif now assumed the role of straight man feeding Tracey lines. He was interested in learning where she was going with this contrived conversation.

"Exactly. Two years for Adams to earn the job in his own right," Tracey said.

"Two years of uncertainty, even if the old man lives that long," Gif said.

"That depends on how wisely our acting president uses his powers," Harrington said.

"What role does Sperry play in all this?" Gif asked.

"He probably has his own game plan," Harrington said. "As best as I can tell, Adams is using Sperry to deal with the country's problems while Adams gives all the speeches and uses his public relations team that he installed in the White House to make sure he gets all the credit when/if things go right."

"And give Sperry all the blame when/if things go wrong," Tracey said.

"You think that is why Adams has Sperry managing things using all of Harrison Tate's staff and appointees?" Gif asked. He knew that neither Tracey nor Harrington was a naïve academic who dreamed up fanciful plots.

"If things go the way Adams wants," Tracey continued. "Sperry may have his own agenda. He wasn't one of Harrison Tate's supporters. In fact he lost a very bitter primary campaign to Harrison that must have hurt very much because he had fancied himself the front runner until Tate emerged as the accidental president."

"I find all of this academically plausible and politically believable, but at the same time it seems to me to be terribly fanciful," Gif declared. "Does either one of you have any plausible evidence to support your speculations? Christ, this would mean that Walker's death wasn't natural or accidental."

Harrington and Tracey exchanged glances. Each waited for the other to respond.

"I think you now understand why the two of us needed to talk with you," Harrington said.

"You didn't answer my question," Gif answered rudely. The subject was too delicate for the three of them to hedge.

Harrington looked again at Tracey before responding. "The two of us agree that someone with police powers in Virginia should investigate the Walker death in depth."

"You're serious?" Gif looked at Tracey for an answer.

Tracey nodded.

"And you have no evidence?"

"Nothing that we can use, Gif," Tracey answered, this time gravely, not as an old flame or competing investigator.

"What makes you suspicious?"

"The coincidence, the circumstances," Harrington answered. "If we had anything concrete, we would be all over it."

"But Walker's death is just too fortuitous for it to be coincidental," Tracey said.

"And you want someone other than yourselves to stick their necks out," Gif declared.

"If you want to put it that way, Gif," Tom Harrington said. "If you could just take a look at the case, under the media radar of course, we would all appreciate it."

"And support me?"

"As much as we can," Tracey said. "Tom and I agree that the key to both deaths lies somewhere in the Walker thing."

"Haven't the media chewed the situation to death?" Gif asked, privately wondering if his two friends were trying to jointly use him for a yet to be stated purpose.

"They have, and no one has identified the person who was with Walker at the time. He didn't swallow all those little blue pills just to take an afternoon nap," Tracey said.

Gif was tempted to give a smart retort to that remark but did not.

"How many?" Gif demanded.

"Too many," Walker said. "We don't have an exact number, but combined with the alcohol he imbibed it was enough to put enough pressure on his system to cause his death."

"Self administered?"

Harrington shrugged.

"It wouldn't have been easy to force a handful of those pills down his throat," Tracey said.

"Was his companion male or female?" Gif asked.

"We don't know," Tracey answered.

"Who does know?"

"The one person who was there with him at the time."

"Who was that?"

"We don't know," Harrington answered.

"Christ, the two of you make a great team," Gif said.

"That's why we need you," Harrington responded before his friend said more than he wanted him to. "We've got the media all over us. We rather hoped that you could come in under the radar."

Gif laughed. "Any police officer who goes near that apartment will have cameras looking over his shoulder."

"Would you consider assisting the bureau as a consultant?" Tom asked. "We could give you any credentials you need."

"Are you really that desperate?" Gif asked, not masking his surprise.

"We are," Tracey answered. "We have nothing on the Tate shooter. We're convinced the cases are linked, but we need someone, like you, to take an independent look at the Walker thing and tell us if we're looking in the wrong direction."

"And you suspect the acting president and acting vice president are behind the whole thing?" Gif demanded.

Tracey and Harrington exchanged pained looks before Harrison answered his question.

"We're probably wrong, Gif, but we can't rule out any possibility. They could be colluding, acting separately, or none of the foregoing. Maybe, the Secret Service is right. Some nut shot President Tate, but our instincts tell us not. What do you think?"

"I don't know enough to have an opinion," Gif answered honestly.

He got up and fetched three more beers from the kitchen fridge. When he got back, Tracey had docilely vacated his recliner and joined Harrington on the couch. Gif handed them the beers and sat down in his recliner without thinking about it. They sat in silence while Gif considered their request. Finally, Gif spoke.

"There's no need for a public announcement about my involvement," Gif declared.

"Of course not, Gif," Tracey said. "We'll cover your backside."

Gif laughed. "Of course, I know how that works."

"We admitted we need your help," Harrington said. "I know you want to find out who killed Harrison. So do we."

Gif glared at Harrington for saying the obvious. When Tom did not back down, simply continued to watch Gif in silence, Gif leaned back and took a deep drink of Budweiser.

"Martha ordered me to get involved. She made it clear that she thought it was my duty," Gif admitted. "But, honestly, I don't know what I can do that you and your investigators have not already done."

"Neither do we," Harrington admitted. He looked at Tracey who for once kept silent, only nodded assent. "But we know how you operate and that sometimes you take chances and get lucky."

Gif did not respond to that gibe. He mused for several more seconds. He wanted to get involved, felt an obligation to do so, but reluctantly wanted to leave the inevitable spotlight to those paid to perform in it. Finally, he decided. "Martha wants me involved, so I will take a look, starting with Walker."

"Good," Harrington declared and stood up. He glanced at Tracey, who remained seated. Harrison without speaking another word started for the door.

Gif immediately recognized that his friend, knowing of his past disputed relationship with Tracey, was discreetly giving them a chance to work out a necessary peace.

Gif waited for Tracey to make a smart aleck remark, but she remained uncharacteristically silent. Finally, Gif broke the uneasy quiet.

"Aren't you leaving with your friend?"

Tracey downed the last of her Budweiser, handed the empty bottle to Gif rather than placing it on the table between them, and answered with a question.

"What do you want me to do?"

"Tracey, we have so much broken ground between us," Gif began but did not finish, not knowing what to say next.

"I know, Gif," Tracey said. "I regret some of it."

She stood up and looked around her. "Surprisingly, I miss this place and some things in it," she said, looking directly at Gif.

He stood up and waited, not trusting himself to try to respond to that ambiguous comment.

"Maybe I'll come back sometime and see if I can figure out what I miss about this dump," Tracey smiled.

As she walked towards the door, Gif obediently followed.

"I'll try to make a lot of noise and keep the media off your back," Tracey said as she pushed on the screen door. "Don't screw up."

She let the door slam in Gif's face and joined Harrison in the car. As they drove away, Tracey fluttered a hand out of the open window.

Gif imagined her thinking: "See you, lover."

"Shit!" Gif swore as he returned to his recliner to worry about his spur of the moment decision.

Chapter 9

The next morning Gif called Tom Harrington on his private line at the office.

"Hello," Harrington picked up promptly.

"Hi, I'd like to start by reviewing your files," Gif said, dispensing with the polite preliminaries.

"Fine. I'll arrange for security to have a badge for you at the front door. Come on up and…"

"I'm not coming anywhere near that squirrel cage of yours," Gif laughed, referring to the odd tetrahedron monstrosity known as Hoover's Revenge which stood seven stories in front on Pennsylvania Avenue and eleven in the rear.

Harrington greeted that tart comment with a brief silence before asking: "What do you propose."

"I know you have enough to occupy your time without serving as my messenger," Gif said, referring to past cases when he and Harrington used to meet wherever and whenever it was convenient. "Can you have one of your errand boys bring the files over to the scene of the crime, say about ten."

Again, Harrington hesitated before chuckling. "I don't think you want all the files. That would take a truck."

"Christ no. Just the one or two important ones."

"I've got the perfect messenger for you. I think you will remember her."

"Oh no, not …" Gif immediately realized who Harrington was referring to and started to protest before he realized his friend had hung up on him.

An hour later Gif had deposited his Prius in the parking garage in the basement and taken the elevator to the eleventh floor before he realized he did not know the room number of Walker's Crystal City hideaway. The media had frequently referred to the eleventh floor and identified the building above Metro Station as the site, including pictures, but Gif did not remember the room number. When he exited the elevator, he was pulling out his cell phone and preparing to punch in Harrington's number when a familiar voice greeted him.

"Good morning, inspector."

Gif turned and found a smiling Reggie Crawford watching him closely.

"I was afraid he might send you," Gif said, smiling back.

During the Capital Hill serial killer investigation, Harrington had assigned Special Agent Reggie Crawford to serve as Gif's FBI assistant. Gif had protested then, knowing that the eager young agent would also serve as his watchdog, keeping the bureau briefed on Gif's activity. Gif, who insisted on conducting his own investigations, alone, to parallel any official effort, federal, state, or local, of course complained, but over time Reggie's usefulness as a driver and general factotum gradually wore him down. They developed a rather close but structured working relationship, based on mutual distrust, which included an occasional promise from Reggie not to report those things that Gif wanted unshared.

"It's something seeing you again," Reggie replied noncommittally.

"We're not a team," Gif insisted.

"Believe me, Gifford. That's the last thing I want. Once was more than enough," Reggie said, demonstrating that she remembered how to handle the prickly Gifford.

"Good," Gif smiled. "Now that we have that out of the way, I want to say I'm pleased to see you again. Is that the material I asked for?" Gif glanced at the large briefcase Reggie was carrying.

"For what it's worth."

"Have you been working this investigation?" Gif asked.

"I'm afraid that's classified information, inspector." Reggie smiled sweetly.

"Where are you assigned these days?" Gif asked, trying another tack.

"1900 Half Street, Southwest," Reggie answered, referring to the headquarters of the FBI's Washington Metropolitan Field Office.

"Good for you," Gif said, meaning it.

Reggie had been a young officer with only one trainee tour behind her when they had previously worked together. Reggie had claimed then she had met Gif in Richmond where Tom Harrington, her mentor and first boss, had been Special Agent in Charge, but Gif honestly admitted he did not remember her.

"Shall we move inside," Reggie said, turning before Gif could respond.

"Lead the way, Special Agent Crawford."

Gif pretended he was in charge while covering the fact he did not know the number of the apartment they were visiting.

Reggie turned left, took ten steps, and stopped in front of apartment 1102. She ripped down the police tape and unlocked the door. She stepped aside and let Gif enter first.

Inside, Gif stopped abruptly, blocking the doorway, interested in a first impression. The place was a mess, and the air, despite the air conditioning, was stale. It was a typical crime scene after the techs had created their havoc. Gif turned.

"Find anything?"

A silent Reggie opened her brief case and offered Gif two bulky files.

Gif ignored the gesture, which he assumed was Reggie's declaration of independence. Again, he wondered what he had done that offended the order of things and required him to be constantly affronted by stubborn women. The place struck him as a typical apartment of convenience. He was sure the French would have a better word for it, but he did not speak French. "Place de rendezvous" and "pied-a-terre" rattled around in his head, but Gif did not dare try the words on Reggie. He assumed that if he did, she would correct him in flawless French. Instead, Gif pretended to study the room which austerely lacked anything that indicated the occupant cared about his surroundings. Better decorated than a hotel room, it lacked warmth, displayed no books, showed nothing that reflected the user's personality. It was just a place to spend a few hours out of the public view. He found it ironic that a potential president found the place convenient, particularly to die in.

Gif continued on into the bedroom, which was a mess. The techs had torn the place apart, looking for clues. Gif wondered what they really expected to find. Certainly, it was an odd place to die in. If anything, it was a convenient site for a high profile politician to meet his temporary mistress out of the public view, nothing more. Gif didn't find that odd. Gif envied Walker for having the clout and ingenuity for finding a way for others to fund his recess.

"In whose name was the apartment registered?" Gif asked Reggie.

Again, she silently offered the two bulky files.

"Reggie, humor me," Gif said, firmly, not pleading.

"The vice president's campaign committee, certainly not Walker's." Reggie challenged him.

"Whose name is on the lease?"

"The Committee for the Election of John F. Walker."

"Who signed the checks?"

"Mr. James Dexter."

"And who is James Dexter?"

"Christ, you don't know anything."

Reggie's words, mannerisms, and tone were designed to tell Gif she resented his being called into the investigation. Gif understood. He had once been an aspiring journeyman investigator himself. Rather than reacting, he waited patiently for her answer.

"Dexter is…was Walker's chief of staff. A thirty year old kid from Walker's senate staff and campaign who served as Walker's gofer."

Gif raised his eyebrows.

"Dexter doesn't know shit," Reggie exclaimed, her disgust evident. "He wasn't chief of anything. He had a lofty title so he could better do anything his lord and master wanted."

"Like renting and maintaining little hideaways like this one. Are there any others?"

"Not that we know. Walker used this one frequently. It was handy to the office."

"Does that bother you?"

"What makes you think it bothers me?" Reggie asked.

"Your attitude," Gif said, holding out his hand for the two bulky files. "You come across as very unsure of yourself, Reggie. It's unbecoming in a special agent. Now withdraw to the other room and let me read this crap."

He sat down on the bed and began to read. He ignored Reggie who had done what he had ordered, just barely. She stood in the living room a foot from the doorway, frowning at Gif. Gif scanned very quickly, and it did not take him long to learn that the bureau really had no idea what had happened. The one thing that was clear was that Walker had died under strange circumstances with one other person present. The fluids on the sheets determined that, and if they were not enough, the two used condoms were. The coroner's thorough report indicated that Walker had an enlarged heart, the kind that occasionally developed in long distance runners. The report speculated that in Walker's case it had simply gone undetected. Some considered an oversized heart a source of pride, but medical opinion sided with the conclusion that it was a very mixed blessing indeed. Walker had in his system an excessive amount of sildenafil citrate, a drug used in medicines such as Viagra. Walker was also a regular user of an alpha-blocker to prevent high blood pressure. In the coroner's opinion, the drugs combined with an excess of alcohol and prolonged exertion to cause Walker's heart to fail. In the medicine cabinet in the bathroom, investigators had found a bottle half filled with large blue tablets which analysis had determined to be triple sized sildenafil citrate, a version not sold or prescribed in the United States.

After reading that, Gif closed the file, set it beside him on the bed, and looked up at Reggie who was watching him from her living room vantage point, an amused expression on her face.

"Well?" Reggie asked.

"What do you think?" Gif countered.

"That Walker was a silly male who caused his own death."

"Really? A suicide?"

"Hardly. Just another chauvinist determined to show masculine superiority."

"Were you able to determine where the blue pills came from?"

"We're still working on it. Most likely the internet. Canada is a very real possibility."

"Was Walker computer literate?"

"He used one at the office. He did not have a laptop or personal computer at home. He depended on others to do his grunt work."

"Who?"

"One of two people, either Beatrice his executive secretary, or Dexter, his chief of staff. Both had worked in his Senate office and on the campaign staff. I doubt that he would have Beatrice order that stuff for him, so it was probably Dexter. Both deny it."

"You said Dexter signed the check to pay for this apartment."

"Dexter signed and used campaign funds to pay the rent. It's all in the file."

Gif ignored Reggie's sharp comment. She obviously took personally the fact that Gif had been brought into the investigation to look over her shoulder.

Gif opened the second file and glanced at the rather lewd photographs of a nude Walker, first those from several angles showing Walker lying on this very bed and others with Walker on the coroner's table. They all featured Walker's enormous erection. After viewing every photograph, Gif looked up and this time found Reggie smiling.

"I don't find this situation very funny," Gif remonstrated, losing patience with her lack of professionalism.

"Everyone else who looks at those photographs does," Reggie smirked before turning around and abandoning the doorway vantage point.

Gif continued to sit on the bed. Two things bothered him. One, the coincidence: the two most powerful men in the United States died on the very same afternoon; and two, the connection: he needed a connection to help him find Harrison Tate's killer. Since the circumstances of Walker's odd demise were all he had to investigate, he was determined to do so thoroughly, no matter whose feelings he might hurt.

Gif left the bedroom to find Reggie waiting impatiently in a chair in the living room. It was certainly not decorated to his taste, and probably not to Walker's. The period furniture was selected for display not comfort and indicated to Gif a woman's touch.

"Have you identified his companion?"

"No," Reggie answered bluntly.

"Why not?" Gif, now irritated, asked.

"Because Dexter claims he doesn't know anything about her. He states that if there was a woman here, she was the vice president's friend not his."

"Do you believe him?"

"Until I can prove otherwise."

"Have you tried?"

Reggie responded with an angry glare. "Of course."

"And you failed," Gif drove the dagger home.

Reggie did not reply.

"And nobody in this building ever saw her come and go."

"No. Do you want to re-interview them?"

"No, but I do want to talk with Dexter. Where can I find him?"

"Presumably at his office or his home."

"Then let's go. I've seen enough here."

Reggie hesitated, and Gif assumed she was debating internally, asking herself whether she should tell him to find Dexter by himself or to assist him. He waited out the small mutiny, standing by a fragile French period chair. Finally, Reggie took a deep breath and stood up. When she did so, Gif sat down, leaving Reggie now on her feet waiting for him. They both stubbornly let silent seconds drag past until Reggie finally capitulated.

"Are we going or not?"

"Sit down, Special Agent Crawford; I have something I want to tell you."

Reggie sat down.

"Do you remember those wild boys in high school whose parents could not control them?" Gif asked, surprising her.

"Of course," Reggie snapped, biting her lip to avoid commenting on such a stupid and irrelevant question, not able to predict where her difficult, temporary partner was heading. She was sure, wherever it was, she would be the one to end up with a short stick.

"Their parents, usually out of desperation, sent the most difficult cases off to a private school that specialized in fixing boys."

"Are you going to suggest that I need to be fixed?" Reggie demanded.

"Of course not. Do you think you need to be fixed?" Gif asked, not hiding his amusement at Reggie's attitude.

Reggie did not reply.

"Sometimes those boys graduated with their problems resolved while others emerged unfixed, so to speak."

Reggie nodded, trying to keep Gif talking, so she could learn the purpose of his nonsensical story.

"But the parents of the unfixed boys were perplexed to learn that their offspring had enjoyed the experience. Do you know why?"

"No, but I know you are going to tell me," Reggie said, trying to keep from smiling.

"Because the private school for difficult boys was filled with companions just like them. In the new school's environment, they thrived despite all the efforts of the school authorities to alter their behavior patterns." Gif smiled.

"And what the hell does that little parable mean?"

"I was just trying to tell you that we are dealing with politicians, and you know what? They all need fixing, and probably always will."

"And in Washington they live among their unfixed peers and enjoy it fully," Reggie laughed despite herself.

"Exactly," Gif said, waving a hand in a circle illustrating his point by encompassing the playpen apartment.

Reggie, using her special White House pass, gained them entrance to the confined parking area behind the Executive Office Building where they commandeered the last two open visitors' spaces. She led Gif into the entrance to the West Wing of the White House where she arranged for Gif as an investigator for the Tate Task Force to be granted a limited pass authorizing him access for a thirty-day period. This process required almost a full hour and by the time they were finished an exasperated Gifford had come close to walking out several times.

"Damned bureaucracies," Gif swore as they were walking down the hall towards the vice president's office.

Since Reggie was enjoying his discomfort, she did not reply. She tapped on the door and stepped back to allow Gif to enter first, which he did. His appearance startled the matronly, fiftyish woman with short white hair who had been sitting behind her desk staring out the window. Her desk was paper free, and she clearly did not have much to occupy her time.

"Beatrice, this is Inspector Gifford, another member of the task force investigating Mr. Walker's death," Reggie dutifully introduced him before sitting down in one of the leather visitor's chairs.

"Oh God, oh no," Beatrice groaned. "I've nothing more to say."

"I'm very sorry, ma'am," Gif tried to sound contrite. "I know this is a very difficult time for you."

"You don't know anything," Beatrice reacted.

"I'm sure many people would agree with you," Gif said, glancing at Reggie who nodded her head in agreement. "I am in the process of back-tracking the investigation," Gif said. "I am double checking to make sure we didn't miss anything."

"I've told Special Agent Crawford everything I don't know," Beatrice said, making a little joke.

"I'm most interested in that apartment," Gif said.

"So's half the world," Beatrice said sourly. "I know nothing about it. For that, you will have to talk with Dexter."

"I certainly want to," Gif said. "What do you know about the apartment?"

"Dexter handled all that. I know the vice president had a secure phone installed, and I can give you the number." She glanced at the secure green phone on the console behind her.

"Who else had the number beside you? The president? His secretary?" Gif asked.

"Oh no," Beatrice reacted. "I had the number and no one else."

"Not even Dexter?"

"Oh," Beatrice said. "Yes, Dexter probably knew the number, but it didn't do him any good. He would never use it. Not ever. Anyway, he had to come in here and use this phone because it is the only one that connects to the secure line the communications people installed in the apartment"

"The the communications people had access to the number?"

"I guess, but they would have to use this phone."

"Are you sure?"

Beatrice hesitated. "I'm not really sure, but they wouldn't have dared use it. The vice president insisted that I be the only one to contact him on this line."

"Not even Dexter?"

"Well, first I would place the call and if the vice president agreed I would hand the phone to Dexter. But that did not happen more than once or twice because the vice president went to the apartment to relax and he would get angry if disturbed, even with me, and Dexter didn't want to face that. He was afraid of Mr. Walker, if you know what I mean."

"After all these years working for Mr. Walker?"

"Oh yes." Beatrice leaned forward and began to whisper. "Dexter wasn't really a chief of staff. He just had the title so he could get done what the vice president wanted. He never made any decisions on his own."

"Really?"

"Yes. Dexter was just a messenger, an errand boy. That's why he is having so much trouble finding a new job."

"A new job?"

"Oh yes. We all have to find new jobs. Nobody has told us anything, not yet, but that is the way things work here. The new man always brings in his own staff, and the old people just pack up and leave."

"What about you?" Gif asked. "Are you having any difficulty?"

"Oh, no. I worked on Capitol Hill long enough that I have friends. I have a job waiting for me, nothing with anything like the status here, but that's all right. I'm old enough that I will be able to make it to retirement. Then, I'll leave all this political nonsense behind."

"Can you tell us who you will be working for?" Gif asked.

"I'd rather not. Not without permission."

"That's all right," Gif said, matter-of-factly. "I do have a delicate question to ask. If I may?"

"They all do," Beatrice said, pleased with herself as she glanced at Reggie for support.

For what it was worth, Reggie nodded affirmatively.

"Do you know the name of the person who was in the apartment with the vice president?" Gif asked bluntly.

"This one?" Beatrice shook her head negatively. "Mr. Walker was a man who liked women. He always did, and they kept changing. He never once told me their names."

"Do you think his wife knew about these other women?" Gif asked quickly, now that he had Beatrice confiding.

"Probably. Like all wives, she put up with a lot," Beatrice hesitated before continuing. "And I don't blame her. Mr. Walker always treated her decently."

Gif heard Reggie shift in her chair behind him but did not turn. "Why do you think she knew?"

"Oh there have been times, particularly when we were in the senate, when Mr. Walker was not as discreet as he has been since he got to the White House."

"Discreet?"

"Oh yes. Before, he didn't have the money for secret apartments and access to secure telephones and all that."

"What did the vice president's protective detail think about all this?"

"I don't know. I'm sure they didn't know about the apartment. The vice president always left them behind when he went there, and after the …after …the president was shot, they didn't know how to find the vice president and they were really in a panic. I told Special Agent Crawford all about that. I thought they were going to explode before I called the vice president for them."

"They talked with the vice president at the apartment?"

"Oh no, the vice president did not answer when I called. He must have already been …" She let her voice trail off.

"When do you move to your new office?" Gif asked just to change the subject.

"I don't know. My new senator wants me to stay on here so I can learn what is happening …" Beatrice hesitated, worried she had said too much.

"I understand," Gif said. "A lot of us would like to know what is happening."

This time, a more cautious Beatrice did not try to educate him.

"Is Dexter here now?" Gif asked.

"No, I don't know where he is. He doesn't tell me anything, now.

He shows up once in a while, but with nothing to do I suspect he's spending his time looking for a job."

"Do you know where I can find him?"

"I can show you his office. I am sure Agent Crawford knows about his phone numbers and home address."

Gif glanced at Reggie who nodded affirmatively.

"If you can't think of anything more to tell me, Beatrice," Gif said, standing up. "I won't trouble you anymore."

"I don't know anything," Beatrice repeated her mantra.

Gif and Reggie shook hands with Beatrice and closed the door behind them.

"I think she enjoyed having some company," Reggie said. "You were kinder with her than I thought you would be."

"I'm not impressed with our former vice president's personnel judgment," Gif said.

"Wait until you meet Dexter," Reggie laughed. "I assume that's where we go next."

Chapter 10

Nan Starbright—Maria Fernandez back in her more glamorous blonde guise – was in the kitchen of her Dupont Circle apartment when someone knocked on the door. She had been living discreetly in her home, the one she occupied in her alter ego disguise, for two days, praying that no one discovered she was back. She peeked through the keyhole, saw two, large, muscular, black men wearing clean tee shirts that bore the bold, red letters "Two Men and a Truck," and relaxed. She had feared that her visitor was her next-door neighbor Terry who had been watching her apartment for her. Terry, she wanted to avoid. For that reason, she had scheduled the move, escape really, for a Monday morning when she was confident that Terry would be at the office. Maria, hated doing this to Terry, but she felt it necessary for Nan Starbright to disappear into an untraceable void. Two weeks living with her disagreeable sister in Miami Beach confirmed something that she already suspected—she could not leave the lovely possessions she had worked so hard to acquire behind. For that simple reason, she took the risk.

"Hello," Nan opened the door.

"Ms. Starbright?" The larger of the two men asked.

"Yes."

"Two Men and a Truck," the brute said.

"Come in," Nan stepped back. "I'm ready to go." Nan pointed at the boxes she had stacked with her most valuable possessions. "Take everything and get me out of her as quickly as you can."

"Problems?" The first man smiled.

"Just do it," Nan ordered.

"Right," the man agreed. "Let me take a quick look."

Nan nodded and followed the two men through the apartment.

"Two thousand dollars," the man said when he completed his survey.

Nan nodded affirmatively. She was prepared to pay any price just to get her goods away from the building without incident.

"Is the destination local, in the metropolitan area?" He asked.

""Silver Spring," Nan said, not willing to give the exact destination until they were away from this building. "Will a check do?"

The man nodded.

Nan wrote a check for twenty-five hundred, adding the extra five hundred for good will and silence. She handed the check to the man.

He looked at it and smiled, showing it to his partner. "This is too much," he said.

"Not if you have me out of here before noon and keep your mouths shut," Nan said.

"Don't worry lady. The supe will learn nothing from us. Times are tough, and we understand back-rent problems."

"There might be a bonus for you if we don't have any problems. The supervisor always goes downtown on Monday morning and meets with the owner."

Without another word, both men started to work.

Six hours later a much-relieved Barbara Dolle was settled in her Silver Spring high-rise with Nan Starbright only a bitter/sweet memory. Her furniture was in place; her boxes neatly stacked, and her appointment book in hand. Her first call was to a senior senator from Wisconsin.

"Hi," she said when he answered his direct line. "It's me."

"Where in the hell have you been?" The senator recognized her voice and let his irritation show.

"Sorry, baby, but I had a death in the family and been out of town," Barbara said.

"You should have let me know," the senator complained.

"I know, baby, but when I got back I had to move."

"Move? Nan, where?"

"It's Barby, now, and I have a new cell phone."

"Ahh. Business problems?" The senator, no neophyte, asked.

"I'll tell you all about it when I see you," Barbara lied.

"When?"

"That's up to you," Barbara, anxious to get back into business, purred.

"Tomorrow?"

"At your apartment," Barbara said and hung up.

⁂

Despite Gif's best intentions, it required three visits before he found the elusive Dexter at home. After Beatrice warned him of Gif and Reggie's interest, Dexter avoided the office and determinedly refused to answer the door. Frustrated by their failure to locate the elusive Dexter, Reggie and Gif had gone their separate ways, a mutually acceptable arrangement. On the third morning, Gif pounded on the door, and a hung over Dexter forgot he was in hiding and irritably responded to the irritating racket.

"Go away."

"Mr. Dexter, open the door," Gif knocked again. "I have a special delivery."

"Slide it under the door," Dexter replied.

"I need a signature," Gif said.

Dexter opened the door and held out his hand.

"My name is Gifford, and I am following up the initial Walker investigation," Gif introduced himself, waving his credentials.

"Shit," Dexter said as he hesitated.

Not waiting for Dexter to react, Gif pushed past him into the apartment.

"I've tried to reach you several times at the office," Gif said, trying to further divert the already distracted young man. "But Beatrice said you haven't been coming in."

"Why should I?" Dexter said defensively.

"Isn't the taxpayer still paying your salary?" Gif asked, amused at the way the interview was beginning.

Dexter responded with silence as Gif sat down on the sofa, making it clear that he was there until he got his questions answered. While he waited for Dexter to volunteer something, giving Gif insight into what might be worrying him, Gif studied his ill at ease host. He was surprised at James Dexter's youth. Gif knew Dexter was in his early thirties, but he looked like a teenager, an odd choice to serve as a vice president's chief of staff. The fact that it was eleven in the morning and Dexter, who everyone seemed to call by his last name, was still dressed in his pajamas did not speak well for his alleged job-hunting effort.

"There's nothing to do there, and sitting around looking at the ceiling is boring," Dexter finally blurted.

"I can sympathize with that," Gif said. "I've had my down periods too."

"I'll bet," Dexter surrendered and sat in a chair facing his tormentor.

"I promise I will not take up much of your time," Gif lied, prepared to ask as many questions as it took.

"I've told the Secret Service and the FBI and the lawyers everything I know, several times," Dexter almost whined.

"Do you have any coffee?" Gif asked amiably, trying to soften the confrontation and entice Dexter into a discussion between two like-minded conspirators working through a necessary exercise.

"No," Dexter resisted Gif's efforts.

Gif shrugged. "Then we better try to get this ordeal over quickly. Why is your name on the lease of Walker's apartment?"

"It's not."

"But you write the checks for the rent. That's the same thing."

"No it isn't."

"All right, Dexter, let's start over. Why are you the one who paid the rent?"

"Because the vice president told me to."

"Where did the money come from?"

"The Committee to Elect John Walker."

"Was that a legal use of campaign funds?"

"The apartment was used for committee meetings."

"And for other things."

"The vice president did a lot of his thinking there."

"Thinking?"

"Why is who wrote the check for the rent so important to you? Are you investigating campaign finances?"

"In a murder case every little detail is important."

Gif's words clearly jolted the young man. He sat up straight, pulled his bathroom tightly together, and stammered. "M..m.murder?"

Gif did not comment.

"That's not what the papers say. It was just a dumb accident."

Gif smiled, implying silently that the media didn't know what he did.

"What does my name on a check have to do with anything?"

Gif took a notebook and pen from his jacket pocket and made a show of preparing to take notes. "Give me the names of the committee members who used the apartment. My superiors will insist that I check with each one for times and dates." Gif shook his head, trying to convey the impression that he thought this was an unwanted imposition.

They sat in silence for two minutes until Dexter relented. "OK, the apartment was for the vice president's personal use. I just do what I'm told. If there was something wrong with that, charge Walker." Dexter smiled, trying to show that he thought that was amusing.

"How often did the vice president use the apartment for personal meetings?" Gif persisted.

"Ask Beatrice. I didn't keep a log."

"Who kept the apartment in order for these meetings?"

"A cleaning lady, I assume."

"The vice president arranged for that himself?"

Dexter's laugh was more bravado than genuine.

"What was her name?"

"Who's name?"

"Maybe you better get dressed, Dexter. You don't want to go to headquarters dressed in your pajamas."

"Maybe I better call my lawyer," Dexter bluffed.

"You can call from headquarters," Gif felt some sympathy for the nervous young man but did not relent.

"OK," Dexter surrendered. "I kept the apartment clean. Walker didn't want anyone else to know about the place."

Gif pretended to write that response down, giving it more

significance than it actually deserved. "Before or after Walker used it for his meetings?"

"Both. The vice president liked to impress his guests."

"What was her name?"

"Which one?" Dexter said derisively.

"The last one."

"I don't know. Walker never told me anything like that."

"Where did the vice president find these girls?"

Dexter shrugged.

Gif closed his notebook and placed it and his pen on the sofa cushion beside him. He stared hard at Dexter, waiting for him to elaborate.

"He usually had a new one every month or two."

"Look, Dexter, we're both grown men and understand this sort of thing. The vice president was under a lot of pressure and needed to relax now and then. We all do. It's none of my business how he did it. What was the last girl's name?"

Gif watched as Dexter considered whether to keep lying or not.

"Just answer my simple questions, and we can get this over with. I'm not enjoying it any more than you are, but understand one thing. I'm not very smart, but I'm stubborn. I'm not leaving here until you do answer my questions."

Dexter looked one direction and then the other, almost as if he were trying to find some way to escape from his own apartment in his pajamas. Finally, he relented. "Nan something."

"Where did you find Nan? An escort service?"

Normally, Gif asked only one simple question at a time during an interrogation because a person under pressure tended only to focus on the last question letting the others slide by, but Gif deliberately threw in the second this time to see if Dexter would seize on the suggestion.

"Escort service? Nothing like that. Walker always found his own dates. He was too cautious to let anyone know what was going on."

"Where did Walker meet this Nan?"

"We never discussed anything like that, and Walker never let me meet them if that's what you're thinking."

"How did he arrange his appointments?"

"He called her."

"What was the number?"

"I don't know."

"Did Beatrice ever call her for him?"

"I don't know."

"What phone did he use?"

"His cell."

"How do you know that?"

"He always used it for personal calls. I know he did this last time." Dexter suddenly shut his mouth, realizing he had said too much.

"This last time?"

"I think so. I entered his office just as he finished a conversation."

"And this was just before he took the afternoon off?"

Dexter nodded.

"And there is nothing else you can tell me about this Nan?"

"Usually, Walker turned over his dates pretty fast. Nan lasted longer than most. I think Walker dumped them fast because of his wife."

"Because of his wife?"

Again, Dexter hesitated, obviously worried he was really talking too much.

Gif waited, giving him time to sort out his fears.

"Yes, I think she tolerated his … his …whatever it was as long as it never grew into something serious. You know how it is here in Washington."

"No, how is it?"

"Most of these politicians think they are above everyone else. That they can do whatever they want just as long as they do it discreetly. Look at Kennedy, LBJ, Clinton, probably most of the others. When these guys get to the White House or even Capitol Hill, they think different rules apply. There's a lot of money floating around and their wives like being big shots, just like their husbands, so they tolerate a lot of crap."

Gif nodded as if he agreed and thought about his next question. He assumed that Dexter was still holding back. Certainly, he knew more about Nan and the pills than he was admitting. Deciding that he had probably learned as much as he was going to this time, he changed the subject, willing to give the nervous young man time to worry.

"And you, Dexter, what are you going to do now? Return to a big job on the Hill?" Gif asked.

"I don't know," Dexter said. "Nobody seems to be interested in me, now, so I'll probably just hang around as long as they keep me on the payroll at the White House. The acting president and acting vice president don't seem to be in a hurry to make any big changes."

"Well, I wish you luck," Gif said. "I'll give you a call if I think of any more questions to ask. Do not leave town without first contacting me." Gif gave Dexter his card

"I hope you don't call," Dexter said ungraciously.

"I know, and I apologize for inconveniencing you," Gif said as he made his withdrawal.

Chapter 11

After his conversation with Dexter, Gif rechecked the files Reggie had given him searching for the results of the bureau's check on the numbers called from Walker's cell phone. Unable to find the list, he had Tina Belosi, who was manning his Richmond office, use her phone company contacts to find the number for him. Gif deliberately did not use FBI resources, not because he did not trust Tom Harrington, but because he knew the only way to avoid a leak in a sensational case was to keep all details to himself. Tina discovered that the Walker household had five cell phones from three different companies. Walker's wife had one, each of his two children had a phone, and that left two unaccounted for. Of these two, only one had been used on the day of Walker's demise, and the number called was another cell phone listed in the name of one N. Starbright who lived in an apartment located on New Hampshire Avenue near Dupont Circle, a well-known D.C. streetwalker's locale. Thus, it was not until the Saturday after his talk with Dexter that he drove to Dupont Circle, found a rare street-side parking place, and made his way to the apartment listed in the name of N. Starbright,

Gif knocked on the door, softly at first, then progressively more loudly, but got no response. After about three minutes of futile rapping, Gif swore to himself and was turning to search for the building supervisor when the door across the hall opened and a middle aged, overweight lady with white hair curled in a tight permanent stared at him.

"Hello," Gif smiled. "I'm looking for your neighbor who doesn't seem to be home. I hope I didn't disturb you with my knocking."

The woman looked at Gif suspiciously.

Gif took out his credentials case and held it up for the woman to see.

"May I ask why you are looking for Nan?" The woman relaxed slightly. "I hope there is no problem."

"Oh no, just a background investigation," Gif equivocated, pleased that he now had a name, Nan Starbright. The catchy name really piqued his interest. Nan Starbright sounded like the kind of sobriquet that a working girl would adopt.

"Just a routine check," Gif repeated.

The neighbor relaxed.

"I'm a government employee, so I understand background checks," she said."One of Ms. Starbright's friends gave her name as a reference," Gif said, trying to look disappointed. "I've called Ms. Starbright several times but got no answer. I hate letting these interviews drag out because sometimes the applicant really needs the job, and the process takes entirely too long as it is."

"That's the God honest truth," the neighbor said. "With the economy in the shape it's in, jobs are hard to come by."

"And I don't like to be the one who's responsible for any delay," Gif agreed.

"You say you've tried several times to reach Nan?" The woman asked.

"Yes," Gif said. "I've even called in the evening."

Gif's comment appeared to trouble the neighbor.

"It's strange that you would mention that," the neighbor frowned.

"Really?"

"Yes," she said. "I've been a little worried about Nan myself. Would you have the time to discuss it with me?"

"Of course," Gif said. "Maybe you know something that would assist me in contacting Ms. Starbright," Gif said. "I would really like to clear this interview."

"Please come in, Mr. Gifford," the woman used Gif's name, which she had only glanced at when he waved his credential case in front of her, thus proving that she was more astute than her appearance indicated. "Maybe I can be of assistance."

She stepped back, and as Gif entered her small apartment, she said:

"My name is Caldwell, Terry Caldwell. Nan is, was, an acquaintance.

I wouldn't say we were intimate friends, but we did favors for each other. May I offer you a cup of coffee, Mr. Gifford?"

"Yes, thank you," Gif replied.

"Please have a seat, sir," the woman said as she turned to the small kitchen alcove.

Gif sat down on a couch covered with a satin fabric featuring large red roses and waited.

The woman returned carrying a plastic tray with two cups of coffee, a bowl filled with envelopes of sugar substitute, a small carton of half-and-half cream, and two napkins. She set the tray down on the coffee table in front of the couch and sat herself in a chair opposite. "Please help yourself, Mr. Gifford. I hope you don't mind instant."

"My favorite," Gif said taking a cup of foul looking coffee and ignoring the cream and sugar substitute.

The woman sat back and waited for Gif to take a sip of coffee. Just as he got the cup to his lips, she spoke. "I haven't met many of Nan's friends, just one or two. What is the name of the person you are doing your check on?"

"I'm sorry, Ms. Caldwell," Gif played the game. "But regulations prevent me from divulging that. The Privacy Act."

"I understand," the lady said primly, clearly not liking the answer. "I'm afraid I have some bad news for you."

"Oh?"

"Yes. I'm afraid Nan has moved. It's all quite strange. Almost three weeks ago, she left town without warning. Normally, we kept each other informed so we can look after each other's apartment. You know, bring in the mail and the like. I have Nan's key, and she has mine."

"Hmm." Gif nodded and sipped the terrible coffee again so he would not have to respond.

"I was really worried because that was so unlike Nan. Then, she called and explained. Her sister Benita had an accident."

"I hope it was nothing serious," Gif said.

"She broke her leg, Nan said."

Caldwell paused, giving Gif a chance to comment. He nodded, waiting for the woman to continue.

"I guess it wasn't too bad. Anyway, Nan said she had to stay with

Benita for a while, and after we chatted a little she asked me to keep an eye on her apartment for her. She was worried that in her rush to get to her sister's bedside that she might have left a light on or something. I said I would, and that's about it."

"Did you check out the apartment?"

"Right away and everything was fine. Nothing out of order."

"Ms. Starbright didn't say when she would be returning?"

"No, but something is odd. I checked the apartment again a week later and nothing had changed. Then, I looked again two days ago, and everything was gone. The furniture, everything. I was really worried. I didn't want to be held responsible if there had been a robbery or something, so I immediately phoned the building super. He said I shouldn't worry, that something had come up, and Nan had moved out lock, stock, and barrel on Monday. What do you think about that?"

"I am as surprised as you are," Gif let his disappointment show.

"That is so unlike Nan. I would have thought that she would at least have knocked on the door or given me a call to thank me for looking after her things while she was out of town."

"Maybe she will," Gif said. "Did she by chance give you her sister's phone number in Florida?"

"No, but I know she lived in Miami Beach."

"I assume her name was Starbright also," Gif said. "Maybe I could call her and ask how to contact her sister."

"I think she said her sister's name was Benita. I can't say about Starbright." Caldwell hesitated. "Somehow, I doubt it."

"Why do you say that?"

"I'm not sure I should say. I'm not a gossip, you know."

Gif waited for her to continue.

"Well, she was rude, leaving like she did," Caldwell tried to explain her rationale for what she was about to say next. "You know Nan was a very beautiful girl, much younger than I am. She had lovely blonde hair, peroxide I suspect, because Nan was very dark complexioned."

She again waited for Gif to comment, and he remained silent, giving her the opportunity to tell her story.

"She said her sister's name was Benita. That's a Hispanic name. Thinking about it, I find it odd that one sister is named Nan and the other Benita."

"Do you think Nan was short for Nancy?" Gif asked.

"Mr. Gifford, I think Starbright was a name for a working girl. Nan was very nice to me, but she lived in a big apartment with expensive furnishings and kept very odd hours. She didn't have a nine to five job like most of us single girls."

"That's very interesting," Gif smiled. "You have been very helpful. It's too bad Nan didn't give you Benita's phone number." Gif forced himself to drink the last of his coffee and stood up, saying: "Delicious. Ms. Caldwell, do you still have the key to Ms. Starbright's apartment?"

Terry pleased at the attention and the opportunity to be helpful, nodded, leaped out of her chair, and hurried to the kitchen where she opened a cupboard door and took out a solitary key. She waved it in the air and led Gif out of her apartment. She unlocked the door to what had been Nan's apartment and stood back, letting the official investigator precede her. She already had carefully inspected the apartment and knew what it contained, nothing.

Gif entered, paused, and studied the empty apartment, finding what he had expected. Nan had obviously cleared out in a hurry, taking everything she valued, leaving only dirt and rubbish behind. He noted the marks on the rug outlining where furniture had stood. The windows had shades, but no curtains or drapes. A filled black plastic garbage bag leaned against the kitchen sink. He opened the refrigerator and was struck by the odor of soured milk.

"It looks like Nan left in a hurry," Gif said.

Ms. Caldwell nodded.

Gif checked out the bedroom, master bath, glanced at the empty second bedroom, and didn't bother to test the telephones. He already knew they were disconnected. Suddenly, he remembered something Ms. Caldwell had said. "You said that Nan did not give you her sister's phone number. Did she by chance tell you how you might contact her if you found something amiss in her apartment?"

"Oh yes," Ms Caldwell replied matter-of-factly. "Nan said she had a new cell phone, and I could reach her on that."

Gif sighed. "Do you still have that number?"

"Oh yes," Ms. Caldwell replied and headed back to her apartment to retrieve it.

Gif did not bother to ask if she had ever tried to call Nan on that number.

Back in his Prius, Gif called Tina in Richmond and had her check out the cell phone number that Caldwell had given him. As he anticipated, it led him to Nan's sister Benita's home in Miami Beach, which Nan had listed as her home address. Gif then had Tina track down the phones listed at that address and finally learned a number he could call.

"Hello," a tired female voice answered on the fifth ring.

"Benita?" Gif asked, taking a chance.

"Who the hell is this?" The female asked.

"I'm a friend of your sister," Gif said.

The female hung up before Gif could continue. Gif smiled and dialed the number again.

"What?" The very irritated Benita answered.

"I am very sorry to bother you," Gif began again.

"Why you wake me?"

"It's exactly eleven fifteen."

"Me work night. Sleep now," Benita complained.

Suddenly, Gif realized that Benita spoke the truth. She was in the same business as her sister, only she worked the night shift.

"I've lost touch with Nan," Gif spoke quickly.

"Lucky you. You call Maria, not me. Goodbye."

"Wait," Gif pleaded. "Nan has moved."

"Me know. Call Silver Spring."

"Do you know her number? This is really important."

Benita laughed. "You call Barby Doll." Still laughing, she hung up.

After pondering that odd conversation, Gif once again called Tina.

"OSI," Tina answered pertly.

"Tina," Gif said. "Please see if you can locate a number for Nan Starbright in Silver Spring, Maryland. It's probably a new number issued in the past week. Nan has changed apartments."

"Right," Tina said.

"Please don't laugh, but the number might be listed under the name Barby Doll or Maria Doll."

"You're kidding," Tina laughed as Gif knew she would. "Barby Doll? A working girl, right?"

"I don't name them, Tina. Just do me a favor and find her," Gif chuckled as he hung up.

Confident that Tina would find what he needed quickly, Gif headed down 16th Street towards the Maryland suburbs, calculating it was worth the risk because it was a much longer trip back to Loudoun and the day was only half over. By the time he reached Silver Spring, his cell phone buzzed.

"Gifford," he answered.

"Gif, Tina," his efficient secretary greeted him. "Believe it or not, I've located Barby Doll. Barbara Dolle, Doll with an e, just registered a new cell phone."

Armed with the information that Tina had given him, Gif checked his Metropolitan Washington mini-atlas, struggled with the small print, but eventually located his destination in Silver Spring. Maria lnu (last name unknown), aka Nan Starbright, aka Barbara Dolle now resided in a modern, ten story, brick building, the Bancroft Apartments, located on East West Highway not far from the Metro. Gif had more difficulty finding a street parking space than he had locating the building, but eventually he compromised on a water hydrant protected by broad paint stripes. He tossed his Official Police Business placard on the dash and walked the block back to the apartment complex. There, he passed through the unmanned lobby and took the elevator to the tenth floor. He tapped lightly with the knocker and waited. To his surprise, the door opened almost immediately, and he found himself face to face with a blond beauty in a fetching black linen mini-dress that highlighted what must be a perfect figure.

"Yes?" The woman demanded, not masking her irritation at the interruption.

"Ms. Dolle, Barbara, Nan," Gif said, displaying his credentials. "My name is Gifford and I have a few questions for you."

Nan/ Barbara tensed, frowned, took one step back, stared wide-eyed at her visitor and then visibly slumped. She took a deep breath, looked to her left, and right, giving Gif the impression she was searching for an escape route. He stepped into the room and closed the door.

"We can talk here or we can go downtown," Gif said.

"Shit," Nan/Barbara declared. "What is this all about? Let me see your credentials again," she ordered as she recovered from her initial shock.

"I think you know what this is about, Ms. Starbright," Gif said, ignoring her demand.

"How in the hell did you find me?" Nan/Barbara asked.

Her question told Gif that she knew exactly why he was there.

"It wasn't easy."

"Benita should keep her damned mouth shut," Nan/Barbara grumbled.

"How do you know I talked with your sister," Gif acknowledged his source.

"Because she is the only one who knows this address and the name Barbara."

"I like Nan Starbright better," Gif said. "Mind if I call you Nan?"

"You can call me anything you want, asshole."

"Can we sit down?" Gif asked as he lowered himself into the chair that stood with its back to the door, placing him between Nan and the only exit from the apartment. He had no doubt that she would run if given half a chance.

"I've nothing to say without my lawyer present," Nan blustered.

Gif reacted by taking out his handcuffs. "Then, Ms. Starbright, I have to read you your rights before taking you to headquarters."

"What did you say your name was?" Nan smiled, apparently preparing to try another approach, charm not confrontation.

"Inspector Gifford," Gif replied. "I am a member of the task force."

"What task force?" Nan sat on the edge of a fragile, gold-gilt chair with striped silk cushions, another imitation French creation.

"The investigation into our national calamities," Gif said, deliberately not explaining the obvious. "What can you tell me Nan?"

"I don't understand."

"Yes you do," Gif said. "For the moment, only you and I know that you are the last person to see Vice President Walker alive."

Gif did not believe it necessary to elaborate on the threat implicit in his last statement.

"Oh shit," Nan demonstrated her limited vocabulary while signaling that she understood.

Under similar circumstances, Gif was confident he could elaborate with much more eloquence the consternation Nan undoubtedly suffered at that moment.

"Tell me precisely what happened," Gif said. "And maybe…"

He did not promise anything but tried to imply with two words that the possibility of maintaining anonymity might exist.

"Oh shit," Nan repeated.

She hesitated, and Gif waited.

"I didn't do anything I wasn't paid to do… ." Nan began.

Gif did not comment.

"A mutual friend introduced us." Nan reverted to her rehearsed story. "John was an important man in a high pressure job, and he needed a safety valve. That's all I was."

Nan paused and looked at Gif with sad, innocent eyes, trying to determine if he was buying her line. Gif nodded encouragement.

"I was discreet, and that was what he needed, among other things."

She again tried to read her tormentor, but Gif did not react, not positively, not negatively. Encouraged, Nan continued.

"We met regularly for the past month or two, but it was all coming to an end. Not soon enough, as it turned out," she said sourly. "He called me; we met at the apartment, and he had a drink or two, too much if you ask me. He swallowed more pills than he should. I warned him to be careful with those damned things. He was too proud of his performance, as if it meant a damned thing to me. He went on and on for at least an hour. I asked him to stop, but he refused to listen, and he finally collapsed. I asked him what was wrong. He didn't answer. I slipped out from under him, turned him over, and he didn't move. I just panicked and ran. That's all I know."

"Who was the friend who introduced you?" Gif asked congenially.

"Oh, I can't tell you that."

"Yes you can."

Nan stared at him, realizing how important this first interview would be to her future.

"Will you protect me?"

"As much as I can," Gif promised nothing, implying whatever Nan wished to assume.

"Senator George Ames." Nan whispered.

Gif nodded. "When and where?"

"At a Georgetown cocktail. Three months ago. Please don't tell Senator Ames I mentioned his name. He is still one of my clients," Nan admitted.

"Did you call Walker or did he contact you?"

"He called me."

"Your Dupont Circle apartment?"

"Yes."

"Where did he get the number?"

"I don't know. I assume Senator Ames. Please, don't discuss this with Ames."

"Nan, do you realize the situation you are in?" Gif asked, taking a little pity on her.

"Of course," Nan bristled. "Why do you think I am answering so honestly?"

"If the media learns your name…" Gif threatened.

"I know. Will you protect me? I'll do anything you want." Nan tested her ability to manipulate him.

Gif smiled. "What did Walker say when he called?"

"He invited me to a party at his apartment."

"And when you arrived?"

"There was no party, just Walker."

"What happened then?"

"I'm a working girl. I know it, and Walker knew it. We negotiated and went to bed."

"What did he pay you?"

"Do we have to go into that?"

"Yes."

"You'll get me in trouble with the IRS."

"That's the least of your worries."

"Five thousand dollars."

"Each visit?" Gif let his surprise show.

"No, a month."

"For how long?"

"That was up to Walker. We didn't have a damned contract."

"Was this the first time that Walker took the pills?"

This question obviously worried Nan because she hesitated. Gifford waited. "No," Nan finally admitted. "Each time we met Walker's performance got a little weaker."

"So each time he took more pills?"

"Yes."

"How many this last time?"

"How the hell do I know? I wasn't his nanny." Nan lost her temper, or at least pretended to do so. Gifford waited. "Too many, obviously," Nan finally blurted.

"Why do you say that?"

"It's obvious, isn't it? Something killed him, probably the pills and the alcohol."

"Did you provide the pills?" Gif continued to press.

"Hell no. Most of my customers don't need them."

"Where did Walker get them?"

"I don't know. Ask Dexter."

"Dexter?"

"You don't know anything, Gifford, do you?"

Gifford waited.

"Dexter is his flunky."

"Did you ever meet Dexter?"

"No."

"Nan, don't lie to me," Gif warned. "Who paid you?"

Nan stared at Gifford, no longer sure how much he knew. "Dexter," she admitted.

"Cash or check?"

"Cash. I don't take credit cards."

"How did he get the cash to you?"

"Carrier pigeon, how the hell do you think?" When Gifford did not react, Nan continued. "He handed it to me."

"Where?"

"At Walker's apartment."

"After every session?"

"Hell no. Once a month. Dexter would call me, and I would meet him there. It was the least I could do."

"You described Dexter as a flunky. What makes you say that?

"Because I heard them talk on the phone. One time Walker went into the bathroom and discovered the bottle was empty. He called Dexter and hollered at him, ordered him to order more, extra strength."

"Where did Dexter get the pills?"

"How do I know? I assumed the drug store like everyone else."

Gif thought about that answer, and Nan fidgeted as she waited for the next question. Finally, Nan asked; "What happens now?"

"You should have come forward and told the authorities what happened," Gif said.

Nan laughed. "You're kidding. Are you going to reveal all this to the media?" She asked.

Gifford studied her thoughtfully, not quite sure what to say. "Nan, I'm going to investigate everything you told me. I can't promise you anything. I have to report your involvement to my superiors, and I can't guarantee how they will react. You know as well as I do how big this whole thing is."

"Oh shit, I'm dead," Nan said.

"Relax, if you can," Gif ordered. "Don't even think about leaving town. As soon as I leave here, I will have you placed under surveillance, but don't talk to anyone but me. I promise you I will protect you as much as I can. If what you told me is true, you don't have much to worry about. You didn't commit a crime other than leaving and not reporting Walker's death. No one is going to arrest you for that."

"The media will hang me for just being there," Nan moaned.

"Yes, but you stay tough and talk to me and you will eventually be able to leave town and change your name, again. I suggest one thing, though."

"What's that?"

"Find something more plausible than Barby Doll."

"I have only one other question for now," Gif said as he stood up. "What is your real name?"

A pained look shot across Nan's beautiful face.

Gif waited.

"Won't Nan do?"

"Of course not. I know that Benita is your sister, so don't play games with me."

"Maria," Nan grumbled. "You have something against Hispanics?" She challenged.

"No, I don't Maria. You can call yourself anything you want, but being Hispanic is nothing to be ashamed of."

"It is for a high class working girl," Nan said.

Gif sat back down.

"Fernandez," Nan said softly. "But nobody knows me by that in D.C."

"I do," Gif smiled, standing back up. "Here are my phone numbers," he handed her his card. "Call if you decide to move again or leave town."

Back in the Prius Gif thought about calling Tom Harrington and arranging a meeting to discuss what he had learned and to set up a discreet surveillance of Nan Starbright aka Barbara Dolle. He knew that he could trust Harrington not to leak the information he had learned about Nan Starbright to the media, but he also understood that Harrington would have to share it with his investigative team and brief his new boss, the acting president. He was confident that once that happened the sensational revelation about the identity of Thatcher's companion would leak. Harrington would presumably protect Gif's involvement, but Nan's life would become a virtual hell, and her ability to earn a living would be endangered. He doubted that few of her customers would take a chance on being identified as a client. Gif decided to hold off on his meeting with Harrington and give the situation more thought.

As Gif followed 16th Street across the District on his way home, he made a spur of the moment decision. He decided to drop in on Dexter's New Hampshire Avenue apartment and push him on the source of those potent blue pills. Although it came as no surprise, Gif was still irritated by the fact that both Dexter and Nan Starbright were lying to him on key points, one of which being the pill provider. He doubted very much that Walker had ordered them himself. He had too many people around him monitoring his activities, the Secret Service, his staff and probably most inhibiting of all, his spouse.

Gif took the elevator to Dexter's dingy apartment, again marveling at the fact that Walker had trusted his chief of staff position to a young, unimpressive man like Dexter. That choice certainly reflected badly on Walker himself. Walker had to know that men in high office were judged by the quality of their appointments as well as by their own actions and statements. Gif made a mental note to check deeper into Walker's own background. The whole situation made him wonder why Harrison Tate had selected Walker as his vice president.

Gif rapped loudly on the door but got no answer. He checked his watch, three o'clock, and wondered if Dexter had finally gotten up the nerve to return to the White House. He thought about going down 23rd Street and visiting Dexter at his office. As he was returning to his car, he noted the increase in the volume of traffic on New Hampshire Avenue, a little surprised at the early start of rush hour, and decided to put off Dexter for another day. He hated sitting in stop and go traffic and opted to head for Loudoun County forthwith.

Gif, the pessimist, surprised himself by making it back to his private retreat in little under an hour. With a couple of hours to kill before getting his usual frozen meat loaf dinner out of the freezer, he decided to get a little exercise. He thought about a jog, dismissed that as an option as he changed his clothes, and instead went out to the barn to exercise his ride-on mower instead. He had made several turns around his too large back yard and was heading for the house when he noticed a familiar figure watching him from the patio. Dick Simmons. That surprised him. He and Dick were close, but their relationship had never extended beyond the sheriff's department or official business. They shared an occasional lunch in the past, but that had been all. Gif considered himself one of Dick's mentors. Dick had worked for him when Gif had been chief investigator for the department and had followed along behind as Gif himself had moved up the ladder until eventually Dick had succeeded Gif as sheriff when Gif had bailed out after one term. Since then, they had gradually grown apart.

Dick waved before sitting down in a patio chair and waiting for Gif to head the mower back towards him. Gif completed his circuit and stopped beside the patio, turning off the noisy engine.

"Hi Dick, join me in a beer?" Gif sat on the mower and waited for his visitor's answer.

"If you're having one. I'm almost off duty," Dick smiled.

As Gif headed for the kitchen, Dick called after him. "I really envy you this place. You even have the weather thermostat set on perfect."

Gif laughed. He fetched the two frosty bottles of Budweiser, handed one to his visitor, and sat down in the chair opposite. "If you've got time, I can throw a steak on the grill."

"That sounds great, but I promised the wife I would be home early tonight."

Gif sipped his beer and thought about asking how he could help the Loudoun Sheriff's Department but did not, recognizing that would be a little abrupt and a trifle heavy handed.

"I suppose you wonder what I'm doing here," Dick obviously picked up the unspoken message from his host's silence.

"I'm sorry, Dick," Gif apologized. "I'm a little preoccupied these days, and small talk has never been one of my strong points."

"You can say that again," Simmons laughed.

"Small talk has never been one of my strong points," Gif smiled, trying to make it sound like a joke.

"You haven't been around to see us for a couple of days," Simmons said. "And I hear that you're working with the task force on the Tate investigation."

"Where did you hear that?" Gif asked.

Simmons gave Gif a sharp look that reminded Gif that Simmons was no longer a subordinate.

"A mutual friend in a position to know, Gif. We're all determined to catch Harrison's killer." Simmons did not back down. "If we can help in any way, let me know."

Gif sipped his beer and waited for a more precise response to his question. Simmons reacted with a silence of his own.

"What mutual friend?" Gif insisted.

"Director Schultz dropped by the office today," Simmons finally capitulated, taking his own deep swallow of beer. "This sure tastes good," he softened his response slightly.

"Tracey Schultz should keep her damned mouth shut," Gif said. "At a minimum she should get her facts straight."

"I'm not sure what that means," Simmons said, not the least concerned that he had agitated Gif.

"I was planning on dropping in on you tomorrow," Gif covered himself. "To tell you they asked me to take a look at the Walker case."

"Really? The director didn't say that. I assumed you were working on the Tate investigation. She just said you were helping out and that I should assume you spoke for her if you requested support."

"I'm staying as far away from the Tate investigation as I can," Gif said. "Harrison and I were too close for me to even pretend I could be objective. Martha would expect me to kill the bastard who shot her husband."

Simmons gave Gif a disbelieving look. "Sorry, I misunderstood."

"Tracey may have thought she was being helpful, but I don't want anyone to have any misconceptions," Gif said.

"I've got it straight now," Simmons smiled. "I thought the Walker thing was pretty cut and dry."

"I guess that is why they passed it off on me. I'm not heading the investigation or anything, just taking an independent look."

"I didn't think they could keep you out of the Tate investigation," Simmons persisted.

"Aren't you involved in that?" Gif asked.

"The bureau is handling it, but they asked us to help with the grunt work, and that appears to be about over."

"Really?"

"Isn't that what you hear from your bureau buddies?"

"I haven't discussed the Tate investigation with them," Gif said, wondering why Simmons was pressing him. "Tracey and Tom Harrington asked that I join the task force informally and take an independent look at the Walker thing. I think they are hoping that if there is any media kickback they can point a finger in my direction."

"Oh I doubt that," Simmons said. "It's been my experience that you can't get between the bureau and the media. Do they think there is a connection between the two investigations?"

"I'm serious, Dick. I haven't discussed either investigation with them. I'm just poking around on my own."

"Don't bullshit a bullshitter, Gif," Simmons laughed. "I know how you poke around a little. You dig and dig on your own until you solve the damned case. Then, you drop it in someone's lap and run."

Gif shrugged his shoulders and held his hands in a "what can I do" gesture. "What can you tell me? Assume I don't know anything about the Tate inquiry."

"As I told you, we were involved in the grunt work. We helped with the roadblocks, the neighborhood canvass, the site search, and nothing else. The Feds don't tell us anything."

"Do they have any leads?"

"My boys tell me the river and the shoreline searches produced nothing."

"Then all they have is the Secret Service crank threat list."

"If you say so," Simmons sympathized. "That's why I was hoping you could share something with me."

"They weren't interested in anything from the neighborhood canvas?" Gif asked, hoping Simmons might have produced something.

"Nobody saw anything. You know the area doesn't have many residents, and most of those were not home at the time of the shooting. They don't farm the land these days. Most of the homes are occupied by suburbanites, and they all work, husbands and wives."

"What about the kids?"

"There was only one school bus in the area at the time, and we interviewed the driver in depth. She saw nothing extraordinary."

"Not even a car that was parked someplace unusual?"

"Believe me, Gif, nobody saw anything. You know as well as I do that if the shooter got away before we set up the roadblocks, he's long gone."

"Shit."

"I agree," Simmons finished off his beer. "Now you know why I was hoping you could tell me something. I'm glad to hear you're involved with the Walker investigation. Coincidences like that don't happen, not the president and the vice president at the same time. Please keep us in the loop. You know the feds. They don't share unless they have to."

"I agree that it seems terribly odd for both men to die within an hour of each other."

"Was the Walker thing really an accident?"

Gif hesitated before answering, unsure how much he should share with Simmons. "The only reason I'm looking at Walker is that I wasn't invited to participate in Harrison Tate's investigation," Gif hedged. "I don't see any connection except for the horrible fact that both men died in the same afternoon. As best as I can tell, Walker was a playboy who died doing what he enjoyed most."

"Have you made any progress in finding out what actually happened?"

Again, Gif hesitated. He trusted Dick Simmons, found his judgment solid and suggestions useful, but he just seemed to be pushing a little too hard. "Frankly," Gif compromised with himself. "I've got a couple of things I want to check out before I make any judgments."

Simmons nodded with understanding at that statement but surprised Gif by asking another question. "Have you located the girl?"

Since Gif had not confided that information to anyone, he did not immediately respond, and too late realized he was telegraphing his answer by not commenting.

"Not yet, but I'm getting closer," Gif compromised with the truth.

"Good," Simmons nodded and stood up. "Let me know if we

can help you in any way. We all considered Harrison Tate a friend, a colleague, a neighbor and one of our own."

After Dick Simmons had departed, Gif worried that somehow he had divulged more than he should have and that made him angry. Simmons was a colleague, and this was the first time Gif had felt so inhibited in his presence.

Chapter 12

Acting President Hiram Alphonse Adams was sitting in his office enjoying his morning coffee when someone tapped on the door to his office, the Andrew Johnson Suite in the Treasury Department. The interruption irritated him because every member of his personal staff knew how much he treasured his early morning interlude.

"Yes?" He looked up before turning his back deliberately on the door in order to convey a message to the interloper who he was confident would be his acting vice president, the arrogant and self-important Alexander Hamilton Sperry.

As he waited for the door to open, Adams wondered just when Sperry would get the message. He was now a tool, one being used by Adams, not an almost co-equal partner.

"Good morning, Mr. President," Sperry announced his presence to Adam's back.

Adams took a deep breath and grimaced as he turned to face Sperry.

"Good morning, Mr. Acting Vice President."

"Please excuse me, but I thought it imperative that we discuss a few vital matters," Sperry said, sitting down without permission in the chair facing Adams' desk.

"I hope, sir, it is none of those economic hieroglyphics," Adams said. "You know I don't understand any of that nonsense. I'm not sure that economists themselves do," he tried to warn Sperry off.

"Yes, but this is very important," Sperry said.

Adams noted he again failed to use the honorific sir but said nothing.

"It's about our financial subsidy program," Sperry said.

"The bailout," Adams called the program for what it was. "I pray for our grandchildren who will have to pay the bill. Trying to visualize a trillion dollars is beyond me. It's more than a handful. I know that. Would it fit on the top of this desk, fill up this room. Someday, you are going to have to take me down to your vaults and show me a trillion dollars."

"Yes, Mr. President," Sperry's tone indicated he was patronizing Adams. "We will have to do that one day. Meanwhile, our parties in Congress–he referred to their respective Democratic and Republican Parties–are dragging their collective feet. We need this legislation passed."

With that comment, Sperry tried to place the burden for managing Congress squarely on Adams' back. Given the fact that the speakership stood vacant, Adams remained the de facto Speaker, whether he admitted it in public or not. Only Jake and a few party leaders were aware that Adams himself was deliberately keeping the post unfilled.

"We'll let our legislative office handle that," Adams said, announcing what Sperry believed was his first substantive decision since taking the oath of office.

"But we don't have one. Not our people." Sperry referred to the fact that Adams had left all of Tate's staffers in place in the White House except for the Public Affairs Office which Adams personally managed.

"But they are your people, Mr. Acting Vice President," Adams smiled. "They were all appointed by your party's president, Mr. Harrison Tate, and I asked you to stay on to manage them."

"That's not..." Sperry started to protest before catching himself.

This was not the time for him to get into a pissing contest with the man who had appointed him acting vice president. Sperry needed the stature of his new office to guarantee his nomination as the Republican's Party candidate for president in the next election. By then, he assumed, Adams would have degenerated into senility leaving Sperry on top.

"I suggest we select my replacement as secretary of the treasury and let him start managing some of this economic stuff."

Adams nodded but did not speak, leaving Sperry unsure whether he had won or lost.

"Then you want me to continue to manage the economic crisis until we agree on my successor," Sperry said.

Adams smiled. "I'll give some thought to your replacement.

Meanwhile, you continue to worry about the economic crisis," Adams said. "Now, was there anything else?"

He sipped on his coffee as a hint it was time for Sperry to withdraw.

'I was wondering if there had been any updates on the investigations." Sperry referred pointedly to the Tate and Walker probes.

"Which investigations?"

Sperry stared at Adams, wondering if the old man was already senile.

"Are they making any progress in finding out who shot President Tate and what happened to Walker?"

"Not that I've heard," Adams shook his head as if they were discussing the weather.

Sperry waited for Adams to elaborate. Instead, the acting president turned in his chair and stared out the window, blocking Sperry's view of the broad smile on his face. Adams pretended to study the scenery until he heard the outer door close behind him.

In the outer office, Sperry found Adams' crony Jake Tyrone chatting with Miss Mary. Sperry hesitated and waited for Tyrone to acknowledge his presence. Tyrone ignored him.

"Good morning, Tyrone," Sperry spoke coldly, deliberately using the chief of staff's last name.

"Sperry," Jake replied in kind.

The two had clashed bitterly and repeatedly over virtually every policy question that was tabled during Sperry's many Capitol Hill appearances. The rigid New Yorker and the good old boy from Missouri just didn't like each other, and neither took the trouble to conceal their mutual disregard.

Sperry watched as Tyrone turned his back on him and entered the acting president's office without knocking.

"How has the President been feeling?" Sperry attempted to learn something useful from Miss Mary.

"Like a frisky ten year old," Miss Mary, who had turned to face her computer monitor, answered without troubling to look at the acting vice president.

Sperry frowned at the back of Miss Mary's head and was tempted to ask why she didn't like him. She treated all the other visitors to her office with exaggerated southern charm. Sperry deliberately waited for the nervy assistant to acknowledge his continued presence and pay a little respect to his position as the second most powerful man in the country. Mary pretended he was not standing behind her and began tapping her computer keyboard. Sperry tried to see what she was working on so dutifully but could not from his position on the other side of her desk. Finally, he cleared his throat, got no response from Miss Mary, and departed. When the door closed behind her, Miss Mary turned, a broad smile on her face, and began to file her nails.

Inside the Andrew Johnson Suite, Jake Tyrone and the acting president had moved to the more comfortable chairs in the conversational corner where they chatted while sipping coffee laced with Jack Daniels from dainty coffee cups.

"I really don't like that arrogant sonovabitch," Jake said.

"You're not alone," Adams agreed. "But he has his uses."

"For now," Jake said.

"For now," Adams agreed. "He wanted me to pat him on the head for the good work he's doing on his economic crisis plan. Do you have everything lined up in the House?"

"Yes, sir," Jake nodded. "We'll steamroller his proposals as soon as he submits them and pass our own."

"You've got the votes?"

"Of course. Our side is so happy to have its man in the White House, they'll do anything you say."

"That's a change."

"Everybody's got their eye on the next election."

"And we're going to surprise them, too," Adams chuckled. "This old man still has some miles on him. I rather like this idea of yours, my sitting here in Old Andy Johnson's office with one foot on the Hill and the other firmly planted on the White House's neck, so to speak."

"I'll bet Old Andy is turning over in his grave, his being a Republican and all that."

"I'm rather glad his friends treated Andy so badly," Adams said. "I can hardly wait to get started on Sperry and his merry band of lame ducks. Sperry wanted to know how the investigations are proceeding. Do you think I should let that little lady brief me?" Adams referred to former FBI Director Tracey Schultz who he had appointed to front the Tate Task Force.

"That was an inspired choice," Jake chuckled because the idea had been his. "The female person Tate appointed as his first director is now investigating his untoward demise."

"No one can accuse us of playing politics," Adams laughed as he sipped his bourbon.

"They could never do that Hiram," Jake addressed Adams by his first name when they were in private. "Politics is not a game."

"You didn't answer my question, Jake," Adams reminded his friend and subordinate who was boss.

"Yes sir, Mr. Acting President," Jake responded sarcastically.

The two were a team and had been for over thirty years. In Jake's mind, he was as much the acting president as Adams. Hiram served as the image and voice and Jake provided the muscle and brains.

Adams smiled. He enjoyed giving his friend the needle as much as he ever had. He, too, recognized how much he needed Jake, particularly now that they had reached the summit.

"Despite her advanced age, she still has great legs," Adams referred to Tracey Schultz.

"That's why you want a briefing?"

"Don't worry about the reason. Just set it up," Adams said.

The next morning Gif decided to drop in without warning on his friend Tom Harrington at the office where the FBI Director spent most of his days. As he was crossing Key Bridge heading for Hoover's Revenge on Pennsylvania Avenue, Gif impulsively changed his mind and turned towards the White House. He still had some questions to drop on young Mr. Dexter and assumed that was where he was hiding out when he was not at home. The bureau badge that the petulant Special Agent Reggie Crawford had arranged got him past the uniformed Secret Service Guards and to the Executive Office Building entrance with only a minimum of irritating inconvenience. There, he encountered a more skilled Secret Service security bureaucracy. Gif had not helped his cause when at one point of high exasperation he had declared:

"I hope the Secret Service will eventually realize that the task force was appointed by the acting president to determine who killed one of your protectees."

Gif, leaving the frowning guards behind and with his badge pinned to his lapel, finally made his way around the Executive Office Building to the entrance to the West Wing. There, the forewarned guards quickly cleared him, and he proceeded to the vice president's office, now occupied only by Beatrice, the deceased Walker's secretary, and presumably Dexter when he reported for work.

Gif rapped lightly on the door and entered to find Beatrice and a Secret Service Protective Detail member watching CNN on television. The Secret Service man glanced at Gif's badge and returned his attention to the television, which was featuring a press conference being held by the new presidential spokesman.

"Good morning, Beatrice," Gif greeted the bored secretary. "Can you tell me where I might find Dexter?"

The Secret Service man chuckled, and Beatrice frowned. "That's hardly the question of the year."

The answer puzzled Gif, but he persisted. "I have a few follow up questions I need ask him."

"I'm afraid you are out of luck," Beatrice said. "We haven't seen Dexter for a week."

"Really? Think he might be at home?"

"I doubt it," Beatrice shook her head. "We sent someone around yesterday. Dexter wasn't in his apartment and the building supervisor said he saw Dexter climb in a taxi a couple of days ago with two suitcases."

Gif sat down, making it clear that such a disappointing answer would not suffice. "Think I should put out an all points bulletin on him?"

Beatrice looked at Gif with surprise on her face. "Why would you want to do that?"

"Because I have some questions for him. Where do you think he might have gone?"

"Dexter's entire life was limited to that apartment and this office," Beatrice said unhelpfully.

"Do you know of any friends Dexter might have decided to visit?" Gif asked.

"Dexter?' Beatrice laughed. "Dexter didn't have any friends."

"Not even a girl friend?"

"Never heard him mention one."

"Where do his parents live?" Gif asked.

"Alabama."

"City?"

"Dothan."

"Address? Phone?"

Beatrice shrugged.

"Who keeps his personnel file?"

"Personnel?"

The Secret Service agent who was finding the exchange highly amusing chuckled. Gif turned on him and demanded: "Were you on Vice President Walker's protective detail?"

"I don't see that is any of your business," the man replied.

"It is if you were one of those who lost their man," Gif said gruffly.

"Well, I wasn't. All of those unhappy gentlemen have been reassigned."

"That should tell you something," Gif said and turned back to Beatrice. "Please call Personnel and have them bring Dexter's file here forthwith."

The look on Beatrice's face told him she didn't like being ordered around by the likes of him and was considering whether she should take issue with his demeanor. "Now," Gif said. "Or I will directly raise the issue with Acting President Adams," he bluffed.

Beatrice reached across her empty desk and picked up the phone.

Ten uneasy minutes later a clerk appeared and dropped a large brown envelope stamped "Top Secret" on Beatrice's desk. "I will need this back by close of business," the clerk said and departed.

Beatrice slid the envelope across the desk in Gif's direction. He retrieved the envelope, sat back in his chair, and extracted a thick green file folder. He scanned it quickly, pausing to read the bureau's background check report and the list of names that Dexter had provided noting the names of those who could be interviewed as part of the process. As best as Gif could tell, they were all members of Walker's staff, past and present, and a few acquaintances from his college days. The only useful item he saw was an address and phone number for Dexter's parents in Dothan, Alabama.

"Is there a desk somewhere I can use while I go over this in detail?" Gif asked Beatrice.

"Try Dexter's office." She pointed at a door on Gif's right.

Carrying the file, Gif opened the door to find himself in a closet sized cubbyhole, just big enough for a desk and a chair. There wasn't even room for a visitor's chair or safe. *Some office for a chief of staff,* Gif thought to himself as he seated himself at the small metal desk. Obviously, Dexter did not carry the usual chief of staff supervisory duties.

Gif looked at the file and then at the telephone. He chose the latter, deciding that he might save himself some time with one quick call. He stood up, opened the door, and called to Beatrice.

"How do I get an outside line?"

"The usual way," Beatrice smiled snidely. "Dial nine."

Gif shut the door without thanking her. He slid around the desk, sat down and dialed.

"Hello," a woman answered promptly.

"James Dexter, please," Gif said without identifying himself.

Gif heard the woman take a deep breath. "Just a minute," she gasped.

As Gif waited, he visualized Dexter's mother conferring with her son. If he were hiding out with his parents, he would undoubtedly refuse to answer the phone until he knew who was calling.

"James isn't here," Mrs. Dexter said. Her voice sounded unsure, and Gif was confident she hated lying for her son.

"Mrs. Dexter," Gif said. "This is Inspector Gifford of the FBI and it is imperative that I speak with your son."

The woman took another deep breath and covered up the phone mouthpiece.

After another long pause, she came back on line. "I'm sorry, sir, but my son is not here. May I take a message?"

"Mrs. Dexter, I have agents en route to your house," Gif bluffed. "If you don't put James on the line, you will force me to charge you with hiding a fugitive."

Mrs. Dexter reacted immediately by speaking to someone else in the room with her. "Here, you talk with him. He has someone coming to arrest you, and I'm not getting involved."

"Oh shit," Gif heard James Dexter exclaim.

The phone clattered, giving Gif the impression that the mother had dropped it. He waited and was rewarded when Dexter came on the line.

"What?" Dexter demanded.

"What?" Gif repeated Dexter's one word. "What are you doing in Dothan? I told you not to leave town."

"So what?"

"So what?" Gif again parroted Dexter's words. "I'll tell you what since you are too dense to realize the position you have put yourself in. I told you not to leave town without checking with me. Do you realize what that means?"

"What?"

"It means you are a fugitive. I can now have you arrested and brought back to D.C. in handcuffs."

The silence that followed told Gif that his words were finally getting through to Dexter. "Is that what you want me to do?"

"No." Dexter answered weakly.

Gif could hear Dexter's mother speaking to him in the background. "James, what does the FBI want with you?"

"I have some more questions for you," Gif said, answering his mother's query for him.

"He just wants to ask me some questions," Dexter spoke to his mother.

"Then, tell the truth," his mother ordered.

"Please mother. Let me concentrate."

Gif waited for Dexter to return his limited attention to him.

"What questions?" Dexter asked.

"I want to know where you got those pills." Gif said.

"What makes you think I got them anywhere?" Dexter tried to bluff.

"I've had a long conversation with Nan Starbright," Gif said. "And among other things she told me she heard Walker tell you to get him some more of them."

"Oh shit," Dexter groaned.

"Dexter, this is not a conversation we should be having on the phone," Gif said, softening his tone.

"You called me," Dexter whined.

"And you fled the jurisdiction," Gif said. "I'll give you just one day to get your ass back here."

"All right," Dexter capitulated.

"Now tell me where you got those pills," Gif ordered.

"The internet."

"If you are not back here by tomorrow morning, I will have you escorted back," Gif threatened.

"I'm telling the truth," Dexter said. "I ordered them on the internet from Canada,"

Gif waited.

"From timeofyour life.com," Dexter said.

"How many times?"

"Four."

"On Walker's orders?"

"Of course."

"Get to the airport, now," Gif said. "There's something you're not telling me."

Dexter's silence told Gif he was right.

Gif waited.

"I didn't get the strong stuff," Dexter finally capitulated.

"Who did?"

"I don't know."

"Dexter, I'm calling our Dothan office now," Gif said, not even sure the bureau had an office in Dothan.

After a brief silence, Dexter said. "Ask Beatrice."

Those words surprised Gif. "I will. Dexter, if you are not being truthful… ." He threatened.

"I am."

"Get your ass back here," Gif ordered and hung up.

He thought about confronting Beatrice, but he hesitated, wanting to learn more before he approached the long time secretary who he had underestimated.

"Did you find the squirt?" Beatrice asked when Gif left Dexter's cubbyhole.

Her attitude gave Gif pause, made him wonder if she had monitored his conversation with Dexter. He glanced at the Secret Service agent who still pretended to be absorbed with CNN's report about former D.C. Mayor Marion Barry's latest escapade. Gif decided that Beatrice had listened in but also opted to let her worry a little about what he might do with the small piece of information he had just acquired.

"Will we be seeing you again, Inspector?" Beatrice called after him, and Gif answered with a wave.

Gif parked in the underground lot opposite the FBI headquarters and walked around to Pennsylvania Avenue where he opened the door to the public entrance. He waved his badge at the security guards and ignored their curious scrutiny as he proceeded to the elevators in the back. He rode with three young ladies to the seventh floor and went directly to the director's office. He opened the door and entered to find an unfamiliar face guarding the inner office. He glanced right and was surprised to see Special Agent Reggie Crawford sitting with hands folded on her lap. Reggie frowned; Gif nodded, and then ignored her. He had already had his fill of Reggie and her insolent attitude.

Gif approached the attractive young lady guarding the entrance to the inner office. He did not recognize her, and she obviously did not know him. Gif glanced out of the corner of his eye at Reggie who appeared to be watching the approaching confrontation with bemused interest.

"Is he in?" Gif demanded, heading for the door to the inner office.

"Sir," the girl demonstrated spunk and agility as she leaped to her feet and blocked Gif from the door.

"What?" Gif demanded.

"Do you have an appointment?"

"No," Gif said as he feinted a move to her left.

She ignored it. She took two steps backwards and stood with her hand on the doorknob and back to the door.

"May I ask the nature of your business with the director?" She persevered.

"No," Gif said. "Get out of my way."

"If I must, sir, I will call security and have you ejected," she said as she eyed Gif's gold badge.

"Young lady," Gif smiled. "I was visiting this office when you wore diapers."

"I'm sorry, sir, but the director is busy and left word that he was not to be disturbed."

"He will see me," Gif said.

"Sir, what is your name?" the secretary refused to bend.

At that point, Reggie intervened. She approached the determined girl and whispered in her ear. Gif waited. The girl nodded at Reggie and again spoke directly to Gif.

"Please have a seat, Inspector Gifford, and I will inform the director that you are here."

Gif glared, but the girl did not move away from the door. Gif made a feint to his right, and she once again jumped in front of him. Gif smiled and stepped back, pretending to move towards a chair. The girl hesitated briefly before returning to her desk and pushing a button on the intercom. Reggie, who had returned to her chair, watched it all with a smile on her face.

As soon as the girl looked down at the intercom, Gif moved to the door, opened it, and entered, closing it behind him. Inside, he found Tom Harrington and Tracey Schultz sitting in the conversational corner with Harrington now occupying the command chair and Tracey the couch. Every previous time Gif had met with the two, their positions had been reversed. Both looked up in surprise at the sudden interruption. Before one of the three could speak, the door behind Gif opened. The girl, her face flushed, spoke first: "Mr. Director, do you want me to call security?"

Tom Harrington laughed. "Thank you, Audrey, that will not be necessary. Inspector Gifford is a member of the task force, and I should have warned you about him. I apologize."

The girl glared at Gif and retreated.

"I don't think you've made a friend there," Tracey laughed. Tracey patted the couch cushion next to her.

Gif deliberately sat on the opposite end of the couch as far from Tracey as he could get. Harrington smiled.

"We were wondering what had happened to you?" Tom said, referring to the fact that neither he nor Tracey had seen or talked with him since they pressured him to join the investigation. "Even Reggie is curious what you have been up to."

"I hope you don't have that child involved in the investigation," Gif changed the subject. "I noticed she's cooling her heels in your reception room."

"Reggie is a member of the team. Jeff Cohena, our Washington Metro SAC, is heading up the investigation," Tom said. "Did you and Reggie have a spat?"

Gif responded by raising his chin and making a rude sound with his tongue, a Near Eastern negative that he had learned on one of his abortive travels to Israel during a previous investigation.

"Never heard of a Jeff Cohena," Gif said.

"An outstanding officer," Tracey said. "The fact you haven't heard of him raises him even higher in my estimation."

Gif thought about responding in kind to Tracey but decided against it. "How is the investigation coming?" He directed his comment to Harrington, acting as if Tracey did not exist.

"The task force commander and I were just discussing that subject when you so fortuitously decided to join us," Harrington, who was amused by the exchange between Gif and his former director, said.

"Yes," Tracey, not one to be ignored, said. "Tom and I have been summoned to brief the acting president. Now that you are back in touch, you can join us and maybe share your recent experiences. I hear you have been nosing around, so don't try to deny it."

"No thank you," Gif answered quickly. "I've had my fill of briefing politicians. I leave that to those equipped with a similar nature to communicate with the type. Have you identified the killer?"

"Unfortunately, no," Harrington tried to put the conversation on a professional level. He checked his watch. "We have to leave in just about fifteen minutes. We can't keep the president waiting."

"You've developed no leads whatsoever?" Gif challenged Tracey, trying to provoke her into telling him how the Tate investigation was progressing.

"I regret to say, Gif, we haven't," Tracey responded. "We are as determined to catch him as you are. Our divers found nothing in the river, which is not surprising, and our search teams on the shore found not a single clue."

"The shooter took his weapon with him?" Gif asked. Something about Tracey's response troubled him. He sensed that she was not telling him everything.

Tracey shrugged. "Like you we hoped that he had left the weapon behind to avoid carrying anything with him when he made his escape, but we have been over inch of land between the shore and the road. We found nothing."

"And the canvas of the residents?" Gif pressed.

"All thirty families," Tracey frowned. "And before you ask, Gif, we set up road blocks for seven successive days covering the attack time period and interviewed every commuter and casual traveler through the area. Not a single person noted a thing out of the ordinary, not a vehicle parked in an unusual place, no one walking along the Lovettsville Road, nothing. We also checked with the one business in the area, that farm restaurant on the hill overlooking the Potomac. Again nothing."

Gif did not comment.

"The Loudoun Sheriff's Department had four cars in the area reacting to the Secret Service alert that the president would be visiting, and we interviewed them in detail. Even your old friend Sheriff Simmons had taken upon himself to drive through, and he saw nothing."

"To be frank," Tom Harrington said. "We're back to double checking all the names on the Secret Service's watch list of cranks. So far, we and the Secret Service have not identified a single nut who was within a hundred miles of Washington that day."

"Well one nut slipped through, that's obvious," Gif said.

"We'll keep looking until we find him," Tracey said. "If you know of something we've overlooked, don't be shy."

"I'm sorry. The killer had to make a mistake somewhere," Gif said. "They always do."

"What have you come up with on the Walker thing?" Harrington changed the subject.

"I don't believe in coincidences," Gif replied but did not elaborate. "I assume you are still working that investigation too."

"I don't believe in coincidence either," Tracey declared. "Of course, we've got a hundred agents on that case too. That's why Jeff Cohena is in Dothan."

"Dothan?" Gif pretended he had never heard of the place.

"Yes," Tracey smiled. "Dothan, Alabama, the Peanut Capitol of the World."

"I'm not sure Jimmy Carter would agree with you," Gif said dourly.

"What does he know?" Tracey said.

"About peanuts?" Gif responded. "Probably more than he does about anything else."

"I've that said," Harrington said.

"Heard what said?" Gif asked, suspecting that he was being set up.

"That Carter doesn't know peanuts about anything."

Gif and Tracey exchanged bemused glances before Tracey continued.

"Jeff reports that Dothan has a giant gold sculpture proclaiming Dothan to be the Peanut Capitol of the World and five foot high, green, cement peanuts on every corner of town."

"I hope that's not all Jeff has to report," Gif said, tiring of the peanut chatter. "What's he doing in Dothan other than taking in the local sights?"

""You may not have noticed," Tracey smiled sweetly. "But Walker's chief of staff has skipped town."

Gif said nothing, waiting for her continue.

Tracey remained silent, determined to make Gif ask the obvious question.

Harrington sighed and pointed at his watch, indicating his friends were wasting valuable time.

Tracey, who had been Harrington's boss and had recommended his appointment as director, paid no attention. She turned back to Gifford.

"Dexter, who was more an errand boy than chief of staff, is from

Dothan. Jeff found him hiding out at his parent's home just outside of town."

"And why does that matter?" Gif asked. "Do you have something that links him to what happened to Walker?"

"The Crystal City apartment is registered in the name of Walker's election committee. Campaign funds pay the rent, and Dexter is the one who negotiated it all," Tracey said.

"That sounds plausible," Gif said.

"Dexter paid all the bills for the apartment, including the girls," Tracey said. "There was a string of them, Nan being only the latest."

"You've identified her?"

"Nan Starbright. She seems to have disappeared too, lock, stock and furniture, but we are working on it." Tracey stared hard at Gif. "This is where you are supposed to stop the games, Gifford, and admit that you have been working on Nan and Dexter also. What have you learned?"

Gif smiled and answered with a question. "I assume you talked with Terry Caldwell, Nan's neighbor and learned that I had knocked on her door. Did she tell you Nan's new address?"

"She doesn't know it," Tracey frowned. "Do you?"

"Nan is now living in Silver Spring under the name Barbara Dolle," Gif smiled.

"You're kidding me," Tracey said.

Tom Harrington laughed. "And what does Barby have to say?"

"Only that she had been servicing Walker for about two months and had a decent pay scale, five thousand a month," Gif smiled.

"Christ, she must be some girl," Tracey declared. "I better talk with Barby and see what I can learn."

"I don't think I will touch that," Gif chuckled.

Tracey frowned at him again. "And what does Barby say about the last session?"

"That Walker had too much to drink and swallowed too many performance enhancers. What do your chemists say about the pills?" Gif looked directly at Harrington, letting him know that Gif realized he too was holding information back.

"Sildenafil nitrate," Harrington admitted. "The pill bottle we recovered had a mixture of pills; the little blue ones are available under trade names like Viagra, and the larger triple strength fellows are of indeterminate origin. The latter are the ones that lifted Walker over the edge, so to speak. What did Barby or Dexter tell you about their origin?"

Gif smiled, noting that Harrington had cleverly included Dexter's name in his question and indirectly acknowledged they knew Gif had talked with Dexter.

"We might as well stop referring to Maria Fernandez by her working names," Gif casually dropped a little more information he knew the task force would find useful.

"Where the hell did you learn that from?" Tracey demanded.

"From Benita and Maria herself," Gif smiled, pleased with himself.

"Who the hell is Benita?" Tracey asked.

"If you drop the profanity, I'll tell you," Gif said calmly.

Tracey waited.

"Benita, Maria's sister, lives in Miami Beach."

"You've been busy," Harrington said, standing up. "We have to go. Care to join us? We can continue this interesting chat in the car."

"Not on your life," Gif said. "I don't intend to have another conversation with a politician that I can possibly avoid."

"That's not what Reggie reports. I understand you are now carrying a White House pass which Special Agent Crawford unwisely arranged for you," Tracey said.

"What did you learn from Walker's computers and phones?" Gif asked as the two FBI directors, one current, and one former, headed for the door.

"We can discuss all that when we get back and debrief you in detail," Tracey said, turning her back on Gifford.

"I suggest the first thing you do when you get back is put a protective surveillance on Maria," Gif called after her.

Tracey replied with a raised finger.

Gif, who had no intention of marking time in Hoover's Revenge waiting for their return, did not trouble to respond. Instead, he remained seated, giving them time to exit the building, before he made his escape. Gif was sitting alone in the director's office when to his surprise Special Agent Reggie Crawford entered with a frown on her face.

"I suppose you know that you have me in the penalty box," Reggie declared as she shut the door behind her. "I thought we were supposed to be friends."

"Reggie," Gif chuckled. "We were never friends, exactly. You were supposed to be my watchdog."

Reggie shrugged and sat down opposite Gif.

"That's the way the game is played," Reggie said. "I pose as your handmaiden, and you tell me what the hell you are doing."

Reggie," Gif smiled. "You're a big girl now. You know the score. Nothing is ever that simple."

"So I've learned. Now, all I do is sit out there," she pointed towards the outer office. "And pretend I'm the director's special assistant."

"Congratulations," Gif said. "Most special agents with your limited experience would give their right arms to have that job. It means you have been tapped for bigger and better things."

"Bullshit, Gifford," Reggie snapped. "I'm an investigator. I was involved in the biggest investigation of the century when you came along and destroyed my career."

"How did I do that?" Gif asked innocently.

"By making it clear that we were never going to be partners on that first day."

"I got the impression you were not pleased to be in my company," Gif said.

"I tried to tell them you wouldn't work with me, but your old girl friend wouldn't listen. She's convinced that any woman can have you dancing just by snapping her fingers."

"That's your problem," Gif laughed. "You didn't snap your fingers.

"She's the one who sidetracked me." Reggie ignored Gif's feeble attempt at humor.

"Relax," Gif said. "She won't be around long. As soon as the investigation reaches a conclusion of some kind, Director Schultz will go back to her nursing home or wherever she's living these days."

Reggie reacted with a begrudged chuckle.

"What did you learn from Dexter's and Walker's phones and computers?" Gif asked abruptly.

"Nothing," Reggie smiled.

"Make sure you don't let something come back to bite you in the ass, Reggie," Gif smiled back and departed.

At the Treasury Department, Harrington and Tracey were forced to cool their heels while they waited to deliver their command performance. After half an hour, Tracey stood up and started for the door, confident that as a temporary appointee she did not have to put up with this kind of bureaucratic gamesmanship. An irritated Harrington stood up to join her, when the outer door opened and Acting Vice President Alexander Hamilton Sperry entered, a broad smile on his face. Clete Clapp, his executive assistant, followed.

'Good morning, directors," he greeted them. "I apologize for keeping you waiting."

Sperry nodded at the watchful acting president's secretary. "Sorry about that, Miss Mary," he acted as if he were in charge and opened the door to the Andrew Johnson Suite's inner office without knocking. His executive assistant followed.

Tracey and Harrington exchanged sour glances. They preferred that this briefing be for the two principals only.

"You may go in now," Miss Mary said.

The two directors entered the inner office in time to find Sperry sitting down in the conversational corner and Acting President Adams rising from his chair behind the huge desk. Clapp and Adams' chief of staff, Jake Tyrone, were already seated along the far wall.

"Finally," Adams declared, pretending that Tracey and Harrington had been responsible for the delay.

"What do you have to report?" Sperry asked as Adams sat down in the chair opposite him leaving Tracey and Harrington standing halfway into the room.

After a momentary hesitation caused by the absence of the standard polite invitation to join them, Tracey and Harrington seated themselves on the couch between the two acting presidents. Both were surprised by Adams' uncharacteristically stolid demeanor and Sperry's apparent assumption of command. The two were exchanging confused looks when Adams broke the growing silence.

"Who wants to go first?"

"Well, sir," Harrington looked at Adams as he spoke. "It would be best if this briefing were restricted to principals only." Harrington glanced at Clapp and Tyrone.

Adams looked at Sperry.

"Mr. Clapp and Mr. Tyrone hold clearances you have not even heard of," Sperry said.

"Please proceed, director," Adams said.

Harrington hesitated as he debated whether to appeal the decision or not.

"We don't have all day, director," Sperry pre-empted Harrington's appeal.

Harrington glanced at Tracey who rotated her head, only slightly, from side to side.

"Our investigators have yet to identify the shooter," Harrington said.

"I hope that is only a temporary situation," Sperry declared coldly.

"We do too," Tracey decided to take some of the heat off Harrington. "There has been some progress on the Walker investigation."

"It's about time," Sperry said.

His tone gave Tracey pause. She had spent limited face time with Sperry but had heard that he was an arrogant sonofabitch.

Tracey turned and addressed Adams, ignoring Sperry. "The coroner has determined the cause of death, and we have identified the person who was with the vice president at the time."

"He obviously screwed himself to death," Sperry declared.

"Not quite," Tracey said, her tone making clear she did not appreciate the sexist interruption. "The coroner reports that the vice president died of a heart attack caused by the interaction of an excessive intake of alcohol and sildenafil nitrate enhanced by physical exertion."

"Sildenafil nitrate?" Adams said.

"Viagra," Harrington said.

"That's what I thought," Sperry looked at Tracey. "What does his companion have to say about that?"

"We are in the process of interviewing her," Harrington said, unwilling to let Tracey Schultz take all the heat.

"Do you conclude that Walker's death was accidental?" Acting President Adams asked.

At least the old goat is thinking, Tracey thought to herself. "We are withholding judgment on that," Tracey answered.

"Much depends on our in-depth questioning of James Dexter, Walker's chief of staff, and the girl," Harrington said.

"I know Dexter," Sperry interrupted. "Why Walker chose him for that job I don't understand. What is the girl's name?"

Harrington and Tracey exchanged looks. Both were reluctant to identify the only potential witness to the vice president's death until she had been debriefed in detail. Neither spoke.

"Well?" Sperry demanded.

"Her name when she was with the vice president was Nan Starbright," Tracey answered equivocally in an effort to protect Maria's real identity.

"I assume she was a working girl and that Starbright is an alias," Sperry said. "What is her true name?"

"She's living now in Silver Spring under the name Barbara Dolle," Harrington said, attempting to distract Sperry.

"Barby Doll," Adams laughed.

"And?" Sperry insisted.

"Sir, do you really want us to go into these details?" Harrington appealed to the acting president.

Adams did not respond, giving both Harrington and Tracey the impression the acting president and Sperry were working as a team despite their opposing party loyalties. For a few seconds, the silence deepened.

"Well, director," Sperry said coldly. "Are you going to answer my question or not?"

"Her name is Maria Fernandez," Harrington admitted.

"Just as I suspected," Sperry exclaimed. "A damned illegal."

"We don't know that, sir," Tracey said, her tone reflecting her disapproval of Sperry's insistence.

"Why are you devoting so much time and attention to the Walker investigation?" Adams interrupted. "It appears to me that Walker's death was accidental. It was all a terrible coincidence. Why put all your effort on the Walker thing, as tragic as it was, instead of learning who shot our president?"

"That's very unfair, sir," Tracey responded. "We are thoroughly investigating both deaths."

"Was it a coincidence or not?" Sperry demanded.

"We cannot definitively answer that question at this point," Tracey answered coldly. "That is what we are attempting to determine, and when we do the president," she looked at Adams, "will be the first to know."

"Presumably before you leak the information to the media, Ms. Schultz," Sperry said.

"Of course," Tracey replied, letting her anger show. "Leaks are something that concern us very much," she threw Sperry's accusation back at him in an implied accusation.

"Leaks concern all of us," Adams said. "Do you have anything more you can tell us now?"

"No sir," Harrington answered, trying to give Tracey time to cool down.

'Very well," Adams said. "We can defer any further discussion until you acquire more definitive information."

"And I hope that will be soon," Sperry got in a final thrust.

As they were leaving, both Tracey and Harrington heard Sperry declare: "I don't trust either one of them."

"Why do you say that?" Adams asked.

"Both were appointed by your predecessor."

The door closed behind them before they could hear Adams' response.

"Thank you for coming, directors," Miss Mary said as they passed her desk.

"I hope the acting president moves over to the Oval Room soon," Tracey said to Harrington as they left the Andrew Johnson Suite.

"Me too," Miss Mary said to herself as the door closed on her visitors.

Chapter 13

Gif returned home that night in an uncertain mood. Now, the task force knew everything that he did. He spent a quiet evening trying to determine what he should do next. The investigation of the Walker incident—the evidence indicated that it was an accident not related to what happened to Harrison Tate--was not something that really interested him. He thought about paying another call on Martha Tate, but he did not know what he could possibly say to her that he had not already said. After a restless night, he woke up with a course of action in mind. He would return to Richmond, get on with his life, and leave all the federal investigation and politics to Tom Harrington and Tracey.

After a breakfast of burnt bagel and coffee, he cleaned out the fridge, tossed all the perishables he had accumulated in the trash, set the green plastic bag out front by the mailbox, turned off the air-conditioning, loaded his two bags in the Prius, and departed for Richmond.

Two hours and forty-five minutes later, he arrived home, the Riverside Apartments. He parked the Prius in its usual place, noted that Marjorie's SUV was not there, and assumed she was where she should be, the Commonwealth Teaching Hospital. With his luggage in hand, he took the elevator to the eleventh floor apartment that they shared. Gif had several times suggested that they legitimize their relationship, but Doctor Marjorie Bliss had resisted. It was only after considerable debate that she agreed to move from her sixth floor apartment into Gif's much larger eleventh floor home that overlooked the James River. Gif viewed the compromise as a major victory, privately deciding that eventually Marjorie who was preoccupied with her career would eventually come to her senses.

As he anticipated, the apartment was empty, and the bedroom

a mess. Marjorie, despite all her pretenses to the contrary, was not a neatness freak. A strong-minded woman, Marjorie lived her own life style; Gif was the one who made the necessary adjustments. As a condition of the compromise, Marjorie had insisted that Gif accept her decorating taste which ran to flowered drapes and pink and red whatnots. Gif did not like the frilly, brocaded stuff—it was definitely unmanly--but as long as Marjorie accepted his green leather recliner and oversized television that played only sports and cop movies, he was willing to accept what Marjorie called superficial changes.

Gif tossed his two cases on the unmade bed, moved Marjorie's nightgown to her side, thought about giving the good doctor a call at the hospital, dismissed that almost immediately because Marjorie did not like to be disturbed at work, and headed for his office on the third floor of the Commonwealth of Virginia Police headquarters. With all of the political nonsense of the nation's capitol behind him--he thought--he was ready to get back to real cop business, catching Virginia's serial killers and seriously demented miscreants.

Twenty minutes later, he walked into his office and was greeted with an enthusiastic "Gif!" by Tina Belosi, his executive assistant, really his secretary.

"Hi Tina," Gif replied, relieved by the relatively low-key reception. Usually, Tina embarrassed him with her overdone welcome homes.

Tina jumped up from her desk, raced towards Gif, and threw her arms around his neck while presenting her cheek for an obligatory kiss.

"Hey, everybody, he's back," Tina shouted while clutching Gif tightly.

With difficulty, Gif extracted himself and stepped back before the rest of the office responded to Tina's announcement.

"What's happening?" Gif asked.

Before Tina could answer, the walking hulk that was his deputy, Truman Johnson, emerged from the office next to Gif's. "Christ, I'm glad you're back."

Gif looked at Johnson and shook his head. "Jesus, Truman, you've put on another ten pounds."

Truman when Gif had selected him had stood an imposing six

feet four inches and weighed two hundred and fifty pounds. Now, he topped the scales at three hundred."

Truman shrugged. "I've been waiting for you to get back from your very extended vacation so I could go on a diet."

"Where are we going for lunch?" Gif asked.

Truman smiled his answer.

Before Gif could say another word, a dour Sarah Whitestone joined them from the third office down the hall. Sarah, forty odd years of age, an aggressive Lesbian, was Gif's chief investigator. He knew that many bigots outside his office liked to make fun of Sarah, but not in his presence, or Sarah's either for that matter. She was a tough, determined investigator with a tart tongue--not a tart's tongue as Sarah's detractors liked to say--a razor sharp mind, and an intuitive edge.

"It's about time," Sarah declared. She glanced at Truman Johnson. "This oversized gorilla is driving all of us crazy."

Truman laughed. Together, he and Sarah formed a formidable team that few dared challenge.

"Come into my office, and we'll discuss things," Gif smiled, now convinced that he had made the right decision when he left Washington and its problems to Tracey and Tom. Still, the thought that he had let Martha and Harrison down nagged him.

"The colonel's been looking for you," Tina said.

Gif shrugged. "What's his problem? He knows where I've been."

"Josie called," Tina referred to Colonel Harris Townsend's secretary.

Gif looked at Truman and Sarah. "You two come in and brief me on what's been happening, and then I'll give Josie a call," Gif said. He turned to Tina. "And you join us," he invited.

"Don't worry," Tina laughed. "I won't tell Josie you're back until you're ready."

As soon as they were seated in Gif's office, Gif, ignoring the towering stacks of paper on his desk, turned to Truman.

"What's been happening?"

After Truman reported on the more interesting cases around the state that Gif's staff had handled without Gif's input, a situation that both pleased and disappointed him, Truman asked the question that obviously was on the minds of all three of his key staff members.

"How is the investigation progressing?"

All three had personally known and respected President Harrison Tate from his days as governor of Virginia.

Gif, assuming that they wanted inside information on a break through, hesitated before responding. "I'm sorry, guys. Just between us, the task force is still on dead center. They don't have a single lead to Harrison's killer, and the Walker thing is a real mystery."

"The shooter was a singleton," Sarah observed. "Since there were no early announcements, we assumed he got past the roadblocks."

Gif nodded.

"And we heard they had you working on the Walker thing," Truman said. "That told us they didn't have a clue pointing at the shooter."

Truman's bland statement of fact told Gif they wanted to hear more than he could tell them.

"Mystery is the right word to describe what happened to Walker," Gif said.

"He didn't just screw himself to death," Sarah asserted.

"There were alcohol and pills involved," Gif said.

"The media told us that much," Sarah said. "What kind of pills?"

"Sildenafil citrate."

"How many?" Sarah pressed.

"A handful of triple strength."

"Hey, where did he get those?" Truman laughed. "I might be able to use a couple myself."

"That's what all your girl friends confirm," Sarah said. "Obesity is your problem, and the solution isn't triple strength sildenafil citrate."

"I'm surprised your kind even knows about such things," Truman struck back with an indelicate reference to Sarah's sexual preferences.

"I talked with the girl," Gif admitted.

Truman, Sarah, and Tina all looked at Gif and waited for him to elaborate.

"I think Nan was a high level call girl, that's all. I doubt she contributed to Walker's death."

"Other than exercising him to death," Sarah laughed.

"You know what I mean," Gif said.

"Do you think there was some kind of conspiracy, chief?" Truman asked. "Did Walker buy those pills himself?"

"I frankly don't know," Gif answered honestly.

"No conspiracy would make it a mighty big coincidence," Truman said.

"And that makes us wonder what you are doing back here if you don't know yet what's going on," Sarah challenged.

"Frankly, I decided there was not much I could do there. I told the task force everything I learned and left town leaving the experts to investigate," Gif said.

All three looked at him waiting for more.

"I was too close to Harrison to get involved in the investigation of his shooting," Gif said.

"We understand that, chief," Truman said dutifully.

Sarah stared at him in disbelief.

"Now, I think I better check in with the colonel," Gif said, fully aware that his three subordinates doubted his story.

"Good to have you back, chief," Truman said as he led the others out of Gif's office.

As they departed, Gif heard Sarah question his report.

"The bastard knows something he's not sharing," Sarah said.

"So what do you expect?" Truman defended Gif.

"I expect him to trust us," Sarah said.

After briefing Colonel Townsend and chatting about what had happened in Richmond in his absence, Gif returned to his office and spent the rest of the day wading through the accumulated paperwork. This consisted mainly of signing what seemed to be an endless stream of vouchers and overtime requests. The only high points of the day occurred when various staff members dropped in to update Gif on their investigations and learn about Gif's involvement in the nation's and the media's sensational preoccupation with the chaos in Washington.

As soon as Gifford left, Nan/Barby packed a bag and once again abandoned her prized possessions. She took the elevator to the basement

and exited the building via a rear entrance that led to the building's loading dock, which was primarily used for move-ins, move-outs, and garbage pickup. She followed the alley to the corner, turned right, and proceeded two blocks to the nearest motel where she registered under the name Theresa Thomas.

As soon as she was alone in her room, Nan took an envelope out of her suitcase. She wrote a name on the front and a brief note on matching paper. She placed the note in the envelope and sealed it. Next, she took a piece of motel stationary and wrote a brief letter to Benita. She then folded that letter over the envelope containing the first note and put both into a larger envelope from her suitcase. She added Benita's address to that envelope and sealed it. After affixing three first class stamps, she returned to the motel office and deposited the envelope in the mail slot. That simple act failed to calm her. She returned to her room, concerned that she had just made a mistake. Benita was terribly unpredictable, but at least she was family.

Nan/Barby hid in her shabby room, watched the television, and worried. Once, someone knocked at her door, but she did not respond. There was no one in Silver Spring that she wanted to see, particularly not any authorities Gifford might have alerted. She spent the day and early evening pacing the floor, nibbling at Chinese carryout, gnawing at the fear that Gifford's identification of her produced, trying to decide what to do about it. Since the authorities had obtained her true identity, she knew that they would contact and interrogate her, and her involvement would inevitably become public. She considered flight, but she could not decide where she could go. Returning home to Mexico, her birth country, was an option, but not an appealing one. She had enjoyed being Nan Starbright, and to give it all up to become Maria Fernandez again was not something she was prepared to do.

The atmosphere in her room became oppressive, almost cell like. When she had first crossed the border illegally, she had earned a meager living as a common prostitute. Twice, the cops had arrested her, so she knew firsthand what life in jail meant. She tried to sleep, but her mind kept churning. Thoughts of all her lovely possessions kept intruding on her worry. In order to obtain some relief, Nan decided to chance a late night visit to the apartment, not to stay, but to gather more of her goods. Nan already missed her lovely, expensive clothes and expensive jewelry.

The more she thought about her predicament, the more determined she was that she was not going to leave everything behind. She rose from the bed, combed her hair, thought about changing colors, but fought her mind's cautious streak. She liked being a blonde; it made her feel glamorous while just contemplating returning to her natural brunette seemed like admitting failure because of something she had not done. She hated her former drab self.

Jan's watch said one AM when she retraced her steps, quickly covering the two deserted blocks and the empty alley. She entered through the unlocked loading dock door, took the elevator to her apartment, and breathed a sigh of relief when she was safely back inside without having met a single other person.

She was reaching for the switch on the nearest table lamp when a voice spoke to her from the dark living room.

"Honey, I wouldn't do that if I were you. There are two FBI agents parked out front."

Maria pulled her hand away from the lamp and stumbled backwards. Her heart thumped in her chest, and she had trouble breathing. She tried to speak but failed.

"Pull the blinds and the drapes, Barbara, and then turn on that damn light," the voice ordered.

Maria was too scared to move.

"Wwwho are you?" She stammered. "Wwhat do you want?"

"Don't be afraid. We need to have a little chat, that's all," the voice said. "Just sit down in that chair by the table. I'll close the drapes and turn on the light and you will be able to see for yourself that I mean you no harm."

Maria hesitated.

"Do it!" The voice ordered.

Maria carefully did as she was told. As soon as she was seated, she sensed motion as the other person moved to the window. She heard her blind being lowered and drapes drawn.

Maria waited, still trembling, too afraid to think about running. She didn't have a clue who the man was, but she assumed he wasn't a cop. The fact that he might not be gave her hope. If he was just a common thief… .

Suddenly, the table lamp came on, and Maria found herself staring at a large, sober-faced man in a dark-off-the rack suit holding a cheap briefcase.

"Ms. Dolle," the man smiled at her.

"The fact that he called her by the name on her mailbox was a good sign. Maria assumed another FBI agent would know her true name by now.

"I've got money in my wallet," Maria said, holding up her purse.

"I'm not interested in your money, Ms. Dolle," the man said. "I only need a few minutes of your time."

"I don't have time right now," Maria said, regaining some of her composure. Now that she could see the man, she felt she might be able to deal with him. Manipulating men was her specialty.

"I won't take long. Please, just answer my few simple questions," the man said as he sat down on the couch facing Maria and placed the briefcase on the coffee table in front of him.

"What do you want?" Maria demanded. She was damned if she was going to pretend that this was a social occasion.

"Be calm, be quiet," the man ordered.

"Ms. Nan Starbright, or should I call you Barbara Dolle?" The man asked. "Or should I address you as Maria Fernandez?"

"Damn Gifford!" Maria swore, trying to hide how much the man's use of her real name shook her. Instead of robbing her, he was making a veiled threat, opening up the whole illegal immigrant thing. Maria was glad she had the coffee table between her and the intruder. She glanced at the door trying to guess if she could get to it before the man could get around the table and grab her.

"Don't even think about the door," he warned. "Do you confirm that you are Nan Starbright, Barbara Doll, Maria Fernandez?"

"And if I am?" Maria challenged, her natural courage returning as the sudden fright diminished. The man was going to do what he was going to do and nothing she said would make it easier, so she decided to make him work for his answers.

"Good. I am going to take notes," he reached for his briefcase.

"I've nothing to say that I haven't already told Gifford," Maria declared.

The man ignored her belligerent attitude. Maria watched as he opened his briefcase. His hand disappeared from view, and when it reappeared, it held a gun with an extension attached to the barrel.

"Don't make a sound, Maria, and we will get this over quickly," he said gruffly.

Maria clasped one hand over her mouth and stifled a scream.

That was the last voluntary action Maria/Nan/Barby ever made. The man pulled the trigger, the silenced weapon hissed at Maria, and one jacketed slug hit her squarely in the forehead, knocking her backward into the chair. She slumped, slid downward, and died.

The man stood up, leaned over Maria, and ignored the bubbling blood that was dripping off her nose and staining the front of her blouse. He carefully checked the pulse in her neck, nodded satisfaction at his handiwork, turned, put the weapon back in the briefcase, closed the lid, and then methodically searched the apartment.

Six PM arrived and departed while Gif struggled with his accumulated backlog. It took a tap on his door by a smiling Tina Belosi to rescue his day. A preoccupied Gif looked up, saw Tina, checked his watch, and raised his hands in surrender.

"Is there anything I can do for you before I leave?" Tina asked.

Gif glanced at Tina, at the still imposing columns of paper on his desk, and then rechecked his watch. He tossed his pen down, stood up, smiled at Tina, and asked:

"Mind if I walk with you to the parking lot?"

"There's nothing there that can't wait another day," Tina chuckled as she looked at the paper, knowing how much Gif hated this part of his job.

They chatted on their way out of the office.

"We weren't sure you were coming back," Tina said as they waited for the elevator.

"There was no risk of that. Loudoun is one of my favorite places in the world, but there's not much for me there, now." Gif spoke almost wistfully remembering the good days at the sheriff's department.

"Do you regret moving to Richmond?" Tina asked, picking up on Gif's mood.

"No, of course not," Gif said.

"Good," Tina declared. "We need you here."

The elevator arrived, and they left that touchy topic behind.

After bidding goodnight to Tina, Gif unlocked the Prius and headed for his apartment looking forward to the surprise on Marjorie's face when he appeared without warning. He checked the dashboard clock and calculated that he would be able to arrive just as the good doctor completed her evening jog. Marjorie ran her life on a strict timetable making it possible for Gif to predict just what his apartment mate was doing at any given moment during the periods she was away from the hospital and office. He had long ago learned that this was how she coped with the chaos that enveloped her when practicing her profession, which was driven by patients with their broken bones that resulted from accidents that usually occurred at the most inconvenient times.

Gif parked in the Riverside Apartments lot in his usual slot, checked to his right looking for Marjorie coming down her regular route, saw nothing and hurried inside. He decided he still had time to get to the apartment, change clothes, and meet Marjorie in the exercise room where she always lifted weights before returning home.

At seven o'clock exactly, he entered the weight room and found Marjorie sitting at her usual machine.

"Surprise!" Gif announced. "Wipe away the lonely tears, the master is home."

'Surprise, tears, master, my ass," Marjorie greeted him as she wiped her sweaty brow with a towel.

Gif pretended to be disappointed at that reaction. "How did you know?"

"You left your damned suitcases on my bed," Marjorie frowned. "This is sweat running down my cheeks, not tears, and no man is my master."

"Pardon me if I say it is my bed too," Gif smiled.

"You can't prove it by me, old man. I've been sleeping alone for almost a month."

"I would hope so," Gif said. "What's for dinner?"

"Pizza or Chinese. You order."

"I was thinking more along the line of something special."

"What's the occasion?"

"My homecoming," Gif grinned.

"There's nothing special about that," Marjorie said, flipping the towel over her shoulder as she stood up and started for the door.

"That's not nice," Gif chided, trailing along behind like an obedient puppy.

"Not nice is not calling me," Marjorie said.

"Phones work both ways," Gif countered.

"Not when you have yours turned off," Marjorie got in the last word.

"Guilty," Gif admitted. "I was trying to avoid somebody."

"Me!"

"No, the feds."

"I think I read someplace that you had joined a federal task force of some kind," Marjorie did not look back as she headed towards the elevator with Gif dutifully following behind her. "Aren't you going to do your exercises?" Marjorie asked, knowing the stock answer.

"I think I'll take a rain check today," Gif said.

Exercise was not Gif's concern as it was Marjorie's. She had to keep her muscle tone in order to deal with the broken bones and stuck joints. Gif on the other hand had passed the point in his career where he felt physical intimidation gave him an advantage with the bad guys who tended to look as his graying hair and excess weight and decide they could take him. If he needed muscle, he used that of his young deputies.

They returned to their apartment exchanging their casual banter. It wasn't until they were dressing to go out for dinner that the conversation turned serious.

"Gif, I was so sorry to hear about Harrison," Marjorie said. She of course knew Harrison Tate casually, but the close period of Tate and Gif's relationship had occurred in the years before she and Gif had worked out their arrangement.

"I know," Gif said. "I wish they could catch the bastard who did it."

"I assumed you were working the case," Marjorie said. She didn't gush over the Tate tragedy because she dealt with death virtually every day at the hospital. She was more concerned about the impact on Gif.

Gif shook his head. "I declined the opportunity. I was too close to Harrison to be objective."

"Then what were you doing?"

"The Walker thing."

"Ohh," Marjorie said and let the matter drop.

They went to a nearby Italian restaurant, which served spaghetti with a meat sauce prepared by an Italian mama that Gif praised as the best he ever tasted, and he always supplemented the pasta with meatballs that he ranked equally highly. Marjorie had a glass of Chianti with her pasta, and Gif indulged himself with two draft Budweisers. Afterwards, they returned to the apartment, chatted for a while longer and then went to bed, a requirement for Marjorie who always rose at five in order to prepare for her early morning of operations.

They had been asleep for only an hour when suddenly the bedside phone rang.

"You get it. It's for you," Gif grumbled.

The house phone was an issue with them. Gif always turned it off as he did his cell phone when he went to bed, and Marjorie regularly turned it back on.

"I'm on call tonight," Marjorie silenced Gif's complaining.

"Bliss," she said, picking up the phone on her side of the bed. She listened briefly, turned, looped the cord under her pillow, and dropped the receiver over Gif shoulder since he had his back to her as a sign of mute protest.

"It can't be," Gif said rolling over.

The headquarters duty officer had firm orders not to trouble Gif at home unless the world was about to self-destruct and there was solid evidence that Gif was the only person who could do something about it. One of the perks of working in the Office of Special Investigation was not being a first reactor. OSI only entered cases after others encountered obstacles they could not resolve, and Gif had made it crystal clear this could only happen during daylight hours, preferably during a normal workweek.

"Who is it?" Gif asked, holding the receiver away from him.

"Your old girlfriend," Marjorie smiled sweetly as she turned to watch Gif's reaction.

Gif frowned.

"I mean the really, literally speaking, really old one," Marjorie patted Gif on the cheek.

"Do you know what time it is?" Gif growled into the phone.

"Hi lover, did I disturb you at an intimate moment?" Tracey Schultz said pertly. "Tell that young broad that only really, literally speaking, really old girls have the experience to…"

"What do you want?" Gif interrupted what he feared was developing into a catfight with him in the middle. Knowing that Marjorie would listen to his half of a conversation and imagine quite accurately what the other person on the line was saying and use it against him, Gif decided that brusque was the way to go.

"What do you think of the news?" Tracey countered question with question.

"What news?" Gif retaliated.

"Get CNN on the God damned television," Tracey ordered. "I'm not your local news repeater."

"Would you please turn on CNN," Gif appealed to Marjorie.

Marjorie, instead of turning on the television, rolled over and aimed her backside at Gif.

"The remote is on your table," Gif protested.

"Having a domestic problem, lover?" Tracey laughed.

Marjorie reached out her left hand, grabbed the remote, and tossed it over her shoulder. Gif caught it and hit the buttons. While he waited for the television to come on, he complained into the phone.

"Why don't you just tell me what's happened?"

"Shut up and see for you," Tracey snapped.

CNN came on with a "BREAKING NEWS" banner racing across the screen. The picture focused on an attractive young lady facing the camera with a building behind her that looked familiar to Gif. After a few seconds, he recognized the building as being the one in Silver Spring he had recently visited. He sat up straight, fully alert. The street in front was filled with Silver Spring Police Department vehicles interspersed with a smattering of unmarked black sedans.

"What happened?" Gif demanded.

"Shut up and listen," Tracey ordered.

"The building behind me contains the apartment of an attractive young lady with multiple names including Nan Starbright and Barbara "Barby" Dolle," the reporter turned and gazed at the apartment. "Ms. Starbright has been identified as the person who was with Vice President John F. Walker at the time of his rather spectacular demise. In a shocking development, the body of Ms. Starbright was discovered this afternoon in her apartment in the building behind me. Ms. Starbright had been shot by person or persons unknown. A source tells us that a FBI investigator was the person who found the body. That is all we have been able to learn at this time. We understand that authorities wished to interview Ms. Starbright about the circumstances surrounding Vice President Walker's most surprising death in a Crystal City apartment at the very same time as the attack on President Harrison Tate. Already, speculation is rampant with some questioning the almost unbelievable coincidence that the two most powerful men in the free word would die at virtually the same time."

Gif muted the television and returned his attention to the phone.

"What in the hell is going on?" Gif demanded, the heavy burden of being the one who identified Nan and therefore responsible for her violent death apparent in his tone.

"Lover boy," Tracey's barbed response was an attack. "You are the only person I know who interviewed the lovely Barby about what happened in the Walker apartment. Since you only deigned to share a brief and unsatisfactory report of your conversations with the now deceased Barby before you skipped town, I suggest you get your mangy ass out of that damned bed and back to D.C. forthwith."

Gif was not sure who hung up first, he or Tracey.

"Lover boy," Marjorie mimicked Tracey. "Hang up the damned phone and turn off the light. Unlike some people who play phone tag all night long, I need my sleep. Sick people depend on me, and I can't operate with my eyes closed."

Gif thought about replying, decided he was in no mood to spar with Marjorie, and turned off the light as ordered. He tossed and turned for hours, repeatedly reviewing his conversation with Nan, and had just fallen into a deep sleep when Marjorie's alarm went off.

"Shit," Gif cursed.

"See you when I see you, lover boy," Marjorie reminded Gif she had not forgotten his nocturnal conversation with Tracey as she rolled out of bed. "We'll talk about your friends and future when you get back."

Hoping to avoid the inevitable debate, Gif feigned sleep until Marjorie left the apartment. As soon as the door slammed behind her, he pushed himself out of bed, took a shower, and shaved. He hurriedly repacked his bags with clean clothes, perversely dropped the dirty ones in a pile in the center of the floor next to some of Marjorie's discarded ones, and gulped down his usual unsatisfactory breakfast of burned toast and lukewarm instant coffee. Finally, he called the duty officer and left a message for Tina and Josie, the colonel's secretary, advising those stalwarts of his plans, and took off in the Prius for Washington.

Despite the early hour, the traffic on I-95 was horrendous, as usual. The long distance commuters—the late season tourists, the truckers with fresh produce from the southland, the oldsters from Florida--all raced the locals down the highway, bumper to bumper. Not a single driver dared to slow to within ten miles of the speed limit; none that is but Gifford. Gif dutifully kept the Prius at sixty-five miles an hour until the tail winds from the passing trucks shook him to distraction. At that point, some ten miles east of Richmond, a mere fifteen minutes into his trip, he joined the competition, darting from one lane to another, daring each of the other white knuckled drivers to challenge him. He made exceptionally good time until he reached a point twenty miles from the metropolitan Washington beltway where he encountered a solid phalanx of commuters. There, he joined his stalled companions in their angry denunciation of the Department of Transportation, the Virginia State Police, the Redskins, the IRS, all other commuters, and suburban life in general. As an addendum to his personal denunciation list, Gif included Director Tracey Schultz, Dr. Marjorie Bliss, and all female drivers under the age of thirty-five.

After an hour and a half spent traversing the last twenty miles into Washington, Gif gave the Pentagon a raised finger, crossed the 14th Street Bridge and turned right on Pennsylvania Avenue. At exactly nine o'clock, he turned left at Hoover's Revenge on to 9th Street and right into the commercial parking lot where a smiling attendant greeted him with a raised palm.

"Sorry buddy, the lot's full," the young man declared.

Gif flashed his credentials, the attendant apologetically shook his head negatively, and Gif turned the tired little Prius around and forced his way across the street to the parking lot under the Hoover Building reserved for senior officers. He again waved his credentials, ignored the guard's stern negative shake of his head, and parked in the first reserved slot that he found empty. He jumped out, locked the Prius, and headed for the elevator with the guard shouting at him from the entrance. Fortunately, the elevator opened just as Gif arrived; he entered and waved at the approaching, angry attendant.

"The director's office," Gif called, confident the guard would not believe him but hoping that implied threat might inhibit him nonetheless.

The empty slot and the timely arrival of the elevator were the first things that had gone right for him all morning.

Gif punched the button for the 7th floor, and the obedient elevator took him nonstop to his destination. There, he turned left, walked briskly down the hall and entered the director's office without knocking. The young girl, Audrey, who on his last visit had decided she did not like Gifford and his failure to buckle to her authority, looked up at him from behind her desk and smiled.

"Inspector Gifford," she greeted him. "The parking attendant wishes to speak with you." She pointed at the telephone.

Gif ignored her and headed straight for the door to the inner office. Audrey surprised him by making no attempt to intercept him as she had last time.

"I suggest you talk with him," Audrey called after Gif. "He plans to tow your car. It's parked illegally."

Gif pushed open the door and entered to find Tracey and Tom Harrington sitting in command chairs in the conversation corner facing each other with Special Agent Reggie Crawford sitting alone on the couch. All three looked up as if they were expecting him. Tom Harrington smiled, and the two women frowned.

"It's about time," Tracey Schultz said. "Where in the hell are your written reports on your conversations with Barby Dolle?"

Gif ignored her. "Hi Tom," he greeted Harrington."

"Gif, thank you for joining us," Harrington said.

The door to the reception room opened. Audrey, still smiling sweetly, looked at Gifford.

"Tom," Gif said. "Would you please instruct your secretary to order the parking attendant not to tow my car."

"Audrey," Harrington said. "Please ask the attendant to make an exception this time and to leave Inspector Gifford's car wherever he might have parked it."

"Yes, sir," a severely disappointed Audrey frowned as she backed out of the office.

A smiling Gif nodded at the sour faced Reggie Crawford and joined her on the couch. Gif turned to Tracey.

"What in the hell happened?"

"You tell us," Tracey replied.

"Who in the hell did you tell where Nan Starbright was living?" Gif demanded.

Tracey, Harrington, and Reggie all exchanged concerned looks.

"So that's going to be your defense," Tracey said.

Gif did not reply but waited for an answer to his question.

"We briefed the acting president, the acting vice president, and two of their staffers, Clapp and Tyrone" Tom Harrington answered Gif's question calmly.

"Why didn't you just hold the briefing in the press room?" Gif asked.

"The choice was not ours, Gifford," Tracey reacted sharply. "The director suggested that the briefing be limited to principals only and Adams overruled him."

"Then you should have walked," Gif said, realizing that he was being unfair.

"As you would have?" Tracey challenged.

Gif glared at her, thought about pointing out that their decision had led to the death of an innocent working girl, but held back. He recognized he was trying to find someone other than himself to blame. He was the one who had failed to protect Nan.

"Who else did you tell about Nan's identity?" Gif asked, softly, less accusatorily.

"Only Special Agent Crawford," Harrington nodded at Reggie. "She was the one who found the body."

"And who did you brief? Cohena?" Gif referred to Reggie's boss, the task force chief investigator, as he looked directly at Reggie.

"No one," Reggie answered coolly.

"So one of seven people knew Nan was with Walker when he died and where she currently lived," Gif said. "One of the seven is responsible for her death."

"I assume you are including four people at the White House, Tom, Reggie and me in your allegation," Tracey snapped. "I suggest you revise your estimate to eight and add yourself. Who did you confide in?" She demanded.

"Let's all calm down," Tom Harrington tried to exert his authority and add a little reasonableness to the discussion.

The others, Gif and Tracey still angry, waited for him to continue.

Harrington took a deep breath. "We are entering troubled waters here. Let's assume that the four of us are professional enough to keep our mouths shut on such a highly sensitive issue." He paused and waited for the others to comment.

"I told no one," Reggie, the junior office present, spoke first.

"Neither did I," Tracey declared and stared at Gif.

Gif hesitated before answering. He tried to remember if he had mentioned Nan's name to Dick Simmons, didn't think he had, and finally responded. "No one outside this room," Gif said.

"I'm sorry to hear that, frankly," Harrington said. "We're left with the likelihood that Acting President Adams, Acting Vice President Sperry or one of their two chief assistants leaked or ordered the hit. Who wants to handle that part of the investigation?"

No one volunteered. Finally, Gif reacted. "I suggest the two people who did that briefing conduct the investigation," Gif glanced at Tracey and then Harrington.

"Let's cut the bullshit," Tracey reacted. "No one in this room is going handle that investigation. The task force will, and Tom and I will select the investigators." She cast a cold look at Gif, daring him to challenge her.

Gif said nothing.

Reggie took a deep breath, clearly relieved that unenviable task would not be assigned to her.

"Why don't you just tell us what Starbright told you?" Tracey asked Gif.

"I already have," Gif reacted. "Your real problem, Schultz, is that you have a political mess on your hands. How long do you think it is going to be before the talking heads and the media start shouting cover up?"

"This is not getting us anywhere," Harrington said. "The real problem is that we have three deaths to investigate. What people say and what they allege should not concern us. If there was a conspiracy, it is up to us to prove it without being concerned about what the media is reporting. No one is going to cover up anything."

"Well said, Tom," Tracey said.

"Agreed," Gif said.

Reggie who sat wide-eyed listening to the strong exchanges between the senior officers said nothing.

"And, Gif, you know as well as I do," Harrington said. "That political complications are a way of life in this town. This is not a first for any of us."

"And when politicians are investigated," Tracey said. "What do they do? They blame the investigators. It's their first line of defense. If you can't stand the heat, Gifford, climb back in that little car of yours and head back to Richmond."

"There is no question that the three deaths are related," Harrington said, subconsciously reverting to his investigator's approach. "Are they a part of a conspiracy?"

"Who gained from the murders?" Tracey asked.

"No one in this room, certainly," Gif said.

"That's right," Harrington agreed. "Let's stop beating around the bush and say it. Adams and Sperry gained from the deaths. Tate's and Walker's deaths opened the top slots for them."

"I doubt that they planned this together," Tracey said. "If there was a conspiracy, it was organized by either Adams or Sperry. Neither of them would have joined a conspiracy of this magnitude to make the other guy top dog."

Harrington laughed. "I can't conceive Adams, a Democrat, conspired to make Sperry, a Republican, the president or vice versa, and I doubt that anyone including the two principals planned the situation we have now, a Democratic acting president and a Republican acting vice president."

"Why would Sperry kill two people in order to make Adams, a Democrat, president, and why would Adams do the same and then compromise his actions by appointing Sperry, a Republican, as vice president? The logic escapes me," Gif shook his head.

"Let's leave this kind of speculating to the talking heads and the media. It won't get us anywhere. What should we do?" Tracey asked.

"What we're paid to do," Harrington said. "Find the killers and put an end to whatever the hell is going on."

"Speak for yourselves," Gif said. "The only payroll I'm on is that of the Commonwealth of Virginia."

"Don't kid yourself," Tracey said. "You're the one who identified Barby, and you're the only investigator who talked to her. The way things are going that makes you a target. The killers don't know what she told you. Somebody killed Barby because she knew something, not because she slept with Walker."

"Don't be so sure," Gif reacted. "I'm confident that Nan was just an innocent working girl caught in something way over her head."

"Then why did they, whoever they are, kill her?" Reggie asked.

"They got worried, given the stakes, and decided not to take a chance. They don't know what Walker may have said to her or what she might have inadvertently learned," Gif said.

"Maybe," Tracey said. "I can't think of another reason to kill her unless there is some kind of conspiracy.'

"It would be a very big coincidence if Nan's murder is not related to Walker," Gif said.

"And that would give us two very big coincidences when you add Walker and Tate's death," Tracey said. "And I can't buy two coincidences. I say they are related and we have a conspiracy."

"If the killers are that concerned, who else is on their list?" Harrington asked, tacitly agreeing with Tracey.

"How did your lead investigator make out in Dothan?" Gif responded to Harrington. His question focused their attention on Walker's death and indicated that he agreed with their conspiracy hypothesis.

Harrington looked at Tracey. "You talked with Jeff on the phone. What did he say?"

"I haven't talked with him yet this morning. Cohena planned to fly in late last night with Dexter in tow. He intended to return Dexter to his apartment before continuing on to Toronto."

"I hope he's going to assign someone to keep an eye on the boy," Gif said.

"Why is he going to Toronto?" Harrington asked simultaneously, inadvertently talking over Gif's statement.

"We met them at Dulles at one this morning, and we have two people on Dexter round the clock," Reggie answered Gif. "You could …" she started to challenge him, caught herself and turned towards Harrington. "Dexter identified the web site in Toronto where he purchased the pills."

"Not the extra strength ones," Gif interrupted. "He's wasting his time."

Tracey turned on Gifford. "Where the hell did Walker get the triple strength …"

"Nan didn't know. Walker got them from someone else," Gif answered before Tracey could finish her question. Tired of her attitude, he stood up and started for the door.

"Come back here, Gifford. Where are you going?" A truly angry Tracey shouted at him.

When he reached the door, he paused and smiled at the others who were still seated.

"Back where I belong," Gif answered Tracey. "You now know everything I do, and you have a very delicate investigation ahead of you. You don't need this old sheriff trampling all over your evidence."

"Gif, please come back and help us sort this out," Tom Harrington tried to add a little reasonableness to the meeting that several times threatened to get out of hand and finally had.

Before Gif could respond, the knob turned in his hand, and the door pushed inward. Gif stepped back, and Harrington's secretary rushed into the room, bumping into a surprised Gifford. She frowned and moved around him, apparently too excited to trouble with common courtesy.

"The acting president's secretary just called. President Adams wants the director and Ms. Schultz in his office forthwith," the girl spoke to Harrington.

"I guess they mentioned Ms. Starbright's untimely death at the morning briefing," Harrington shrugged.

"Good luck," Gif said and started for the outer office.

"Gif, just a minute," Harrington said as he pushed out of his chair, prepared to follow his friend if necessary.

Again, Gif hesitated.

"Are you sure you don't want to come along with us?" Harrington asked.

Gif laughed.

"Tom, I'm the last person you need on this investigation now. You've got to unravel a political conspiracy involving three murders. Not one of those deaths was a coincidence. The motive was political ambition, and you know how well I get along with politicians on good days. This is going to be a landmark investigation, one for the history books, so grab it, and run with it. Tell those conniving killers down the street what they can do with their forthwith bullshit."

"This is your kind of case, Gif," Harrington said.

"Let the shit go," a still angry Tracey declared. "He's running scared."

"You don't need me, Tom," Gif ignored Tracey. "I shouldn't be involved in any part of an investigation that includes Harrison's murder, and that appears to me to be what you've got on your hands now."

"Let's not make any hasty decisions we might later regret," Harrington said. "Unfortunately, I don't have time to debate the issue. Even if our lord and master is a prime suspect, and in this instance he is, I have to respond when he calls. Where are you going to be?"

"I'm going stop in Loudoun, make a few arrangements about the house, and head home, Richmond," Gif said. "Give me a call if something comes up that I can help with, but keep your predecessor out of my hair, please."

Gif glanced at Tracey who had truly irritated him. Tracey responded by turning her back on him.

"But my mind is made up," Gif continued. "Good luck and don't tell those guys down the street anything that you don't want to read about in the newspapers."

"Reggie," Tracey said. "Some people are just full of shit."

"That's true, Reggie," Gif said. "And it's not difficult figuring out which people that might be."

"Please leave me out of this," Reggie said.

Harrison's secretary followed Gif out of the office, closing the door behind her. Gif glanced over his shoulder and smiled when he saw her guarding the door in a pose that indicated she was willing to risk life and limb to deny him reentry.

"Good riddance," Gif heard Audrey say as he continued down the hall towards the elevator.

By the time he reached the Prius, Gif, who had been debating the issue with himself, was convinced he had been correct when in the heat of the moment he had decided to pull up stakes and move to Richmond leaving all of this Washington political nonsense behind him, Tracey to the contrary. In retrospect, Tracey's anger amused him; she didn't know what she wanted. Gif waved nonchalantly at the sour faced parking attendant as he drove past and headed for the ramp to 9th Street. All things considered, Gif decided as he drove around J. Edgar's ugly building, he was leaving the place for the last time on a high note.

Unfortunately for his peace of mind, Gif continued to rehash the meeting. After crossing the Potomac, he found himself mentally reversing directions, primarily because he sensed Harrison Tate's spirit calling him back. Gif knew that if he could Harrison would join his widow in demanding that Gif catch the bastard who shot him. Tate wouldn't have put it quite the same way Martha had—kill the bastard—but Harrison would expect Gif to make sure that justice got what the law prescribed. Gif pondered what to do all the way to the exit that took him to the Dulles Toll Road, and it was as he was approaching the Beltway that he remembered that Nan had told him that Senator George Ames had introduced her to Walker. Gif immediately decided that was a loose end he had failed to mention to Tom Harrington, and he turned off on the beltway, circled back to I 66 and headed once again towards D.C. and Capitol Hill. With luck, he would find Ames in his office, ask his questions, and be back on the road before Harrington and Tracey completed their briefing of Acting President

Adams. Besides, a worn Emerson quote popped into his mind: "a foolish consistency is the hobgoblin of little minds."

Gif's preliminary research had told him that Ames had an office in the Hart Office Building that he knew was located on Constitution Avenue between 1st and 2nd Streets. He had no difficulty locating the relatively modern structure but finding a parking place was something different altogether. After repeatedly circling the surrounding blocks, Gif was ready to forget the whole idea and complete his escape from the heart of the country's political milieu when a tourist surprised him by abandoning a spot that Gif was able to maneuver the Prius into with a minimum of difficulty, an action that surprised him because it had been years since Gif had parallel parked any kind of vehicle.

He quickly walked the six blocks to the Hart Building, used his complimentary bureau badge to clear security, and to learn that Ames' office was located on the sixth floor. He glanced at the skylight atrium, joined a group of visiting constituents at the elevator bank, and arrived at his destination in a relatively relaxed mood. Previous investigations had taught Gif that conducting interviews with self-preoccupied politicians was almost always a very irritating and frequently futile process, and he anticipated that his conversation with Senator Ames would not prove to be an exception.

Exiting the elevator, he turned left, quickly discovered he was heading in the wrong direction, reversed himself, and walked to the end of the hall where he located the Ames office. He tapped politely on the door and entered to find himself in an imposing reception room, which told Gif that Ames was a ranking senator. All that Gif knew about him was that he represented Montana, a western backwater.

Gif found himself facing two secretaries and a slender man in shirtsleeves who was leaning over the desk of the girl on his left. Gif took a chance and addressed the man.

"Senator Ames?"

"Yes," the man grinned at Gif, presumably assuming that Gif was a visiting constituent.

"Sir," Gif grinned back, wondering how many voters from Montana ever visited this office. Ames' response told Gif not many. "My name is Gifford, and I represent the Tate Task Force."

The man's grin vanished.

"And if you can give me just a few minutes..." Gif continued to smile, knowing he had his quarry cornered. He assumed this interview was going to be easy.

"Do you have an appointment, sir?" The executive secretary tried to intervene.

"I'm just a few minutes ahead of the media," Gif improvised.

"Come in, I only have a few minutes," Ames grimaced. "Hold my calls," he ordered the secretary.

"What can I do for you Mr. Gifford?" Ames said, seating himself behind the huge desk.

"I need to know about your relationship with Nan Starbright," Gif said, going for the throat.

Ames' blanched and began tapping his fingers on the desk. "Nan?"

"Starbright," Gif said briskly, sitting down in the chair facing the Senator's desk.

"Nan Starbright," Ames said softly.

"Yes, the call girl who was murdered yesterday and who was present the day Vice President Walker died," Gif said, almost feeling sorry for the man.

Ames hesitated before deciding that Gifford was not fencing. "Yes, I knew Ms. Starbright."

"Intimately," Gif said, pushing while he had the senator on his heels.

Ames stared at Gifford and decided to fight back. "I think I want my chief of staff to sit in on this interview. He's my legal advisor."

Gif shrugged.

Ames picked up the phone and said. ""Claire, have Clifford join us."

Ames watched the indifferent Gifford closely while he waited for his aide to join them. The door burst open, Ames relaxed and spoke: "Cliff, Mr. Gifford is from the Tate Task Force and has some questions. I thought it best if you joined us as my legal advisor."

"Yes sir," Clifford read the situation accurately and turned to Gif. "May I see your credentials, sir?"

Gif held up his credentials case for Clifford to read.

"You represent the Virginia Office of Special Investigations," Clifford said.

"And the Tate task force," Gif said.

"What can the senator do for you?" Clifford asked.

"Tell me about his relationship with a call girl named Nan Starbright who was with the vice president when he died and who was murdered last night," Gif hit the young man between the eyes.

His reaction told Gif that this was all news to him. Clifford turned towards the senator.

"I will answer that question, Cliff. Yes, I had a relationship with Nan Starbright," Ames tried to brazen his way out of a difficult situation. "So what?"

"Ms. Starbright told me that you introduced her to Vice President Walker," Gif said.

"I did," Ames admitted.

Gif noticed that Clifford kept looking from Ames to himself, a virtual admission that Clifford's ostensible client was peeling back a very large onion, layer by reluctant layer.

"Senator, I'm not sure you should be answering these questions," Clifford tried to caution his ostensible client.

"And Ms. Starbright admitted under oath," Gif exaggerated, "that you were the one who gave the vice president those triple strength blue pills."

That accusation shocked both the senator and his aide/lawyer. The ominous implications of such an act were obvious. If true, Ames had contributed to Walker's untimely death.

"That's nonsense," Ames reacted, his voice quivering.

Clifford stared at his superior/mentor/alleged client.

The fact that Ames had not actually denied giving Ames the pills was not lost on Gif who waited for Ames to say more, but Clifford intervened.

"I think this interview should stop right now," Clifford said.

"That's all right, Cliff," Ames said, taking a deep breath.

Gif had the uneasy feeling that Ames was preparing to lie.

"Sir, I advise that you do not answer any more of Mr. Gifford's questions," Clifford said

"Was Nan Starbright the only girl you and Vice President Walker shared?" Gif forced the issue.

"I'm a married man, Mr. Gifford," Ames declared.

"We're all adults, here," Gif said. "The fact that you have female friends is not the issue. Your sharing of those friends with Vice President Walker is pertinent to my investigation. Even more importantly, I need to know about those pills. Did you also share them with your friend?"

Ames shook his head. He looked at Clifford, silently pleading for help. Clifford reacted:

"Mr. Gifford, this interview is over. Please leave."

Ames's reaction confirmed Nan's story and Gif's suspicions. Ames had given his friend Walker the pills.

"Senator, where did you get those pills?" Gif demanded.

"Sir, please don't say another word," Clifford said.

Ames clasped his hands and stared mutely at his visitor.

Gifford smiled, stood up, and bluffed: "We will be talking again, senator. Don't admit to the media anything you don't tell me first. I can't guarantee privacy, but I might be able to help."

Gif took the elevator back to the ground floor and was heading toward the door when he noticed a small commotion to his left. An attractive, shapely woman with extensive makeup and carefully groomed hair stood with her back to the atrium talking to a television cameraman with a small crowd watching in rapt fascination. Recognizing a television news team at work and given his bland media threat to Ames, Gif stopped, curious about the occasion. He found the reporter quite striking even though a closer examination revealed that she had to be at least in her forties, the small lines around her eyes defied the age concealing makeup. Although Gif spent little time watching television news, the woman for some reason was vaguely familiar.

Gif shrugged indifferently and was turning away when the woman looked directly at him, reacted for some reason, giving Gif the uneasy feeling that she had recognized him. She stopped talking, drew her index finger across her throat signaling the cameraman to turn off his equipment, and startled her onlookers by pushing through them. She marched directly for Gif. Gif started for the exit door but halted when he felt a tug on his coattail.

"Inspector, Inspector Gifford I believe," a throaty, very distinctive voice addressed him.

Gif turned and only then recognized the woman. He had seen her on network television. Working out of New York City, she was some kind of co-anchor/investigative reporter. He tried to remember her name, but failed, maybe because he had never liked her. She always handled the more sensational news and had a pushy style that most of the time came across as hostile, giving Gif the impression that she did not like her subjects and knew they certainly didn't like her.

She flashed a bright smile filled with false promise intended to overwhelm the viewer. Gif didn't react. Insincerity no matter how it was packaged always turned him off.

"My name is Mavis Davis," the woman declared, offering her hand to him.

Realizing that her entourage was now watching, Gif took the hand, not wanting to appear boorish. After a quick touching of flesh, Gif tried to pull back, but the woman held on tightly, surprising Gif with the firmness of her grip. He looked sharply at her, and she squeezed his hand two quick times before releasing it. While Gif was considering what that meant, she stepped closer and spoke softly.

"Who have you been visiting?" She almost whispered in his ear.

Gif did not reply.

"Let's you and I have a quick chat, off the record," she continued, undeterred by Gif's non-response.

"No comment," Gif said, catching a whiff of her seductive perfume.

"Look big boy," Mavis changed her approach. "I know you're working the investigation with the Tate task force. Give me something I can use, and I'll protect you. If not, I'll lead off the evening news with a report that you were in the Hart Office Building investigating a senator. Everybody knows we've got a political conspiracy on our hands."

Despite himself, Gif laughed at the pushy broad's impertinence.

"I'm not sure what everybody knows or how you learned it, lady, but you can report what you damned well like. I get the impression that's your thing." Gif rather liked his impromptu answer.

Mavis smiled and glanced back at her cameraman to see if he was getting her on tape. Gif looked up in time to see her assistant with his camera perched on his shoulder nod back. Mavis again leaned toward Gif and whispered conspiratorially so that only Gif could hear her words. "You're a shit, Gifford."

Mavis stepped back, turned toward the camera, and spoke in a loud voice.

"I thank you very much, Inspector Gifford."

Gif realized she was pretending to address him while actually speaking for the benefit of the small group of onlookers as well as the camera.

Gif turned away and walked briskly toward the door. He heard Mavis still talking in a loud voice behind him. "Ladies and gentlemen," she announced. "You are witnessing history being made."

As soon as Gifford was out of hearing, Mavis Davis signaled her cameraman to cut it off and pulled her cell phone from her purse. She hit the number for her office and instructed her assistant to begin calling all the senatorial offices in the Hart Building and to find out which office Gifford had visited.

Gif returned to his car, irritated by the contrived scene with the reporter, but satisfied that he had identified the source of the pills that had contributed to Walker's death. He doubted that Ames would voluntarily admit it. To do so would involve him in the conspiracy, at least in the eyes of the media and the voting public. Gif headed back to Loudoun, wondering what he could do with the information. To pass it along would only involve him more deeply in the investigation, and that was something he was determined to avoid, particularly given the fact his last report had provoked the death of a marginal participant. At the very least, he assumed, Tracey and Tom Harrington would be obliged to brief the two people that Gif considered primary suspects.

Gif again directed the Prius back across Memorial Bridge to I-66, the Dulles Toll Road, and home. By the time he reached his mountain retreat, he had decided that his first reaction after leaving Harringon's office had been the correct one. He should return to Richmond and leave the political treachery to those being paid to deal with it, Tracey and her negative opinions to the contrary.

Gif arrived at his mountain sanctuary in a relaxed mood. Just to reassure himself that he was making the right decision, Gif circled the house. He noted the damp rot on the sills and the shutters that needed paint, major chores that he had planned to handle before the tragic events of the past week had intervened. Having to defer those labors to others troubled him because he believed that he owed his retreat better. The old house had always treated him well, and it was the one thing he would now miss most about leaving Loudoun. Gif thought briefly about keeping the place, but rejected the idea. He needed a clean break. Cruel fate had taken those who had made his Loudoun life acceptable from him.

Gif went inside, checked the Yellow Pages, and at random selected a realtor. He dialed the number, got a friendly female response, and scheduled an appointment for the next morning to discuss the sale of his mountain paradise.

Chapter 14

Gif changed his clothes and started a list of the things he would have to do to make the place more attractive to prospective buyers. High on the list was painting, inside and out, dealing with the wood rot, and the addition of a new garage door. The old one was showing its age, and the automatic opener was inoperative. Gif decided he could handle the painting himself, but he would have to delegate the other chores to skilled handymen. He estimated that replacing the rotting wood, a never-ending task when dealing with an old settler's house like this one, and installing a new garage door would cost him at minimum five thousand dollars, an amount he assumed he could recover when he set a fair sales price. Although painting was a drudgery that Gif usually postponed, he persuaded himself that the best way to deal with the problem was to start immediately. He collected some old touch-up paint cans and a stiff brush before deciding that he needed to prepare a list of the items he had to purchase at Lowes before he could commence work. The process quickly overwhelmed his initial weak enthusiasm for the project. Gif tossed the list aside, promising himself that he would return to it with renewed enthusiasm after talking with the realtor.

Consoling himself with the shaky thought that he had made real progress, Gif lit the charcoal, helped himself to a frosty Budweiser, and stuck a frozen steak in the microwave to defrost it. While the coals were lighting, Gif's cell phone buzzed. He checked, noted that it was Tom Harrington, decided he didn't want to hear any more about the investigation, not even feedback from the meeting with the acting president, and turned off his phone.

After another two beers and a delicious steak, rare and loaded with garlic salt, just perfect, he retreated to his recliner and turned on the television to discover a Redskin pre-season game just starting. The day, which had begun so badly, was turning into a perfect evening, persuading Gif he was making the right decisions. Although only a preseason contest, the game surprised him modestly. The first team offense played only two series, enough to confirm that the sportswriters were correct; the offensive line for the fourth year in a row doomed the Redskins to mediocrity. The defensive team showed promise, just enough to guarantee that the Redskins might make the playoffs, but that didn't interest Gif. One game and out offered nothing to cheer about. The moderate surprise came with the performance of the second team quarterback, a rookie nonetheless whose name Gif had never heard mentioned. Despite the fact that the second team offensive line was even worse than the starters, the young quarterback showed poise under pressure and the ability to use his legs to evade the behemoths that tried to crush him. Not only that, the rookie, whose name was Stan Muncy, had a surprisingly strong arm capable of flinging the ball some seventy yards downfield, a skill that had been in short supply for the Redskins since the 1970's and Sonny Jurgensen.

Gif watched Muncy perform for almost two full quarters before growing disgusted with the dismal overall Redskin performance and going to bed.

Following the game, a bruised and battered but understandably exuberant Stan Muncy rode with Boozer Jankowsky, a fellow rookie who was trying to make the team as a defensive back, in Boozer's ten-year-old Ford pickup from FedEx Field in Landover to their apartment in Ashburn, Virginia, a good fifty plus mile drive. Since Boozer had surprised everyone with his performance during the second half, Boozer shared Muncy's high spirits.

"Christ, you looked good," Boozer praised his new friend. "You keep playing like that and you'll put the Lip on the bench." Boozer referred to the first string quarterback, Bruno the Lip Hauptman, who hadn't completed a single pass.

Muncy slapped the dashboard hard, spontaneously demonstrating his shared enthusiasm, but he characteristically downplayed his performance, which had been better than even he had expected, when he replied:

"I was just lucky. I feel for the Lip. Our offensive line stinks. If one of them threw a single block, I didn't see it." Muncy spoke the truth. He had spent the entire time he had been in the game running for his life. "I've never thrown the ball so far in my life, out of desperation and fear."

"I've seen you throw the ball in practice that far," Boozer defended his friend from himself. Boozer as a novice defensive back spoke the truth. It was his job to defend against the receivers that Muncy was throwing to. "You've got the strongest arm I've ever seen."

"I'm in no hurry to start," Muncy said. "I don't know how the Lip has lasted this long with that kind of protection."

"Maybe after they see how you can throw the ball, and tonight should help, the boy owner will go out and spend some of his millions on the offensive line," Boozer said.

"Between you and me, I wish somebody else had drafted me," Muncy said.

"Don't talk like that," Boozer cautioned.

"Let's not talk about me," Stan said. "You made the team tonight, the best cornerback on the field."

Boozer laughed. "I was pretty lucky, but don't get carried away." His tone made clear, however, that he liked Stan's praise, particularly since it came from a player who was an odds on bet to become one of the leagues preeminent superstars.

"Christ, who would have thought it. Our first game. Nobody at Cornell ever thought I would get a chance to play in one game, not even a preseason game," Stan spoke honestly.

"That's true," Boozer could not resist the opportunity to needle his friend. "Cornell, for Christ sake, a potted Ivy School. I thought all you guys were supposed to be brains not muscle."

Stan Muncy laughed. "New York State has its share of musclemen. Look at Syracuse. They've had some big time ball players. Ernie Davis went to high school in Elmira and played for Syracuse."

"You should have seen the brawn in the locker room at Ann Arbor," Boozer said, referring to his alma mater, Michigan. "Not a single working brain among us, including mine."

"Jesus, some of these linemen are monsters," Muncy said, remembering the behemoths who had tried to crush him earlier in the evening. "I weight two hundred and thirty pounds, and some of those guys weigh twice as much."

"You're not telling me anything I don't know," Boozer said. "I stand six feet and weight two hundred and ten pounds, and I have those elephants coming at me too. I'm fast but these guys in this league are as fast and quick as I am."

"Don't kid me. You looked good tonight, Boozer. Besides," Muncy laughed at the memory. "You only have one or two trying to flatten you. I have the whole line plus the linebackers and safeties too."

"That's why you get paid the big bucks," Boozer said

The two chatted about the game for the entire hour plus it took them to get back to Loudoun County where the Redskin practice field was located, the primary reason they were living in Ashburn, that and the lower rent for apartments.

"I'm sore, but I'm not ready to hit the sack. I'm too keyed up," Muncy said as Boozer turned off the Dulles Access Road on 28 heading for Waxpool Road and home.

"Me too," Boozer said. "Want to stop in Tiny's and grab a few?" He referred to Tiny's Bar, a favorite Redskin hangout near the Ice Rink not far from the practice field.

"Why not?" Muncy agreed.

Five minutes later Boozer turned off Waxpool Road and parked the truck behind Tiny's between a Lexus SUV and a Hummer.

"Looks like some of the guys beat us here," Boozer said.

Both players knew that the Hummer belonged to Bruno Hauptman, the starting quarterback, the man whose job Muncy was trying to take, and the Lexus was driven by Bruno's best friend, Hippo Krizinski, the starting left guard who weighed in at three hundred and fifty pounds.

Boozer and Stan exchanged looks, each waiting for the other to suggest that maybe it might be best if they tried another bar. Neither was sure that the starting quarterback was in any mood for small talk with a young competitor, not after the evening's terrible performance.

"We've got to play with these guys," Stan said, using more bravado than he felt. He wasn't sure that Bruno's presence would add to the evening, particularly given the mood he and Boozer were sharing. "We should probably not pat ourselves on the back too much tonight," he cautioned.

Once inside, Stan glanced at the bar and noted the usual alignment. Bruno Hauptman, the team's leader stood in the middle. On his right were four offensive linemen, all African Americans, bulky, muscular, and frowning. On his left were four whites, two receivers, a fullback, and the center."

"Let's take a table," Stan suggested.

Before the two rookies could quietly find a table in the rear, Winchester Johnson, an enormous black tackle standing two places to Bruno's right spoke" "Hey, rook, the drinks are on you."

All nine players at the bar turned in Stan and Boozer's direction. All were smiling.

"That's right," Stan called to the bartender. "The drinks are on me."

"You don't have to do that," Boozer said.

"It's OK, Booze," Stan cautioned his friend. "That's just their idea of hazing."

"Hazing, my ass," Boozer glared at the men at the bar. "If those assholes had done their job, they wouldn't have to take it out on you, the only one on the team who did what he's paid to do."

Hippo Krizinski, an enormous guard on Bruno's right, leaned on the bar as he turned his head and frowned. "You have a problem with protocol, rook?"

"No," Boozer glared at the monster who outweighed him by two hundred pounds. "My problem is with offensive linemen who don't know how to block."

"Want to see how I block, rook," the guard took a step in Boozer's direction.

"Come on Boozer, forget it," Stan played the peacemaker. He

tugged at his friend's arm and pulled him further from the bar. "The drinks are on me," Stan called again, trying to make peace.

Hippo turned back to his drink, mumbled something that Stan could not hear, and his teammates responded.

"They're all a bunch of shits," Boozer declared as soon as they were seated. "Teammates my ass."

Stan, who knew he would need the help of the linemen at the bar if he ever got a chance to showcase his abilities in a real game, tried to calm his friend down. "It's OK, Boozer. We need them as much as they need us."

"I don't buy this rookie shit," Boozer said. He played a position where everything depended on his own talent.

"I know," Stan said. "But I have to. I depend on them. I just wish they would do their jobs."

"You don't think they are trying to make you look bad, do you?" Boozer asked, almost as if the thought had just occurred to him.

"No," Stan answered honestly. "They need to win just as much as we do."

The bartender helped calm things down by serving double drinks to every man at the bar. Just as the waitress was delivering two beers to Stan and Boozer's table, another person joined them.

"Mind if I join you guys," Jaws Kraver, the team's third quarterback joined them. Jaws had been in the NFL for fourteen years, two and one half years as a starter. He had never lived up to his collegiate promise and appeared to be content to serve out his time at a big salary as a backup, waiting for the starter to get injured. In reality, Jaws and Stan were competing for the backup's job. The third string quarterback seldom got to play in a regular season game.

"Hi Jaws," Stan said amiably, welcoming the diversion, hoping it would cool Boozer down. The last thing he needed was a brawl with the players he would need to defend him if he ever got to call the signals for the first team. He was smart enough to recognize that could be as soon as the next play, preseason or regular.

"Don't pay any attention to the boys," Jaws looked at the backs of the behemoths at the bar. "They had a bad game and know it."

"Christ, they made us look bad," Boozer admitted.

"Not buddy boy here," Jaws patted Stan on the back. "You really looked good," he smiled.

Stan turned and stared, wondering if the older player was really serious. After all, they were fighting to see who might have a job when the season began in earnest.

"It's just a game," Jaws said, giving Stan the impression that he knew exactly what he was thinking.

"I know," Stan nodded. "But sometimes it can really hurt." He patted his knees to stress his point.

"Wait until you are my age, buddy boy," Jaws laughed. He raised his empty glass. "Waitress, another of these on my friend here."

"I don't know how you do it, Jaws," Stan said.

"What? Stand all this easy money and the adulation?"

Stan noticed that Jaws was smiling at two young girls who were sitting alone at a table to their left. "You married?" Jaws asked.

"Me?" Stan asked. "No way."

"Got a girl friend?" Jaws asked.

"No sir," Stan answered.

"Then get ready, son, you are about to have the experience of your life," Jaws said and waved at the girls to join them.

To Stan and Boozer's surprise, the two girls who looked to be eighteen at the most immediately stood up and walked over to their table.

"Can the man of the day buy you girls a drink?" Boozer asked, looking from the girls to Stan.

"If we can have his autograph," the older of the two said as she sat down on Stan's right.

"You bet," the younger girl said, sliding into a chair between Boozer and Stan.

"See how easy it is boys," Jaws said, downing his drink and rising from his chair. "Have a good time."

"Hi guy," the girl on Stan's right slid her hand under the table and grasped his knee. "You really looked great tonight."

Stan, embarrassed, turned towards Boozer and was surprised to see that the younger girl already had her hand behind his neck and was kissing him.

"What are you rooks doing?" A deep voice demanded.

Stan looked up and found Winchester Johnson, the big offensive tackle, looming over their table.

"No poaching, rooks," Johnson declared, pulling the younger girl away from Boozer.

"Hey," Boozer leaped up from his chair and pushed Johnson.

Johnson did not even bother to push back. He pulled a huge fist back and swung at Boozer before he realized a counterattack was coming.

Stan, knowing he had no choice, leaped to his feet. Before he had a chance to decide what to say or do next, one of Johnson's mates hit him on the side of the head, knocking him to the floor. Within seconds, Boozer and Stan were on their backs and being dragged to the door. The huge linesmen dumped them outside where the bar bouncer took over.

"And don't come back," the bouncer said, raising his fist in a threatening manner even though he had had nothing to do with the confrontation.

The bar door closed and Boozer and Stan found themselves sitting on the ground, bleeding, hurting, wondering what to do next.

"Want to give it another try," Boozer, the defensive back, asked.

Stan, the quarterback, who was not sure what it had been all about rubbed the side of his jaw and shook his head negatively. "Tomorrow's another day," he said.

Boozer didn't respond, giving Stan the impression that he really didn't want to try again either. After a few minutes, the two rookies made their way back to Boozer's pickup and drove the five blocks to their apartment.

The next morning Gif woke with a terrible taste in his mouth, a throbbing headache that indicated he had consumed too many beers while watching the Redskin game, and to the sound of his cell phone, which he had turned back on. He gently shook his head in an effort to clear his thoughts, but that made matters worse. He leaned over and grabbed his phone.

"Yes," he tried to speak but his voice did not respond. It only made a rasping sound. He tried again. "Yes,"

"You bastard," a male greeted him. The voice sounded vaguely familiar, but Gif had no idea who the rude caller was.

Gif turned his head from one side to the other, regretted it because his sinuses drained and his head throbbed, and he demanded: "Who the hell is this?"

"Who do you think it is, you bastard."

"I don't have a clue and don't care, you bastard," Gif tried to match the caller's intensity, but failed. His head hurt too much. Gif hung up and dropped his head back on the pillow.

The cell phone rang again, but this time Gif ignored it. He leaned back, tried to sleep, but his body resisted the effort. Finally, he got up and paid an obligatory visit to the bathroom before going to the kitchen where he burned a bagel and heated some instant coffee. He sat down at the table, took a bite and a sip, had difficulty swallowing both, and heard his cell phone ringing in the bedroom. He let it ring and ring but finally could stand it no more. He stood up, went into the bedroom, grabbed the phone, and demanded again: "Who the hell is this?"

"Who the hell do you think it is," a woman's voice said.

This time, Gif recognized the caller. "Christ, Tracey," Gif swore. "What the hell is going on?"

"You tell me, you shit," Tracey said.

Gif hung up and returned to the dining room table taking his cell phone with him, confident that Tracey would call back if it were important. He sipped the lukewarm coffee; it tasted terrible, and bit into the dry bagel. It tasted like sand. The cell phone rang again. Gif picked it up.

"Tracey, what the hell is going on?" Gif asked.

"Tracey, my ass, you lying bastard," the male voice that had woke Gif from a troubled sleep declared.

"I don't know what you are talking about or who you are, you bastard," Gif replied in kind.

"This is Senator George Ames, and I'm going to sue your sorry ass," the voice declared.

"Be my guest. Mind telling me why?" Gif relaxed.

"Your goddamned allegations about me on national television," Ames said.

"I don't know what you're talking about, senator," Gif replied.

"Bullshit, Gifford. Your ass is mud," Ames said and hung up.

Gif, deciding the man had gone off the deep edge, dropped the cell phone back on the table and took another bite of the burned bagel. Before he could sip his coffee, the phone rang again.

"What?" Gif demanded as he lifted the coffee to his lips. This time he was prepared.

"Have you lost your mind?" Tracey demanded.

"I don't know what happened at your meeting with Adams," Gif said. "But relax, and stop calling me a shit. Whatever is troubling you, I had nothing to do with it. I quit. The investigation is all yours, and I'm going back to Richmond for good."

"Then why don't you keep your damned mouth shut," Tracey demanded.

"I still don't know what you are talking about," Gif said, now relaxed.

"Then you better turn on the damned television, Channel 4. It's all about you, shit face," Tracey said and hung up.

Gif shrugged. He turned on the television, switched to Channel 4 and saw himself standing in the lobby of the Hart Building chatting with Mavis Davis. He watched and heard himself say: "Report what you like."

Gif immediately realized that the comment had been edited. He definitely remembered trying to discourage her by saying: "Report what you damned well like," among other things.

The picture showed Gif strolling away, a self-satisfied smile on his face. Mavis turned toward the camera and said:

"Inspector Gifford, a key investigator for the Tate/Walker Federal Task Force, has just visited Senator George Ames's office in the Hart Office Building where he questioned Senator Ames in detail about his intimate relationship with Ms. Nan Starbright who was with Vice President Walker when he died. Sources confide that Senator Ames may have been the person who introduced Ms. Starbright, also known as Ms. Barby Dolle, to the vice president. Listeners will recall that Ms. Starbright/Dolle was found with a hole in her forehead in her

Silver Spring apartment by a lead FBI investigator. This reporter has also learned that the task force is now deeply engaged in sorting out what is alleged by responsible political commentators to be a political conspiracy the likes of which this country has never seen. This is Mavis Davis reporting from Washington."

Gif turned off the television and leaned back in the recliner to consider the implications of what he had just seen. He now understood Senator Ames's and Tracey's angry reactions. They both blamed him for Mavis Davis's sensational report placing them in the public hot seat; Gif knew he was blameless. The news anchor/investigative reporter had cleverly edited the tape of their brief encounter in the Hart Building lobby and had somehow learned who Gif had visited. He considered calling Ames and Tracey back and explaining his innocence, but he recognized that would be futile. The tape confirmed his brief contact with Davis who had used his edited parting comment to ostensibly validate her release of the alleged confidences he had shared. Although Gif expected such distortions from the media, he had to admit that Mavis Davis had adroitly exploited their chance encounter. The experience also made Gif more determined than ever to sell his most prized possession, his mountain home, and move to Richmond leaving the Washington phase of his life far behind him.

That thought gave Gif small solace, but that was enough for him to decide to make one personal call before he escaped. He was reaching for the phone to find out if it would be possible for him to visit Martha Tate at her Leesburg home en route to I-95 when a knock on the door interrupted.

"Mr. Gifford?" A cheery feminine voice called through the open screen.

"Coming," Gif responded as he pushed out of his chair. That simple act gave him pause. He would really miss that chair along with his other Loudoun possessions. He knew that Marjorie would fight against his moving a single thing into their already crowded apartment. On the other hand, leaving them behind would be like closing the door on an entire phase of his life, one that he had enjoyed most of the time.

When he reached the front door, Gif remembered his appointment with the realtor.

"Mr. Gifford, I'm Gloria Shepherd of Blue Ridge Realty," she said as she offered her hand.

Over her shoulder, Gif saw her Lexus sedan parked near his Prius. He understood why realtors drove expensive cars, presumably to impress clients and take advantage of the business tax write-offs, but he didn't know why most of them were pudgy, round faced women in their early forties. He suspected it was because they were recent divorcees doing something unaccustomed, supporting themselves.

'Colin Gifford," Gif took her hand and returned her forced smile. "Please come in Ms. Shepherd."

"This is a great place you have here," the realtor said as she studied the interior of the house.

Gif looked around and tried to see the place through her eyes. It looked a little shabby. "I'll have to do some touch up," Gif said.

"Mind if I just do a brief walk through, get a first impression to guide our discussion," Gloria said as she moved toward the kitchen taking Gif's acquiescence for granted.

Gif remembered the dirty dishes in the sink and the unmade bed in the bedroom. "I slept in," Gif said as he followed his intrusive visitor.

Gloria took in the kitchen with a quick glance, nodded her head, and moved on with Gif in tow. She made fast work of her initial survey and returned to Gif's combination den/living room where she sat down on the couch and opened her briefcase. She took out a folder and extracted several brochures.

"These are properties we have recently sold in the county," she said as she handed the professionally designed sheets which featured mountain homes far grander and more pretentious that Gif's.

"This is an original settler's home," Gif said. "The first owner built the log cabin himself in 1760 when this area was still threatened by the Indians. In fact the room in which we are sitting and that fireplace were part of the original structure."

"I know," Gloria said. "I can tell from the mixed construction, the logs of the original cabin and the wood shingles covering the later additions. I'd wager that the subsequent owners did much of the work themselves."

Gif looked sharply at the realtor, assuming that she was critically appraising his home in order to influence the asking price, downward of course, making it easier to unload.

Correctly reading Gif's sour expression, Gloria ignored it. "Don't misinterpret my comments, Mr. Gifford. The mixed architecture is a standard for these older houses. Personally, I like them very much."

"They are really priceless," Gif said. "Just imagine the history they could tell. Why John Mosby himself operated across this very land." Gif referred to the Confederate raider who had made the area uncomfortable with his surprise raids.

"I know. I grew up in Loudoun reading about John Mosby. The Quakers who lived here supported the Union—they opposed slavery you know—while the big plantation owners backed the Confederacy. I'll bet you even have a secret cellar under your kitchen flooring which was used to support the underground railroad."

"There might be," Gif agreed reluctantly. "I've never pulled up the kitchen flooring."

"Then I have news for you," Gloria said. "I did a little research on this property after you called and learned that a family of Quakers named Miner lived in this very house in the mid eighteen hundreds."

That was news to Gif, but he was not about to admit it. He nodded and changed the subject. "I've got forty acres of prime land here. How much do you think I can get for it?" Gif tried to make it clear that he was disinterested in continuing the chatter.

"For the land alone, or for the land and the house?" Gloria asked.

"Both. I'm thinking of moving from the area," Gif said. "Please understand this conversation is just exploratory at this time."

"I understand, Mr. Gifford," Gloria smiled as she collected her literature and slid it back into the file folder.

"But if we can work out a reasonable price…" Gif let his voice trail off.

The realtor placed the folder on the coffee table beside her briefcase. Gif was not sure if she was leaving it for him to peruse or preparing to pack it away.

"What price did you have in mind, Mr. Gifford?"

"I was thinking in the neighborhood of eight hundred thousand," Gif said. He had paid a hundred thousand for the property twenty-five years ago, and, given appreciation, he estimated that was a fair price."

Gloria frowned. "I must speak frankly with you, Mr. Gifford. I know that two years ago property in the area went in that price range, depending of course on its condition. Yours is going to require considerable upgrade and repair. And we have our current economic situation. We are selling houses–thank goodness we live in a prime area with the mountains and our proximity to Reston and the District—but not as many as we have in the past."

"You are saying the market is not very good now. I know that."

"Yes, unfortunately, I am. If you want or need to sell in this market, you will have to accept a reasonable price and invest some thirty or forty thousand in upgrades and repair."

"This house is in excellent condition," Gif said, frowning to let the pushy realtor understand that he was not pleased with her comments.

"I know how you feel, Mr. Gifford, but we are talking about a different generation of buyers. Most of those looking at the market today are younger people, much younger than you or I…"

Gif assumed she was talking about him, not herself, and he didn't like it. He didn't consider himself old or even older.

"And they have different tastes. If we take another brief walk through, I will explain what I mean with some specific suggestions."

Gif stood up and gestured with his hand, inviting the know-it-all realtor to lead the way.

Gloria went directly to the kitchen where she waved her hand to include the whole room. "The kitchen will have to be gutted, new cabinets and counters installed along with all new appliances."

"There's nothing wrong with these cabinets, counters and appliances," Gif said defensively. "I installed them myself only ten years ago." He exaggerated. The cabinets were at least thirty years old, the counters twenty, and the appliances of mixed vintage. "Everything is in working order."

"I know," Gloria smiled, trying to accommodate her potential client. "But the appliances don't match. Black refrigerators are out of style, the dishwasher is white and the stove is a hideous yellow, and the sink is stained."

"When I replaced the fridge and dishwasher," Gif said defensively they didn't have any yellow ones."

"Remember we are selling to young housewives who have their own views about colors," Gloria said.

"Then sell it to a bachelor," Gif groaned in exasperation. "I'm perfectly comfortable here, and don't see any need to fix things that aren't broken."

"And the floor," Gloria resumed her appraisal. "What's under that carpet? Old tile?"

"I don't know," Gif said honestly. "The floor was carpeted when I bought the place, and I replaced it once. I like carpet."

"Modern housewives don't. They want the new hardwood flooring in the kitchen."

"It'll scratch and spot," Gif said.

"Have you taken a look at the new materials, Mr. Gifford?" Gloria asked.

Gif shook his head, and Gloria dismissed his reaction by continuing on her tour.

By the time they were finished and back in the living area where they were seated in front of the huge fieldstone fireplace, Gloria had recommended the gutting of two bathrooms along with the kitchen, new carpets for the two bedrooms, and hardwood floors for the rest of the house along with lots of paint and plaster work.

"Christ," Gif said. "You're talking about a lot more than forty thousand in repairs. More like a hundred thousand or more."

"We do want to sell, don't we, Mr. Gifford?"

"Sell? Yes. Give away, no."

"Should we take a look at the outside Mr. Gifford?"

"I don't think that will be necessary, Ms. …" Gif was so irritated that he could not remember the pudgy realtor's name.

"Shepherd," she smiled brightly. "If we are going to be working together Mr. Gifford, please call me Gloria."

Gif took a deep breath, decided the realtor was just doing her job, though he found her most irritating, in part because she sounded like she was getting all of her ideas out of the realtor's handbook and women's magazines. He tried to respond calmly.

Ms. Shepherd, you've given me a lot to think about," Gif said. "Let me consider your suggestions and I'll get back in touch with you." *Probably never,* he thought to himself.

"Very good," the realtor nodded as she set the folder with the brochures on the area houses that had sold to one side. "With your permission, I'll leave these for you to assist you in making your decision," she closed her briefcase and stood up.

"I thank you very much for taking the trouble to educate me," Gif said, not meaning a word of it.

"Please call when you make up your mind," the realtor said. "I know at first blush all this is very overwhelming, but with Blue Ridge Realty's assistance the process will be quite pain free."

As the surgeon said to the patient whose legs he was about to amputate, Gif thought.

"I will call when I make up my mind," Gif said as the realtor waved before climbing into her Lexus.

Gif watched as Ms. Shepherd turned the Lexus around, swinging too wide and leaving a rut in Gif's front lawn. He returned to the house, picked up the file folder, tossed it into the fireplace, and considered his options. It took him ten seconds to decide he would not be selling the house.

If the modern generation doesn't share my taste in kitchens and bathrooms, screw them.

Chapter 15

The head coach walked into the room filled with aching players and announced curtly:

"Your performance yesterday was bad, so damned bad that we aren't going to look at the films. Everybody in pads and out on the field."

Not a player uttered a word. The coach turned his back, and Winchester Johnson groaned. The angry coach spun around and glared at the players.

"Does somebody have a problem with that?" he demanded.

Not even Winchester Johnson answered.

The coach waited and the players obediently retreated to the locker room where they silently donned their pads before jogging out onto the practice field; all knew what lay ahead of them; they would suffer.

Boozer Jankowski with his enlarged black eye was more worried than most despite the fact that he was one of the few who had had a good preseason game. As a first time starter for the defense at cornerback, he knew the offense would not treat him kindly.

"Hey rook, how's the eye," Winchester Johnson, the huge offensive tackle who had sucker punched Boozer asked.

Boozer turned, balled up his right fist, and glared at Johnson.

Johnson laughed and jogged away from Boozer. "Son, tighten your sphincter. I'll be greeting you soon enough."

Boozer glared after the monster, fully aware of what he meant. At cornerback, Boozer was responsible for the offensive team's pass catchers. He liked to hit them hard, catch them unaware, knock the ball out of their hands and damage them if possible. His advantage lay in his speed and his ability to read the field. His disadvantage came after making the initial hit. That was when the other team's muscle men punished him for his transgressions.

The coaches lined up the first team offense and the first team defense against each other. On the opening play, Boozer spotted the team's premier tight end cutting across the center of the field and hit him low about fifteen yards behind the line of scrimmage. It was a solid hit, and he was feeling real good about it when a ton of offensive lineman landed on his back. Fortunately, he had his knees in position to absorb the blow, but his relief was short-lived. A huge hand ripped his helmet from his head and a fist smashed into his good eye. Boozer's unprotected head bounced twice against the ground, the fist struck him a second time, and he lost consciousness.

"Tough shit, rook," Winchester Johnson said as he pushed Boozer's face into the ground and levered himself to his feet.

None of Boozer's first team defense teammates said a word. They returned to the defensive huddle leaving the unconscious Boozer lying where he fell.

The coach, disgusted, blew his whistle. He waited until two trainers rushed out, grabbed Boozer by the arms, and dragged him off the field.

"Another rook eats dirt," a backup offensive guard standing to Stan's left laughed.

Stan, who had seen the brutal after action hit on his roommate and friend, turned. "Good luck, rook, you're going to need it," the guard said.

Since the lineman was one of those he needed to protect him, Stan did not reply. Fortunately for him, the coach arbitrary demoted him to third team quarterback, and he spent the rest of the practice running plays at the opposite end of the field while his competition, Jaws Kramer, the old guy, took the battering.

After three hours in the late August heat, an exhausted Stan was jogging off the field wondering if Boozer had suffered a major career ending injury when again a teammate challenged him.

"Hey, rook, you lucked out today. Your turn comes tomorrow." Winchester Johnson shoved him, causing Stan to stumble as the huge tackle jogged past him.

Stan entered the locker room wondering why he bothered. With teammates like these, not even the big money made it worthwhile.

Stan checked out the training rooms and was beginning to worry when he found Boozer sitting on a bench outside the team doctor's office. Both of Boozer's eyes were swollen almost shut.

"Hey, how are you?" Stan asked.

Boozer peered at him through squinted eyes. "Did you see that?" He asked. "The fuckers sandbagged me."

"I know," Stan said, worried about his friend.

"Can I help you son?" The team doctor asked from behind him.

Stan spun around. "How is he? Will he be all right?"

"Just a couple of bruises, son. All in a day's work."

"Dirty shits," Stan declared. "They sandbagged him."

"I didn't see it," the doctor smiled. "Football is a man's game."

"Come on," Stan grabbed Boozer by the arm and helped him off the bench. "I thought this was supposed to be a team game," Stan glared over his shoulder at the doctor.

The doctor answered with a shrug. "Get used to it, son."

"Stuff the clichés and get a job," Stan said and walked Boozer out of the examining room.

Later, while he and a still weak Boozer were getting dressed, Stan saw the coach walk into the room with the doctor. Both looked in his direction. The doctor whispered something to the coach who shook his head negatively before turning and leaving the room.

After the chubby realtor departed, Gif gathered the unopened paint cans and stiff brush and returned them to the garage. He thought about calling Senator Ames to explain that he had not been the source of the accusing story, but he decided against it, knowing that Ames would not believe him. He also considered calling Harrington and/or Tracey to register his denials, but his pride won after arguing the negative. If his friend and his former friend did not know him better than that, he decided, they would have to live with their misconceptions.

Angry with Mavis Davis, disappointed about his session with the realtor, and irritated with Tracey and Harrington, particularly the former, he devoted the rest of the day to prepping his refuge for another extended period without him.

Tired and sore from the day's practice and still furious about their treatment by alleged teammates at practice and at Tiny's the night before, Stan and Boozer picked up some Chinese carryout and ate dinner at their apartment. After the largely unsatisfactory meal, they retreated to the small living room where Boozer, who resembled a raccoon, stretched out on the couch, and Stan settled into the one comfortable chair facing the television. He grabbed the remote and flipped through the channels, moving from one tired old rerun to another. None of the movie channels was any better.

"Comcast sucks," Boozer, who lay with a pillow shielding his eyes, declared.

"Want to try the NFL Channel?" Stan asked trying to remember the number.

"What is it? 738?"

"Screw it," Boozer said, throwing his pillow at the television set. "I've had all the football I can stand for one day."

"Are you up to a couple of beers?" Stan asked.

Boozer answered by pushing himself up off the couch. "These damned walls are crushing me."

Stan, who shared the feeling, stood up. "Let me get my shoes and my wallet," he said, heading for the bedroom.

"Bring mine, too," Boozer said, dropping back on the couch.

When they reached the parking lot behind their apartment, Boozer made the next decision for them. "I'll drive," he said and headed towards his pickup.

They rode in silence until they reached the Waxpool Road intersection. Neither noticed the nondescript Japanese car with a single occupant that had followed them out of the apartment parking lot.

"Tiny's all right?" Boozer asked.

"Those shits will be there. Are you game?"

Boozer answered with a defiant stare through his swollen raccoon eyes.

"If we take them on, we're going to need some muscle to help us," Stan said.

"Spoken like a true quarterback," Boozer muttered.

"Don't get angry with me. I'm just being realistic," Stan said. "They've got us outnumbered."

"I know."

The battered, old Honda continued to trail their pickup, carefully staying two cars behind them.

They parked behind the building and entered Tiny's to find it already hopping. Winchester Johnson, the hulking offensive tackle who had tormented them the previous night and who had assaulted Boozer on the practice field, was already at the bar surrounded by several of his muscle bound friends, one of whom spotted Stan and Boozer as soon as they entered and poked Johnson with his elbow. Johnson turned, saw the two rookies, and smiled.

"Our evening's entertainment," he said. "Hey rooks, back for some more?"

"Ignore him," Stan grabbed the bristling Boozer by the arm and pulled him to an empty table in a back corner of the room.

As soon as they were seated, the same waitress approached.

"Two beers," Stan ordered.

He watched the waitress as she swiveled away from them.

"Great ass," Stan said as he glanced towards the bar and noticed that Winchester Johnson had his massive back to them, apparently content to ignore them for the moment. He turned to see how Boozer was reacting.

"Hi guys," a familiar voice said.

Stan looked to his right and found Jaws Kraver, the third quarterback who had joined them the previous night just before the one sided fight, sitting with two of the team's second string running backs at a table nearby.

"I hope I wasn't the cause of last night's contretemps," Jaws said. "I was the one who spoke first to those two girls."

"No way," Stan said, even though he wasn't completely sure that Jaws hadn't precipitated the one sided fight. Jaws, who was at the tail end of his career, had been giving Stan a lot of good advice.

"Anyway, I brought along a little muscle as insurance," Jaws said. He nodded at the two large backs who flanked him. Each weighed a good two hundred and fifty pounds, not in Winchester Johnson's class, but large muscular men in any case.

"Let's unite forces," Boozer said, standing up and making a show of shoving the two tables together. The noise attracted Winchester Johnson and his fellow linemen's attention. Johnson smiled, waved, and turned back to face the bar.

"This might prove interesting," Tank Stalloni, the third string fullback grinned, showing his missing front teeth.

"Are all teams this way?" Stan asked Jaws.

"Football is a contact sport," Tank Stalloni laughed.

The waitress delivered Stan and Boozer's beer, and Stan graciously ordered three more for Jaws, Tank and the third back, a muscular African American who smiled a lot but said very little.

"Christ, the coach worked us hard today," Stan tried to make conversation.

"Yeah, but the pay is damned good," Jaws said.

"Be glad you're not starting," Tank Stalloni said. "Those guys are going to get us all killed." He nodded in the direction of Winchester Johnson and his offensive line stalwarts.

"I wonder why the boy wonder doesn't spend some of his big bucks on the O line," Stan said.

"Son, get used to it," Jaws smiled. "The O line is the last place they worry about. They stack up the three hundred and fifty pounders and order them not to move."

"As if they could," Tank said. "You quarterbacks are expected to take three steps back and throw the ball."

"And?" Jaws said.

"And then run like hell as if your life depended upon it," Tank laughed. "Do what you're told, and you'll survive."

"Don't pay him any attention, kid," Jaws said, looking at Stan. "Either take your three steps and throw fast or hand the ball off to Tank here and watch him run for his life. He's paid to take the pounding, not you."

"I'd rather to see you guys," Boozer said, referring to quarterbacks, "throw the ball. If you don't, little guys like me have to tackle bruisers like him." He nodded at Tank and his silent companion.

To Stan's surprise, the next three hours passed quickly, dominated by football chatter and no challenge from Johnson and his friends. In fact, Johnson and his entourage left first, followed by Jaws and the two running backs, leaving Boozer and Stan the last team members in the bar. Stan and Boozer finished yet another beer before calling it a night, and both were staggering slightly when they exited Tiny's and rounded the building. The parking lot was dark when they turned towards Boozer's pickup.

Halfway there, Stan felt the call of nature and stopped between two parked cars to relieve himself. By the time he finished, Boozer was seated behind the wheel waiting for him. Stan opened the door on his side and paused.

"Are you sure you don't want me to drive?" Stan asked. He had deliberately paced himself, taking only one bottle to every two by Boozer.

"Hell no, get in," Boozer responded predictably.

"Hey kid," a voice called from the dark behind him.

Stan turned, saw the outline of a figure leaning on the hood of the car behind him, pointing something at him.

"What …" Stan started to reply when something smashed into his chest knocking him backward against the pickup.

Inside the pickup, Boozer saw a flash of light followed by a loud blast.

Boozer spun to his left and jumped out of the car.

When his feet touched the ground, he turned and was hit with a thunderous blow to his chest.

He dropped without uttering a sound.

The attacker trotted off to his left, stripping the gloves from his hands as he ran. He tossed the gloves and his weapon into the open trunk of the small red car, climbed into the driver's seat, and drove off into the dark with his lights extinguished.

"What in the hell was that?" the waitress called to the bartender.

The bartender shrugged. "Who knows? Probably a truck backfiring. Just mind you own business."

"Yeah," the waitress agreed. "We're lucky those damned Redskins got through one night without another damned fight."

Forty-five minutes later, the bartender locked the door behind him, started for his car. Almost there, he tripped over Stan's body.

"Shit!" He complained as he grabbed his cell phone.

⁂

The next morning a still depressed Gifford locked the door behind him, climbed into his Prius, and headed down Route 15. His primary regret was that he still had his mountain real estate on his back. He followed 15 until he hit 17 and continued on until 17 crossed 95. There, he turned west towards Richmond. It was the long way, adding miles to his trip, but at least it cut the arduous 95 in half. He was west of Fredericksburg when his cell phone rang.

"Shit," Gif complained. In the haste of his escape, he had made a mistake. He had turned on one of the major irritants in his life.

Gif had a tendency to blame inanimate technology and not the callers. He thought about ignoring it, assuming the call was from someone in the life he was leaving behind him. The damned thing persistently ignored his inattention, and he finally surrendered.

"Gifford." He answered curtly, saying not a word more, not a smattering of a courtesy he did not feel.

"Gif, it's Josie," Colonel Harris Townsend's secretary announced.

"Hi Josie, what's up?" Gif greeted one of the few persons who made his life more tolerable.

"Hang on," Josie ordered.

"Gif," Townsend came on the line. "Where are you?"

"Oh shit," Gif reacted, knowing that question meant he was about to be turned in another direction.

"I'm on the way home," Gif replied.

"Which one?"

"The only one I have," Gif said.

"Good," Townsend misunderstood.

At least Gif could not tell if he truly misunderstood or did so deliberately.

"Best that you pull over so we can chat," Townsend said.

Gif obediently pulled to the side of the road, ignoring the irritated blast from the twelve wheeler that protested his abrupt maneuver.

"OK," Gif said.

"I know you're a Redskin fan," Townsend said. "What do you think of the news?"

"What news?" Gif asked, assuming that Townsend was just making small talk.

"You're kidding?"

"No I'm not," Gif said, getting tired of people asking if he had heard the news. "I just shut down my Loudoun place, maybe for the last time, because I'm thinking about putting in on the market. I spent the morning locking up, didn't have the television or radio on, and haven't read a newspaper."

"Are you serious?"

Gif assumed he meant serious about selling the Loudoun house.

"Of course. I've had my fill of all the bullshit that comes out of Washington, and right now I'm parked on I 95 outside of Fredericksburg. Just getting off this highway will be justification for moving to Richmond for good."

"What about the Tate investigation?"

"It's in good hands. I was never involved in that anyway."

"I thought you were," Townsend said. "The word on the street and the television is that you're carrying the task force on that broad back of yours. I've been telling everybody you were our representative in the investigation and to funnel everything through you."

Gif laughed. "Sorry, Harris, you better keep an eye on those everybodies of yours. Nobody funneled anything to me."

"Guess we never came up with anything to funnel."

"It doesn't matter," Gif said. "You're not alone. They don't have a clue who the shooter was. They're back to checking out the crazies list. I took a look at the Walker thing. There might be more to it than I initially thought. We can discuss all this when I get there which will be in an hour."

That comment was met by silence.

"Are you still there?" Gif asked wondering if the connection had broken.

"Sorry," Townsend answered immediately. "I was thinking."

"That's a positive," Gif laughed. "I'm not sure anyone in Washington is."

"Would you mind turning around and going back to Loudoun?" Townsend surprised Gif.

"Hell yes," Gif reacted. "I just made my escape from the place."

"I'm afraid I committed you," Townsend said.

Gif let his silence convey his displeasure. He and Colonel Harrison Townsend were friends, quite close friends, but Townsend still commanded the Virginia State Police who paid his salary, something he needed more than ever since he had just burned some bridges behind him.

"Gif, I was serious when I referred to the Redskins. Last night two of their players were murdered, and Dick Simmons just called and asked for your help."

"Simmons?" Gif let his surprise show. "Why didn't he call me directly?"

"He said he tried your cell phone, but you obviously had it turned off."

"He's right," Gif admitted. "I made the mistake of turning it back on when I cleared Loudoun. There are people in the area I wasn't interested in talking with, but Simmons wasn't one of them. He knows where I live."

"Dick says this Redskin thing is big. The media are all over him, and he already has his hands full with the Tate investigation. Apparently his parking lot is filled with network satellite trucks, and half his staff is busy keeping them out of the building."

Gif chuckled at the image. "Simmons can handle it. Dealing with the media isn't my thing."

"After seeing your performance on network television, I have to agree with you," Townsend said.

"That's not fair. I was set up," Gif protested.

"I was serious when I said I made a commitment for you," Townsend persisted. "Investigating difficult murders is our job too, you know."

"You really want me to turn back?"

"I do. I'm sure if it weren't for …this other thing, I would have difficulty keeping you away from the Redskin case."

"Shit," Gif said.

"Sorry."

"Who got shot? It wasn't the Lip was it?" Gif referred to the starting quarterback, Bruno the Lip Hauptman."

"Close. Somebody used a shotgun on second string quarterback Stan Muncy and linebacker Boozer Krzinsky."

"There goes the future," Gif said.

"And if the person responsible was another Redskin?"

"The fans will lynch the investigator responsible for destroying their team," Gif said.

"What do you think will happen when the finger pointing reporters start to work?"

"No wonder Dick Simmons wants to unload this sucker."

"Interested?"

"Do I have a choice?"

"Not really, old friend."

"The good doctor is going to kill me. She's not speaking to me now," Gif groaned.

"It's my experience that communal silence is not always a bad thing," Townsend laughed as he terminated the conversation.

Gif drove ten miles down I-95 looking for a turn off that would let him reverse directions, cursing every foot of the way.

Acting President Hiram Adams and his chief of staff Jake Tyrone were sitting in the Andrew Johnson Suite sipping their bourbon, Adams with his feet propped on a side drawer of old Andrew's desk, Jake sprawled on the sofa with his feet on the polished coffee table.

"Do you think it's true that Johnson used to drink his bourbon from these very cups?" Jake asked.

"That's what I'm told. Old Andrew, a loyal North Carolinian, appreciated his bourbon like the good ole boy that he was."

"North Carolina? I thought he was from Tennessee."

Hiram laughed. "I've always cautioned you, Jake. Do your homework."

Tyrone frowned, sipped his bourbon, and waited, knowing his boss, mentor and friend liked nothing better than the chance to educate him.

"Andrew Johnson was born on December 29, 1808 in the kitchen of a small house on Fayetteville Street, Raleigh." Adams paused, raised his delicate cup in a good-natured salute to his friend and waited for the obvious question.

"How the hell did he get to Tennessee?" Jake accommodated him.

"At the age of seventeen he moved to Greenville, Tennessee, where he opened his own tailor shop."

Jake laughed as the old man expected and waited for him to continue. One of his more onerous duties was listening to the garrulous eighty year old demonstrate how smart he was.

"As a twenty-two year old, he was elected Mayor of Greenville, beginning a political career that carried him to the United States Senate and ultimately to this lovely room and this beautiful desk where he sat when he sipped his barrel aged bourbon." Adams smiled as he leaned back and waited for Jake to praise the depth of his knowledge. He didn't admit that he had learned what he had just recited from a pamphlet he found in the drawer of his desk.

"I wouldn't bet a dime on the Redskins this year," Jake changed the subject.

Adams frowned at his assistant, showing his displeasure at not being granted his due admiration.

"Two murders, that must be a first," Jake said as he ignored Hiram's unspoken admonition.

"A distraction," Adams agreed.

"Particularly for the task force and the media," Jake said.

"The public has a short attention span," Adams declared, using the cliché as if it were an original thought.

"Not when it comes to the Redskins," Jake said. Over the years both he and Adams had become ardent Redskin supporters.

"Do you think it's possible we may never learn who shot poor President Tate," Adams smiled as if the idea might please him.

"Why don't we call in those two FBI directors and ask them," Jake suggested, finally arriving at the question he intended to ask when he started this discussion.

"An ex FBI director and a director who is about to become an ex whether he knows it or not," Adams agreed. "Good idea. Have Miss Mary give them a call and tell them to get their butts over here."

In Director Thomas Harrington's 7th floor office, he and ex-Director Tracey Schultz sat in the conversational corner as they discussed the lack of progress in the Tate and Walker investigations. Chief investigator Jeffrey Cohena, the Special Agent in Charge of the Washington Metropolitan Field Office, had returned from his quick trip to Toronto where he had personally interviewed the pharmacist who peddled cut rate drugs on the internet. The man had frankly admitted he had provided the sildenafil citrate ordered by James Dexter on three separate occasions, but he denied supplying anything stronger than those little blue bills readily available with a doctor's prescription. The pharmacist had shown Cohena the records which included the dates and the dosage for the pills he had sent, and Cohena, an experienced investigator, had believed him.

"What do you think about Jeff's report on the pills?" Tracey asked.

"I respect Cohena's judgment," Harrington answered. "Jeff believes the super strength pills came from a second source."

"And Dexter claims he didn't have anything to do with them," Tracey Schultz said. "I don't trust everything the kid says, but it is possible somebody else gave them to Walker."

"Nan Starbright," Harrington used the name he preferred over Barby Dolle.

"She is not going to tell us anything now," Tracey referred to her untimely death.

"I gather that Gif accepted her denial about the pills," Harrington said.

"She told him Walker got them somewhere," Tracey agreed.

"I wish Gif hadn't bailed out on us," Harrington said.

"I wish he hadn't been so frank with Mavis Davis," Tracey said.

"Is Ames still denying he had a relationship with Ms. Starbright?" Harrington asked.

"Senator Ames is not admitting anything. He refers all questions to his legal advisor."

"Do you think Ames is the one who gave Walker those super pills?" Harrington asked.

"Who gave them that name, super pills?" Tracey asked.

"I did, just now," Harrington smiled.

"I suggest you don't give the media any ideas," Tracey said. "I can see the headlines now. 'Superpills Kill Supersackman."

"I'll let you handle the media," Harrington said. "You and Gif seem to have a knack for it."

"Ha, ha. Those two playboys, Ames and Walker, shared everything else including Barby Dolle," Tracey said. "I wouldn't be surprised if Ames gave Walker the pills to try."

Suddenly, the door to the reception room opened, and Harrington's young secretary appeared.

"The acting president's secretary just called and invited you two to a session at the White ...at the Treasury Department," the girl announced.

"Oh shit," Tracey reacted. She glanced at Harrington.

"We've got to go," Harrington said. "Please tell them we are on the way," he spoke to the secretary who withdrew.

"What in the hell are we going to say?" Tracey asked. "Do you think that if we report that Gifford has had a breakthrough, someone would pass it on, and Gifford might come face to face with the killer? It would teach one of them a lesson. We couldn't lose."

"We could do that, but knowing Gifford, he would shoot the sob and arrest half the White House."

"Would that be all bad?"

Then who would we report to?" Harrington laughed as he rose from his desk. "Meanwhile, I suggest we say as little as possible and rush back here before our report becomes Breaking News."

"Why don't you handle it yourself this time, Tom?" Tracey asked.

"Adams will expect you to be there," Harrington answered. "He appointed you to lead the task force. Do you want to handle the briefing this time?

"You do it so well, Tom," Tracey deferred.

"Maybe we should get Gif back here," Harrington said. "If nothing else he would distract our masters with his unorthodox style."

"And the media, too," Tracey said, unable to let go of the Mavis Davis thing.

"Do I detect a hint of jealousy, Tracey?" Harrington asked.

"Jealousy? I'm too old to be jealous," Tracey said as she stood up. "Are you sure you need me for this exercise in futility?"

"I do, as the Christian said to the lion as they entered the Coliseum."

"What the hell does that mean?" Tracey asked.

"I don't know," Harrington said as he followed her out the door. "I'm getting punchy. I thought it sounded erudite."

"I'd put that line the same place you can put the super pills," Tracey said.

Chapter 16

When Gif arrived back in Leesburg, he drove directly to the sheriff's office. There, he found the situation exactly as Colonel Townsend had described it. The old bowling alley that should have been replaced years ago as the county's answer to law enforcement was under siege. Network satellite vans surrounded the place waiting to support the deployed teams of talkers with blow dry hairdos who jostled with a horde of shabbily dressed print reporters carrying notebooks and pens, all searching for a single malleable source.

As Gif drove around the building, they all stared hopefully at him. He ignored them. Because the rear lot was congested, he parked in front of the back entrance in a clearly marked No Parking zone. He assumed that if Dick Simmons really wanted his assistance, he could fix any ticket.

"Inspector, Inspector Gifford," a female voice called as he climbed the steps and approached the door.

Gif turned, found a smiling Mavis Davis with her cameraman behind her pointing his equipment in his direction. Gif waved and entered. "Under no circumstance let that person in the building," he ordered a grim faced female deputy guarding the entrance.

"Yes sheriff," she replied, telling Gif that she knew who he was.

Gif nodded.

"Sheriff, do you want me move your vehicle?" The deputy asked.

"Leave it where it is, but please keep an eye on it for me," Gif answered.

Gif charged up the steps to the second floor, entered the reception room to his old office, waved casually at the new face manning Kitty's old desk, and growled:

"Is he in?"

Before the pretty young thing could answer, Gif was past her. Too late, he remembered that her name was Gloria.

"Yes, sir, please go right in," she called after him.

Gif entered and found Dick Simmons behind his polished new desk facing an unfamiliar lieutenant sitting at attention in the subordinate chair. The mere sight of Simmons's new furniture irritated Gif.

"Gif, I'm not sure that you ever met Brian Sadler. I think I mentioned him to you," Simmons greeted him. "Brian is my chief investigator."

Gif nodded at Sadler. Before the man spoke a single word, Gif took an instant dislike to him. Sadler, an outsider, now occupied a slot that Gif had created and should now belong to a deputy that Gif had personally trained.

"Colonel Townsend tells me you have a little problem," Gif spoke directly to Simmons before dropping into a chair along the back wall.

"Take this chair, please, sir," Sadler leaped to his feet offering the chair directly in front of Simmons to Gif.

Gif waved a hand in dismissal and waited for Simmons to respond to his reference to Townsend.

"Brian, I would appreciate it if you would give Sheriff Gifford and me a few minutes," Simmons, recognizing his old superior's mood, dismissed his chief investigator.

Gif waited until the door closed behind the former military policeman who had usurped the job that should have gone to someone like Billie Williams.

"Townsend said you asked for help," Gif said.

"We need some expert assistance," Simmons said, accurately reading Gif's mood.

Gif, irritated at having his personal plans derailed, was tempted to ask why Simmons hadn't come out to the house if he wanted to talk with him. He resisted the impulse, however, because he knew that an unscheduled visit would have irritated him also. As much as he hated having his personally set schedule disrupted by others, Gif had to admit that he had been the one who had turned off the phones. Still, he was beginning to feel that the familiarity he had always shared with Simmons had vanished, and he was not sure what had changed with his old subordinate whose career he had mentored. Gif assumed that years of command had colored Simmons' views of his old boss, and he did not like that feeling. Simmons no longer acted like the deferential junior he remembered. Although he told himself that was a natural development and that he should now take pride in the fact that Simmons was now his own man, it still bothered him.

"Have you heard the news?"

"Somebody iced a couple of Redskins," Gif said, leaving the burden of explanation on Simmons.

"Last night, a party or parties unknown blasted two Redskin players outside of Tiny's in Ashburn," Simmons said. "With a twelve gage pump. Do you know Tiny's?"

"Did you recover the weapon?" Gif ignored the question. He could visit the scene later.

Simmons shook his head.

"No witnesses?" Gif assumed there were none, or 103.5 reports he had listened to on his return journey would have mentioned them.

"No. The two victims closed the bar and were leaving when the perp ambushed them in the parking lot."

"What happened in the bar before they left?" Gif asked, wanting to know if the two had gotten involved in a drunken brawl with somebody.

"Nothing, not that night," Simmons said.

Gif immediately picked up on that answer. "But they had a problem before."

"Muncy and Jankowsky were both rookies," Simmons said. "The night before they had a problem with the usual hazing."

"But not the night of the shooting," Gif said, tired of pulling the story out of his old subordinate. He had taught him how to give a terse but complete report, but Simmons had apparently forgotten the lesson.

"That's right. We're told that they had a small fight with a couple of teammates and got tossed out on their asses. But nothing happened last night. The two drank at a table with a couple of other players, the older teammates stayed at the bar, and all was calm. The older guys left a good half hour before the two rookies. They were apartment mates and stayed on."

"You interviewed the older guys?"

"Yes. Brian Sadler, the lieutenant you just ran off, did. They all had alibis for the time of the shooting."

"Convenient. They covered each other." Gif ignored the reference to Sadler.

"Convenient, yes. Brian thinks they were truthful."

"Who do you think did it?"

Simmons shrugged. "A disgruntled fan. A jealous boyfriend. We don't have a clue."

"There was a girl involved?" Gif picked up on the jealous boyfriend comment.

"Two groupies were involved in the previous night's dispute. A couple of teenage girls. They were not present last night."

"OK," Gif said, standing up. "Mind if I take a look around the crime scene and visit Redskin Park?"

"That's why I asked for you, Gif. We need experienced help. Mind if Brian tags along? He's handled the investigation to date."

"I'd prefer to take an independent look," Gif said. "What's Billie doing these days?" Gif referred to Billie Williams, another ex-subordinate who had worked closely with Gif's chief investigator, Gizzie Kane.

Simmons answered by tapping a button on his fancy intercom.

"Ask Billie Williams to come in here."

"Billie's still working investigations," Simmons turned back to Gif. "I'm not sure what he's up to right now, but you can have him if you want him."

"I do," Gif said. "I know Billie."

Gif immediately got the message. The new guy, Brian Sadler, was Simmons' boy and would keep Simmons informed of what Gif was doing. Billie's loyalty presumably rested elsewhere, an attitude that placed him outside the confidence of the current regime. No more than two minutes later, a smiling Billie Williams appeared, all six feet four inches, two hundred and seventy-five pounds of him.

"Gif," Williams greeted Gif enthusiastically.

"Christ, Billie, you've put on weight," Gif smiled.

"I know. I spend a lot of time shuffling paper these days," Williams said, glancing at Simmons.

"Billie is office manager for investigations," Simmons said.

Gif had trouble understanding that. Billie had been one of his brightest, most perceptive investigators, but he let the comment pass. He and Billie could discuss that situation later.

"Billie, Gif has agreed to work with us on the Redskin case. Would you mind assisting?" Simmons asked.

"Excuse me, Dick," Gif interrupted. "I would like to be perfectly clear. I did not say I would take over the case, work with you, or assist in the investigation. The murders happened in Loudoun County and your department clearly should take the lead. Given the high profile being given the case," Gif glanced out the window to emphasize his point, "and since Ashburn is located in the Commonwealth of Virginia as well as the County of Loudoun, the Office of Special Investigations has been tasked by Colonel Townsend to take an independent look, and that is what I intend to do."

Simmons frowned, Billie stared, and Gif hated having to play the law enforcement bureaucrat with the man who had been his personal choice to succeed him as sheriff. He needed, however, to make perfectly clear what his chain of command would be. Gif waited to see how Simmons would respond, not really caring, but curious to learn how much Dick had changed. Gif hoped that the dramatic turnover in sheriff department personnel was not a true indicator.

"That's right, Gif," Simmons finally reacted with a false smile. "You have always been your own man. We'll take your help anyway we can get it."

"Good," Gif said. "I'll leave all contact with the media up to you and your public relations staff."

"If that's the way you want it," Simmons agreed, surprising Gif.

If Gif had been in Simmons' shoes, he would have tried to pass the burden of dealing with the media off to the Commonwealth representative. However, to be fair to Simmons, Gif knew first hand that the post of sheriff was an elective office, and no politician could pass up any opportunity to exploit media attention. Gif actually remembered sitting in this very office and looking out the window and watching Sheriff Tate hold spontaneous press conferences. Still, while Simmons said the right things, the false smile on his face told Gif that something was not right.

"So, Billie," Gif turned to his old subordinate. "If you have the time, I would appreciate your helping me get up to speed."

"Of course, Gif," Billie answered. "If the sheriff agrees…"

Simmons nodded.

"Then, that's settled," Gif said as he stood up and started for the door.

Billie glanced uncertainly at Simmons. When he did not react, Billie jumped to his feet and followed Gif out the door. Gif did not speak again until they were in the outer hall.

"Where should we start?" Gif asked.

"Redskin Park," Billie answered immediately.

"Shall we take my car?" Gif asked.

"Sure thing, Gif," Billie said. "Let me grab a couple of things from my office, and I'll join you."

"I'll wait at the back door," Gif said.

"We've kept an eye on your vehicle, sheriff," the female deputy guarding the rear entrance smiled as Gif approached. She glanced out the window at Gif's Prius still conspicuous in the No Parking zone at the foot of the steps.

"Never know what the animals out there might do to get attention," the deputy chuckled, referring to the media who were now herded back some twenty yards from the steps.

Gif chatted with the deputy about the vagaries of the media until Billie rejoined him a few minutes later. This time Billie was wearing his belt, which included his holstered weapon, handcuffs, radio, and other paraphernalia.

"Feels good dressing like a real deputy for a change," Billie declared.

"I like your choice of partners, sheriff," the female deputy said, nodding her approval at Billy.

"It's a relief to get out of purgatory now and then," Billie said as he pushed open the door.

As soon as Gif appeared, the media started shouting questions at him. He led Billie down the stairs and heard the distinct voice of Mavis Davis addressing him:

"Are you taking over the investigation, Gif?"

Gif did not look in her direction. He climbed into the driver's seat, and Billie with a little difficulty because of his size climbed in beside him.

"These are great little cars," Billie said. "Been thinking about buying one myself."

"You can't go wrong," Gif said as he started the engine. "And they're not as little as they look." He glanced at Billy and corrected himself. "They might not fit you," he laughed. "But they're roomy enough for normal sized people."

As Gif headed toward Route 7 on his way to the Loudoun County Parkway, he noted that one of the satellite trucks was tracking them, carefully staying three cars back, trying to be inconspicuous.

"We've got an escort," Gif said.

Billie turned and peered out the back window.

"Damn right," Billie confirmed. "Why don't we pull them over and give them a ticket for following too closely.

Gif laughed. "Three cars behind us?"

"Why not? Just writing it will make me feel good."

"I know, but it's not worth the effort. They'll just tear it up. They know your boss won't push it. He's an elected official and needs good publicity too."

Gif continued down Route 7 for eight miles, jockeying with the traffic flow that was packed into red light jams, meaning the red lights created a patchwork effect of rushing cars. Racing blocks of traffic moved with huge gaps between the masses so that from above the highway looked like a checkerboard filled with a mile of space separating the bumper-to-bumper cars.

He turned right on Loudoun County Parkway at the intersection where the developer subsidized county board had authorized the construction of world class, high-rise offices, upscale shopping, expensive restaurants, parks, luxury apartments and single family homes.

"You've heard about One Loudoun?" Billie asked.

Gif nodded and glanced at the scarred fields on his right. Bulldozers had done their work and departed, leaving nothing behind but exposed dirt. Every single piece of green had been dug up, felled, and hauled away, but not a single sign of construction could be seen.

"Appears that bad economic times have thrown a wrench into their plans," Gif said.

"Remember the working farms and all the beautiful fields?" Billie asked.

"Progress," Gif shook his head.

"Somebody's losing a lot of money," Billie said.

Gif glanced in his mirror and saw the satellite van still trailing them, now exposed with no vehicles between them and their rabbit. Despite the parkway's four lanes, it appeared to Gif to be underused.

Billie noticed Gif's rear view check, turned, and peered into the mirror on his side of the car. "Doesn't that sexy network reporter friend of yours work for Channel 4?" Billie referred to Gif's brief television appearance. "She's pretty well preserved for her age."

"Mavis Davis," Gif confirmed. "A real pain in the ass."

"You know her well?"

"Not the way you're implying, Billie. I had a brief chat with her, that's all."

"Oh," Billie said. "She's the one that stuck it to you. I missed that newscast, but I heard about it."

"You didn't miss anything," Gif said sourly.

About three miles down the road, they approached the turn off to the Redskin practice field. They passed a parked Sheriff's sedan, and Billie waved.

"We set up traps here regularly," Billie laughed. "It's like shooting fish. For a couple hundred yards, right there, the road becomes two lanes. We have the speed limit set for twenty-five miles an hour with forty-five miles an hour on each side."

"For that short distance?"

"Yes," Billie said. "It was the sheriff's idea. You'd be surprised how many tickets we can unload just about any time we want."

"Doesn't seem fair," Gif said.

"Sheriff says life isn't fair, and he has to fund the department. Turn left," Billie ordered."

Gif glanced at the small sign that said "Redskin Park" and turned left. He followed the narrow road about two hundred yards and was stopped by a civilian guard standing by a small traffic control booth.

"Sorry, no entrance," the civilian said. "You can circle around the booth and head back the way you came."

"Police," Gif said and pointed at Billie's uniform.

"Sorry, we're closed to the public today, and we are not hiring any part time security. This is private property," the unimpressed guard declared. "Turn around and head back out."

"What's happening?" Gif asked.

"Team meetings. Come back on a public day."

"This is an official visit," Gif said. He was tempted to ask Billie why they were stopping here in the first place, but the officious guard was beginning to annoy him.

"Sorry," the guard replied. "My orders are to admit only authorized personnel."

'Back off, buster," Billie leaned forward giving the guard a view of his imposing bulk.

Unimpressed, the guard laughed. "I'll check," the guard said and turned to enter his booth, presumably to call his supervisor.

"Don't bother," Gif said as he stepped on the accelerator. In the mirror, he saw the guard dutifully talking on the phone.

"Who do these guys think they are?" Gif asked rhetorically.

"The Redskins," Billie smiled. "They do just about whatever they want around here."

"Including murdering each other," Gif said.

"I hope not," Billie said. "They've lost two key rookies already."

"The world won't end if the Redskins have another losing season," Gif said. "Their offensive line sucks."

"Well they are the Deadskins," Billie laughed.

"I don't recommend using that phrase around here today," Gif said, assuming that Billie was referring to the reason for their visit.

Billie turned and looked out the back window. "The guard stopped the satellite truck."

"I'll bet he's not in the mood for a friendly chat."

"You're right," Billie said. "Our escort is turning around."

"I guess up close Mavis's legs didn't turn the trick," Gif said.

"Now who's trying to be clever," Billie said.

Chapter 17

In the Andrew Johnson Suite, Acting President Hiram Adams listened patiently as Acting Vice President Alexander Hamilton Sperry ended his harangue of the Director of the FBI and the Chairman of the Tate Task Force following their command briefing.

"I don't know what the hell you two are doing down there in that ugly building of yours, but I suggest you get off your asses and find out who is murdering our citizens," Sperry ordered. "I particularly want to know if this Redskin thing has anything to do with the other murders."

"Do you folks need any help? More manpower? Anything at all," Adams played the Mr. Nice Guy to Sperry's heavy.

"No sir, thank you. We have all the manpower we need," Tracey ignored Sperry and answered Adams. She had to fight to control her temper in the face of Sperry's rude arrogance.

"We're fine for now," Harrington added. Harrington was enough of a bureaucrat to avoid being too definitive with a negative.

"Then I strongly recommend that you two begin earning the big money the citizens are paying you," Sperry got in the last word.

Tracey and Harrington obediently got up and filed out of the office, leaving Sperry, Adams and their two assistants behind.

"That guy's a jerk," Tracey declared after the door closed behind them.

"The acting vice president, of course," Harrington said.

Having noted that Acting President Adams secretary was listening, Harrington spoke for her benefit while pretending to respond to Tracey. Tracey looked sharply at him, angry enough to take on her former subordinate, saw him glance in the direction of the wide-eyed Miss Mary, took the warning, and stomped out of the reception room.

In the Andrew Johnson Suite, the acting vice president continued his rampage:

"Those two are incompetent. We should unload them," he declared.

"If you would please excuse us," Acting President Adams spoke directly to Clete Clapp, Sperry's primary aide.

Clapp looked at his superior, Sperry, who nodded affirmatively, confirming Adams' order. Clapp responded by staring meaningfully at Jake Tyrone, Adams' chief of staff, who remained seated. Clapp again glanced at Sperry to see if he noticed that Tyrone had not moved, but Sperry did not react. Having no choice, Clapp departed, not a happy man. He privately vowed that when the day came, and Sperry was president, Adams and his flunky Tyrone would get repaid for this insult.

"I don't think Mr. Clapp appreciated that," Adams smiled at Sperry.

"I don't either," Sperry answered ambiguously

"Are you stating that you support Mr. Clapp's reaction, or are you saying you agree with my thought that Mr. Clapp did not appreciate my request?" Adams challenged Sperry.

"A little of both," Sperry smiled, standing up to Adams for the first time.

"Mr. Acting Vice President," Adams said, placing strong emphasis on the "acting" in Sperry's title. "If you have you have a problem, you have a clear choice," Adams declared.

"And what is that?" Sperry demanded curtly. Sperry was not sure if Adams was actually threatening him by suggesting that he consider resigning.

"You can leave if you wish," Adams used a little of his own ambiguity, congenially ignoring his acting vice president's demeanor.

"Leave?"

"Yes."

"This room?"

"Or your acting position, whatever you wish," Adams challenged the rude New Yorker.

Sperry blanched, revealing his shock at the sudden confrontation.

He quickly analyzed his position. He could protect his pride and resign or he could capitulate. Unprepared, he quickly compromised.

"Yes, sir," he said, sitting down making it necessary for Adams to fire him.

Adams, amused that Sperry took advantage of the option conveyed by the phrase "if you wish," smiled and pretended that the heated exchange had not taken place. It was obvious to all three men in the room, however, that Sperry had bowed under pressure.

"All right," Adams said, acting like a good politician. "That briefing was very informative."

Adams looked at his chief of staff, Jake Tyrone, silently ordering him to handle the heavy lifting.

"Yes, Mr. President," Jake leaped to his feet. "The investigators don't have a clue who killed President Tate."

Adams nodded approvingly.

"There clearly is some kind of political conspiracy afoot, and it is our obligation to unravel it. Mr. President," Jake paused. "May I suggest to the Secret Service that they increase your security?"

"Do you think that necessary, Jake?" Adams asked, keeping a close eye on Sperry's reaction.

"Sir, you are the only president we have, and until those people," he referred to Harrington and Schultz, "get their act under control we can take no chances."

"What do you think Mr. Acting Vice President?" Adams again stressed the acting.

Shocked by the abrupt question while still reeling from Adams's sudden assault, Sperry hesitated, not knowing what to say. He had his own vision of the future, but for next few weeks he needed the almost senile old man's continued support/tolerance to achieve it.

"I of course agree with Mr. Tyrone," Sperry said, silently wishing any potential assassin good luck.

Adams smiled. "Very well, Jake. Take care of it. What do you make of that briefing?"

"As I said, they don't have a clue," Jake played the game.

"I know, Jake," Adams said. "Please speak frankly. Acting Vice President Sperry is a member of our team."

That misstatement almost made Sperry smile, but he caught himself.

"Very well," Jake said. "Those two," he referred to Harrington and Schultz, "fully realize although they don't say it that only one person has the knowledge that can help us catch the killer."

Adams nodded and turned towards Sperry who was having trouble determining what game the two were playing.

"Young Mr. Dexter," Adams said.

"Dexter?" Sperry blurted. These two yokels were suddenly outmaneuvering him, and he didn't have a clue where they were heading.

"Yes," Jake said. "He's the last man standing, so to speak, who can tell us what really happened to Vice President Walker."

"Really?" Sperry said. "What do you know that I don't?"

Adams laughed. "Mr. Secretary of the Treasury, did you think of checking Mr. Dexter's bank account?"

"His bank account?" Sperry suddenly realized he was playing a game that had already been programmed.

"Yes. Young Mr. Dexter had a very strange deposit to his Dothan bank savings account," Adams said.

"One hundred thousand dollars that appeared out of nowhere electronically and just as fast moved on to a Barbados offshore bank of dubious reputation."

"Where did the money come from?" Sperry asked. "Where did it go?"

"We hoped that you might help us answer that question, Mr. Secretary of the Treasury," Jake smiled.

"Why would you think I could answer that question?" Sperry asked.

"You are our money expert, our banker," Adams smiled, leaning back in his chair and waiting for Sperry to react.

Sperry looked at each of his tormentors and laughed. "You want me to track that deposit?"

"Of course," Adams said. "What else did you think?" He let his comment hang in the air as an accusation or a request for help.

"I'll get right on it," Sperry said and hurried from the room.

"That went well," Jake laughed as Adams lifted his bourbon/coffee cup in the air in salute.

James Dexter nervously paced the floor, a prisoner in his New Hampshire Avenue apartment. Outside, a weary FBI agent sat in his car allegedly providing him protection. In Dexter's opinion, the man was his watchdog, keeping him in, rather than keeping others out. For the first few days after the bureau had forcefully returned him to D.C., Dexter had been grateful for the protective federal presence. Nan's death had been a shock. Now, however, Dexter, who had not even ventured to the office, had grown bored with the entire business. He talked on the phone with his parents, reassured his worried mother, stared out the window, and complained to himself as he paced from wall to wall. Even Dexter, a loner by personality, needed some company, and his uncongenial watchdog provided nothing.

Finally, Dexter made up his mind. He had to get outside his four oppressive walls, have a solitary drink, a quiet walk, get mugged, anything for a change. He decided to take matters in his own hands. He dressed in his most inconspicuous outfit, jeans, a black sports shirt, his blue Nikes, even colored sweat socks. He peeked out the front window, saw the bored FBI agent dozing in his parked car, took the elevator to the basement, went out the back door that led to the alley, slipped past the green garbage bags, and was free, or so he thought. As he hurriedly made his escape, Dexter failed to notice a man in a dark shirt and wearing a Redskin baseball cap pulled low over his face sitting in a nondescript red Toyota.

Anticipating that his subject would catch a cab at the far intersection, the man waited until Dexter almost reached the corner. He started his engine, but not his headlights, and slowly followed Dexter. As anticipated, Dexter rounded the corner, hailed the first cab that came down New Hampshire Avenue from the direction of Dupont Circle, and climbed inside.

"Georgetown," Dexter ordered.

"Anyplace in particular?" The cabbie asked, frowning. Georgetown was only a ten-minute hop away at this time of evening.

"M and Wisconsin," Dexter replied.

The cabbie grunted, hit the accelerator, and raced away, determined to make this a quick trip. He assumed that this fare would be a small tipper.

Behind the cab, the red car followed.

Dexter, pleased with himself, relaxed in the back seat of the cab. Nine minutes later the cabbie pulled to the curb at the corner of M Street and Wisconsin Avenue. Dexter got out and handed the cabbie five bucks through the front window.

"Thanks," the cabbie said, pocketing the money, and speeding away.

Dexter, who had been expecting change, hollered a feeble "Hey" after the departing cab. He watched until it disappeared around the corner heading up Wisconsin Avenue.

"The shit," Dexter grumbled about being taken yet again.

Dexter crossed the street and began a casual stroll up Wisconsin Avenue. The college kids with a sprinkling of middle-aged tourists and off duty servicemen flowed through the area. The bars seemed to be hopping, and everyone was having a good time. Dexter thought about continuing up Wisconsin Avenue to one of his favorite places, the Old Europe. It wasn't the Georgetown in-place it had once been, and it catered to the older set, but Dexter liked the ambiance, which he used to impress his occasional date. Deciding it would be best to avoid places where he might be known, Dexter impulsively turned into a small bar that he had never frequented before. Dexter entered and found himself in a dark, noisy, narrow, but long room that had a bar on the right manned by three bartenders. A single row of tables lined the wall on the left. The place was crowded with what looked like college students, all drinking beer and talking loudly, apparently trying to impress their colleagues with their volume.

Dexter wondered what the kids would think if they knew who had just joined them, one of the recently crowned media celebrities whose name was featured on the front page of both the *Post* and the *Times*. A tall boy pushed back from the bar and made his way to the rear of the room, obviously heading for the john. Dexter slipped into the just vacated space, waited until he got a bartender's attention, and ordered a Miller's Lite draft.

Dexter sipped his beer, leaned against the bar, and relaxed for the first time in days. Quiet anonymity in a public place was just what he needed. He stared at the mirror in front of him, watched the bartenders working quickly and efficiently, and listened to the kids on his left debating the merits of Emerson and Thoreau. They were even discussing Emerson's famous essay, Self Reliance. Dexter remembered when he had been their age and had participated in similar beer fueled discussions. He recalled a quote he had used himself: "Society is always pawing man with its filthy institutions"—or something like that. Dexter listened to the kids, waiting for one of them to repeat the lines that had become a cliché. By his third beer, Dexter was growing disappointed when he realized maybe he had disremembered the quote. He decided that maybe Emerson had not used it in the essay under discussion, and it came from Thoreau, possibly "Walden." Before he could decide, a boy, the third on Dexter's right, declared: "Society is always pawing man with its filthy institutions." That made Dexter's night. He himself had liked that one and was pleased that he remembered it.

Dexter turned his head, getting ready to join the debate, when someone jostled him on his left. Dexter pivoted, a disapproving expression on his face.

"Pardon me, fellow," A rather large man in a dark shirt much like Dexter's own and wearing a Redskin hat nodded at him.

"No problem," Dexter said and turned his attention back to the kids.

"A draft," the man in the Redskin hat called to the nearest bartender.

The foaming glass appeared quickly in front of him, and he took a deep drink.

"To be great is to be misunderstood," the kid who had delivered the hobgoblin quote announced.

That comment really appealed to Dexter, given his current problems, and he was waiting for a chance to chip in when the newcomer on his left spoke again.

"Kids, they'll soon learn what life really is about."

Dexter frowned and thought about challenging him.

"Don't you agree?" The man asked Dexter directly.

Aware of a silence on his right, Dexter glanced at the kids and was surprised to see that they were watching him, waiting for his reply. Now caught in the middle, Dexter didn't know what to say. Kids were excitable in bars, usually ready to show their peers how tough and smart they were, especially after several beers, and the guy in the hat looked like a blue collar tough.

"Excuse me," Dexter backed away from the bar. "Nature calls."

The man in the Redskin hat smiled, waited until Dexter entered the men's room, turned back at the kids and winked, and then followed his prey. The kids shrugged and returned to their debate.

The place smelled of urine; the sink was filthy, and the single mirror cracked. Dexter hesitated, made sure the two stalls were empty, and gingerly stepped around the pools gathered in front of the urinal.

He unzipped his trousers and was concentrating on the stream of expelled beer in front of him when the door behind opened. Self-conscious, Dexter glanced back and was dismayed to find the tough in the Redskin hat smiling at him. He watched as the man checked the room, slid a small wedge between the door lock and the frame, and turned. Dexter thought about asking about the wedge, but he did not, afraid the tough might take offense.

"Those kids are something else," the man said.

Dexter nodded, turned his attention back to the urinal, worried about splashing his trousers and about the tough and did not see the man reach behind his back, lift his shirt, extract a large automatic pistol, take a silencer from his pocket and screw it on the weapon.

"Don't look, Dexter," the man ordered.

The use of his name alarmed Dexter, and he froze.

"My wallet's in my pocket," Dexter's voice cracked with emotion.

"Don't worry about it," the tough said.

Wasting no time, the man held his weapon several inches behind Dexter's head.

The revolver made a quiet hiss and pop. Dexter fell forward, hitting his head on the dirty wall of the urinal. The man grabbed Dexter by the collar, pulled him backwards, stepping to the side to avoid the streaming blood. Dexter fell flat on his back landing in the pools of urine. The man fired a second shot into Dexter's forehead. He leaned over, admired his handiwork, stood up, unscrewed the silencer from his weapon, shoved it into his pocket and tucked the gun back into his belt under his shirt. He retrieved the wedge, opened the door, turned right, and hurried out the rear exit.

Chapter 18

"Billie, what are we doing here?" Gif asked. "Where's the crime scene?"

"At Tiny's," Billie chuckled.

"And why are we at Redskin Park?"

"I've always wanted to see this place," Billie said.

"Billie," Gif cautioned.

"This is where the suspects are," Billie said.

"What are their names?"

"I was hoping you would tell me that. No one else has a clue."

"Lead the way," Gif shrugged.

"Shall we start with the top?"

"The boy owner?" Gif asked.

"If you think he's here."

"Billie, I think I'm beginning to understand why Dick has you tied to a desk," Gif said. "Was the boy owner at Tiny's when this went down?"

"That dump. You're kidding."

"Where is Tiny's?" Gif asked.

"A mile down the road."

"That's what I want to see first," Gif said, halting at the door to the main building.

"Do you think they'll let us back in?" Billie asked. "It might be worth seeing since we are already here."

Billie's disappointment was so transparent, that Gif relented.

"OK," Gif said. "Let's start with Nails and see what he has to say."

Gif referred to Nails Burkosky, the Redskin coach, a former Miami Dolphin linebacker who made his reputation with Kansas City where he earned his name, Nails, a play on the timeworn cliché, so tough he can eat nails. An opposing player tried to denigrate him by saying Burkosky is so tough that he can eat snails. While most opposing teams simply called him the dirtiest player in the league, the hometown press liked to provoke Burkosky by printing the slightly altered cliché before season games.

Gif followed Billie into the rectangular building, which was nothing fancy, merely a brick box with windows.

When they were inside, Billie stopped and turned towards Gif, obviously waiting for him to take the lead.

"Which way?" Gif said.

"Don't ask me?" Billie said. "I'm a paper pusher, remember. I've never been here before."

"Doesn't look like the boy owner is wasting his money on administration," Gif glanced down the stark, deserted hallway.

They approached the security desk and asked: "Where's the head man's office?"

"Owner or coach?" The surly guard asked without looking up from his newspaper.

Gif noticed he was reading the sports pages. "Learn anything in there?"

"Offensive line needs help," the guard patted his newspaper. "Don't tell anybody I said so."

"Coach," Gif said.

"Lots of luck," the guard smiled for the first time. "Snail's that way," he said, pointing with his thumb. "Corner office."

Gif, who found the ambiance at Redskin Park odd, underwhelming at best, was beginning to enjoy himself. He rapped on the door and entered to find himself facing a familiar craggy face with hard, hostile eyes. The solitary man at the desk looked like a pro linebacker who had put on weight, which was exactly what he was.

"Get lost," Nails Burkosky greeted him.

"Mr. Burkosky," Gif held up his credentials. "I am Inspector Gifford and this is Deputy Williams." Gif began his deferential song and dance.

"I recognize the uniform," Nails interrupted. "So what?"

"I'll tell you so what?" Gif said as he sat down in one of the two chairs facing Nail's desk. "We're going to interview you, take as much of your valuable time as we feel necessary, and if you don't cooperate we'll take you in handcuffs to headquarters and conduct our discussion there in less congenial surroundings."

"A man after my own heart," Nails laughed, surprising Gif. "I'll answer your brief questions if you get right to it. I've got a lousy team, and I'm trying to figure out what to do about it. Know where I can find four good offensive linemen?"

"I wish I did," Gif answered. "I'm not sure four will be enough."

"What should I tell my lawyer that you are threatening to charge me with?" Nails asked.

"Impeding a murder investigation, conspiracy, illegal parking, anything that comes to mind," Gif answered. "Are you still beating your wife?"

"Not the newest one, not yet," Nails answered before turning to Billie Williams who had taken the second chair. "Play any offensive line, deputy? You've got the size."

Before Billie could answer, Nails stood up, walked around the desk, and stopped by Billie's chair. Gif had not realized how big Nails truly was until he was on his feet. He stood a good six feet three or four, weighed at least three hundred pounds, had hands the size of tennis racquets and a neck that looked to be at least a size 26.

"A little high school and college," Billie answered standing up so he could look down on Nails.

"How old are you?" Nails asked.

"Thirty-two."

"You're over the hill. Where did you play your college ball?"

"University of Virginia."

"That explains why I never heard of you," Nails said.

"You don't even know my name," Billie challenged him.

"If you were any good I would have heard of you," Nails ignored the irritation in Billie's voice.

"It's Billie Williams."

"Still doesn't mean anything to me," Nails said as he punched Billie's stomach with a huge forefinger. "Too much blubber," Nails declared.

Billie delighted Gif by hitting Nails' stomach with an equally large forefinger. "Whales shouldn't talk about blubber," Billie said.

Nails laughed and returned to his chair behind the desk.

"Why do you say your team is lousy?" Gif asked.

"Too soft, just like your deputy. The two of you couldn't get me in handcuffs if I held one hand behind my back for you. If I can't find me a couple of dinosaurs for the middle of the offensive line, we'll be lucky to win six games. And you know what that means."

"You're out on your ass," Billie answered before Gif could.

Nails pointed a meaty forefinger at Billie and said: "You've got that right, Moby Dick." He turned towards Gif. "Now ask your questions, Inspector, because for starters I've got to get busy and find me a backup quarterback and starting corner. I just lost two good ones."

"Do you have any idea who might have killed them?" Gif asked.

"I've already answered all those questions," Nails frowned.

"I'm taking charge of the investigation, and I want to hear those answers for myself," Gif surprised Billie who had wondered precisely what role Gif was going to play.

Billie smiled. With Gif taking charge, he assumed he would now have a little more active involvement himself.

"Makes sense," Nails grumbled. "If you want something done right, you have to do it yourself. The answer to your question is that I don't know who killed them. I'm told that the two rookies didn't take to the usual hazing. Damn fools, the players I mean, not the rookies. Grown men making big bucks and they behave like a bunch of immature fraternity boys."

"What kind of hazing?" Gif asked, trying to get a feeling for the kind treatment that could have motivated the killings.

"As I said, the usual stuff. Tying rookies to goalposts after practice, involuntary ice water baths, wet towel snapping, Gatorade showers, all that crap, harmless but silly."

"It could be very provoking," Gif suggested.

"Most players tolerate the little stuff," Nails said. "The meaner things my staff and I try to keep an eye on."

"Meaner?"

"Football is a violent game. A hard hit provokes payback, and sometimes it gets out of hand among veterans as well as rookies. Wrestling matches and fistfights between teammates are not uncommon."

"Are you saying that Muncy and Jankowsky were both involved in some of the meaner stuff?"

"I didn't personally witness any of it, but a lot goes on that I don't see," Nails said.

"But there have been incidents."

"I understand that both men were involved in some kind of disagreement at Tiny's the night before the shootings, and that there had been some rough contact that afternoon on the field."

"Who should I talk to about this?" Gif asked.

"You are talking with him now."

"Give me a name."

"Winchester Johnson should be able to help on that score. You've heard of Johnson?"

Gif laughed. "Of course. Was he an observer or a participant?"

"The latter."

"On the field or at Tiny's?"

"Both, I'm told."

"Give me the name of an observer," Give said.

Nails hesitated. "Try Jaws, he's got more brains than most of these guys."

"Jaws Kraver, the quarterback?"

"Our backup quarterback," Nails answered. "But don't go pointing any fingers at him. I'm going to need him real bad one of these days." As soon as the words were out of his mouth, Nails looked sternly at Gifford. "And don't go around quoting me on any of this shit."

"Coach, I'm conducting a murder investigation, and I don't gossip or chat with the media," Gif said.

"Hey, I watch television too. I saw you whispering in the good-looking reporter's ear. The one with the great legs. I couldn't see where your hands were."

"Coach, that was staged. If you want to go see those legs in person, take a walk out to your front gate, and check out the satellite truck," Gif said.

"Just kidding, Gifford. I know the media. Use it or ignore it, but don't trust it. I'll bet that reporter told you it was all off the record."

"She tried. I didn't bite. She threatened to make up her own story; I told her to report whatever she wanted and left."

"I guess that's just what she did," Nails chuckled. "She made up her own story. Bet you don't use that line again."

"Where can I find Kraver and Johnson?" Gif asked.

"Practice is done for the day, and the boys are working on their physical conditioning. They'll all be coming in before long."

"They're still out on the practice field?" Gif asked.

"The backs and the receivers will be running, and the linesmen are prone on the grass moaning and groaning and pretending to be exercising and stretching," Nails said.

"Coach," Gif said as he stood up. "Thanks. We may be back."

"Don't rush," Nails said.

As soon as they were walking down the hall, Billie spoke: "You let him off pretty easy."

"We can always come back. He's a man with problems that I would like to see solved, and I want to talk with those who had a firsthand view of what happened."

"Do you really think it was something that grew out of a simple hazing?" Billie asked. "All the new players go through it to one degree or another without getting involved in a dispute that leads to two murders."

"I know, but we have to follow our noses wherever they take us," Gif said.

"When did you start using all these clichés?" Billie asked.

"It's either the company I keep or the environment of this place. You got to learn, Billie, to fit in."

"Yeah, I'll watch closely and see how you accommodate," Billy laughed.

When they reached the practice field, Gif was disappointed to see that a field was all there was. No bleachers. The situation was just as Nails had predicted. The smaller men were jogging around the field in packs with the pass catchers and the smaller running backs leading followed by the corners and safeties with the heftier of the running backs trailing. The massive linesmen were gathered in groups at two ends of the field, the offense at one end, and the defense at the other. All were prone, groaning impressively as they occasionally lifted an arm or a leg, pretending to exercise or stretch tired muscles.

"It all looks like a big act," Gif turned to Billie.

"Much of it is," Billie chuckled. "Remember, those big guys weight in these days at three hundred to four hundred pounds. Their bodies aren't designed for this kind of work. They are at the end of a two practice day, and they are exhausted."

"I remember the day when a big lineman was two hundred and eighty or ninety pounds. Nobody knew these mastodons could even move let alone play football," Gif said.

"Times change. Imagine what it must feel like to have two or three of those guys jump on you."

"I guess that's why the ball carriers are running so hard," Gif said as a group of sweating backs trotted past them."

"I wonder why they don't have any bleachers." Gif said as he glanced around the field, noting that there were not many fans standing and watching the apparently open practice.

"I guess they don't want anyone here to get too comfortable," Billie said. "Besides, the fewer people they have here watching the practice, the happier they are. The teams all spy on each other, you know."

"Do you think one of those guys might be Jaws Kraver?" Gif nodded in the direction of two men standing on the opposite sideline chatting. Both were in relatively clean uniforms, neither wore a helmet, and if they had on shoulder pads, they were very small ones. The player on the left wore number 19 and the other number 11.

Gif and Billie circled the field and approached the two from behind.

"Mr. Kraver?" Gif announced their presence.

"Please, no interviews during practice," Number 11 replied without looking back.

"This won't take long," Gif said.

Number 11 turned, glanced at Gif, took in Billie's uniform, and said: "Oh."

"In private, please," Gif said.

Number 19, who had to be Bruno the Lip Hauptman, the starting quarterback, reacted first: "See you later, Jaws," he said and jogged towards the clubhouse sanctuary.

Gif laughed. "I didn't mean to chase your friend away."

"That's OK," Jaws said. "The Lip knows what's going on. He feels as bad about Stan and Boozer as the rest of us. Both would have had a great future with the team," Jaws Kraver said.

"We have a few questions," Gif displayed his credential case.

"Ah shit," Jaws said. "I want to catch the bastard who did this as much as you do, but I already told those other investigators every single thing I know."

"Mr. Kraver," Gif spoke firmly. "I'm now in charge of the investigation and want to hear your answers myself."

"OK," Jaws acquiesced.

"What do you remember about last night?" Gif asked.

"Everything. The same bunch was there who participated in the brawl, except last night nothing happened. Winchester Johnson and his gang were there when I arrived with two of the backs, Willie Johnson and Tank Stallone. I brought along Willie and Tank, mainly as a precaution. If they had been there the night before, none of that nonsense would have happened. Willie, Tank, and I were at a corner table, and Johnson and his fellow linemen were at the bar when Boozer and Stan arrived. Boozer looked like a damned raccoon with those black eyes."

Already, Gif had follow-up questions, but he held back, letting Jaws tell his story his way.

"Johnson spotted them right away, made a couple of dumb rookie wisecracks, but backed off when Boozer and Stan joined our table. Willie and Tank aren't walking houses like Johnson and his gang, but they are big men who are all muscle not flab and beer bellies." Jaws smiled as he remembered the scene.

"Then what happened?" Gif encouraged.

"Nothing, that's it. We sat there for a couple of hours, drinking our beer and bullshitting a lot, just football crap. Johnson and his gang left first, and Willie, Tank and myself followed not long after. We were all worn out from practice. The coach, angry about our lousy preseason game, worked us hard. Nails can be a mean sob when he wants, and yesterday at practice he wanted."

"Boozer and Stan didn't leave with you?" Gif asked.

"No sir. They stayed to finish their beers. That's all I know. I guess they got ambushed in the parking lot." Jaws hesitated, frowned, and then added. "I wish Willie and Tank and I hadn't left them alone."

"Was there anyone else in the bar when you left?"

"The bartender and a couple of regulars, an old guy, and two or three rednecks, locals not players."

"Did any of the regulars or rednecks have a problem with Stan and Boozer?" Gif asked, starting to use the names like old friends.

"Not that I know of."

"Where did Boozer get the black eyes? The brawl you mentioned?" Gif asked.

"Oh those. Boozer got one in the fight and the other on the practice field. Boozer, a cornerback, nailed the tight end crossing the field pretty good, and Winchester Johnson gave him some payback. The tight end hangs out with Johnson and his linemen buddies."

"Must have been some payback. Two black eyes," Gif encouraged Jaws to elaborate.

"Just one. Winchester was rushing downfield to block for the tight end caught Boozer from behind, flattened him, jumped on top of him, pulled his helmet off, slugged him, and then jammed Boozer's head into the ground. I wish he would save that stuff for the other teams," Jaws said.

Amazed that Jaws would admire what appeared to him to be a dirty play, Gif shook his head. "Christ, if that happened out on the street, we could charge Johnson with felony assault."

"That's football," Jaws laughed. "You won't believe what goes on at the line of scrimmage. The whole game is just one big felony assault."

Gif looked at Billie who was smiling, apparently enjoying the first hand descriptions of athletic violence.

"And the brawl?" Gif asked Jaws.

"That happened the night before. It was probably my fault. I set the two rookies up with a couple of girls, and Johnson and his gang who had been riding the two rookies all evening used it as an excuse to jump on Boozer."

"If you made the move, why did they take it out on Boozer?"

"Boozer, Stan, and I were sitting at the same table, Winchester and his O line buddies were at the bar. They had nothing to do with the girls, they just pretended, acting like we were poaching on their turf."

"But why Boozer? Was there something going on between him and Johnson?"

"Not that I know of. I think it was just the beer and a rookie thing. You know, hazing."

"Why did they focus on Boozer and not Muncy?"

"I can answer that," Jaws laughed. "Boozer was a defensive cornerback, the natural enemy of offensive linesmen, and Muncy was a quarterback, one of those Johnson and his guys are paid to protect."

"But you are on the same team."

"Football's not a complicated game," Jaws said. "When Johnson and his buddies pretended that Boozer and Muncy were poaching they called them on it. Boozer took offense, and Johnson nailed him. I guess that's when Boozer got his first black eye."

"And Muncy?"

"He stood up for Boozer, and someone else—I don't know who—decked him. Then, the bunch of them tossed Muncy and Boozer out the door."

"Where were you during all this?"

"Me, I introduced the boys to the girls and took off. I'm a quarterback, and I'm not stupid. Now, do you mind if I get back to the locker room. I've got a couple of hours to spend in the ice. Practice is hard on these old muscles."

Gif waited until Jaws had jogged out of hearing range before turning to Billie: "You're an ex football player. What did you make out all of that?"

"Sounds like football to me?"

"Do you think enough went down between Boozer and Muncy and those other guys to make somebody angry enough to take them down with a shotgun?"

Without even considering the question, Billie replied. "If somebody had taken the shotgun to Johnson and his buddies, I would look hard at Boozer. But it sounds to me like Johnson was just having a little fun."

"That's strange fun."

"People that play the game of football are strange."

"Let's leave Johnson and friends for later," Gif said. "I've had all the football talk I can stand for one day. Let's see what the locals have to say. Where's Tiny's?"

"It's just up the road. Want to take a look at the scene?"

"And to talk with the bartender or whoever was there the night of the shooting and the night of the fight." Gif turned and headed for the Prius. "Have you ever met this Tiny?"

Billie shook his head. "Never been in the place."

"I'll bet Tiny is an ex lineman," Gif laughed.

Chapter 19

Twenty minutes after the shooting in the men's room, a reeling patron entered, spotted the body sprawled on the floor near the urinal, staggered over to it, cursed because it was blocking his access, and kicked the body's foot.

"Wake up, man," the drunk mumbled. "Nature calls."

When the man did not moved, the drunk, assuming that the offender was just somebody who had had too much to drink and was sleeping it off, a perfectly logical reaction from his point of view, grabbed two feet and dragged the sleeper into the nearest cubicle. Under considerable bodily pressure himself, he grunted as he jammed the sleeper into the stall and pulled the door shut. Oblivious to the trail of blood and urine that stained the floor, he hurried to the urinal where he had trouble unzipping his fly, He released a strong stream that stained his trousers, partially hit his target, and made a sizeable contribution to the mess on the floor. When finished, he pulled his zipper half up, did not notice the stain that ran down his right pants leg, and staggered out of the men's room grumbling about the inconsideration of others.

A full hour passed before a patron sober enough to react to the scene entered the bathroom. He took one look at the mess on the floor, which bore the contributions of a number of drunks, was repulsed, turned away from the urinals, and opened the cubicle door to find the crumpled mess that had been James Dexter. The man, forgetting why he had entered the men's room in the first place, rushed back into the bar, whispered to the bartender and then hurried out the front door, determined not to get involved in that mess.

The frowning bartender strolled back to the men's room, trying to appear as nonchalant as he could, not wanting to alarm the other patrons and cause a rush on the door. He cautiously entered, cursed at the stench and mess, wondered who was going to clean that up, and then saw the open cubicle door.

"Holy shit," he exclaimed and backed out, shutting the door behind him. He hurried to the bar, where with one eye on the entrance to the men's room, he phoned 911 and reported his problem.

Knowing the Metropolitan Police as he did, the bartender hurriedly used a black marker to scribble a do not enter sign on a sheet of paper which he taped to the men's room door. He then pulled one of the small tables over to the door and turned the table on its side, effectively blocking entry. Whenever a drunk subsequently tried to circumnavigate the blockade, the bartender would call advice from his place behind the bar.

"Use the lady's room. The plumbing broke."

One hour and ten minutes later a police cruiser pulled up outside. Two tired cops, weary from a night of dealing with muggings, a drug shootout, and countless stumbling drunks, entered.

"Christ, about time," the bartender greeted them.

"Where's the stiff?" The first cop asked.

"The men's room," the bartender said as he pointed with his thumb.

"I'll check it out," the second cop said.

"What happened?" The first cop demanded.

"How the hell should I know," the bartender answered.

The second cop shoved the table to one side, pushed into the men's room, took one brief look, and came out holding his nose. "Close the front door," he called to his partner. He whispered into his radio, waited, nodded, and sat down on the end barstool.

"Gimmie a beer," he growled.

An hour later the crime scene inspectors and two detectives arrived.

"What's up?" The first detective asked.

"A stiff with two holes in his head, one in front, one in back," the second cop, who still sat at the bar nursing his beer, answered.

"Who did it?" the portly detective asked.

The cop shrugged. "You tell me. We shut down the place and waited for you heroes to arrive."

"Where's the stiff?" The detective asked.

The cop sipped his beer as he pointed behind him.

The detective turned to his partner and inclined his head. They went to the back of the bar, checked out the table and the sign, and pushed open the door.

"Christ," the portly detective declared, reaching for his handkerchief. "When in the hell are these guys going to learn to hit what they aim at."

Two hours later, the medics hauled Dexter out of the bar in a zipped up rubber bag. Nobody knew that it was Dexter. He had left his wallet with his identity at home.

At Dexter's apartment, the FBI watchdog dozed through the night behind the wheel of his car. At seven AM, his relief arrived.

"What's happening?" The unsuspecting day man asked.

"Nothing. The jerk spent a quiet night in his apartment," the weary night man answered and drove away.

The day surveillant spent the morning tapping the steering wheel, reading the *Post* sports pages, drinking coffee from paper cups, and watching the girls walk by. At noon, he grew hungry. He decided to check on his subject before breaking for lunch, took the elevator to Dexter's floor, knocked on the apartment door, and got no response. The silence worried him. After about ten minutes of futile pounding, he opted to cover himself and call headquarters.

"What?" A bored voice demanded.

"This is K 22. I've been on duty since seven, haven't seen my subject, and am now standing outside his apartment. He doesn't respond."

"Try again."

"I've been here for half an hour," he exaggerated. "And I get no response."

"Just a minute."

The day watchdog waited. After ten minutes, the voice came back on the line. "Kick the damned door in and report."

"Are you sure?"

"Kick in the God damned door and report."

The day watchdog did as he was told. Even though he was a husky man, it required several kicks to break the frame holding the lock. He pulled his weapon and entered, carefully following FBI procedures.

"Dexter?" He called.

No response.

The day watchdog worked his way through the apartment. After assuring that the apartment indeed was unoccupied, he called headquarters again.

"The shit's not here," the watchdog reported. Now, he was worried. His rabbit had hopped.

"Are you sure?"

"I'm sure."

"Standby," the voice ordered.

A minute later, another voice came on line. "Are you sure?"

"He's not here."

"Where is he?"

"How the hell would I know?"

"Standby."

A few minutes later, the first voice came back on line. "Help is on the way."

"Shit," the day watchdog hit the off button on his cell phone and stuck it in his pocket. Everything was about to hit the fan, he knew, because this case was major. He immediately worried that the director himself might appear and re-assign him to Big Flats or some such place in never, never land.

The Metropolitan Police who assumed they had another gay drunk case on their hands sent Dexter's body to the morgue where it was placed on a slide and shoved into the cooler where they could get around to it in due process. The Washington Metropolitan Morgue was renowned for its backlog.

Chapter 20

Gif stopped the Prius in front of the bar that was located several hundred yards from a closed ice rink. He turned and looked at his companion.

"Are you sure this dump is what we're looking for?"

Billie Williams pointed at the small neon sign in the front window. "That says Tiny's."

"And those Redskin millionaires hang out here?"

"It looks too pricey for me," Billie laughed.

"Let's check it out," Gif said. "Where's the crime scene?"

"Probably around back."

Gif followed the narrow alley to the right of the shabby building. As soon as they reached the rear, they spotted the police tape, but nothing else. The parking lot was empty.

"I guess CSI did what they do," Billie said.

Gif parked the Prius near the tape.

"I'll bet Tiny's owner is pissed," Gif said. "Where do you think his patrons are parking now?"

"Over there," Billie said, looking at two cars parked behind the ice rink.

Gif ducked under the tape and held it up for Billie to follow him. "I guess it would be too much to ask where they found the bodies."

Billie shrugged. He looked to his left and right before spotting the small yellow flags near the center of the lot. He pointed. Gif nodded, and then followed Billie to the spot protected by the flags. Gif glanced at the blood in two separate spots about ten yards apart, saw nothing that caught his attention, and turned to his companion.

"What do you think, Billie?"

"I don't see anything to think about," Billie shrugged.

"Let's talk with the bartender," Gif agreed.

"Right," Billie said. His puzzled expression indicated that he was still waiting for Gif's renowned intuitive investigation technique to kick in.

Gif ignored him. Nothing he had learned thus far piqued his interest. He doubted that the double killings had sprung from the hazing or teenage games the Redskin players had amused themselves with, and he too was waiting for his instinct to tell him that something was amiss.

Inside, Tiny's was almost deserted. A middle-aged bartender with a giant red nose glanced at them when they entered, and the two oldsters propped on stools staring into their half-empty beer glasses did not even look up. Behind the bar, a television tuned to CNN droned on, but no one was watching. The drab scene reminded Gif of the old first year philosophy question: if a tree falls in a forest and no human is present to hear it, does it make a sound? Certainly, the two oldsters didn't appear to be in a condition to have heard any untoward noises. If he had to depend on their testimony, Gif was certain he would have to conclude that no tree had fallen, hence no murders committed. Therefore, Gif opted to address his questions to the bartender.

"What'll you have officers?" The bartender greeted them as he rubbed his nose and moved to stand in front of the draft beer spigot. "I was on duty last night, told the other officers everything I know, which is nothing. I was closing up after those last two left, heard the shots, ran out back," he looked in the direction of the rear door, saw the two bodies, hurried back inside, and called 911."

"I'll take a Budweiser," Gif said. "A bottle and a clean, frosty glass if you have one."

Billie, who had been waiting for something more substantive out of his leader, turned and stared at Gifford.

"What about you, deputy?" The bartender stood with his hand still on the draft spigot.

Billie pointed at the bartender who slid a glass under the nozzle.

The bartender delivered the draft to Billie with a flourish, fetched a Budweiser and frosty glass from the cooler at the end of the bar, and set them down in front of Gif.

"On the house," the bartender declared.

Gif nodded affirmatively, surprising Billie again. Gif held the glass up to the ceiling light, approved the frost as it formed, then poured his beer. Gif took a deep drink.

"I like a good cold beer on a hot August day," Gif declared.

Before Billie or the bartender could react, Gif turned towards the bartender and smiled as he said:

"Now, tell us what happened both nights before I haul your ass off to jail."

The bartender, apparently accustomed to surly cops, did not ask on what charge.

"OK, you don't have to throw a tantrum." he said. "The first night a bunch of Redskin linemen were at the bar, bullshitting each other, when the two rookies came in. Immediately, the big guy, Johnson, jumped them and started the hazing nonsense. After a while, Johnson got bored, and the rookies sat down at that table over there," he pointed, "and the only grownup of the bunch, Jaws Kraver, joined them. A couple of local girls came in and started to flirt with Jaws. Jaws passed the girls off to the rookies and moved to another table. Johnson jumped in and challenged the rookies. As usually happens when you mix a half dozen beers, a bunch of oversized adolescents with muscles, and only two broads, somebody punches somebody."

"Who punched whom?" Gif demanded.

"Johnson slugged the cornerback Jankowsky. Why? I don't have a clue. Now, you know everything I know," the bartender smiled and turned away.

Before Gifford could call him on it, the front door opened, one of the regulars woke up and whistled, and Mavis Davis sashayed in. She walked right up to Gifford and Billie, smiled, and asked. "Mind if I join you boys?"

Mavis turned to the staring bartender. "Give me a frosty Bud," she nodded at the bottle standing in front of Gif.

"Only if you want to get hauled out of here in handcuffs," Gif answered her initial question gruffly.

"Do what turns you on, big boy," Mavis chuckled. She pointed her finger at the bartender. "I'm waiting, buster."

"Don't I know you?" The bartender, still impressed, asked.

"Only on network news," Mavis smiled too sweetly. "You don't look like the news-watching type to me," Mavis said. "So you don't know me like Inspector Gifford here does."

The bartender blinked at the put down, glanced at Gifford with new respect, and turned to fetch the frosty Bud as ordered.

Mavis pushed her way up to the bar between Gif and Billie. "Excuse me, big fellow," Mavis said when her shoulder brushed against Billie's chest. She turned her head at Gif: "On what charge?"

It took Gifford a few seconds to grasp that she was responding to his handcuff threat.

"Stalking," Gif replied, trying not to smile.

Mavis laughed. "Our lawyers will eat you alive."

"You definitely followed us to Redskin Park and then to this dump," Billie joined the discussion.

"Just visiting the crime scenes," Mavis said, reaching for the Budweiser the bartender had deposited in front of her. She drank a deep swallow directly from the frosty bottle. "Damn, that tastes good," she approved.

"What's a big time news hen like you chasing a little story like this one," Gif asked, stressing he word hen.

"Because a big cock like you is hopping around the farmyard," Mavis replied, not missing a beat.

That sally made both Billie and the bartender laugh. The two regulars at the other end of the bar applauded.

Gif lifted his glass in salute. "Where's your cameraman?" Gif looked around the bar. "I had the impression you liked to have him taking pictures you could later edit and misrepresent," he referred to Mavis' unprofessional use of their brief contact at the Hart Building.

"I didn't misrepresent anything, Buster. You said what you said, and I had no trouble finding out who you visited, Senator George Ames. Then, I just added one plus one, a big time cop investigating a major crime and a playboy politician with a reputation for sharing the favors of call girls with his friends."

"You learned all that just from my no comment in the lobby?" Gif laughed. Privately, he was impressed with the aggressive television anchor's perceptiveness. "You didn't answer my question."

"What question?" Mavis asked. She looked at the bartender.

"Bring my friend another beer." She pointed at Gif's empty bottle. "This one is on me."

"So is your first one," Gif said. "And my friend will have one too. The question was: where have you hidden your cameraman?"

"Don't worry about my cameraman. We've already bounced all the pictures we need for tonight's news off the satellite. There, I answered your question. Now it's your turn. "What do think the connection is?" Mavis again surprised Gif.

By this time, Billie and the bartender were looking from Gif to Mavis watching the two spar.

"What connection is that?" Gif asked.

"Between all these murders, Tate, Walker, Starbright, and the two Redskins," Mavis flashed her sweet smile again, obviously pleased with herself.

"You asked what I think." Gif was beginning to enjoy himself.

"I did," Mavis said.

Before Gif could generate a response, his cell phone buzzed.

"Excuse me," Gif said taking two steps away from the bar and turning his back on the others. He glanced at his phone, saw the caller was his Richmond apartment mate, thought about not answering because this was certainly an inconvenient time for a chat but realized Marjorie probably wanted to know when he was coming home.

"Hi," Gif answered.

"Where in the hell have you been?" Marjorie demanded.

"Let me call you back later, and I'll explain," Gif tried to calm Marjorie.

"You said you were coming home today, and I broke precedent by leaving the hospital early, skipping my exercise routine and cooking you a real dinner."

"I'm afraid I won't be able to make dinner, hon. I'll call you in a few minutes."

"Tell me now," Marjorie insisted. "Everything is on the stove. Where are you?"

"Oh just tell your girl friend you are having a beer with a good looking broad in a bar," Mavis spoke loudly for all to hear, proving to Gif that she really was perceptive, intuitive, or something, probably the latter if something was a witch.

Despite himself, Billie joined the bartender and the two regulars in laughing loudly at Gif's obvious predicament.

"I heard that, you shit," Marjorie declared and hung up on him.

Gif turned, shrugged, and tried to cover himself: "Just the office."

"I suggest you better start looking for a new office," Mavis laughed.

Billie and the bartender joined her, and the two regulars applauded.

Gif glared at Billie, ignored the others, and grabbed his fresh beer.

"I better summon my cameraman," Mavis said. "I'll definitely want to review this scene later."

"There is no damned connection," Gif declared angrily, referring to the discussion, which the telephone call had interrupted.

"Sure there is honey," Mavis patted Gif on the sleeve. "You."

After that oral triumph, Mavis drained her bottle, stepped back, turned, lifted one hand, announced "Ta, Ta, boys it's been fun" and swiveled towards the exit.

"I think she won that round," Billie chuckled.

Gif glared at him, took another swig of beer, frowned at the smiling bartender, and started for the front door himself. Billie, still smiling, chugged his beer and followed.

"Come back anytime, gents," the bartender called after Gifford and Billie.

Gif ignored him and kept walking.

"Hey," the bartender called, concern in his voice, as Gif pulled the door open. "Nobody paid the tab."

"Send the bill to the news hen," Gif replied, suddenly feeling much better.

"Where?" The bartender pleaded.

"Try Channel Four in New York," Billie said as he followed Gif out the door.

"Where we going now? This investigating is fun," Billie said as Gif backed the Prius out of its space.

"What's that?" Billie pointed at a note tucked under the wiper.

Gif stopped, got out of the car, grabbed the folded paper, and opened it. To his surprise, it contained a local phone number written with an obvious female slant. Below the number were two letters.

"MD." Gif crumpled up the paper, started to toss it, then changed his mind and stuck it into his pants pocket.

Gif got back into the car. Billie looked at Gif, waiting for an explanation. He got none.

"I'm taking you back to the bowling alley," Gif referred to the headquarters of the Loudoun Sheriff's Department, and then I'm going home."

"I hope all that back there didn't persuade you to drop the case," Billie said. "I'm in no mood to go back to that damned desk and all that paper."

"We'll give it another go tomorrow," Gif relented.

"Good. I was just starting to feel like a real deputy again," Billie said. "Good conversation, cold beer, you know."

They drove in silence back to Leesburg. As Billie was climbing out of the car, Gif called after him. "Run a check on the names of everyone connected with this case for tomorrow," Gif ordered.

"That'll take me all night," Billie protested.

Gif smiled. He didn't admit that he was punishing Billie for laughing at his discomfort.

"What am I looking for?"

"Someone at Redskin Park with political connections."

"You don't think that Mavis Davis was right; that these cases are all connected?" Billie called after Gifford as the Prius pulled away.

Gif answered with a wave.

As he mounted the steps to the bowling alley, Billie grumbled: "Someone connected to these cases other than Gifford."

Chapter 21

Throughout the day Dexter's urine soaked body with a John Doe tag attached to its toe resided in a locker in the city morgue. Business was always brisk in the nation's murder capitol, and considerable time usually passed before the somnambulant pathologists got around to determining cause of death. Even though in Dexter's case the two holes in his head rendered this determination obvious, it still had to be made and the requisite paperwork filed, just in case.

Back at Dexter's apartment, a panicked agent waited. If the stupid shit in the watched building wanted to slip away, everybody knew that there was nothing he could do about it, everybody that is but his superiors. One guy sitting in a parked car out front might signal the bad guys to keep away, but if the dork himself wanted to slip out, he could. A singleton agent on a job like this was simply a symbol, nothing more. Ten minutes after his panicked call to the operations center, the buzzards descended. They arrived with "what in the hell is going on" on their lips and after a quick tour of the apartment they joined the agent in the sitting room.

After two hours, the heavy lifters appeared. First came Former Director Tracey Schultz and not far behind her the current director, Sir Thomas Harrington, as the working stiffs referred to him, not to his face of course.

"What the hell is going on?" Schultz demanded.

Now tired of the same refrain, the agent answered with a shrug. What the hell Schultz was a former-been despite her lofty title as task force director.

"Where is he?" Harrington asked.

The director had chief investigator Jeffrey Cohena in tow. Those two commanded the agent's attention. If he didn't respond to them, he could find himself in Polar Bear Alaska or on an ice floe in the Arctic Sea.

"The shit slipped out the back door," the agent who didn't have a clue as to Dexter's whereabouts responded.

"Where did he go?" Cohena demanded.

"I don't know sir," the agent answered. "My post was the front door."

Harrington glared at Cohena. "Was there only one agent on this detail?"

"Yes sir," Cohena acknowledged. He now was the man in the gun sight. "I didn't specify a full protective detail." Despite his reputation as a hard head, he knew when to kneel.

Showing mercy, Harrington did not ask why.

"Do we have an all points out on him?" Schultz, who had been waiting for the opportunity to strike, demanded.

Harrington looked at Cohena who glared at the trembling agent. The unfortunate was unaccustomed to dealing with so much brass.

"Yes, sir, ma'am," he answered crisply. At least he had done one thing right. He had called help.

"We'll find the little bastard," Cohena assured Harrington and Schultz. Being confident was the chief investigator's prerogative.

"We're in deep shit," Harrington, exercising the authority of his office, spoke to Tracey.

Tracey shook her head and sat down on the sofa next to the agent. He reacted by leaping to his feet. "I'll check with operations," he said as he headed for the door.

"Oh let him go," Tracey said. "I don't know how we expected one guy to shut down this building."

"Me neither," Jake Cohena declared as he followed the agent out the door. Since he was the man who assigned the detail, he was just escaping.

"We screwed up." Tracey spoke to her protégé Harrington.

Reacting honestly, Harrington shrugged and answered: "We did."

"Don't let Cohena put the burden on that poor guy's back," Tracey said. "Where do you think the little shit went?"

"Probably to get a beer. This place would close in on me fast," Harrington said as he looked about the small apartment.

"I would think the vice president's chief of staff could afford better than this," Tracey said.

"Dexter was just a gofer," Harrington said.

"If I were him," Tracey sighed. "I would gofer as far as away from here as I could."

"I know," Harrington agreed. "He's just a little guy caught in something far bigger than he anticipated."

"He or his boss," Tracey said. "And the boss is dead."

"Let's take a look around," Harrington said.

"OK." Tracey's tone told Harrington she was as depressed about the silly situation as he was.

Harrington led the way into the bedroom where they found three large crime scene investigators and one female standing in a tight circle, all with guilty expressions on their faces. Their director had caught them listening to his private conversation with the task force commander.

"What do you have?" Harrington asked.

"I don't think the little shit has gone far," the female, an Asian, responded, indicating she was the team commander.

Harrington waited.

"We've got his wallet, an envelope with one hundred thousand dollars in small bills, and all his clothes. I don't think he took off and left all this stuff behind. I sure wouldn't," she waved an envelope that probably contained the money."

Harrington turned to Tracey. "That money might represent good news. Maybe we should all relax and wait for Mr. Dexter to come back. He probably slipped out for a beer."

Tracey's skeptical look conveyed her doubt, but her words let the bureau off the hook. "Maybe you're right," she said. "I'm going back to my hotel. Give me a heads up if you find the little shit, and I'll come over and kick the crap out of him myself."

Harrington nodded, a relieved expression on his face. He knew firsthand how difficult his old boss could be when angry, particularly with a new president on her back.

Tracey returned to her car, wondered what she would do for dinner, her last supper so to speak, and decided only one man would know what really was going down. She followed New Hampshire down to M Street and then on to Key Bridge where she hooked up with I 66 which took her to the Dulles Access Road. Ignoring the exorbitant charges, which she paid, she took the Greenway to Route 15 past Leesburg and turned west heading to Gifford's shack that he considered his mountain palace. She knew he would not welcome her unheralded arrival but didn't care. Her old apartment mate and lover at least owed her a decent drink and meal, which she assumed, would be his damned meat loaf TV dinner. The thought of what lay ahead of her made her smile. At least she would enjoy tormenting the bastard if she caught him at home.

Gif was relaxing on his patio with two burgers on the grill when he heard the grate of heavy tires on the gravel out front. Before he could check it out, his cell phone buzzed. The caller's identity worried him. The good doctor's last call had been a bust.

"Hi, I was just getting ready to call you," he lied, putting as much warmth and sincerity in his voice as he could muster.

"Really?"

The brevity of Marjorie's response failed to tell him if she was still angry or not, leaving him unsure how he should cover himself.

"I'm home with a couple burgers on the grill," Gif chose a neutral defense. He knew from experience that trying to explain too much right away would give Marjorie the advantage.

"Two burgers?"

"Yes, I'm really hungry. I wish you were here to share." Gif ignored the accusation inherent in the way she gave emphasis to the number two.

"Poor boy. All alone?" Marjorie pressed.

"Yes," Gif answered truthfully. He was alone when he spoke.

Unfortunately for Gif, at that very moment Tracey came out the back door and called: "Hang up the phone, lover, I'm famished."

Gif turned his back on Tracey.

"Marjorie," he said, stalling while he waited to learn if she had heard.

The dead line gave him his answer. She had hung up on him again. Gif folded the phone, stuffed it into his pocket, took a deep breath, and turned to confront the uninvited guest.

"You're burning dinner," Tracey said as she turned over the burgers.

"Your timing is exquisite as usual," Gif said, amused at the situation despite Marjorie's over-reaction.

"These are ready," Tracey said, pretending that Gif referred to the burgers. She dropped slices of cheese on the sizzling meat. "Bring me a thick slice of extra onion and some catsup when you fetch my beer," Tracey ordered.

Gif thought about challenging Tracey's untimely and unheralded arrival but did not. He found her demeanor an improvement over that of Mavis Davis and Doctor Bliss. Besides, he welcomed the company.

When he returned from the kitchen, Tracey was seated at the picnic table with both burgers on the only plate, waiting for Gif to deliver the onion and catsup. Two fresh burgers were on the grill. Gif deposited the Budweisers, a fresh one for him and a first for Tracey on the table in front of her, sat down beside her, and pulled the plate to a neutral position between them. While Tracey slopped catsup on her burger, Gif carefully applied mustard to his.

"Why people insist on ruining a good burger with catsup, I'll never understand," Gif said. He added a slice of tomato and a wedge of onion to his.

"Where did you get this table?" Tracey countered.

"I made it," Gif answered. That project had taken him two months some twenty years previous and he was proud of the results despite the weathering.

Ignoring the response, Tracey took a large bite of her burger. "Not bad," she declared. "It needs more garlic salt."

Gif pointed at the garlic salt bottle that stood on the table next to the grill.

Tracey glanced at the bottle, at Gif, and ignored both as she turned her attention back to the burger. They ate in silence until Gif stood up to turn the burgers on the grill. He deliberately overloaded one burger with garlic salt, challenged Tracey with a look, and returned to the table.

"All right, what do you want?" He capitulated.

Tracey deliberately finished chewing her burger and sipped from the Budweiser bottle before she answered with a question.

"Where the hell is the little shit?"

Gif laughed. "Which little shit is that? Have you misplaced somebody I don't know?"

"Dexter."

"Why ask me? You and your bureau friends are supposed to have him in hand."

"Why aren't you lounging in your Richmond love nest with that muscular doctor child you are cohabiting with?"

"Are you enjoying your golden years wherever it is you have your walker parked?" Gif counterattacked.

"At least I'm not retired in place ripping off the taxpayers," Tracey finished her burger.

She stood up and turned over the burgers. "Where is the potato salad?"

"There is no potato salad," Gif said.

"Chips?"

Gif shook his head before remembering a long opened bag of chips, which were so stale he planned to toss them. He stood up and returned to the kitchen.

"More onion," Tracey called after him.

When Gif returned with the onion and stale chips, he found Tracey back at the table with the two fresh burgers on the plate in front of her. Gif tossed her the chip bag. Tracey reached to catch it, and Gif deftly pulled the plate back to a spot on his left beyond Tracey's reach.

Tracey smiled sweetly and waited.

"What's with your only lead?" Gif referred to Dexter.

"We had him stashed in his crummy apartment with a protective watch parked out front and last night, sometime, the little shit slipped out the back."

"Clever of him. Where did he go?"

Tracey shrugged as she loaded her new burger. "Strange thing, he left his wallet, an envelope filled with cash, his clothes, everything behind."

Gif stared at Tracey, waiting for her to elaborate. She ignored him, concentrating on her burger.

Gif added mustard, onion, and tomato to his own burger and pretended to ignore Tracey. They stubbornly ate in silence.

"I assume you don't have him," Tracey said when she finished her meal.

"I've got nothing to do with your damned investigations, none of them," Gif reacted.

"Do you still have television out here on your mountain top?" Tracey asked.

Gif did not answer. Tracey knew damned well that he did.

"While you clean up, I'm going to catch the news," Tracey said.

Gif watched her enter his house and disappear. He heard the refrigerator door open, the click of the beer bottles, and the slam of the door closing. Shaking his head in frustration, he cleaned up the mess and joined Tracey in his den just as Mavis Davis' familiar face appeared on the screen below the caption:

BREAKING NEWS

"The following network news is now preoccupying the nation's capitol," Mavis declared. "Channel 4 sources report that a key witness in the Vice President John F. Walker investigation has disappeared. Last night, James Dexter, Walker's chief of staff, mysteriously vanished from his home. Dexter, one of the last persons to speak with the vice president, left behind his wallet, an envelope containing $100,000 in hundred dollar bills, his unpacked suitcases, and all of his possessions. Given the unresolved murder of Nan Starbright, who was with Walker at the time of his yet to be explained death, investigating officers decline to speculate where Dexter might be or even if he is still alive. At the time of his disappearance, Dexter was under the protection of the Federal Bureau of Investigation."

"Damn, she's good," Gif said, enjoying the look of pain on Tracey's face. This report made him doubly relieved to be disassociated from the Tate and Walker investigations. Despite the pain he still felt over the loss of Harrison Tate, he rather enjoyed the freedom to sit back and watch Tracey agonize.

"Some shit is leaking," Tracey glared at the television.

"An all point stop and detain bulletin has been put out on James Dexter," Mavis continued. "Although authorities decline to comment on the reason for the arrest bulletin, political circles in the nation's capitol are buzzing with speculation that Walker's death may not have been an accident and were indeed part of a conspiracy. Those supporting this conjecture point out the extremely odd coincidence of the sudden violent deaths of the president and vice president at virtually the same moment."

"What do you in know about your friend's sources," Tracey turned on Gif.

"Don't look at me," Gif glared back. "She's an acquaintance, nothing more," Gif hesitated. "Let me amend that last statement. She bought me a beer the last time I saw her. If that makes me a friend, consider your own position," Gif glanced at the beer bottle setting beside Tracey's chair.

Tracey did not react.

"In a related development," Mavis Davis continued. "Your investigative reporter has learned that the recent shooting of two prominent Washington Redskin players may well be related to the aforementioned conspiracy."

The picture on the television then left Mavis Davis and focused on two men standing in a parking lot.

"Oh shit," Gif groaned as he sat up straight in his chair and stared. He immediately recognized himself and Billie Williams standing in the parking lot behind Tiny's Bar.

"I assume Mavis bought that beer this afternoon," Tracey said

Gif did not reply.

"Your reporter," Mavis continued, "recently discussed this rash of murders with Inspector Conor Gifford of the Office of Special Investigations of the Commonwealth of Virginia State Police, a unique unit that specializes in high profile crime. A former FBI special agent, Gifford served as chief investigator of the Loudoun Sheriff's Department under then Sheriff Harrison Tate before ultimately replacing Tate as sheriff. Subsequently, Gifford followed his mentor Governor Tate to

Richmond where he assumed his current position. Some of you will remember Inspector Gifford as the man who led the investigation that apprehended two serial killers who were operating on Capitol Hill. Inspector Gifford--whose friends refer to him as Gif the Terrier, those who have fallen under his scrutiny call him the Terror-- initially led the investigation into the death of Vice President Walker. The picture on your screen shows Gifford at work in the parking lot behind Tiny's Bar in Ashburn where the Redskin players were so brutally slain."

"Gif the Terrier," Tracey smiled. "An apt name for a real dog. What was that you were saying about not being an authoritative source?"

"It's all news to me," Gif shrugged. Privately, he seethed at being used again by the devious Mavis.

"How much are you paying that broad to serve as your personal publicity agent?" Tracey asked.

Gif ignored her.

"For unexplained reasons," Mavis continued. "Gifford withdrew from the Walker investigation. Sources who prefer to remain unnamed confide to your reporter that Inspector Gifford, unhappy with the conclusions being reached by the task force appointed by Acting President Adams, angrily withdrew and was returning to Richmond when the Loudoun County Sheriff's office commanded by a Gifford protégé, Sheriff Richard Simmons, requested the assistance of his old mentor, an investigator renowned for his lone wolf investigative style, to assist in the high profile Redskin investigation."

"What the hell are you up to?" Tracey demanded.

"It's all news to me," Gif repeated.

Tracey's cell phone chimed.

"What?" She answered. "I'm watching," she said and hung up.

Gif looked at her, but Tracey did not elaborate.

"This afternoon your reporter discussed the Tate, Walker, Starbright, Dexter, and Redskin cases with Inspector Gifford at Tiny's Bar in Ashburn, Virginia, the site of the Redskin slaughter," Mavis continued.

The picture on the screen showed Mavis exiting the bar followed by Gifford and Billie Johnson. Editing made it appear that the three came out together.

"Given Gifford's lengthy association with President Tate and his involvement in the Walker and Redskin investigations," Mavis continued, "your reporter contacted the inspector to obtain his unique insight into the sensational events that have traumatized the nation's capitol. Understandably, Inspector Gifford was loath to speak on the record about the ongoing investigations, but the conversation left little doubt in this reporter's mind that there is more to the concern about conspiracy afoot in the nation's capitol than simple coincidence," Mavis said with a knowing smile. "This is Mavis Davis reporting from Washington, D.C."

The screen flashed blank then returned to a silly reality show. Tracey turned off the television, looked at Gif, and said:

"She gave you a big buildup and then peddled her own conclusions."

"She tried to make it sound like I briefed her off the record," Gif said.

"That she did. She's good," Tracey said.

"I need a real drink," Gif declared.

"Make that two," Tracey agreed.

Two cell phones immediately began to page. Without consulting, Tracey and Gif turned them off. Gif went into the kitchen, filled two tumblers half full with ice and topped them off with Jim Beam which he kept in the cupboard for special occasions. He returned to the den, handed one to Tracey, sat down opposite her, and without the usual gratuitous amenities drank half of his in one gulp. Tracey watched and then did the same.

"Shit," Tracey and Gif announced at the same time.

They stared at each other, both grimaced, and then laughed.

"I think someone is manipulating all of us," Tracey said. "Mavis is just riding on the bandwagon."

"I agree," Gif said, lifting his glass.

Tracey responded in kind, and they drained their tumblers.

"More," Tracey ordered.

Gif took her glass, returned to the kitchen, added a little ice to both tumblers, topped them off with Jim Beam, and returned to the den taking the bottle with him. Tracey raised her glass, toasted Gif, and said:

"Screw all the conniving politicians."

Gif lifted his glass, smiled at his old lover who was beginning to look better and better with each drink, almost as she had thirty- years previous, and drank some more.

"I think I'm going to become their worst nightmare," Gif said, slurring his words slightly.

"Then we are in competition," Tracey declared. "Which investigation do you want?"

"All of them," Gif said, surprising himself with his own bravado. "I'm told they are related."

"Dumb shits," Tracey agreed.

"You know," Gif said. "That Mavis isn't a bad looking broad, but you can't trust broads."

"Come on, Buster," Tracey said, standing up. "You don't know nothing. Let me show you the real thing."

"I think I may have seen that real thing, thing before," Gif standing up, nonetheless.

"But you don't know all the new tricks," Tracey countered, leading Gif into the bedroom.

Chapter 22

At the D.C. Morgue, it was morning when a haggard attendant pulled open slot Number 98.

"What makes you think your boy is here?" The attendant asked.

"I don't think," the weary FBI agent answered. "I just do what I'm told and I'm told to check every stiff in this place against this photograph." He held up a copy of a recent photograph from James Dexter's security file.

"You're really going to enjoy this one," the attendant laughed as he slid Number 98 back.

"Holy shit," the agent said, stepping back, gagging on the smell. "What did they marinate this one in?"

"I think you might recognize the odor," the attendant replied.

The fragrance of urine was overwhelming. The agent stepped back five feet and held his handkerchief to his face as the smiling attendant pulled back the cover.

The agent held the photograph in front of him and glanced at the fragrant stiff. "Oh Christ," he declared. "That's him."

"That's who?"

"Don't ask," the agent ordered as he turned away. "And don't let this one take a walk, or it'll be your job."

"Don't worry," the attendant called after the retreating FBI man. "If this one walks, you won't have any trouble finding him."

The attendant shoved Number 98 back into its slot.

Outside, the agent called the ops center duty officer, reported his find, and the weary man immediately phoned Jeff Cohena and advised him they had located James Dexter. Cohena rushed from his Arlington home to the D.C. Morgue where he conferred with the special agent, viewed the occupant of Slot Number 98, choked on the odor, and departed after instructing the agent not to let Dexter out of his sight.

"Just so I don't have to sit next to him," the agent shouted after the door closed behind Cohena.

Outside, Cohena phoned the director, Thomas Harrington, at home and reported that they had apprehended Dexter. As soon as he heard the details, Harrington passed the buck back to Cohena and ordered him to so inform the task force commander, former Director Tracey Schultz. Cohena tried Schultz's cell phone several times, got no response, and decided to hell with it. He returned to his home in Arlington, too tired to worry about an ex-director, and went to bed.

The next morning a very hung over Gifford woke to find someone lying next to him in his bed. Momentarily, he was confused, leaned over, identified Tracey, and silently denounced himself for being a fool. He groaned, sat up, rubbed his temples, and was heading for the bathroom when Tracey called after him.

"Damn you, Gifford."

Gif halted and turned, prepared to defend himself.

"Oh, God," Tracey moaned. "How much did we drink? What did we do?"

She appeared to be suffering so grandly that Gif chuckled and continued on his way.

"Please," Tracey pleaded. "Don't spend all morning in there."

Gif used the john, splashed water on his face, and obediently returned to the bed where he lay back down. Only when he was prone did he realize that he was totally naked.

Tracey slowly pushed herself erect and made her way to the bathroom. After a visit that was even briefer than Gif's, she too returned to the bed where she lay back down, carefully not touching him. Gif was not so miserable that he failed to notice that she, too, wore no clothes.

"You're holding up pretty well for your age," Gif said, thinking he was offering a compliment.

"You plied me with alcohol and took advantage of me," Tracey accused mildly as she covered her head with a pillow.

"I assume I enticed you out here under false pretenses," Gif said.

"Oh don't worry," Tracey replied, her voice partially muffled as it came from under the pillow. "Nothing new happened. It's not as if we didn't live together for two years."

Gif, who didn't know how to reply to that, particularly since his head was throbbing, said nothing.

They lay beside each other in suffering silence for about five minutes until Tracey poked him with an elbow.

"I need coffee."

Gif did not move.

"Now," Tracey ordered.

"Get it yourself," Gif replied, concealing the fact that he too needed caffeine.

"I'm a guest."

"You didn't act like it last night," Gif countered. Tracey did not argue. "Besides," Gif added. "Nobody sent you an invitation."

"Coffee, please," Tracey said, patting Gif's stomach.

"Any lower and you might get more than you bargained for," Gif said.

"Promise?" Tracey said, rolling onto her side, sliding her hand slowly southward.

Gif, who was in no condition to deliver on any kind of threat, groaned, slid away from the ominous hand and out of bed. He stepped around the clothing, his and Tracey's which, intermingled, were strewn across the floor. He grabbed clean slacks and a shirt from the closet and headed for the door.

"Black, hot and strong," Tracey called after him.

Gif hesitated, thought about commenting on the black, hot and strong, decided he could not deliver on any count, and continued out the door.

In the kitchen, Gif dumped a heaping spoonful of instant coffee into a cup, filled it with water from the tap, and shoved it into the microwave. He leaned against the cupboard until the timer dinged. He took the steaming cup from the microwave and was lifting it to his mouth when Tracey emerged from the bedroom wearing one of his old dress shirts.

"Thank you, lover. You're a lifesaver," Tracey smiled as she took the cup from his hand.

She turned and made her way to the drop leaf table that Gif used for all purposes. Gif watched the sway of her still trim hips and admired her shapely legs until Tracey sat down at the table. The tail of Gif's shirt slid dangerously upward flashing a striking amount of flesh at the staring Gif.

"See anything you haven't seen before," Tracey smiled at him before sliding her legs under the table partially obscuring Gif's view.

Gif shrugged, grabbed a cup, added a measured spoonful of coffee, and let the microwave do its work. After the bell rang, Gif grabbed the cup and took the chair facing Tracey. For the first time he noticed that without its concealing makeup, Tracey's face showed her age.

"Where the hell is the newspaper, old man?" Tracey demanded, irritated by Gif's unconcealed scrutiny.

"We are in my country house, old lady," Gif sipped his coffee, wondering if he too showed his fifty plus years. He never gave his age much thought. He felt the same as he always had and only looked in the mirror to shave. "And I don't support the scribbling class."

"Shit," Tracey said. "Turn on the television."

"You know where it is," Gif glanced toward the den.

Tracey stood up, grabbed her cup, and sashayed away entertaining Gif with more exaggerated motion. He watched as she settled into his recliner, picked up the remote, and pointed it at him. She hit the button several times and laughed. "Lover, something must be wrong with this thing. I can't seem to turn you on no matter what I do."

Despite his still throbbing temples, Gif laughed.

Tracey, satisfied with her antics, turned the remote back towards the television, and poked the on button.

"Try Channel 8," Gif suggested.

To his surprise, Tracey did what she was told and the metro area news station came on.

"…the body of Vice President John Walker's chief of staff was found at the District of Columbia mortuary," the newsreader chirped.

Both Stacey and Gifford immediately jerked to attention.

"A reliable source tells Channel 8 News that a body that the morgue had held as a John Doe has been identified by an FBI official as that of Mr. James Dexter, a senior White House aide. Mr. Dexter, one of the last persons to have met with Vice President John Walker prior to his death from yet to be determined causes, was the victim of a homicide. He had been shot twice in the head by person or persons unknown. The FBI has ruled out suicide. Mr. Dexter, who had been under protective FBI surveillance, eluded that surveillance, and had been the subject of an intensive federal manhunt for the past twenty-four hours. Our source reports that Dexter had been listed at the morgue as an unidentified John Doe because he carried no identification whatsoever at the time of his discovery. No further details are available at this time. However, Washington political sources are abuzz with speculation, given the obvious linkage between Mr. Dexter's murder with the vice president's death, the Harrison Tate assassination, and the shooting of Ms. Nan Starbright who was with John Walker when he died. This combination of unexplained and violent deaths has all of the ingredients of a best seller mystery: sex, the demise of a president and vice president at virtually the same moment, and the elimination of a key aide and an apparent call girl."

Gif and Tracey exchanged surprised looks.

"I've got to get out of here," Tracey declared.

"They left out Mavis Davis's report that I am a connection that links all that with the Redskin murders," Gif said.

"Don't worry, lover," Tracey patted Gif on the head as she hurried past him toward the bedroom. "Your media girl friend will take care of that on Channel 4. Too bad you can't clip her comments and paste them in your scrapbook."

Gif leaped to his feet, almost spilling a half cup of coffee.

"Screw Mavis Davis," Gif said, as he followed Tracey.

"I'll leave that to you, old man, if you can get up to it," Tracey laughed. "I get the shower first."

Tracey carelessly tossed Gif's shirt on the bed. "While you're waiting, I would appreciate your gathering my things," she pointed at the discarded clothing strewn about the floor. "And be careful, don't mess them up. I'm not going to have time to get to the hotel to change."

Gif watched with admiration as Tracey broke her suggestive pose and closed the door behind her. Then, disregarding her order, he sat on the bed and tried to sort out what he was going to do today. Too much was happening all at once.

Twenty minutes later, Tracey exited the bathroom, still naked. By then, Gif had impulsively decided what he was going to do.

"Sit down, right here," Gif ordered as he patted a spot on the bed beside him.

Tracey smiled. "Lover, as great as all that might have been, I don't have any time for fun and games right now."

"Give me just five minutes," Gif pleaded. As focused as he was on what he wanted to tell her, he was not oblivious to her charm. He knew she had to work hard to keep her body in that shape. Involuntarily, he pulled his shirt hem lower over his stomach.

"That doesn't hide anything, big boy," Tracey laughed. "You need to get a little exercise."

"Please," Gif said. "This is important."

"OK," Tracey said as she sat down beside him, carefully making sure they were sitting calf to calf, thigh to thigh. She was a girl who never passed an advantage, and she sensed one was coming her way.

"I'm tired of sitting on the sidelines," Gif said.

"Good," Tracey agreed, not sure what was coming next.

"I've done my grieving for Harrison, and now I want to catch his killer. Mavis Davis has everyone in D.C. convinced I'm working the case, so I think I will. Any objections?"

"Of course not," Tracey said as pushed off the bed. Gif's decision was not what she had expected. "You know I wanted you involved with the task force from the very beginning."

Gif placed a large hand on her bare shoulder and pulled her back beside him. "I'm not talking task force. You've already pulled that nonsense on me," he referred to the Capitol Hill Serial Killer case when Tracey had been FBI Director and had maneuvered him into heading the task force as a figurehead where he took the heat while she and Harrington handled the investigation.

Tracey did not comment.

"You, Tom Harrington, Cohena and the task force can do your thing, and I'll do mine."

"OK," Tracey said. "I'll cover you if you promise to keep me informed."

"Don't worry about that. You guys can take all the credit. I can't just sit here anymore."

"What about the Redskin investigation?"

"I'll work that too, related or not."

"Do you really think they are connected?" Tracey asked, not trying to conceal her surprise.

Gif shrugged. "Who knows? Who cares?"

"All right," Tracey said, standing up and facing him. "Tom and I will do what we can to handle our acting president and friends."

"Don't tell them anything important. Someone's leaking, and it's getting people killed." Despite himself, Gif stared at Tracey's erect nipples. He reached out and tweaked one.

"That's not what's leaking," Tracey laughed and stepped away.

"I didn't say I was in any rush to get investigating," Gif said.

"But I am, lover, so turn off all those urges until I get back to you," Tracey said as she began to collect her clothes. "Besides, I think you have a little problem in Richmond you might have to address."

"What do you suggest?"

"You best consult a doctor down there," Tracey laughed as she slipped into her bra.

Ten minutes later Tracey departed and Gif returned to the kitchen where he reheated his coffee and burned a stale bagel. While sitting at the table forcing the unappetizing but usual breakfast into his digestive system, he called Billie Williams.

"Sheriff's Department, Williams speaking," Billie answered on the first ring.

"Billie, Gif," Gif greeted him. "Did you do that little research I asked for?"

"You're kidding. I was here until midnight, and I'm working on it now. I thought you were going to liberate me from this damned desk," Billie complained.

"All things come to those who earn them," Gif paraphrased the cliché.

Billie's silence told Gif he didn't think the subject funny.

"Well, keep working on it," Gif said. "And, there are a couple of other things I want you to do for me."

Billie responded with a grunt.

"I didn't hear you."

"Shoot," Billie said. "Before I do."

"I want to see everything that the department has on the Tate shooting and the Walker thing," Gif said.

"You want me to just walk in and ask for the files?"

"Of course not. You've got friends, use them."

"Shall I tell them why?"

"Sure. Say you're curious and want to learn from the pros."

"And if that doesn't work?"

"Then kiss a couple of the clerks. They always crave attention from brutes like you, and they know more about what's going on than the deputies. The girls talk with each other."

"And if my boss, Lieutenant Sadler, the chief investigator, wants to know what I am poking around for?"

"Lie."

Billie laughed. "OK. What are you going to be doing, Sir Master Investigator?"

"Investigating. I'll be in touch," Gif said and hung up.

Thirty minutes later Gif was in the Prius working his way toward I-95, one of the most dangerous stretches of highway in the country, and the one Gif hated most. He was whistling as he reviewed his plans.

A harrowing three hours later, a tense period filled with bumper to bumper traffic travelling at seventy-five miles an hour, Gif was still whistling as he pulled up behind the relatively new building that housed his office, those of the Office of Special Investigations, and of course

Colonel Harris Townsend, the commander of the State Police. Gif parked in his reserved slot, paused to acknowledge that he had missed the familiar place, and went directly to Townsend's office.

"Good heavens," Josie Warrick, Townsend's assistant, declared as soon as Gif entered her office.

"Hi Josie," Gif smiled.

"Colonel! I've got a stranger out here," Josie called in mock alarm through the open doorway that led to Townsend's office.

Almost immediately, Townsend materialized, smiled broadly when he saw Gif, put his hands on his hips, and declared: "Behold, Josie. The man who's the connection in the three biggest cases to ever shake this country."

"So one misinformed television correspondent alleges," Gif responded.

"Two coffees and no visitors," Townsend spoke to Josie. "I'll close the door, but you can eavesdrop on the intercom like you always do. This should be a really good story." He stepped back and waved his right hand. "Come right in, inspector."

After Josie had served the coffee and shut the door behind her, Townsend looked at Gif and in all seriousness asked: "What in the hell is going on in Washington, Gif?"

"I wish I knew," Gif replied.

"Some people seem to think that you are right in the center of it all," Townsend said.

"I took a brief look at the Walker thing, talked with the two people that were the last to speak with the vice president, and learned very little," Gif said.

"Somebody must have thought they knew something. Both seem to have been killed for a reason," Townsend observed.

"Nan Starbright and James Dexter," Gif confirmed. "I'm still not sure what happened with Walker. I would say it was just a terrible accident if it wasn't for the fact that someone killed Starbright and Dexter. I don't like coincidences, particularly when they involve murder. Anyway, I told the task force what little I had learned and withdrew. As you know, I was returning to Richmond to do some real work when you sent me back to help out on the Redskin thing."

"Sheriff Simmons called and let me know you had taken over the investigation," Townsend said.

"That's not quite true. Simmons knows that I said I would take a look at it. Responsibility for the investigation still rests with Simmons," Gif said.

"I'll reinforce that the next time Simmons calls," Townsend said. "I saw that television news thing saying the Redskin murders were part and parcel of the whole big conspiracy and that you were the connection that tied them together."

"Mavis Davis," Gif nodded. "I talked only briefly with her twice, both times at her instigation. We discussed nothing, but she set me up. She edited the tapes that her cameraman took without my permission and tailored her story to make it appear that I was a source. All her words came from her own imagination."

"Then you don't think the Redskin murders are related."

"I can't prove they are, Harris," Gif said honestly.

"But you can't discount the possibility."

"No."

"Where do you stand on the Tate shooting?"

"I don't know. I continue to believe I was too close to Harrison to objectively participate in the investigation but…" Gif let his voice trail off.

"But…" Townsend pushed.

Gif hated this discussion but realized that Townsend as Commander of the Virginia State Police was entitled to demand his views.

"But, I'm going to find out who shot him," Gif admitted. "I talked with Tracey Schultz last night, and she admits the Tate investigation is still on dead center. They don't have a clue pointing at the shooter despite all the manpower they have thrown at it."

"So," Townsend smiled and nodded affirmatively. "You have finally decided you are going to unravel the whole ball of wax."

"I'm not sure about unraveling any ball of wax, but I'm going to take another look at all the investigations, if you agree."

Townsend chuckled. "I couldn't hold you back if I wanted. Frankly, I was hoping you would take over the task force from the first day."

"Tracey Schultz is more than competent to handle that job. She and Tom Harrington make a team. Together, they will find the shooter if ..." Gif hesitated.

"...if the damned media and conniving politicians let them," Townsend finished his sentence for him.

"Our acting president and acting vice president are giving them fits. Better them than me. Tracey and I discussed this just three hours ago. She will take the heat from the media and the White House this time, and Tom Harrington will push the investigation with all his resources."

"I wish them luck with that," Townsend said. "Meanwhile, you are going to get busy and unravel the damned case."

"I hope so, but I'm going to need your help."

"Anything. What do you want?"

"I want to work without anyone on my back."

"Nothing new about that."

"No announcement leaking from Richmond even suggesting that we might be involved."

"Not until all the dust settles."

"Good. And I would like to have some help from my team in the Office of Special Investigations."

"Take them all."

"We'll have to work out a cover story to explain their absences," Gif said.

"Tell me what to say."

"Harris, I've got work to do," Gif said, standing up. "I thank you for your full support and will try not to disappoint you."

"That's what I'm here for, Gif," Townsend stood up and offered his hand. "I've been waiting for you to make this decision. Good luck and let me know if I can help, and most importantly watch your back."

Gif looked quizzically at the colonel after that last comment.

"Somebody seems intent on eliminating everyone remotely involved in these cases, and as Mavis Davis alleged, you, I repeat you, are a connection in this alleged conspiracy. I repeat, watch yourself."

"I will," Gif said.

"I'mgladyou'retakingsomereliablemusclebackwithyou,"Townsend referred to the officers of the Office of Special Investigation.

When Gif exited the colonel's office, Josie looked up, winked, and made a motion with one hand across her lips, pretending to zip them shut. She raised a thumb to Gif before turning her back on him. He didn't see the trickle of worried tears that streamed down her cheeks.

⁂

On that emotional note, Gif returned to his office, asked Tina to assemble the team, and sat down at his desk. Once there, he noted the stack of paper on the left side of desk had risen several inches. He ignored it and reached for the important stuff that Tina obediently assembled to the right side of the pile. Those were the papers that required his signature. Most were vouchers submitted by his officers, and he always dealt with those first. Gif settled into his chair, pulled the important stuff towards him and was preparing to sign it unread when the team filed in, led of course by his deputy, Truman Johnson. Like Billie Williams, Truman was another six foot four, 300-pound ex-athlete. As he waited, Gif asked himself if a pattern was forming. Was he becoming so insecure that his subconscious was selecting a palace guard to defend him? The thought irritated him, and he tried to cover it by signing the forms as quickly as he could.

Behind Truman came Sarah Whitestone, his deputy's diametric opposite. Sarah was a fortyish something female who stood five four standing on her toes, weighed a hundred and fifteen pounds, and made no secret of the fact that she preferred female company. Sarah was a relentless investigator who gnawed at an investigation until she reached its core. Jerry Quigley, the youngest team member, their tech guru who talked with machines and made them dance to his will, nodded at Gif who depended on him for matters technical even though Gif did not hide his academic disinterest. Joyce Tryon, an African American with a highly honed racial sensitivity, came next. Joyce, whose forte was the ability to read the reactions of a subject like a Dick and Jane book, pretended she did not know Gif had been gone. Last appeared Harold Creighton, more muscle, another former high school lineman. Each had been personally selected by Gif.

"Hi guys," Gif greeted them. "How are things going?"

"As if you cared," Sarah Whitestone challenged him as she always did.

"Down, Sarah," Gif smiled.

"You have to tell us about those Redskins," Harold said.

Sarah, Joyce, and Jerry groaned.

"Everything's under control," Truman declared, trying to put a stop to the posturing. "I'll brief you."

"Don't," Gif said. "I'm just passing through and need your help."

Those words caught everyone's attention. They sat up straight, signaling Gif they were anxious to get involved in his high profile activities.

"I've got more on my plate than I can handle," Gif admitted.

"That Mavis Davis looks like a real handful, boss," Sarah spoke for them all, using indirection to encourage Gif to share his experiences with them.

"Don't believe everything you see on television," Gif cautioned Sarah.

Sarah shrugged.

"What in the hell is happening up there, boss?" Truman asked the same question Sarah had, just using different words.

"I wish I knew, and I need your assistance in finding out," Gif said.

Nobody said a word. All were waiting to hear Gif share some details. Gif's debriefings usually hit the high points of his investigations, and all present were skilled at reading between the lines. Gif knew this, but he was not ready to share the little information that he had.

"Somebody's killing off people faster than I can count," Gif said.

"And some think you are the common denominator," Sarah blurted.

The others nodded agreement and waited for Gifford to elaborate.

"I frankly don't know who or why," Gif said, referring to the killer. "You all know that Harrison Tate was a personal friend of mine, of long standing. I wouldn't be sitting here if it weren't for him."

"I bet you wish you were sitting somewhere else," Joyce Tryon smiled.

No one else laughed.

"That's not true, Joyce. There's no other place I would prefer to be."

"I was just kidding, chief," Joyce reacted.

And I wish that President Harrison Tate was still presiding in Washington," Gif mildly put Joyce in her place.

"What can we do to assist, chief?" Truman tried to get the meeting back on track.

"Pack your bags and come back with me and help me find the killer or killers," Gif said.

Gif's simple appeal caught them all by surprise. Not a one had ever heard Gifford admit he needed help.

"When do we leave?" Truman asked.

"I want you at my place in Loudoun tonight," Gif answered.

"Holy shit," Jerry Quigley, the team's junior member spoke for them all.

"If you can't make it, I'll understand," Gif said.

"Chief, you can't keep us away," Truman said. "Right?" He looked at the other team members.

"You bet your ass," Sarah declared. "Try and keep us away."

"Do we need reservations somewhere?" Joyce Tryon asked.

"No, I'll handle that. We'll work at my shack," Gif said. "Bring what you think you might need for motel living. We'll send out for anything you forget."

"Hot shit," Jerry Quigley declared. "I'll drive."

"Maybe you all should drive. You'll probably be going in different directions while we're there."

"No problem, I'll coordinate," Truman said. "And don't worry about the motel. I'll take care of that. You have enough on your plate."

"Truman and Sarah can be roommates," Jerry said.

Everybody laughed.

"I would really look forward to that," Sarah, the lesbian, said sourly.

"Don't look at me, Sarah," Joyce said.

"Thanks, Truman, we can work it out when you get there," Gif ignored the usual repartee. "We've got five major cases on our hands."

"President Tate, Vice President Walker, the call girl, the guy marinated in urine, and who else?" Sarah asked.

"Two Redskins," Gif answered.

"Jesus, there is a big conspiracy," Jerry Quigley said.

"I frankly don't know what is going on," Gif admitted.

"What about the FBI and the task force?" Truman asked.

"The bureau, the task force, the world media, and everyone else you can think of will also be investigating.

"And what in the hell will we be doing?" Sarah demanded.

"Conducting a parallel investigation and finding the damned killer. I want each of you to bring whatever equipment you think you will need," Gif said, looking directly at their technical guru Jerry Quigley.

"Holy shit," Quigley said, jumping up and leaving the room.

"Truman," Gif looked at his deputy. "You will be supervising the team. I'll take the Tate assassination, and you can negotiate the other responsibilities depending on interest."

"I'll take the Dexter thing," Harold Creighton said. "I've always wanted to check out Georgetown bars. And the Redskins. I could do that too," Harold Creighton said.

"You would have to work with Billie Williams from the sheriff's office on that," Gif cautioned.

"No problem," Harold said.

"I'll work Walker/Starbright/Dexter if there is anything left to do," Joyce said. "I would also really like to help with President Tate if I can."

Joyce surprised Gif with that offer. "I'm certain I could use your help re-interviewing the river residents," Gif said.

Joyce nodded.

"And that leaves the call girl for me," Sarah Whitestone said.

"Sarah strikes again," Jerry said.

The others dutifully smiled, but the running banter about Sarah's sexual preferences was growing old. Sarah ignored him.

"And I would like to help with Tate, if I could," Sarah said.

"OK, but we work as a team out of my place," Gif repeated, not wanting them to get the idea this would be a pleasure jaunt. "I suggest we hold off on setting the assignments in concrete until we get to Loudoun. Your interests sound fine to me, but I defer the final assignments to Truman. We might end up with everyone working on everything, so don't lock yourself in too quickly on any one subject."

"If anyone asks about what we are doing?" Truman posed a good question.

"Right," Gif responded. "Tell your families you are off on a sensitive corruption probe that you can't discuss. There is a big problem in Loudoun with developers, just among us, but don't tell anyone up there that you're investigating local corruption. Nobody around here should care, but in Loudoun there might be a public reaction if the media starts reporting that we are investigating their local bigwigs. Any questions?"

Nobody responded.

"Good," Gif said. His team handled questions about sensitive investigations all the time. "Tina can serve as a Richmond point of contact for families as needed. My place is isolated so we can come and go as we want. We'll coordinate everything else there."

"What about the FBI and the task force?" Sarah asked. "I assume we will have to talk with them."

"I'll arrange the coordination from the top," Gif said.

That comment brought a smile to every team member's face, telling Gif that they knew about his past relationship with task force commander Tracey Schultz.

"Tom Harrington is good people," reliable Truman Johnson filled the embarrassing silence.

"Any questions?" Gif asked.

"I have about a million," Sarah laughed.

"Save them for our first meeting tonight," Gif ordered. "Any questions about logistics, Tina can answer."

"See you tonight," Truman said as he stood and led the team out the door.

"Who's doing the cooking?" Joyce Tryon asked.

The team members laughed as they followed Truman who declared: "I cook mean burgers."

"Don't expect me to do the clean up," Joyce got in the last word.

⁂

Gif grabbed the priority stack of papers. With Tina's expert assistance, he began signing without reading a single document. When he finished, Tina collected the papers and left with the words: "Good luck chief. You can reach me here or at home, and I'll get what you need."

"Thanks, Tina," Gif said as he stood and followed her out of the office.

Gif drove directly to the Riverside Apartments. His watch told him that he was arriving too late to catch Marjorie just as she finished her exercise routine, as he liked to do, but that was copasetic with him. He had too much delicate explaining to do without a drink in his hand. He parked in his usual place and was surprised when he met the building supervisor in the lobby.

"Mr. Gifford, I'm glad I caught you," said Sam Miller, a congenial man who Gif had always found responsive, interested, and helpful.

"Good evening, Mr. Miller," Gif greeted him. "No problems, I hope."

"Oh, no sir. I just need to know what you want me to do with the chair. It's too nice to just toss in the dumpster."

"Chair?"

"The green recliner."

"How did you get it?"

"It was in the hall outside of your apartment and a couple of your neighbors complained, I'm sorry to say."

"Oh shit," Gif said. "Give me a couple of minutes, and I'll get back to you."

Gif took the elevator to the 11th floor, not looking forward to his conversation with his apartment mate. He had no doubt that after hanging up on him Marjorie in a tantrum had shoved his favorite chair into the hall as a symbolic act. Marjorie's temper was her one trait that troubled him the most. He usually tried to ignore her occasional paroxysms by attributing them to the pressures of her profession, but this time he knew what had triggered it, the unfortunate calls that Marjorie terminated when first Mavis Davis and then Tracey had punctuated their conversation with untimely comments intended as humor.

Gif thought about knocking first to give the volatile Marjorie fair warning of his arrival but decided against it. After all, it seemed silly to knock on the door of his own apartment. Now he shared it with Marjorie, but the name on the lease was still his alone. He had lived in the place long before the good doctor agreed to move in and share it. Accommodating Marjorie's feminine taste, all frilly and flowers, had been bad enough, but Gif had negotiated and succeeded in keeping in place his green recliner, his desk, his bed and a few other possessions he treasured.

Gif took a deep breath and slid his key into the lock. At least he tried. The key would only go half way in. Gif wiggled it and tried several more times with no success until he finally tapped on the door. Getting no response, he slapped the door with his palm and called, "babe, it's me."

"Go away," the good doctor ordered.

"Please, just open the door," Gif said, letting his impatience show in his tone. "If you've got a problem, we can discuss it."

Marjorie laughed. "I don't have a problem, you do."

'The damned key doesn't work," Gif complained.

"I know. I changed the lock."

"Why in the hell did you do that?"

"To keep you out," Marjorie said.

"I'll get Mr. Miller to open the door with his passkey."

"It won't work. I didn't tell him I changed the lock. I'd charge you both with breaking and entering, anyway. How do you think that would look? Your women friends would just love it, lover," Marjorie sarcastically imitated Tracey's comment that she had unfortunately heard during the aborted phone conversation.

Gif hesitated and tried to think of some way to get Marjorie to open the door. "It's my apartment, in my name," Gif said. As soon as the words were out of his mouth, he regretted them. They sounded feeble, like pleading, even to him.

"Go away."

"Don't worry, I intend to," Gif said, not admitting that he had planned on spending the night after pacifying Marjorie with logic and cover stories for his contact with Mavis Davis and Tracey. He realized that Tracey would be the harder sell. She had been in Gif's Loudoun retreat when Marjorie called, and Marjorie knew the full story of Gif and Tracey's past relationship. He even felt a little guilty about what had happened after the aborted call, but he didn't plan on trying to explain an accidental one-time thing that meant nothing to him, not really, he rationalized.

"Goodbye."

"Wait," Gif pleaded. "I need a couple of suits. I'm going to be in Loudoun a little longer than I thought."

"You can stay forever, as far as I'm concerned."

"The suits. I need them," Gif insisted.

Marjorie did not answer. Gif waited. Two minutes passed with no response, and Gif was walking back towards the elevator when the door to his apartment opened, and Marjorie tossed two of his suits out into the hall.

"Please calm down and give me a chance to explain," Gif turned back.

Marjorie, still in her sweat suit, stepped into the hall and stood facing him with hands on hips. Gif thought she looked great, just a little angry. The fact that the door to the apartment was now open gave him hope.

"There's nothing to explain. You're up there in that love nest of yours having the time of your life with your ex girl friend and that television pussy while I'm down here working my ass off."

Good, Gif thought. He had her talking. Now, he had to calm her down a little before he tried to explain. Gif took two steps towards Marjorie, and she held up her right palm.

"Stop right there or I'll deck you," she ordered.

Gif stopped. Gif knew that she thought she could take him, given her daily weight lifting and muscle development exercises that she needed to support her orthopedic practice. He was confident he could handle her, but he didn't want to get into a fistfight with her. That would be silly as well as counterproductive.

"Let's talk. It's all just a big misunderstanding," Gif tried again to placate her.

Marjorie responded with a glare. "So talk."

Gif noticed she was standing with her Nikes on his best suit.

"Please don't mess up my jacket," Gif said, smiling thinly so it didn't look like he was begging.

Marjorie looked down, saw the suits under her Nikes, smiled, and deliberately started swiping the soles of her sneakers on them.

Gif was tempted to push her off of them. Marjorie looked at him, read his reaction, and laughed. "Don't even think about trying."

The door on the apartment opposite Gif and Marjorie's opened, and the kindly old lady who lived there looked out. She glanced at Gif then at Marjorie.

"Hi guys, need a referee?" She asked.

Her response embarrassed both Gif and Marjorie. They exchanged looks. Gif shrugged, and Marjorie, who had spent more time chatting with the neighbor than Gif had, laughed.

"No, Laura, just a little domestic disagreement," Marjorie said.

The little old lady smiled sweetly. "I can understand that. I suggest you give him his damned suits, and if you want to slug it out, please don't do it in the hall outside my door." She then turned towards Gif. "I saw you on television, Mr. Gifford. Is that Mavis Davis as lovely as she looks?" She then glanced at Marjorie, winked, and closed the door to her apartment.

Marjorie, now thoroughly embarrassed, glared at Gif. "Well?"

"Can we please step inside so we can discuss this without disturbing the neighbors," Gif said. "I promise I will leave as soon as you let me explain."

Without a word, Marjorie turned, her Nikes grinding the wrinkles deeper into Gif's jacket, and retreated into the apartment.

Gif sighed, retrieved his suits, and found Marjorie standing inside facing him.

"Don't think about sitting down. I got rid of that damned green chair of yours," Marjorie, still angry, warned.

"About my chair ..." Gif began.

"I don't want to discuss the chair."

"Can I just put these down somewhere?" Gif, who still held his rumpled suits, asked.

"No. Tell me your lies and leave."

"OK," Gif tried to sound reasonable. "The first time you called I was in a bar in Ashburn with Billie Williams and a room full of people conducting interviews," Gif began. "That television news person showed up just as you called, and she tried to be funny. She wasn't, but before I could explain you hung up." Gif paused to give Marjorie a chance to react.

She said nothing.

"And the second time you called I was at home fixing me a burger after a hard day of investigating a very difficult and high profile case, the murder of the two football players, and Tracey appeared uninvited. She's the chairman of the Tate investigation task force, and she had some things she wanted to discuss. Since I spend my days talking with people, I usually keep my cell phone turned off. Tracey decided the only place she could find me would be at home. It wasn't a romantic rendezvous or anything like that. Tracey's visit was all business. Besides, as you well know, Tracey and I broke up almost thirty years ago. Anything we once might have had between us, ended then, and not under friendly circumstances."

"Mavis Davis is my age, and your old lover is a good ten years older," Marjorie declared.

"What has that to do with anything?" Gif blurted irritably. As soon as the words were out of his mouth, he knew he had made a tactical mistake.

"Is Mavis Davis as attractive in person as she appears on television?" Marjorie asked sweetly.

Her change in tone surprised Gif. "Can I just sit down so we can discuss this comfortably?" He asked, hoping to take advantage of the apparent change.

"No. Is she?"

"Up close she shows her age," Gif lied.

"And what about your old lover? Is she an old hen too? Up close, that is."

"I don't know what you mean by up close," Gif stalled, knowing that anything he said would set Marjorie off again.

Marjorie stepped up to Gif until their bodies touched and her face was an inch from his. "This is up close," she said and shoved him back towards the door.

"I wouldn't know," Gif lied. He and Tracey had been a lot closer than that.

"For a cop, you're a lousy liar," Marjorie said. "You've explained, now leave."

"All right," Gif lost his temper. He pivoted and left not bothering to shut the door behind him. As he walked towards the elevator, he heard the door slam shut.

⁂

As the elevator descended, Gif quickly reviewed the results of that visit and decided he would have to find another apartment. As much as he liked the Riverside complex, he knew it would have to be elsewhere. A truce with Marjorie did not appear likely. In the lobby, Gif found the building supervisor still waiting.

"Leaving again? So soon?" Sam Miller smiled.

"I've got a lot of work to do in Northern Virginia," Gif said.

"I know. I just saw that Mavis Davis on the television again. I'm sure you know. It was about that Dexter boy who worked for the vice president."

Gif nodded. He would have liked to know how Mavis Davis handled that development, but he didn't want to discuss it with Miller.

"That must have been something to see," Miller said.

"What's that, Mr. Miller," Gif asked despite himself.

"Them having soaked that poor boy in urine. I guess they were trying to make him talk. Did the CIA do that?"

The words surprised Gif, and he didn't know how to respond. Certainly, the garrulous building supervisor would quote him to everyone he met, and a couple reporters for the *Richmond Times Dispatch* lived in the Riverside, always an irritant and something he would not miss when he moved.

"I don't know anything about that, Mr. Miller," Gif responded. "I left this morning before that story broke, but I am sure the CIA would never do something so disgusting."

"That's not what I read in the paper. I see you've got yourself some fresh clothes," Miller nodded at Gif's wrinkled suits. "I guess you're heading back now. Everything OK upstairs?"

"Oh sure," Gif said as he started for the door.

"About the chair, Mr. Gifford," Miller called after him.

Gif stopped. "Oh yes. Do you have someplace you can keep it for me until I get time to deal with it?"

"And all the boxes?"

The question surprised Gif.

"Oh yes," Miller smiled. "There are several of them, one of them was open, and I couldn't help but notice it was a lot of your shoes."

"Oh Christ, women," Gif said.

"I know. I'm on my third wife," Miller said sympathetically.

"Frankly, Dr. Bliss and I are going through a difficult period. She's seen and heard some things that she misinterpreted. As soon as I have time, I'll be able to work it all out."

"That Mavis Davis, I'll bet," Miller smiled conspiratorially. "She really looks like a hot one."

"Just a misunderstanding," Gif said.

Miller winked.

"Mr. Miller," Gif surrendered. "I really have to get back to Northern Virginia. Duty calls. Could you help me out?"

"Sure thing, Gif," Miller used the short version of Gifford for the first time in their relationship.

"Could you arrange to have my things stored in a nearby locker until I get back?"

"We guys got to stick together."

"Could you handle it for me?"

"Including everything else that Dr. Bliss tosses that I think you might want to save?"

"Yes," Gif said gratefully. "Could I give you a check including a little something for you, for your troubles?"

"No problem," Miller said.

"How much do you think?" Gif asked as he pulled out his checkbook.

"A thousand dollars," Miller said.

The amount surprised Gif, but he quickly wrote out the check to Miller. "If it amounts to more," which Gif doubted. "I settle up as soon as I get back."

"Not to worry, Gif," Miller assured him. "And if there is anything else I can do, just give me a call. I could keep an eye out for Doctor Bliss if you want?"

"Don't worry about that," Gif laughed wryly. "Doctor Bliss can take care of herself."

"I understand," Miller said. "I've seen her lift those weights. I wouldn't want to take her on."

"Me either," Gif declared as he made his hasty escape. Things were not turning out exactly as he planned.

Gif barely noticed the trucks, the oldsters in their SUVs from Florida and the speeding tourists as he guided the Prius along I-95 on his way back to Loudoun. His mind wrestled with the sudden life-turn that his visit to his Riverside apartment had precipitated. *I'm too old to play these damned boy/girl games,* he told himself repeatedly.

By the time he reached his Loudoun sanctuary, he had decided several times that he and Doctor Bliss were finished–he had difficulty calling her Marjorie–and he was tempted to call Tracey for an update on the investigation. Just as he reached for his cell phone, he hesitated. The thought struck him that there might be something wrong with him, this damned attraction to tough women who liked sparring with him and pushing him around. While he debated that notion, he pulled a TV dinner from the freezer, his usual meat loaf with soggy peas and a lump of tasteless mashed potatoes, and stuck it in the microwave. He thought about a frosty Budweiser but decided against that. There was too much evidence of the previous nights near orgy to indulge himself again.

Chapter 23

Dusk was falling when the two men dressed in dark suits and carrying identical suitcases approached each other on Haines Point. The lights were coming on in the city, and the Lincoln and Jefferson monuments were fully illuminated. The commuter traffic on Memorial and 14th Street Bridges had tapered off, and the only citizens in the vicinity were a couple of fishermen trying their luck in the Potomac, two young couples in canoes floating past, and a homeless person dozing on a park bench.

The man dressed in jeans and a dark T-shirt and carrying a leather briefcase came from the direction of the golf course. He discreetly surveyed his environment, turned to glance behind him to insure he was not under surveillance, and sat down on a bench some several hundred yards from the sleeping park denizen. Two grey squirrels who had been playing tag paused to check out the newcomer, decided he was not likely to be carrying a bag of peanuts as a treat for them, and resumed their romping. A few minutes later a man with a Redskin hat pulled low over his brow and dressed in dark clothing just like the first man came from the opposite direction. He ignored the first man and continued for several hundred yards before turning abruptly and returning to the bench where he paused, set down his briefcase next to that of the first man, placed his foot on the bench, and pretended to retie his shoe.

"Are you sure you weren't followed?" The first man asked.

The man in the Redskin hat ignored the question. "Is it all in the bag?"

"One million dollars in tattered and dirty bills," the first man said.

The second man smiled, put his foot to the ground, picked up the briefcase closest to the leg of the first man, and turned to leave. "This is the last time we meet," he said, speaking softly out of the side of his mouth.

"Problems?" The seated man asked, a troubled expression on his face.

"I worry about you amateurs. I'm the professional. It's been good knowing you. Goodbye." The second man walked away without looking back.

The seated man remained on the bench, making sure that his contact cleared the area without a sign of surveillance.

Gif woke the next morning after a restless night filled with conflicting thoughts about Tracey, Marjorie, Mavis, the investigations, how to organize his team in the house and the first thing he would do the next day. He burned himself a bagel, heated his instant coffee in the microwave, and sat at the table with his cell phone in front of him. After forcing his breakfast down, he thought about checking the latest news on the television, decided that a potpourri of fact and fiction would only cloud his vision, and phoned Martha Tate at her Leesburg home.

"Hello," Martha surprised Gif by answering the phone promptly herself.

"Martha, Gif," he said.

"Hi Gif," she surprised again him with the vigor in her voice. "I've been watching your shenanigans on television," she said. "I'm beginning to suspect that your life is better than a soap opera."

"Not really, Martha," Gif said, not amused. "I called to see if I could drop by and see you."

"I've been waiting for you to call. Come ahead."

"Right now?"

"I've nothing better to do and need some company. All the important people who visited us at the White House have stopped calling, and my local friends are too intimidated to renew old friendships."

"I'll see you in half an hour. We can chat then," Gif made a quick decision.

He estimated that his team would arrive by eleven, but they could make themselves at home and set up their office without being told how to do it. This wouldn't be the first time the place had served as their base for an investigation. Gif was heading for the door when his cell phone buzzed."

"What?" Gifford answered. The damned thing was more an aggravation than a useful tool.

"What yourself, lover," Tracey greeted him. "Where in the hell have you been? I have been trying to reach you for days."

"Hours," Gif corrected her. "Since yesterday morning, Tracey. Am I that forgettable?"

"I'm not sure. Up for a replay?"

That made Gif hesitate. He had his team arriving to set up an investigative base, and he was not sure he wanted them and Tracey to mix. Deciding he couldn't keep their presence secret from Tracey, and not caring if the team learned that he and Tracey had negotiated a truce, he replied:

"Sure, why not?"

"Don't be so damned enthusiastic," Tracey fired a warning salvo. "Besides, I should warn you. I'm not a one-night stand, not any more at least; it takes too much effort. I'm tired of this damned hotel room, and if I move in, it's for the duration."

"At least," Gif said, hiding his surprise.

"At least?" Tracey repeated with irony in her tone. "Don't get it in your head that I'm that easy."

"Tracey, you never have been easy," Gif said.

"What about your doctor friend?"

"She's not easy either," Gif laughed.

"OK, I'll see you when I see you," Tracey hung up before Gif could warn her about the team's presence.

"Screw it," he decided, turning off his cell phone and heading out the door.

When he arrived at the Tate family home in Leesburg, Gif was surprised to find no one manning the guard post that the Secret Service had constructed at the front gate. He drove unchallenged up the circle driveway and stopped directly in front of the steps, just as he had when Harrison had been sheriff and Gif his first and only investigator. Gif got out, checked the yard behind the recently painted iron fence–the grass needed cut--and climbed the stairs. Politely, he rang the bell. There had been a time when he would have entered unannounced like a member of the family.

Almost instantly, Martha, the former first lady, opened the door.

"I saw you come up the driveway," she said as she turned and led him into the small parlor on the right. "I spend a lot of time these days looking out that damned window," she said as she pointed at her nest beside the large picture window.

"The grass needs cut," Gif said. "Want me to do it?"

"Hell, no. You know what I want you to do."

After she and Gif were seated, Martha again took the lead:

"Have you caught that bastard yet?"

Gif, uncertain how to respond, hesitated. "I came to talk about that," Gif said. "Why are you answering the door yourself, and where is your protection team? The gate was wide open."

Martha laughed, pleased with herself. "I fired the whole bunch of them."

Gif waited for her to explain.

"The Secret Service was the first to go."

"But…" Gif started to protest.

"Gif, I've lived in this house for almost my entire adult life. You know that. I cooked for Harrison, cleaned the damned place, did the washing, and even knew how to answer the phone."

"But the government is obligated to provide a protective team for…"

Martha waved her index finger, indicating she was not interested. "I know. I told them to leave. I don't need them or want them around. They couldn't have been happier. Sitting around this place waiting for me to go somewhere had to be boring, and I got tired of fixing lunch and coffee for them."

"Aren't you afraid living alone?"

"I've got all of Harrison's weapons and know how to use them. I keep the loaded 12 gage in the bedroom. Besides, who is going to attack me, for heaven's sake?"

"But…" Gif not was sure how to refer to the fact that her husband's killer was still at large.

"I hope the bastard shows up here. I'm waiting for him," Martha dismissed Gif's pro forma protest.

Gif decided he would have to rethink his old premise about how soft and Harriet Nelson like the preceding generations of women had been.

"And your house staff?" Gif asked.

"They're gone too," Martha declared firmly.

"Jesus, Martha," Gif started to protest.

"I've got something for you," Martha surprised him by pushing herself out of her rocker. "Wait here."

Martha left the room, crossed the adjacent dining room, and disappeared into another part of the house. Gif heard a door open in the back and assumed that she was in Harrison's study, a room that Gif had spent much time in talking with his then boss. Suddenly, Martha reappeared carrying a sealed envelope, which she unceremoniously tossed to Gif.

"I was beginning to suspect you had forgotten about me and that I was going to have to throw it away," Martha smiled as she sat back down in her rocker. "I don't think Harrison would have wanted me to, but he's not making the decisions now."

Gif doubted that Harrison had ever dominated this crusty lady. He studied the envelope noting his name on the front in Harrison's familiar hand.

"Open it now," Martha ordered.

And they thought that Hillary was tough, Gif thought to himself as he slid a finger under the seal. He cautioned himself to treat the paper carefully because it could be a historical document, a private communication from a slain president to a close friend. The envelope held a single sheet of paper. Gif unfolded and read the message written personally by Harrison.

Gif,

If you are reading this, it is because my suspicions have proved true and Martha has handed it to you personally.

Please, old friend, forgive my subterfuge. I am not sure If I am suffering from an overactive imagination or am simply paranoid, but I fear that I have enemies who are so preoccupied with gaining the position that I now hold, that they are involved in a complicated conspiracy against me. I do not know if they simply despise me so much, or if they are driven by an unquenchable thirst for money and power. Twice now, one of my alleged subordinates has hinted that vast riches could be mine if I only stepped back and allowed certain deplorable actions to pass. Without proof, I could not act, but now with my demise I am sure that you can and will. I dare not cite names. I have not even told dear Martha who the villains might be. Gif, if they have killed me–there I've said it–I am confident they will have left a trail that only you can follow. You have always been an intuitive investigator. I have often wondered where that insight came from. I'm sure that it is a gene thing and somewhere in your ancestry there lived another you, loyal, determined, tough and intelligent. Don't let the Secret Service distract you with its self-protecting hypothesis that this was the act of a madman. If the talking heads are alleging conspiracy, believe them. I don't have to tell you to look at those who benefitted from my death. I have the utmost confidence in my vice president, a loyal man of another generation who is not ready for responsibility, unfortunately. That is another story. Rely on John Walker, he will assist you, but don't believe that he can intellectually figure this mess out. It has been my great fortune to have known you. I regret that you did not let me advance you to the positions of responsibility you and your talent deserve. Avenge me, please.

Your friend,
Harrison

⁂

Gif swallowed hard and looked up at Martha with tears in his eyes. She continued to study him with a grim expression on her face.

"Like I told you on that terrible first day, Gif, catch the bastard," she said in a firm, hard voice.

Gif nodded, not trusting himself to speak. He carefully folder the note, placed it back in the envelope, and grasped it tightly in his right hand. Finally, he spoke:

"Did he show this to you, Martha?" He asked softly.

Martha shook her head. "No, Gif, but I know what it says. Harrison told me his fears before he wrote it."

"Would you like to read it?" Gif offered the envelope to Martha.

"No. You keep it, and do what you must." Gif noted that she did not say "do with the letter what you must." He wondered if she was telling him to kill the bastard not simply bring him to justice.

"Martha…I…" Gif began.

"No, Gif. I don't want to discuss this matter further," Martha said. She stood up giving Gif the impression she was dismissing him.

Gif obediently pushed out of the chair. "Martha, if you ever need anything…"

"I know you have much to do," Martha said in a firm voice as she led Gif to the door.

Outside, Gif with the envelope still clutched in his hand hesitated as he stood at the door to the car. He thought about all the happy times he had enjoyed at this house, his conversations with Harrison, and he glanced at the sitting room window. He saw the determined, lonely old woman looking back at him. Not knowing what else to do, he waved, climbed in the Prius, followed the circling driveway to the street, and headed back to greet his arriving team. All the way home, he chastised himself for not having joined the Tate investigation at the very beginning. He had protested he would be too subjective, that he had been too close to the victim. The note that rested on the seat beside him made that gratuitous excuse ring hollow.

⁂

To Gif's surprise, five cars were parked on the lawn in front of his house. He stopped the Prius near his front door and entered to find the whole team present. Everything seemed to be in motion, his furniture rearranged. Even his favorite recliner had been shoved to one side.

"Hi chief, we didn't touch the bedroom," Sarah Whitestone saw him first. Her comment was a greeting and a warning to the others that he had returned

Truman Johnson, Jerry Quigley, Joyce Tryon, and Harold Creighton materialized from somewhere to join Sarah in welcoming Gif to his own home.

"Hi guys," Gif greeted them. "Continue with whatever you were doing when I got here. I have to make a phone call."

He whipped out his cell phone and punched a programmed button.

"What?" Billie Williams mimicked his idol.

"Get your lazy ass out here," Gif ordered before hanging up.

Gif smiled at his waiting team. "In twenty minutes our local team member will join us, and you can have a staff meeting."

Truman, Joyce, and Sarah stared at Gif.

"Will you be joining us?" Truman asked.

"As I said in Richmond, you guys are going to have to organize yourselves. I've got my own problems."

They all waited for Gif to elaborate. When he did not, the others exchanged knowing glances and resumed what they were doing when Gif had interrupted them.

"We have rooms at the "You All Come Inn" down the road," Truman reported.

"Whatever," Gif shrugged, privately wishing them luck. The "You All Come Inn" was a real dump. Remembering when he had been their age, he assumed they all were trying to make a few bucks off their per diem.

Gif sat down in his recliner, which had been shoved into a corner, and watched while the team worked around him. Sarah and Joyce were exploring his kitchen. Truman Johnson was sorting papers at one end of the dining room table, and Jerry Quigley, assisted by Harold Creighton, was setting up his equipment. Gif took the envelope from his pocket and re-read Harrison's prescient message. He was tempted to share it with the OSI team from Richmond but decided against it. The note was too personal. He carefully folded it and slid it back into his jacket pocket.

Truman moved from the table to the chair opposite him. "Do you really think we have a conspiracy on our hands?" Truman asked.

Gif stared at his loyal deputy, reluctant to share even with him. "That's what we are going to find out," Gif finally said.

Truman waited for Gif to elaborate. When he did not, Truman stood up, and rejoined to his colleagues.

"I'm on line," Jerry Quigley said from his chair at the table. "Whose e-mail do you want me to read?"

Gif smiled. Jerry was kidding.

"Can you read e-mail going to and from specific computers in the White House?" Gif asked

Suddenly, the room grew quiet and everybody waited for Gif to explain.

"Do we have warrants, sir?" Truman asked formally.

Gif smiled but did not answer Truman's question.

"Without getting caught, Jerry?" Gif pressed.

"I don't know, Gif. I'm sure NSA and a half dozen other government agencies have programs that the White House uses to protect their communications. It could be hairy. I can't guarantee anything," Jerry said.

"Let's take a step back," Gif said. "As a test see if you can identify any personal e-mail addresses for the acting president, the acting vice president, and their key assistants, Jake Tyrone and Clete Clapp."

"Just the e-mail addresses, not the messages themselves?" Jerry asked.

"That's right," Gif said. "Stay away from the messages, for now."

"That might be perfectly legal but politically sensitive," Truman cautioned.

"We're looking for threat mail, right?" Gif said.

"That's different," Truman admitted. "Do we have anyone's authority to do this?"

"You have mine," Gif said.

Jerry Quigley nodded and started playing with his mouse.

No one else said a word. Gif assumed their silence meant that all were individually processing the portent behind Gif's exchange with Truman and Jerry. They continued to work silently until Sarah Whitestone came out of the bedroom and called to Gif.

"Boss, we've made a mess of this place. If you are having more company tonight, we should clean it up a little."

That odd comment, particularly the reference to company, caught everyone's attention. Gif stared at Sarah but did not immediately reply.

"I should at least make the bed for you," Sarah smiled.

Gif assumed that Sarah had somehow picked up on the fact that he had had company spend the night. At first, he was not sure how to reply. Finally, he decided to be candid.

"Thank you for the offer, Sarah, but I will clean up in there. I've got a houseguest, and I haven't gotten around to the bedroom yet."

Everyone stared at Gif and waited.

"Tracey Schultz, the task force commander will be camping out here for the duration of the investigation," Gif said.

Gif waited for someone to challenge him on that, but no one, not even the outspoken Sarah, said a word.

Exactly twenty minutes later, as Gif predicted, Billie Williams arrived.

"OK, people, listen up," Gif announced as soon as Billie walked into the room. "This is Billie Williams from the Loudoun Sheriff's Department. Those of you, who don't know Billie, introduce yourselves. Billie will work with each of you as needed. Hold your own staff meeting, decide what you are going to do, and then do it. I will see you later. Find those bastards behind this mess."

Gif left his home leaving Truman in command as usual.

Not quite sure where he should personally start, Gif headed towards Leesburg and was driving down the Dulles Toll Road in the direction of D.C. when he decided to begin with the Secret Service.

Forty minutes later, he turned into the back entrance to the Executive Office Building where he waved his West Wing pass and his credentials at the Secret Service uniformed guard, informed him of his intentions, and waited. Five minutes later the guard answered the phone in his cubicle, frowned his disbelief at Gif, and approached the futuristic Prius.

"You can park in a Visitor's Slot, sir," said the dismayed guard who had expected to be ordered to turn the intruder away.

Gif, ignoring the guard's instructions, slid the Prius into a clearly marked VIP parking space near the entrance leading to the overstaffed security checkpoint.

"Good morning, sir," another uniformed Secret Service officer greeted him. "Do you have an appointment?"

Gif again flashed his pass and credentials and replied. "No."

Confused, the guard hesitated, unsure what question to ask next.

"Who is your boss?" Gif asked.

"Sergeant O'Brien," the guard answered.

"The big man," Gif elaborated.

The guard hesitated. "Acting President Adams."

"A little less big," Gif took pity on the guard. "The Director of the Secret Service," Gif said.

The guard smiled. "The Director is not in this building."

"Just point me in the direction of the man who is in charge of security here," Gif ordered sternly.

"Yes sir," the guard replied, now thoroughly intimidated. He picked up his phone, dialed a number, and said: "I have an inspector here to meet with the colonel," he said.

Gif didn't even try to imagine the response.

"No not termites," the guard said. "He's an investigator of some kind."

He listened some more before looking up. "Who do you represent, sir?"

"The Tate Assassination Task Force," Gif frowned, hating himself for browbeating the poor guard who was just doing his duty.

"He says the task force," the guard reported. He waited, listened, and finally smiled at Gif. "You can go right up, sir."

"To where?" Gif demanded, concealing the fact that he did not know who he was going to meet or why.

"Room 211. Just take the escalator," the guard said, relieved to be free from his problem.

Gif took the escalator to the second floor.

Room 211 proved to be a cramped office with four desks, two occupied by smiling young ladies, and two by tired, frowning men in their mid forties. The men did not acknowledge Gif's presence, and the girls ignored him as they chatted intently. Gif hid his irritation and waited. Finally, he spoke loudly:

"If it is not too much trouble, I would appreciate one of you rude bureaucrats to direct me to the person responsible for presidential protection."

The girls ignored him, presumably because they did not consider themselves rude bureaucrats, but the first man on the left pointed a thumb to his right. "Next office," he said and returned his attention to the stack of papers piled in front of him.

Assuming that he would get more response from the boss, Gif exited and entered the adjacent office without knocking. An older, better-dressed man looked up with an irritated look on his face and waited for Gif to explain his presence. Gif sat down and stared. He had heard that all Secret Service agents shared a common trait, arrogance, but this was his first real experience. Previously, most of his contact with them had been tempered by the presence of the protected official. Common wisdom had it that Secret Service agents acted as they did because they could either use their association with the White House as an intimidation factor or because they knew that the president would always support them in any dispute with other departments and organizations. Of course, the president always ruled in favor of the Secret Service because he naturally believed that his security was paramount.

"State your business or leave," the bureaucrat finally spoke.

"I'm investigating your fuck up, and I'm not leaving until you answer my questions," Gif replied.

The bureaucrat laughed. "You must be Gifford. I've heard about you."

Gif waited.

"My name's Pendergast. I'm the Assistant Director in charge of the Office of Protective Operations. This closet is where I work. When

I'm here, I'm busy and don't have time for chitchat. If that's what you want, see me at our headquarters building at H and 9th. Make an appointment. Good day, Inspector Gifford."

Gif, amused that the man lived up to the Secret Service's reputation, did not move.

After a minute of silence, the man looked up and asked: "What did you not understand? Do I have to call security and have you escorted out of here?"

"Only if you want me to stand out front and announce to the media that the Assistant Director of the Office of Protective Operations refuses to answer questions of the Tate Task Force investigating the Secret Service's failure to protect the president," Gif smiled.

Pendergast tossed his handful of papers at his desk and stared at Gifford. "Ask your damned questions and then get out of here. I have a new president to protect."

"I hope you do a better job than you did last time," Gif said. "Harrison Tate was a personal friend, and I promise you I intend to identify the killer and will not hesitate to make public every lapse in security that I uncover."

"Don't threaten me, Gifford. I assure you that I am as determined as you to apprehend the bastard who shot President Tate. I was not a personal friend, but I am the man responsible for any lapses, as you describe them, that you might discover. I assure you his protective detail did their job as professionally as humanly possible."

"The results don't support that contention," Gif fired back.

"Ask your damned questions."

"I want the names of every man on President Tate's detail that day at the river," Gif said.

"The task force already has the list."

"I said I want the names, now, from you. I'm going to investigate anew this protective disaster from the moment it began. I will not tolerate a single omission."

"You will have a list," Pendergast growled as he made a note. What else?"

"I want to interview each and every man from that detail before I leave this building."

"You might have a long stay. I hope you brought a change of clothes with you."

"I'll stay as long as necessary after I inform the media that the Office of Protective Operations is refusing to make those agents available for interview.'

"Not one of those agents is now assigned to this office."

"Then have them reassigned."

"Or you'll talk with the media. We are aware of your…shall I say close relationship with certain network investigative reporters," Pendergast smiled.

"Say anything you wish," Gif smiled back, ignoring the reference to Mavis Davis. "Am I correct in assuming that the Secret Service has covered itself by reassigning those agents to remote offices to hide them from investigators like myself?"

"Assume anything you like, Gifford," Pendergast snapped.

"Inspector Gifford to you, Pendergast," Gifford responded. "Have them transferred back. I will expect to interview them tomorrow in this office."

"You might find the space inhibiting. And where do you think I'm going to work?"

"Have you thought about moving over to the Treasury Department? I understand that the Secret Service once reported to that department, and that is where your current protectee is now working. You should be able to locate an appropriate closet there."

Pendergast made another note on his pad. "What else?"

"The Secret Service has conducted an independent investigation of that day," Gif said. "I want access to every single file."

"No way."

"The task force lawyers will issue you subpoenas before close of business today," Gif said, standing up.

"I will have our lawyers confer with the White House Legal Counsel."

"Since the task force was appointed by the acting president, I assure you the legal counsel's response will be positive," Gif said. "Members of my team will appear at opening of business tomorrow morning. Arrange to clear them through security, have the protective team members available for interview, and provide appropriate rooms for my investigators to meet with your officers and read files. This room appears cramped. Do you think it will be necessary for Director Schultz and Director Harrington to accompany them with appropriate legal support and subpoenas?"

"You've got to be kidding me."

"Try me," Gif said as he rose from the chair.

"Give me the names of your officers," Pendergast ordered.

"Detective Truman Johnson will call to coordinate the arrangements," Gif said.

Gif closed the door behind him before an angry Assistant Director Pendergast replied.

Already tired of fencing with the Secret Service, Gif returned to his Prius and called Truman Johnson to brief him on the Pendergast confrontation. Gif also told Truman that he would have someone from the task force contact him to set up the team's liaison with Tracey's investigators including appropriate briefings and file reviews there.

Chapter 24

Gif was driving down Pennsylvania Avenue on his way to Hoover's Revenge and an unscheduled, unexpected meeting with Tracey and Harrington when his cell phone buzzed. He picked it up and answered curtly: "Gifford."

"Mr. Gifford," an unfamiliar voice said. "This is Sam Miller."

Gif required several seconds to identify the name. Sam Miller. Suddenly, he remembered, the friendly Riverside Apartments building supervisor.

"Oh, hi Sam," Gif covered his momentary lapse. "Did you get everything in storage?"

"I'm sorry I had to bother you," Miller did not answer Gif's question. "But I need your input."

"No problem," Gif said, wondering what Miller would think if Gif said he was on his way from the White House to the FBI headquarters to discuss the biggest investigation in the country's history.

"I rented a storage locker like you ordered. Got a good deal too, only a hundred bucks a month."

"Great," Gif said, tempted to ask what happened to the rest of his thousand dollars.

"But I don't know if we are going to need it."

Gif was momentarily distracted by a tourist making a left turn in front of him from the far right lane. Gif hit his horn, and the Prius responded weakly. The low-pitched horn was the only thing Gif did not like about his great little car.

"Mr. Gifford, did we lose the connection?" Miller asked.

"No," Gif chuckled for Miller's benefit. "I'm in the car and a damned tourist cut across in front of me."

"I'll bet that's a problem," Miller commiserated.

"You said we may not need the storage locker," Gif encouraged the chatty man to continue.

"Oh yes. I was planning on loading the chair and boxes in my pickup and taking them to storage like you wanted when Doctor Bliss stopped by my apartment. I think she was on the way to the hospital."

Gif pulled into the parking lot across the street from the Hoover Building, waved at the attendant, and descended three levels until he found an empty slot.

"I assume Dr. Bliss had put more of my things in the hallway," Gif said, his phone crackled, making communication difficult.

"No sir. Surprise, surprise. Doctor Bliss gave me a key and ordered me to put the chair and the boxes back in the apartment."

"Did she say why?" A surprised Gif asked.

"No, sir. What do you want me to do? Take everything to storage or put the stuff in the apartment."

Gif hesitated, not sure what to do.

"Doctor Bliss seemed to be in a good mood this morning, but I'm afraid she might lose it again if I don't do what she said. You know how unpredictable women are."

Gif, who didn't have the time to deal with this petty stuff, made a quick decision to keep his options open.

"Do what Dr. Bliss says, but don't give up the storage locker," Gif said.

"Good idea, Mr. Gifford."

After breaking the connection and remembering that he had agreed that Tracey could move in with him for an indefinite period, Gif realized he had only complicated the problem. As soon as Marjorie learned about that, his chair and boxes would be back in the hall, this time with everything else that Gif valued. He thought about calling Miller back but concluded that would be a waste of time. It would be easier to just roll the dice and see what happened. Life with Marjorie was comfortable, most of the time, but Tracey's current attitude intrigued him. Tracey was almost behaving like the girl he knew thirty odd years ago. He also knew he hadn't heard the last of the intrusive and persistent Mavis Davis, and given his off and on unencumbered status, that interested him too.

The hell with it. First things first, Gif tried to dismiss all thought of the Marjorie complication as he climbed out of his car, made his way up the ramp, negotiated with the attendant who recognized him, and headed for Tom Harrington's office, the one guarded by the officious kid.

Despite his best effort, Gif was still musing about Richmond and his quandary there when the elevator reached the 7th floor. He entered the director's reception room, smiled at the mature woman who manned the second desk, turned left, ignored the kid who was in over her head and entered Tom Harrington's office without knocking. After his recent White House experience complicated by Miller's call, Gif was in no mood for little games, not even common civility.

"Sir, you can't go in," the kid called after him.

Gif slammed the door behind him, ignoring the kid's complaint. He found Harrington, Tracey, Jeff Cohena, the Metro Washington SAC who was serving as the task force's lead investigator, and Reggie Crawford, the young agent who had once been a near ally, sitting at the director's conference table. It was obvious they were discussing their various investigations, but Gif was not interested.

"I hope I'm not interrupting something important," Gif said, not really caring.

Tracey smiled and winked, Cohena and Crawford frowned, and Tom Harrington, who was presiding, responded:

"We're discussing the investigations, Gif, please join us. Your timing is perfect."

Harrington sat at the head of the table with Tracey on his right and Cohena and Crawford on his left. The latter two had files opened in front of them and had obviously been referring to them in making their reports. Cohena casually closed his file, and Reggie, seeing her supervisor's action, did likewise. Gif pretended to ignore the obvious slight as he sat down at the end of the table opposite Harrington, deliberately conveying a message to the others present. He was not here in a subordinate role.

"What can you share with us, Gif?" Harrington asked.

"I have members of my team operating out of my Loudoun place," Gif announced. "Tracey, I would appreciate it if you would have someone from the task force contact Truman Johnson and arrange for my investigators to review your files and to establish a working liaison."

Gif's request caught the others by surprise. Cohena frowned and looked at Tracey and Harrington. Crawford smiled as she waited for Gifford to elaborate. Harrington turned towards Tracey trying to read her reaction. Tracey nodded. "Good. I assume that means you are rejoining us."

"If you and Tom don't object," Gif said.

Harrington swallowed hard. He ignored Cohena's obviously negative reaction and said:

"Of course not. We'll just have to coordinate closely so we don't get in each other's way." Harrington turned to Tracey.

"I'll be staying with Gif for the duration," Tracey smiled. "That should take care of the liaison. Special Agent Crawford can handle the files and the routine coordination."

That frank statement caught Harrington, Cohena, and Crawford by surprise. All three stared first at Tracey and then at Gifford. Harrington quickly masked his reaction. Reggie smiled at Tracey's liaison allusion but frowned when Cohena scowled.

"Good." Gif reacted first. He took advantage of the initial shock to seize temporary control of the meeting. "I would like to make this a quick visit." Gif glanced meaningfully at Cohena and Reggie before speaking to Harrington. "Tom, if you and Director Schultz could humor me and allot me just a few minutes of your time…" He let his voice trail off.

A tense Cohena immediately got the message. He grabbed his files and stood up. Reggie, now amused by the bureaucratic coup d'état, followed her supervisor's lead.

"We can wait outside," Cohena said without looking at Reggie.

"Thank you," Tom Harrington agreed.

The three at the table sat silently until the door closed behind Cohena and Reggie.

Gif waited for a sharp rejoinder from Tracey, but to his surprise, none came. She didn't even tap her fingers on the table as she normally did when irritated. Harrington nodded at Gif and waited for him to continue. The two had cooperated so closely in past investigations that neither relied on normal protocol. They sat in Harrington's office and he was now the director, but all three were conscious of the fact that in the past Harrington had been the junior member of the team.

"I'm sorry, Tom, for barging in like this, but I just came from the White House and wanted to compare notes with you two before I make my escape."

"The White House?" Tracey laughed. "I wish I had been there."

"Not the Andrew Johnson Suite?" Harrington said, agreeing with Tracey.

"The reason I ran your investigators off is because I want to keep awareness of my participation on a strict need to know basis. There have been entirely too many leaks about everything on this investigation," Gif said.

"You can assume, Gif, that most of them came from those landmarks further down Pennsylvania Avenue," Harrington said.

"I know, but just to be sure…" Gif said.

"Agreed," Harrington nodded. "Don't worry about Jeff and Reggie. They have their hands full as it is."

"And the media on their backs," Tracey said. "Now tell us what you've been up to."

"I've had a busy twenty-four hours," Gif said. "I made a quick trip to Richmond yesterday," Gif explained his absence for Tracey's benefit.

"Really? That must have been interesting. How is the good doctor? Has she broken any good bones lately?"

Gif laughed, despite his mood. "Doctor Bliss repairs bones; she doesn't break them."

"I was thinking about yours," Tracey said. "She might think she has cause."

"I met with my team," Gif changed the subject. "With the approval of Colonel Townsend, I'm bringing five of my key investigators up here for a while. As I said, they've set up at my place," Gif said, pausing to see how the others reacted.

"You're going to get involved in the investigation," Tom spoke first. "Great. That's what I wanted you to do from the beginning. Although I'm not quite sure what five more investigators will be able to do that my two hundred haven't already."

"They set up at your place?" Tracey asked with raised eyebrows.

"Only an office," Gif answered Tracey quickly. "They won't be there at night." Gif turned to Harrington. "They're just people I'm comfortable working with. They're all competent investigators who will work under the media's radar."

"No problem, then," Tracey said. "I don't plan to sleep in a dormitory with a bunch of kids." She glanced at Gif before turning towards Harrington. "I've decided to move in with Gif for the duration. I'm sick of hotels."

To his credit, Harrington reacted without blinking. "Good, now I know where I can find both of you."

"And it will let Tracey monitor what the team is doing, so that we don't cross wires," Gif added quickly.

"It will let Tracey keep track of a lot of things," Tracey laughed. "What happened at the White House that brought you here in such a snit?"

"Let me tell you what happened earlier than that. It's much more important, for me at least," Gif said.

"The floor's all yours," Tracey said.

"I visited Martha Tate in Leesburg. Did either of you know that she has dismissed all her Secret Service protection, all of her staff, and that she is living alone in the Leesburg house?" Gif asked.

"No," Harrington answered. "Is that wise?"

"I don't blame her," Tracey declared. "She's one tough lady."

"Martha says she's lived in the house without staff for most of her life and that she is not about to change for the last few years she has left."

"But…" The lawman instincts in Harrington started to speak but he stopped abruptly.

"Martha says she has Harrison's arsenal cleaned and ready and that she keeps a twelve gage fully loaded in the bedroom. She gave me this," Gif took the envelope from his suit coat pocket.

Both Harrison and Tracey leaned forward in their chairs.

"This is why I asked Jeff and Reggie to wait outside. It's of importance only to me, but I will share it with you two as friends not as investigators. I know I don't have to ask you this, but please don't mention it to another soul. Not even Martha has read it. Now, I share it with you, but no one else."

Both nodded. Gif handed Harrison Tate's letter to Tracey. She read it slowly and carefully and handed it to Harrington. Tracey and Gif sat in silence until Tom had read it. When he finished, Tracey spoke first"

"Christ, a voice from the grave."

"I see why you are involved," Tom said.

"This makes your involvement a presidential appointment that precedes mine," Tracey said. "What do you want us to do, boss?" The latter was said without a smile.

Harrington carefully folded the note, placed it in the envelope, and handed it back to Gif. "That's priceless. Future historians will go bonkers. It should be put in the National Archives."

"If you put it up for auction, the collectors will kill for it," Tracey said.

"I'm more worried about doing what Harrison asked me," Gif said solemnly. "Martha ordered me to get the bastard, and I don't think she meant just arrest him."

"I was serious, Gif," Tracey said. "How do we help?"

"Cover my back; keep the politicians and the media off me. You recognize, I'm sure, that Harrison was talking about political conspiracy," Gif said.

"A damned bloody coup d'état," Tracey said.

"What happened at the White House?" The practical minded Tom Harrington asked. He, after all, was the one charged with conducting the investigations.

"The Secret Service tried to stonewall me," Gif said.

"Who?" Tracey and Harrington asked simultaneously.

"The Assistant Director in charge of Protective Operations," Gif answered.

"Howard Pendergast, I know him," Harrington said. "I'm told he's a good agent who's been promoted a couple of steps above his ability. Now, he has a reputation as an ass kisser and paper shuffler."

"The Secret Service has transferred every member of Harrison's protection team to God knows where. I ordered him to have them back in his office by tomorrow morning so my people can interview them."

"Want me to lean on him?" Harrington asked.

"Give him a call and instruct him to do everything I asked. You should know I demanded access to all his files dealing with the shooting and the investigation. He declined, and I threatened you two would appear in his office with search warrants if he doesn't produce them."

"Right," Tom Harrington said, looking at Tracey to see if she agreed.

"I'll run interference if necessary," Tracey said.

"You know Jeff's boys debriefed the team members," Harrington said, sounding a little defensive. "Do you want your people to review our files?"

"That would be helpful, Tom," Gif spoke quickly.

Gif turned to Tracey.

"I would like my team to have a look at anything the task force may have that you think is important and to establish a working relationship with your investigators. There is only five of them plus Billie Williams, and they will be looking at all the investigations, so they shouldn't step on too many toes. I would hope your people commiserate with them and help as they can rather than resent them as intruders. I want them to start from scratch, but I'll make sure they proceed with a proper attitude."

"I'll see that our people understand," Tracey said. "Our investigations are at an impasse, and our people are frustrated. If you don't object, I'll simply tell them that the new team of outside investigators was my idea, a fresh look to see if we can come up with some new theories. I'll describe the team as an integral part of the task force." Tracey hesitated. "That would even explain what I'm doing at your house," she smiled at Gif.

"That's a good idea, Tracey," Gif said.

"Don't worry about Jeff and Reggie," Harrison said. "I'll make sure they keep their mouths shut about your involvement, Gif."

Gif, who had been worried about his earlier revelations, nodded assent.

"We don't know who shot Harrison," Harrington continued. "Now that we have your note from Harrison, we have to conclude that the Walker thing was part of a conspiracy not a terrible coincidence. We can't share that knowledge with the task force investigators, but we do have to take another look at Walker's death including the murders of the only two people who might have had useful information. We didn't know who killed them, but we realized it had to have been an attempt to cover up something. The whole thing smells of political conspiracy, and we have to look at that nice, old acting president sitting in the Andrew Johnson Suite. Incidentally, no one's forgotten that he is our boss. Shit."

"We're going to have to work together on all of this," Gif said. "I wasn't kidding when I asked you to cover our backs. If anything starts leaking, and the media gets the idea we're investigating a political conspiracy, that shit will hit the fan."

"Since we're working together, now, Gifford," Tracey smiled. "I've got a question."

Gif nodded, already anticipating what was coming.

"You carefully talked about the team this and the team that," Tracey said. "You never mentioned what the Great Gifford would be doing in all this."

"You two know I'm not a very good team player," Gif admitted.

"You're not any kind of team player, Gifford," Tracey said.

"If you don't object, I'll just do my thing while all you investigators do yours," Gif said.

"Gif, do your thing and if your boat starts sinking, Tracey and I will climb in it with you," Harrington declared.

"That's right, Gifford," Tracey said. "I agree with Tom with one slight exception. That shadow behind you won't be yours. It will be me."

Unable to come up with a response to that warning, Gif stood up and started for the door.

"Wait!" Tracey ordered.

Gif turned to find Tracey and Tom looking at each other. Harrington nodded, and Tracey responded by turning her head towards Gif. "Please give us another minute, Gif," she said.

Gif sat back down at the table and waited.

"We've been holding something back," Tracey began.

"Why does that not surprise me," Gif laughed.

"This is important. Only Tom, myself and the bureau medic who handled Harrison's autopsy are aware of what I am about to tell you.

Not even Jeff out there or any of his investigators know one simple fact."

Tracey now had Gif's full attention.

"We didn't tell you because you declined to participate in the investigation," Tracey continued. "But now, you are fully engaged and should know."

"Oh Christ, Tracey, just tell me," Gif declared. "I know how investigations are conducted."

"We have the slug," Tom said, watching Gif closely.

"You're kidding me," Gif placed both hands on the table in front of him. Having the bullet that killed Harrison was the best news he had heard since that fateful day.

"We do," Tracey confirmed.

"You found it in the river?" Gif let his disbelief show. "How do you know it's not just an errant shot from a hunter?"

"The president was wearing one of those new lightweight Kevlar vests," Tom said. "The shot hit him in the back, went completely through his body, and lodged in the vest. The vest did what it was intended to do, stop the slug, only too late to do Harrison any good."

"Then all we have to do is find the weapon that fired it," Gif declared, slamming his hands on the table. Suddenly, a thought struck him. "Does the acting president or anyone on Pennsylvania know this?"

"Of course not," Tracey responded.

"Keep it that way," Gif said as he again headed for the door. This time his step was much lighter. He now believed he had a fair chance at unraveling this mess. Suddenly, he stopped. "If your investigators don't know about the slug, who is looking for the weapon?"

"Everybody is," Tracey said. "They just don't know we have the key evidence."

"You're going to have some very angry staff when they learn you withheld this from them," Gif said.

"Gif," Tracey called after him. "There is one more thing. There's someone who insists on talking with you."

Gif stopped.

"Nan's sister is in town and says she will talk with no one but you. She's hiding out at Nan's apartment."

Chapter 25

Gif drove directly from Hoover's Revenge to Silver Spring. Benita Fernandez was Maria aka Nan Starbright aka Barbara Dolle's sister, the last link to what had really happened in Walker's Crystal City apartment. Anxious to know what Maria in her desperation had confided to Benita, Gif wasted no time in contacting her.

Gif went directly to Maria's apartment, noted the torn police tape that still hung on each side of the door, and tapped softly.

No one answered. Gif tapped again, harder. He faced the security peephole in the door and waited. This time, he was rewarded.

"What?" A soft, accented female voice greeted him.

"I'm Gifford, your sister's friend," Gif smiled. "We talked on the phone."

"Bullshit, friend. Show badge," the voice responded.

Gif held up his credentials case and waited.

"How know you Gifford?" The uncertain voice challenged.

"Because you told the cops that you would only talk to me," Gif answered. "Maria trusted me and so should you, Benita," Gif used her name for the first time.

"Shit," the voice reacted.

Gif waited patiently and finally the door opened.

Gif stared at the older and much used version of Maria and waited.

"Badge again," the tougher sister insisted.

"Stop the crap and let me in," Gif said, holding out his credential case.

"OK, cop, it you," Benita stepped back.

"You shouldn't be here. This is a crime scene," Gif said, trying to get the edge.

"Who care, arrest me," Benita laughed. "Not be first time."

"I was your sister's friend," Gif tried a different tack.

"Sit down, Gifford," Benita ordered. "Want coffee?"

"No thanks," Gif replied.

"Me want," Benita said. She stood up, poured a cup from Maria's expensive coffee maker, added a healthy shot of her dead sister's bourbon, and sat down facing Gif."

"OK, cop, what you give me?" She demanded.

"Your sister's memory," Gif tried.

"So, Maria more pretty, better lay," Benita smiled. "So what? Me just working girl, want some?"

"Benita, all I'm interested in is catching your sister's killer," Gif suspected that he was in over his head.

"Bullshit," Benita laughed. "You want blame Maria."

"Cards on the table, Benita," Gif surrendered. "I want to catch your sister's killer and to learn what she had to do with Vice President Walker's death."

"Maria did no thing no kill man. Maria tell me man take pills so he get it up. He die because he get it too high, too much pills, too much booze. No new that. He owe Maria, no pay last time. Me want."

"But he's dead," Gif responded weakly.

"She gave all man want and now you pay me." Maria held out her hand.

"How much?" Gif asked.

"Five hundred."

"We'll bargain," Gif said.

"Four hundred," Benita smiled.

"I'm not talking money. I'll pay the full five hundred and throw in everything in this apartment," Gif replied, looking at the expensive furnishing around him.

"No want this shit," Benita dismissed his offer. "Me need carry round money."

"OK, tell me what she told you about Walker."

"No tell me shit."

"What did she say about why she was visiting you?"

"Maria say she scare shitless." Benita hesitated. "Maria no say that, me say, know Maria. She no come me if no have trouble. Maria always think better me, but not now."

"What did she say about Walker?"

"She say big deal, little dick."

"And?"

"He take pills make dick big."

"Did she say where he got the pills?"

"We no talk that. Maria always look down me, say she got more money me.

"Want to prove her wrong?" Gif decided to take a chance.

"You want do me?" Benita smiled.

"As much as that might appeal to me," Gif smiled back. "I'm asking how you would like to make a thousand bucks."

"What you want?" Benita asked eagerly. "Me do ever thing you want."

"Just tell me the truth. What did she say about Walker?"

"Oh, shit," Benita reacted. "What you want Benita say? Maria say man friend give pills."

"What friend?"

"Some man. Me no know."

Gif opened his wallet, took out all the money he had in it, some five hundred dollars. He laid it on the table and looked at Benita. "This is all I have with me. Tell me his name, and I promise you," Gif took off his watch and put it on the table, "that you will get the rest."

Benita looked at the watch and the money. She reached across the table, slid the watch back towards Gif, and touched the bills with a forefinger. She counted them before looking at Gif. "Me trust you?"

"Of course," Gif answered. "I'll pick up the phone and have am officer deliver another five hundred to you."

"OK," Benita said, grabbing the money. "Keep watch. Make call."

Gif took out his cell phone and punched Tracey's number. When she answered, he said cryptically: "Have someone bring five hundred in unmarked bills to Nan's apartment."

To his surprise, Tracey answered respectfully: "Yes, sir."

Gif hung up the phone and turned to Benita.

"Tell me the name."

"Senator George Ames," Benita smiled.

⁂

Gif left Nan Starbright aka Barbara Dolle aka as Maria Fernandez's apartment one thousand dollars poorer, at least somebody was, but knowing nothing more than he had suspected. Senator George Ames was the source of the extra strength pills. Knowing that told him little. A swinging colleague had shared some blue pills with the vice president who had taken them to prove his machismo to a call girl. That did not mean that Walker was an innocent victim or his provider was part of a conspiracy. Suspecting that somehow that James Dexter's demise somehow would provide a missing clue, he turned his attention elsewhere.

As he was crossing Memorial Bridge heading for I-66 Gif violated the law. He punched Billie Williams' button on his cell phone.

"What?" Billie answered immediately.

"Meet me at Redskin Park," Gif ordered and hung up.

A half an hour later Gif turned off the Loudoun County Parkway onto the barely marked road that led to Redskin Park. Billie was already there, waiting in his parked car, chatting through the window with the guard. Gif stopped next to Billie, pointed straight ahead. Gif ignored the guard and pulled away, leaving the exasperated guard with a problem. Billie laughed.

"Don't worry, he's always that way," Billie called to the guard as he followed Gif onto the compound.

Behind them, the guard grabbed his phone and alerted security. Billie pulled his cruiser in next to Gif who was already out of the Prius.

"I wondered how we were going to handle this investigation," Billy said as he joined Gif.

"I thought I made that perfectly clear at the house," Gif smiled.

"I thought you reassigned me to do a little of this and a little of that," Billie said.

"That's what you're doing, isn't it?"

"Yes, but why are you here with me and not Herald?"

"I didn't say I wouldn't do a little of this and that too. Sheriff

Simmons has his team led by Chief Investigator Brian Sadler investigating this case, doesn't he?"

"Yes."

"And he asked us to take a look also?"

"Yes."

"And I asked you and Herald to investigate the Redskin murders, didn't I"

"Yes."

"So what's the problem? Are you telling me I can't investigate too?"

"I'm just not used to having so much divided authority," Billie said. "Do I report to Herald, Sadler, you, who?"

"One of the above."

"But…"

"No buts, Billie. What is Gizzie doing these days?"

Gif's sudden switch of subjects confused Billie. Gizzie Kane had been one of Gif's favorites when he had been sheriff. He had even appointed Gizzie his chief investigator, jumping her over several more senior deputies, and Gizzie had carried her junior partner, Billie, along with her. It was Gizzie's abrupt retirement that had left Billie in the difficult position he now occupied, a favorite of a departed chief investigator.

"She's living in her old house with her husband and kids and seems to be thoroughly enjoying it," Billie answered. "I saw her last week."

"And she has no regrets, doesn't miss it all?"

"I don't think so Gif," Billie hesitated.

"Spit it out, Billie," Gif ordered.

"I don't know really why Gizzie left. She refused to discuss it with me."

"But?"

"Well, I just had the impression that there was something going on between her and the sheriff."

"Gizzie?"

"I don't mean an affair or anything like that," Billie said quickly. "I think they had their disagreements. Maybe Simmons was trying to tell her how to run her investigations. I don't know."

"Let's worry about the Redskins today." Gif turned and headed for the front door of the main building. Privately, he decided to find time for a chat with his old protégé. He too found Gizzie's sudden decision to retire puzzling.

Inside, two security guards blocked their access.

"May we be of assistance, gentlemen?" The guard wearing sergeant stripes on his sleeve asked.

"Yes," Gif replied. "Get out of my way, or I'll have Deputy Williams handcuff you."

That response startled both guards, and Billie learned why he had been invited. "Sir, this is private property…" the sergeant said, his tone less certain this time.

"And it's in the County of Loudoun which is located in the Commonwealth of Virginia," Gif declared. "I represent the commonwealth and Deputy Williams the county. Do you have any difficulty comprehending that?"

"No, sir. But…"

"Where is the owner's suite?" Gif asked abruptly.

"Top floor on the left," the second guard spoke for the first time.

The sergeant glared at his subordinate. When he turned back to face the two visitors, he found them heading for the elevator. After a moment of hesitation, the sergeant shrugged and grabbed the phone from the desk.

Gif turned left when they exited the elevator and pushed open the first door, surprising the occupants, two attractive young ladies who were busy chatting and buffing their nails.

"Where's the boy owner?" Gif demanded.

'Sir," the girl on Gif's right glanced at a closed door. "May I ask…"

Before she completed her sentence, Gif, followed by an amused Billie Williams, opened that door and entered to find himself in a huge room. A couch flanked by four chairs, all covered in rich brown leather stood directly to his right. Against the far wall, was an immense conference table lined with chairs. In the center of the room stood a desk that Gif estimated cost at least thirty thousand itself. The walls were lined with action photographs of Redskin players, many of whom Gif recognized, an awareness honed by hours spent staring at his television screen.

Two men who had been looking out a floor to ceiling window that faced the Redskin practice field turned and glared at the intruders. Gif recognized both men. The larger of the two, Nails Bukosky, the Redskin coach, he had already interviewed. The other he only knew from his intrusive appearances on Gif's television set. For reasons that Gif could not comprehend, Fox Network cameramen believed it mandatory that they transmit shots of the owner's suite at critical moments of the game. David A Douglas was some kind of communications guru who had made a quick fortune by his early thirties when through some kind of adroit maneuvering he had ended up getting the Redskins franchise for a mere eight hundred million dollars, an amount of money that Gif had difficulty comprehending any place outside of the United States Government's debit sheets.

"Who the hell are you?" Douglas demanded.

Nails Buckosky laughed before Gif could reply, raising him in Gif's estimation by a considerable degree.

"Inspector Gifford," Nails answered for Gif, "is responsible for catching the bastard who killed our two boys. We've already had a little chat, so I assume he's here to question you."

"Do you have an appointment?" The arrogant little owner demanded.

Gif smiled, not because he was intimidated, but because he was amused. The boy owner was reacting just as Gif had anticipated he would. Douglas' public image was that of an arrogant little shit whose early success had clearly gone to his head. The one thing that Gif hated most about the Redskin telecasts were the occasional pictures showing the boy owner presiding in his box trying to look concerned while he entertained visiting celebrities. Gif had to admit that those pictures really annoyed him, but they were not the thing he really hated most; it was the constant losing and weak offensive line that bothered him most, but the boy owner ranked high.

"He probably thinks you are responsible for the shootings," Nails again spoke before Gif did.

"Why in the hell would he think that?" Douglas turned on his coach.

"Because he suspects you may have found yet another way to cut costs," Nails laughed, pleased with himself. "Everyone knows we need an offensive line."

"See my secretary. Make an appointment," Douglas glared at Gif.

Gif, still silent, ignored Douglas's order. With Billie Williams following close behind him, Gif joined Douglas and Nails at the window and looked out at the tremendous view of the practice field where the players were pounding the hell out of each other.

"I wish they had done that a few days ago," Gif referred to the abortive preseason game.

"Close the damned door," Douglas shouted at his secretary who was watching from the doorway to the reception room.

Gif mentally added bully to the descriptors he had filed away for the boy owner.

"I think I had better get down there before those guys pare the roster even more," Nails said.

"Stay here," Douglas ordered.

Nails ignored him and left the room. Although Nail's independence raised him in Gif's estimation, Gif doubted that he would set any tenure records with the Redskins. The boy owner was already on his sixth head coach.

Douglas turned and retreated to his chair behind the carrier-sized desk.

"Please have a seat, gentlemen, and we'll get this over with as quickly as we can. My bird arrives in exactly twenty-four minutes."

Although he recognized that Douglas was simply trying to impress his visitors, Gif did as he was told. He took one of the subordinate chairs facing Douglas, and Billie Williams slumped into the other.

"My name is Gifford, and…" Gif said.

"I already know that," Douglas interrupted.

"And if you let me complete a sentence we might be able to get through this in time for you to catch your bird," Gif said.

"OK. Don't worry about the copter," Douglas said. "I was just spouting off. It'll wait because I own it and everything else around here."

"Including the players?"

Douglas glared at Gif but controlled his temper. "That's not the way I would describe the situation. Would you, deputy?" Douglas acknowledged Billie Williams for the first time.

"And as I was saying," Gif interrupted. "This is Deputy Billie Williams."

Billie and the owner exchanged nods.

"Some of them might feel the relationship has certain qualities similar to their ancestors' situation, particularly the black ones," Billie shrugged, answering the owner's question.

Douglas surprised both Gif and Billie by laughing. "I look after my boys," Douglas declared. "I know that the media doesn't like to say that, but I do. As soon as you release the bodies, I will have them flown to their homes at my personal expense in my airplane. I will go with them. I've spoken with their families, and they are waiting. Can I tell them when that will happen?"

"That decision rests with Deputy Williams," Gif glanced at his companion, hoping he did not surprise him too badly.

Douglas shifted his gaze from Gif to Billie. To his credit, he hid any surprise that he felt.

"Deputy?" Douglas pressed for an answer.

"You can have them today. I will call as soon as I leave this meeting," Billie declared.

"Thank you, deputy," Douglas said. "What do you want to know from me?" He turned back to Gif.

Gif nodded to Willie. "Deputy Williams will ask the questions," Gif said.

"Who do you think killed two of your players?" Billie asked.

"I don't know. Do you?" Douglas answered.

"I know that there have been recent disputes among your players," Billie countered.

"Understand two things, if you will," Douglas surprised both Gif and Billie by commenting. "Professional football is a damned violent activity. I deliberately say activity not sport. Participants try to inflict harm on the opposition and protect themselves from suffering it. In order to do so, they must also practice the way they play the game. At times that can be self-defeating for the team. The coaches try to protect the skill players in practice, but that is easier to say than do. Tempers fray. Teammates fight. You can't develop a violent edge and turn it on and off like a light switch. At the same time, some of these grown men act like a bunch of damned kids. I refer to the silly practice called hazing. The coaches tell me the players think it develops team esprit. I don't believe it. The disputes you so nicely refer to, deputy, involving the two unfortunate players that I frankly cannot afford to lose, stemmed from hazing. Sometimes it gets out of hand and carries over in practice and off the field. I know there were fights at that dump known as Tiny's. I can't do anything about that. This stuff happens on every team in the league. If you are asking do I think something that developed within my team led to those terrible shootings, I say no. Of course not."

"Sir, I assume you knew your players well. You obviously care about them. Why do you think someone selected these two players to be his victims?" Billie persisted.

"I don't know. Their personal lives are their business. Now they are your business, so you tell me. Maybe there is a jealous boy friend or husband lurking out there. Maybe we have a nut running around with a shotgun seeking a share of the players' fame. Maybe somebody owed somebody money and didn't pay. Or," Douglas hesitated and looked directly at Gifford. "Or, maybe there is some kind of connection with these terrible Washington murders as some of the media seem to think."

Gif ignored that gibe aimed at him.

"We plan to interview your players individually," Billie changed the subject.

"Your colleagues have already done that," Douglas said.

"We have some follow up questions for a few of them," Billie said.

"I can't stop you. I might hinder you, but remember, deputy, we have another game coming up in two days, and we have a team to rebuild, physically and mentally. The people of Washington expect that. Look out that window."

Neither Gif nor Billie turned toward the window.

"When those players come off that field, they are going to be bruised and tired. Management owes them the opportunity to recover and rest. Go take a look at those battered bodies resting in the ice and being treated by the doctors and trainers and then tell me I'm being unfair or inconsiderate. You have your job to do, and I have mine. I wish you success. If you must ask your questions, please try to select an opportune time."

Billie nodded. "And if we have more questions for you," Billie said. "I assume you will be available."

Douglas stood up, effectively dismissing them. "Of course. Now, if you excuse me I have a bird to catch. I'm due at the White House in exactly twenty minutes."

Gif and Billie shook hands with the owner and departed.

When they reached their cars, Billie turned to Gif: "I'm not sure that man deserves the sobriquet boy owner."

"Shit Billie, I don't even know what sobriquet means, but I agree with you anyway. I think we just met the man who earned eight hundred million dollars before he was thirty."

"What do we do next?"

"Let's take a look at the river," Gif said.

"You mean Sheriff Tate's place?"

"I'll meet you there."

"What's that got to do with the Redskin case?"

"We've all got more than one investigation on our plates," Gif shrugged. "Where does Gizzie live?"

"Same place. Some things change, some don't."

"Since it's on the way to the river, I think I'll stop off and say hello," Gif said.

"You may think you'll be able to entice Gizzie back to work, but I doubt it. Good luck in any case."

Gif smiled.

"Since you're making a stopover, I think I'll see what's happening at headquarters," Billie said, showing that he too had a mind of his own. "Maybe they're making more progress that we are."

I'm sure they'll want to know what you've been up to," Gif cautioned.

"Don't worry boss. You aren't the only one who can dissemble. I'll give you credit for releasing the bodies."

Chapter 26

Just turning into Gizzie's driveway gave Gif a touch of nostalgia. His former sheriff's department protégé had played a major role in virtually every Loudoun County case that Gif had been involved in. He parked the Prius, climbed the steps to the porch, and knocked on the door not quite sure what to expect. Gizzie had a volatile personality and never refrained from expressing her opinion, forcefully and profanely. That tendency combined with her incisive mind made Gizzie the person Gif respected.

The door opened. Gizzie looked out long enough for Gif to see that physically she had not changed, just a few more lines around the eyes and mouth. Gizzie stared at Gif, frowned, and slammed the door shut without speaking, demonstrating that she still packed a lot of dynamite in a small package.

"Gizzie, damn it, open the door," Gif laughed.

Nothing happened. Gif waited.

Suddenly, the door burst open and a smiling Gizzie threw her arms around him.

"I heard you were in town. No, I saw you on television," Gizzie said as she kissed him on the cheek. "You and that old broad make a great team."

"What was that all about?" Gif asked.

"Just a kiss on the cheek. I'm not trying to compete with those media types you hang out with these days," Gizzie chuckled.

"No, I mean that business with the door."

"Oh, that. I was just testing you. Still drink coffee or is it all champagne, snails, and caviar now?" Gizzie stepped back and pulled the door wide before turning for the kitchen.

Gif followed her down the hall.

"I was just getting ready to clean the dump up," Gizzie waved a hand at the cluttered counters and dirty dishes in the sink.

"Billie says you are a devoted housewife and mother these days," Gif said. The kitchen was exactly what he expected.

"Good old Billie is still hanging in there," Gizzie said. "They're treating him like dog shit. What are you going to do about it?"

"I don't understand what's happening at the department," Gif said. "I stopped by and there were a lot of new faces and few of the old." Gif invited Gizzie to comment.

"You're still not very good at priming the damned pump," Gizzie laughed.

Gizzie dropped a spoonful of instant in a cup, filled it with tap water, and shoved it into the microwave. She did not, however, respond to Gif's tacit invitation to vent about the department. She turned and studied Gif.

"You look the same, just a lot older," Gizzie declared. "You ought to try Grecian Formula."

Gif laughed. "Damn it Gizzie it's not the same place down there without you."

"I was stunned to hear about Harrison," Gizzie said. "I'm so sorry."

"I know," Gif said.

"Are you close to catching the bastard who did it?"

"I've kept my nose out of the investigation," Gif said. "Harrison and I were too close for me to be objective."

"Objective my ass," Gizzie blurted. "Just catch the bastard."

"You sound just like Martha," Gif said.

"How is she taking it?"

"She's back at their Leesburg place. She fired the Secret Service and all the staff."

"Good for her."

"That's what Tracey said."

Gizzie gave Gif a knowing look but said nothing.

"You should drop by," Gif suggested.

"Drop by where? Are you and Schultz playing house again?"

"No, damn it. Where did you get that idea?"

"I always felt you were still yearning for wonder woman."

"I was talking about Martha. She's all alone now," Gif tried to put the talk about Tracey to bed. Sometimes Gizzie was just too damned perceptive.

"Me? Martha and I were never close. We traveled in different circles. Besides, she never invited me to the damned White House." Gizzie as usual told the truth as she saw it, bluntly.

"Stop by anyway. She's lonely but won't admit it. A visit by a familiar face will make a big difference."

"Me consoling the widow of a president," Gizzie laughed wryly. "Hell, I haven't even driven down Pennsylvania Avenue since you drafted me for that shitty Capitol Hill thing." Gizzie referred to the serial killer case that she had virtually solved for Gif. At least, she had uncovered the key clues at a critical time.

The microwave buzzed. Gizzie pulled Gif's cup out, spilled a few drops of coffee on the floor, ignored them, and handed the cup to Gif.

"Let's go sit down," Gizzie said leading the way out of the kitchen.

"What about you?" Gif raised the cup.

"I've had mine," she answered.

That was the first sign of change that Gif saw in the new Gizzie. When working, Gizzie had lived on caffeine.

After they were settled, Gizzie asked the first question. "What case are you working on now?"

Gif thought about using the cover story he had recommended to the team but decided against it. This was Gizzie he was talking to.

"I'm working a little bit on all of them," Gif answered honestly.

Gizzie nodded and waited for him to continue.

"Harrison, Walker, Starbright, Dexter, and the Redskins."

"The Redskins?" Gizzie stared at Gif. "How are they connected?"

"Some people think I'm the connector."

"No one believes Mavis," Gizzie laughed. "They just stare at her legs and ass. I don't know why; she's putting on weight. Is she?"

"I'm nibbling around the edges of the other cases," Gif said before Gizzie could go to work on Mavis Davis.

"Just nibbling?"

"The bureau and Tracey's task force and Dick Simmons's boys are all doing their thing. They've got plenty of manpower. I'm just nosing around, and I've brought in a little help."

"Hi O Silver, away," Gizzie chortled. "The Lone Ranger rides again."

"I've got a small team from OSI stashed out at my place, and Billie Williams is helping out."

"You've got Billie playing Tonto? That I would like to see. Don't you think Billie's a little overweight for the role?"

"You weren't available, Gizzie. Mind telling me why?"

"I'm retired, boss, just a happy, fucking housewife."

Gif rubbed his fingers on the table beside his chair, found dust, and made a show of rubbing his hands together to remove it.

"So dusting isn't my thing," Gizzie challenged. "Is it all a big conspiracy like your asshole buddy Mavis Davis claims? You being the big connection and all. I assumed that was a lot of media hyperbole."

"Hyperbole," Gif laughed. "You've been working on your vocabulary since you retired, but you haven't cleaned up your act much."

"So I read a lot," Gizzie said. "This housewife shit isn't all it's cracked up to be."

"Gizzie, would you like to help me out?"

Gizzie laughed as if the suggestion were the most preposterous thing she had heard lately. "Dick Simmons would have kittens if he heard I was involved."

"Assuming that's a negative, would you mind telling me why you and Dick had a falling out?"

"Have you spent much time with our good sheriff lately?" Gizzie answered a question with a question.

"No, why?"

"He's changed, Gif."

"In what way?"

"All of this campaigning to get elected sheriff has made him more politician than cop," Gizzie said.

Gif wondered if Gizzie was simply playing him. She knew that Gif hated politics and that he strongly opposed the idea of electing police officers. The demands and costs of campaigning required the candidate to make too many compromises, something Gif considered that a cop could not do. The law was the law that should be enforced. Period.

"Give me a for-instance," Gif said.

"Drive by his house, sometime, his new house."

"Where is it?"

"Ask Billie."

Gif looked at Gizzie and waited for a better reply, but she sat opposite with pursed lips. Her posture alone told him that was all she was going to say on the subject, and he knew from past experience that Gizzie in that mood was unmovable.

"And he has a new place over on the shore, too," Gizzie surprised him.

"A fancy place?"

"Dick also dresses a lot better and drives expensive wheels," Gizzie said. "And that is definitely all I am going to say on that subject." Gizzie made a show of crossing her legs and folding her arms.

Since Gizzie knew that Gif made a point of watching the body language of those he was questioning, he realized she was sending him a deliberate message.

"OK," Gif said. "I surrender. Are you interested in joining my little OSI team? We could try that and see where it takes us."

Gizzie laughed. She unfolded her arms and legs and looked Gif squarely in the eye. "We both know that the only place that could take us would be Richmond. You don't have OSI investigators stationed in Leesburg, and that is where I live. My husband would kill me. Thank you, but no thank you. I do have one suggestion for you."

"What?" Gizzie made Gif ask.

"Kill the damned bastard that shot Sheriff Tate. Martha's right."

Gif shook his head. He could have observed "Women" but he didn't. Instead, he said:

"We're going to get him. I promise you that."

"I wish I could help, Gif, but I can't."

Not knowing what to say to that, Gif drained his cup and stood up.

"Gizzie, it's been good seeing you again. If you change your mind about anything, give me a call. I've got the same cell number, and you know how to reach Billie."

"Sure thing, boss," Gizzie waved her hand in dismissal.

Gizzie followed Gif to the front door, watched as he went down her steps. Before he reached the bottom, Gizzie closed her door, shutting Gif out.

Gif stopped, looked at the door with a puzzled expression on his face, before climbing into the Prius and heading for Route 15 and his river meeting with Billie.

Gif was surprised when he found the small lane that led from Lovettsville Road to the Tate home place on the Potomac River unguarded. He noticed the police tape that had identified the site as a crime scene crumpled in the gutter. Assuming that had been Billie's handiwork, Gif continued on through the forest that intruded on what once had been farmed acreage. Harrison had kept this place as a private hideaway, not as a rallying point for family outings, and the family had stopped tilling the soil decades ago. Gif had visited Harrison many times here when they had worked together but not for a good ten years. The distance from the main road seemed farther than Gif remembered it. Nothing appeared familiar until he dropped down the last incline and emerged in the graveled parking lot located between the deteriorating barn and crumbling house. Obviously, Harrison had not spent much time here lately because Gif remembered when his friend had been proud of his family's first home in then largely unsettled Virginia. Harrison had liked to point out the exact spot where his great grandfather had ferried escaping slaves across the Potomac as they traveled the underground railroad to freedom.

Gif parked next to Billie's cruiser, and Billie got out to join him.

"I'm not quite sure what we're looking for here, chief. I don't think we'll find many Redskins hereabout these days."

"I don't think there ever were any Redskins of the kind you're thinking about," Gif laughed.

"Yes, and I'm sure those that were here wore feathers not helmets," Billie laughed, amused by his own word games."

"Let's sit on the porch and chat a little," Gif suggested. "Then, if you aren't afraid of the water, we can take a little cruise downriver.

"Try me," Billie smiled.

After they were seated, Gif thought about the revelation about the slug that he had learned from Tracey and Tom, considered briefing Billie, and decided that he best not. Since Tracey and Tom were not sharing that information with their key investigators, Gif could not either.

""What did you learn at the office?" Gif asked.

"Not much. Sadler was interested in what I was up to, and I fed him a lot of crap," Billie said, referring to his departmental boss, the sheriff's chief investigator, a position that by rights should have been his. "The coroner agreed to release the bodies. There's little question about cause of death."

"Good," Gif said.

"And the sheriff dropped by. He asked how we were making out, and I told him about our meeting with the boy wonder," Billie said.

"Did you mention our cover story?"

Billie stared at Gif. "The sheriff knows I'm working with you on the Redskin thing."

"The one I suggested to the team," Gif explained. "That we're investigating a local corruption thing."

"Billie shook his head. "No, it wasn't necessary. Why do you ask?"

"They hadn't heard about my team?"

"No."

"Good. I failed to suggest that we keep a lid on their presence and the corruption cover story. Have you noticed many changes in Dick?" Gif referred to his successor as sheriff.

"A few," Billie stalled. Gif's odd questions were making him uneasy. Sometimes, he found it very difficult to read where the unpredictable Gifford was heading, and Billie did not like to appear stupid. "Did you find Gizzie at home?"

"Yes. What kind of changes?" Gif asked, ignoring Billie's attempt to change the subject.

"Can you be specific?" Billie asked.

"Yes," Gif decided to be candid. "Are you satisfied with all the changes at headquarters?"

"No," Billie answered honestly.

"Let's take a trip downriver," Gif's abruptness, again surprised Billie.

After they launched Harrison's old boat, the one he had died in, Gif turned to face Billie, who was handling the sputtering outboard, and declared:

"Billie, I frankly don't like what I see at headquarters."

"What do you mean, Gif?"

"I miss Gizzie. I'm not sure about all the new guys."

"So do I. Neither am I," Billie admitted.

"Take us down river," Gif said.

Billie obediently headed the boat towards the bridge.

"Do you know where the shooting occurred?" Gif asked.

"About," Billie answered. "Are we investigating the Redskin shooting or the sheriff's department?"

"I'm not investigating the department," Gif said. "Billie, I don't want our silly corruption cover story to get you in trouble."

Billie nodded. "Me neither. That's why I didn't mention that your team was in town. I'm still a county employee and my assignment is to assist you with the Redskin investigation."

"Something's bothering you Billie. Is it the fact that I'm involved in more than one investigation at a time?"

Billie laughed. "That I expect, Gif. It's just that I feel like I'm walking a narrow line. You have the freedom to do what you want. I don't. I've got my own career problems."

"You don't like the desk work."

"There's that and the fact that the sheriff is bringing in outsiders and jumping them over the rest of us. There have been a lot of changes since you left."

"Such as?"

"The standard of living of some of us has really improved."

"Dick?"

"Yes sir," Billie got formal.

"Mind sharing with me?"

"Some worry that politics corrupts."

Gif assumed the Billie was playing to his well-known conviction that police officers should not be forced to campaign for public office, such as sheriff. He waited.

"You want me to speak honestly?" Billie asked.

"That's why we are out here on the river," Gif admitted.

"Dumb me," Billie said. "I thought we were investigating."

"We're multitasking."

"I know that Dick Simmons is one of your boys," Billie said.

Gif did not react.

"But politics has changed him."

"In what way?"

"You didn't answer my question about Gizzie," Willie smiled. "Did you have an interesting conversation?"

"We did. I don't understand why Gizzie retired so abruptly. House work isn't her thing no matter what she says."

"Gizzie surprised us all."

"Did she have trouble with those changes you mentioned?"

"You should ask her."

"We skirted about the subject. She mentioned that Dick Simmons has a new house."

"A new house?" Billie reacted. "It's a mansion. Do a drive-by and you'll see what I mean. Check out his wardrobe these days when he is off duty, and don't forget his wheels. I'm told he has a new place at the shore. I haven't seen it, so I won't swear to it, but I have met his new bride. Now she is really hot, a twenty something hot."

"Dick never mentioned a new wife. What happened to Polly?"

"She's still living in their old place. I hear it wasn't an amicable parting."

Gif made a mental note to drop in on Polly for a friendly chat, ignoring the fact that his agenda was rapidly expanding. "Where is Dick's new place?" Gif asked.

"Waterford, on top of the hill overlooking the village," Billie said.

"That's a pretty high budget neighborhood," Gif said.

"Particularly when you own twenty acres of it," Billie stared at Gif trying to read his reaction.

"Maybe I'll ride by on my way home," Gif said.

Billie smiled. Waterford was a good thirty-minute detour on Gif's ride home.

"This must be about where the shooting occurred," Gif said.

"Yes sir. If I overstepped…" Billie's face showed concern. Everybody knew that Simmons had been Gif's personal choice to replace him as sheriff.

"People change, Billie," Gif reassured him. "If I understand the crime scene, the shooter must have fired from over there," Gif pointed at a knoll that stood about two hundred yards from the shore.

"Yes sir," Billie said as he turned the old boat in that direction.

"Let's land and scout around a little," Gif said.

"The bureau, the Secret Service, and our boys have crawled all over that area," Billie let his skepticism show.

"I know," Gif smiled. "Humor me. I just like to get a feel for where things happen. You can wait at the boat."

"No way, boss," Billie laughed. "What would everyone say if I let you get eaten by one of those big, black West Virginia bears that consider this area their private preserve?"

"It would never happen," Gif responded. "Black bears and I have too much respect for each other to quibble over this place."

Billie ran the prow of the boat against the graveled shore and turned off the engine. Gif jumped out in ankle deep river water and pulled the bow two feet onto land, just far enough to keep it from floating away.

"The river's low," Billie said as he climbed out of the boat, carefully stepping on dry land. "Everyone's going to wonder what you were doing wading around with your shoes on," Billie laughed.

"I'm just an old country boy," Gif shrugged.

"And I live in a penthouse way up in the sky," Billie smiled as he referred to the old song.

"You're too young to remember that line," Gif said.

"You ought to hear my big band collection," Billie said.

Gif turned and started climbing the steep bank with Billie dutifully following. After considerable slipping, sliding, and confrontations with resisting brush that fought unfairly with sharp bristles, they reached the knoll that Billie had pointed out from the boat. The high grass on the knoll top had been flattened and the ground for fifty feet around was spotted with recently dug holes.

"Looks like the searchers reached the same conclusion as you, Gif," Billie said. "They were trying to find where he buried the weapon. If there was any evidence lying around here, it's long gone now."

"Did the files indicate any finds?"

"Not even a footprint," Billie answered.

Gif turned and faced the river. "If the shooter lay prone here, keeping his body below the ridge line, he would have been virtually out of sight from the boat," Gif said. "He fired once and took off in that direction," Gif pointed at the ravine that led up the hill.

"A five minute climb and he would have been back at his car," Billie agreed. "Another two minutes and he would have been on 15, across the bridge and just another traveler on one of those Maryland highways."

"There's no place on that section of Lovettsville Road where he could have completely concealed his getaway car," Gif said.

"Maybe he had a bicycle or a motorcycle," Billie suggested.

"Somebody saw something," Gif insisted.

"There's not much traffic on Lovettsville Road at that time of day," Billie said.

"Housewives returning from a day at the outlets or with the groceries, a school bus, one of the area residents, an old retired guy," Gif said. "Christ, there were four sheriff's department cruisers in the area."

"The Feds and our deputies have debriefed all the residents; they set up road blocks for a week, annoyed every commuter, and interviewed every motorist who passed through during the time frame covering the shooting, and came up empty. Nobody saw anything."

"There are workers at that farm restaurant up there at that time of day," Gif pointed at a local eating place that served dinners only from a site on the other side of the road half way up a steep incline.

"They were among the first debriefed," Billie said, shaking his head.

"We're going to talk to everybody again," Gif said. "Somebody saw something. They just don't know it."

Gif turned and started back down the hill to the river.

A half an hour later Gif turned the Prius toward Route 9 and Waterford, an old village that was settled by Quakers in the early seventeen hundreds. Just before the Civil War, it had been a mill town, the second largest village in Loudoun County. Then, stagnation had set in, and Waterford like most of Loudoun County had dozed through time until the years after World War II when restorationists discovered it. The arty set from the District of Columbia purchased the rotting homes in the old village and set to work recreating their little pocket of old Virginia. By the 1970's Waterford had been added to the National Historic Landmark List, a simple act that locked in the village's exclusive future. Gif had paid little attention to the tiny arts and craft center when he lived in Loudoun, primarily because crime was virtually nonexistent in the village and the residents were preoccupied with their liberal and intellectual causes.

Gif followed the county road past the entrance to the village itself and guided the Prius around a bend and up the hill. While the Waterford patrons carefully guarded the exclusivity of their 18th century architecture, the farmers with acreage overlooking the village sold off their land to the highest bidders, transforming themselves into members of the nouveau riche class.

Lacking an address, Gif slowed so he could read the names on the mailboxes. Billie had said near the top of the hill, and he had been correct. Only Billie's words had not been sufficient to warn Gif sufficiently about what he found there. He had expected to learn that Sheriff Dick Simmons and his new bride had graduated to Loudoun's upper class suburbia, a five bed room house, probably in the seven hundred to eight hundred thousand range, on a big lot with a couple of newly planted trees and an expanse of struggling lawn. Instead, he found a Sheriff's Department Bronco parked in the curved driveway of a modern day mansion that Gif estimated was worth two to three million. It had a four-car garage with every space filled, an Olympic sized swimming pool with a professionally landscaped patio, a house-wide balcony, and at least twenty rooms. Gif admired the three acres of manicured lawn being treated by at least two illegal gardeners.

"Oh Christ, Dick," Gif sighed. If his protégé hadn't married very, very well he obviously had succumbed to the politician's self-destructive disease, dependency on easy access to graft and off the books campaign funds.

Not wanting to alert his old friend to unwanted scrutiny, Gif continued down the road to the first country intersection where he turned around and retraced his route passing the Simmons' modern day castle without a second glance. He had seen far more than he wanted.

Back at Route 9, Gif turned left and directed the Prius, which he had thought an extravagance, towards home. One thought troubled him the whole way. He was very sorry he had selected graft investigation as a cover for his OSI team; clearly, it had not been one of his brighter inspirations. If word circulated that he was investigating corruption in Loudoun, it was sure to create panic in the very office whose support he needed.

Gif turned into the overgrown double path that he called a driveway, passed through the stubby mountain forest that provided him privacy, and emerged in the overgrown pasture that he optimistically dubbed a lawn. Expecting to see the cars of his team, he was disappointed to find a large satellite truck with a turning disk blocking his view of his modest castle. Beside the truck sat a run of the mill, black government sedan. Even more unsettling was the fact that two women were sitting on lawn chairs near his front door, drinking his Budweiser, and apparently chatting amiably. Neither acknowledged his arrival with a greeting smile or a wave.

Gif parked the Prius in its customary place at the side of the house. Apprehensively, Gif got out of his modest machine and approached the women with an apprehensive frown on his face. Neither Mavis Davis nor Tracey acknowledged his arrival or his proprietary rights.

Inside, the house phone was ringing persistently.

"Would you answer that please, lover," Tracey finally acknowledged him. "It has been ringing off the God damned hook."

Gif started for the door. "Hi, guy," Mavis called after him. "That damned thing is really irritating."

Gif took a deep breath, resisted the impulse to say what he really thought, and let the door slam behind him.

"Gifford," he snarled into the receiver. At least he felt free to express himself to the inanimate intruder.

"My, you are in a mood," Marjorie's voice greeted him.

Gif hesitated, not sure what to say. He didn't trust himself to speak, ready as he was to condemn an entire gender.

"So you are back in Loudoun," Marjorie said.

"Where did you think I would be after that reception last night," Gif decided to let all of them, the women, know what he really thought.

"I apologize, sweetie," Marjorie acted as if throwing his possessions in the hall and refusing to let him spend the night was just a little injustice, her right as a female.

Gif stubbornly did not respond. In truth, he didn't know what to say. He had two tormentors chatting out front, a network cameraman hiding behind his truck waiting to catch him at an awkward moment, and Marjorie jousting with him on the phone.

"I've had a trying day," Gif admitted.

"You're not the only one, buster," Marjorie bared her fangs. "Four broken limbs, two replacements, and moving all your crap back in the apartment."

"You're the one who threw it out," Gif said, a moderate response if he ever heard one.

"Gif, honey, bring us two more beers," Tracey called.

"Are you alone?" Marjorie demanded.

"Hell no," Gif declared. "I've got two lonely women sitting out front, drinking my beer, and demanding service."

"What kind of service?" Marjorie demanded. Before Gif could muster a response, Marjorie shouted: "Gifford, you're a shit."

Gif slammed the receiver down, assuming that his damned recliner would soon be back in the hall.

"Gif, honey, we're dying of thirst out here," Tracey called.

Gif grabbed three Buds from the fridge and returned to front lawn. He deliberately handed a bottle, unopened, to each of the smiling women who sat in his chairs. Gif, unwilling to take the trouble to fetch another chair from the back patio, remained standing. He opened his bottle, took a deep and much needed drink, and waited for the fireworks to begin. Neither Mavis nor Tracey was the passive type.

To his surprise, neither said a word. Each twisted their bottle top, lifted the frosted bottle in toast as if cementing a pact, and tossed the caps into the grass.

"Had a busy day, dear?" Tracey asked, playing the part of a well-trained housewife.

"Hell no," Gif growled. "I've had a terrible day."

"I heard you visited Redskin Field," Mavis spoke for the first time.

"Who told you that?" Gif demanded.

"A reliable source," Mavis said.

"Who?" Gif insisted.

Mavis smiled at Tracey. "Shall I tell him?"

Tracey nodded.

"I've got a wonderful interview for this evening's six o'clock news," Mavis said. "Don't miss it. The boy owner is a real charmer."

That told Gif where Mavis had learned about his visit to Redskin Park. He assumed that Mavis had immediately hurried on to Loudoun to squeeze Gif for more local color. Gif looked at Tracey, wondering why in the hell she was humoring the pesky reporter. Only a few hours previous Tracey had solemnly pledged to cover his back with the media.

"It's all right, dear," Tracey smiled as she reached over and patted Gif's knee. "Mavis and I have reached an understanding."

"One concluded in hell," Gif grumbled as he stepped out of Tracey's reach.

"Now, now," Mavis chided Gif. "You can't cover everything up."

"What am I covering up?" Gif demanded.

"You're investigating the Redskin murders and ..." Mavis hesitated and glanced and Tracey who nodded affirmatively. "And a major corruption problem in Loudoun County. I knew there was some kind of connection, I just looked in the wrong direction."

Gif glared at Mavis, looked at Tracey, and tried to figure out how to warn her that the corruption investigation cover story would not work.

"I confided to Mavis that we asked you to lead the federal investigation but you refused because you were too close to Harrison Tate," Tracey said. "She promised not to use that confidence."

"Tracey also promised that you would give me the exclusives," Mavis smiled insincerely.

"Exclusives?" Gif demanded.

"Yes, on the Redskin thing and the corruption investigation," Mavis said.

"You shouldn't have done that," Gif frowned at Tracey.

"But I did dear. Please don't let me down. Besides, Mavis knows that we are back together."

"Oh shit," Gif feigned exasperation.

"Is it a deal?" Mavis demanded. "Or should I call my crewman who's sitting in that hot cab pointing his camera at us. The poor dear is dying of thirst."

Gif glanced at the truck, aimed his worst frown at Mavis, and declared: "OK, it's a deal, with one caveat. You cannot use the corruption investigation story until I say you can. If you break it prematurely, there are a lot of corrupt officials who will crawl into their holes and pull them in after them."

Mavis frowned, giving Gif the impression she was going to negotiate, but instead smiled and turned to Tracey. "He really is a dear, isn't he?"

"Is it a deal?" Gif insisted, recognizing he was dealing from an extremely weak position.

"I normally don't do this, Gif," Mavis said. "I will hold off on the corruption story but will use everything I get my hands on dealing with the Redskin investigation. Agreed?"

"Agreed," Gif relaxed.

"One more thing," Mavis said. She hesitated. "No two things. You have to promise to give me an exclusive on the corruption investigation. Agreed?"

"Agreed," Gif felt like he was still climbing uphill.

"And, right now," Mavis said. "You must pose with me."

"What kind of pose?" Gif asked.

"You and I just stand over there," Mavis pointed to the lawn and pretend we are chatting like friends."

"You're kidding me."

"I need a shot of you for the six o'clock," Mavis said.

"Gif frowned.

"I know, dear," Mavis said. "But my producer insists."

"No voice," Gif said.

"No voice," Mavis agreed. "Deal?"

"Deal."

Mavis smiled, stood up, tossed her empty bottle over her shoulder, and patted Tracey on the knee. She waved to her cameraman and led Gif out on to his lawn where she stood with her back to the woods. Gif reluctantly joined her. The cameraman rushed from the truck, pointed his camera and a little red light came on. Mavis smiled at a frowning Gif.

"See, this isn't so bad. Smile for the birdie," Mavis said.

Gif almost answered but caught himself just in time.

Mavis touched Gif's arm like an old friend, leaned over, and kissed Gif on the cheek.

Gif turned away. The light on the camera went off, and the cameraman gave Mavis a thumbs up.

"Mind if I borrow a beer for my friend in the truck? To seal the bargain?" Mavis said.

Gif nodded sourly, hoping Mavis appreciated his attempt at playing a poor sport, and waited while Mavis raided his fridge. She returned from the kitchen with what were probably the last two bottles off frosty Bud and returned to the truck. Mavis closed the satellite truck door, handed one bottle to the driver, tossed the cap of her beer out the window, and held the bottle up as a toast to Gif.

"Christ," Gif complained as the truck drove away.

"I know," Tracey smiled at him. "She was here when I arrived."

"The team?"

"Fortunately, they were not here. I entertained her with bullshit and a couple of beers, and you, dear, came to my rescue. Did you have a bad day at the office?"

"At this point," Gif admitted. "I don't have a clue. What's for dinner?"

"That's the very question I've had on my mind," Tracey smiled sweetly.

"We've got to quit using the corruption investigation cover story," Gif said

"Why?"

"I wasn't thinking when I suggested it," Gif said. "There are some local officials whose support I need, and I'm afraid the damned cover story will send them all into hiding."

"Dick Simmons?" Tracey's question told Gif that she knew more than she was admitting.

"Yes," Gif answered honestly.

"Want to discuss it?"

"No," Gif said.

"Who was on the phone?" Tracey changed the subject.

"You wouldn't believe me if I told you," Gif said.

"Yes I would," Tracey said. "It was the good doctor, wasn't it?"

"Yes, but she had nothing to say that would affect our plans," Gif smiled. "Let's see if we've got any beer left."

Chapter 27

The next morning Gif and Tracey were still in bed when the first cars arrived. Oddly, they had spent the evening without discussing a single one of the cases that troubled them both. As soon as the front door slammed, Tracey leaped out of bed.

"Me first," she said as she headed towards the bathroom.

Gif, who normally would be mortally embarrassed to be caught in such a potentially incriminating circumstance, simply shrugged. Gif lay back in bed and relaxed as he listened to the various familiar sounds that emanated from the rest of the house, the voices, male and female, that penetrated his bedroom wall. He had so many problems circulating in his head that he really didn't care what the members of his team might think. They were all adults, members of the liberal minded generation.

Finally, Tracey, shiny, clean, and undressed, opened the bathroom door.

"What do you think?" She asked as she posed in the doorway.

"We'll catch the bastards," Gif grinned, deliberately misinterpreting her question.

"Gifford, you're a worse shit than people think," Tracey laughed as she started dressing.

Gif leaped out of bed, stark naked, and headed for the bathroom doorway where he paused to pose, mimicking Tracey.

"What do you think?" Gif asked.

"You better catch the bastards," Tracey laughed. "You've got nothing else going for you."

Gif raised his hands in surrender and closed the door behind him.

Fifteen minutes later, he emerged to find the bedroom deserted.

He dressed and exited the bedroom to join his full team, even Billie Williams.

"You don't look the worse for all that wear," Sarah Whitestone greeted him from her seat at the table.

Gif shrugged. "I need coffee."

"That's what Ms. Schultz said before she rushed out of here," Truman Johnson smiled.

Gif ignored the laughter, heated his coffee in the microwave, returned to his dining table, shoved papers and files to the side, sipped his coffee and then exerted his authority. "All right guys, where do we stand?"

Everybody laughed. "You are a real David Letterman," Joyce Tryon said.

"No, Conan," Harold Creighton said.

"No, Jay," Jerry Quigley said.

"Very funny," Gif frowned.

"Right, boss," Truman Johnson took charge. "Billie has already briefed us on your day. You hit the hot spots in D.C., chatted with the boy owner, and interviewed the fish at Point of Rocks. Do you have anything you want to share with the group?"

Gif hesitated. Truman had caught him without an agenda.

"But he had a good evening," Sarah Whitestone cracked. "The task force commander reported that Mavis Davis dropped by early, and then the two of you had a relatively quiet …whatever. Gif you have to look after than woman; she's showing the strain."

"Of whatever…" Joyce Tryon laughed.

Gif sipped his coffee and waited for the chuckles to subside. "Truman," Gif gave his deputy a chance to report.

"Sarah?" Truman passed the ball to Sarah Whitestone.

"I'm the referent for the Tate shooting," Sarah announced.

"We're all sharing everything, with each investigator responsible for one of the cases," Truman explained.

Gif nodded.

"I'm not quite sure what you expect of us, Gif," Sarah adopted her "I'm being serious now" mien. "Take me," she winked at Joyce Tryon, while letting the extended pause add ambiguity to her comment.

Everybody laughed dutifully.

"Take me," Sarah began again. "I visited the task force where I learned that you had already alerted their troops that one of your representatives would be visiting. Thank you. It would have been helpful, less stressful, if you had shared that little piece of information."

Sarah paused to give Gif a chance to apologize. He did not. He hadn't seen Sarah since his meeting with Tracey and Tom Harrington.

"The bureau has a couple of hundred agents working the Tate assassination, so I'm not sure what you expect me to accomplish," Sarah resumed her report. 'Anyway, a Special Agent Reggie Crawford, I believe you are acquainted with Reggie, arranged a badge for me, and buried me under a mountain of files. That's how I spent my day. As best as I could tell, the bureau covered the crime scene on the river and came up with zilch. The task force has duplicate copies of all the Secret Service files that the Protective Intelligence and Assessment Division maintains on threats. They average ten threats a day, so do the math. It adds up to over 900 threats for a three-month period. The files on the follow-up investigations and name traces hold a ton of paper. I didn't even try to read that stuff. Reggie assured me that she personally has reviewed every page without identifying a single crackpot who could have been near the river on the day in question. I didn't touch the subject of political conspiracy. Bottom line: the task force doesn't have a solid clue as to the identity of the shooter. What did you find out on your visit to the river?" Sarah asked Gif.

"Let me defer to Billie on that," Gif passed the buck to the deputy sheriff, catching him by surprise as he was lifting his coffee cup to his lips.

"Right," Billie set his cup on the table and folded his hands. "We sat for a while on the porch and chatted about the good old days in the sheriff's department. We discussed recent personnel changes and admired the view. I noted that the area was surprisingly underdeveloped, and the inspector observed that the local Redskins were conspicuous in their absence. From where we were sitting, neither of us could spot a single feather, a strange development that the inspector attributed to the likelihood that modern day Indians in the area all wore helmets not headdresses. After discussing this odd cultural phenomenon, the inspector changed the subject and admitted that he might have made a mistake in selecting the team's cover story."

Abruptly, Billie terminated his recitation and grabbed his coffee cup, surprising everyone with the nature and terseness of his report.

After a few seconds of silence, the room erupted in laughter and applause.

"Sounds like a productive visit," Sarah spoke first.

"Rather typical of the way the chief handles investigations," Joyce Tryon added.

"I'm disappointed that you didn't find any feathers," Harold Creighton who Truman had assigned to the Redskin investigation pretended to frown.

"I'm more interested in the problems with the cover story," Truman Johnson, the team leader declared. "Seriously, chief," he looked directly at Gif.

Taken by surprise and still not into the meeting, Gif hesitated before answering. He certainly didn't want to get involved in a discussion about graft, particularly that possibly involving his friend and former protégé Dick Simmons, whose support they all might need as their investigations developed. Gif frowned his disapproval at Billie for dropping this sensitive issue in front of the team without warning.

"Congratulations, Billie," Sarah declared. "Earning a frown with your initial report at your first meeting is a record."

Everyone clapped, Billie smiled, and Gif reacted.

"This is serious stuff," Gif said, trying to get the meeting under control. "I made a mistake in suggesting that cover story. We don't want any of the local media picking up on our alleged investigating of local corruption and getting the wrong people worried. We need all the support we can get from the local authorities."

"Do any of you have any suggestions?" Gif asked.

"Why don't we say we're conducting a statewide investigation into rampant prostitution," Sarah blurted.

"I volunteer to take on the local houses of ill repute," Jerry Quigley raised his hand.

Gif shook his head negatively.

"What about drug trafficking?" Truman suggested seriously.

"That will get the DEA on our backs," Harold Creighton said.

"Why don't we limit it to the recruitment of minors for immoral purposes," Sarah said.

"Let's just say we are conducting a sensitive investigation that we can't discuss," Gif decided. "Refer any questions to me personally. Billie, the floor is still yours," Gif tried to get the discussion refocused on the investigations.

"Yes sir," Billie replied deferentially. "We took a boat ride to the spot of the shooting, identified where the shooter had to fire from, went up, and took a look. Gif decided that we should re-interview every resident, everyone who has been identified as being in the area at the time."

"I can help there," Sarah said. "I made a copy of the list of names of residents and passers-by that the task force interviewed and re-interviewed."

"Good," Gif said. "Sarah, you and Billie can work that list but don't let it control you. Ask everyone for the names of anyone they saw in the area during that time frame in recent weeks. And, Billie, please pay particular attention to any of the cars that your department dispatched to the scene to support the presidential detail."

"Yes, sir," Billie said.

"We're going to need help," Sarah protested, overriding Billie's "Yes sir."

"Just do it, Sarah, we don't have a hundred agents to deploy," Gif ordered.

"You and your yes sirs," Sarah complained to Billie.

Billie answered with a shrug. "You ought to try shuffling papers at a desk in a local sheriff's office."

"I'll help with the interviews," Harold volunteered.

"Good, now let's keep moving along," Gif glanced at Truman.

"Right," Truman reacted. "Time is against us. Joyce, do you have anything to share?"

"I've got the Walker thing, whatever it is, and the call girl, Nan Starbright. I talked with the building supervisor and the other residents in the Crystal City apartment--those that I could find--where Walker died, debriefed Walker's secretary, and I plan to visit Nan/Barby Dolle's apartment before taking on the task force investigators and files. Do you think this Reggie Crawford will open the door for me?" Joyce Tryon looked at Sarah Whitestone.

"I've got her phone number, Joyce," Sarah answered.

"My initial reaction is one that everyone I talked to seem to share. Walker's death was a terrible tragedy that simply coincided with the Tate shooting," Sarah said.

"It's still early times in the investigation," Gif cautioned.

"Are you implying that we really have a political conspiracy on our hands like the media alleges?" Truman asked.

"No, guys, I meant exactly what I said. Nothing more. It is still too early in our investigations to reach a judgment of any kind. We're backtracking the work of professional investigators and we must avoid sending the wrong kind of message," Gif said.

"What you're saying, chief," Sarah interpreted for the others. "Is that we're treading in troubled waters. Tread carefully."

"That's right, Sarah," Gif nodded.

"Wade don't tread," Harold suggested.

"But we sometimes get our feet wet," Billie laughed.

The others looked at him curiously. "Care to elaborate?" Truman asked.

"When we landed the boat," Billie said. "The inspector jumped out into knee deep water. He ruined his best shoes and pants."

Everyone laughed.

"That's enough humor for today," Gif said as he stood up, terminating the meeting. "Like you, I have a few things to do today."

"Don't you have anything to share?" Sarah asked.

"No," Gif smiled as he headed for the front door.

"I've got the Redskin follow-up," Harold called after him. "Don't you want to brief me on your visit there yesterday?"

Gif paused. "You're right. Billie, brief Harold and the team on our meeting with the boy owner."

Gif decided to begin his day with a visit to the Loudoun County Sheriff's Office, an act he had performed every day for a good twenty years of his life.

In the Andrew Johnson Suite at the Treasury Department, Acting President Hiram Alphonse Adams and his best friend and chief of staff Jake Tyrone were engaged in something they did every morning. They were enjoying a coffee laced with Jack Daniels, a little bit of the hair of the dog, while they discussed the day's relatively modest schedule. Unlike most of his predecessors, Hiram Adams was not a hands-on president. Jimmy Carter among others had worried every little detail, a passion that Hiram shrugged off like a casual wave from a disinterested bystander.

"We've got Clark Kendall scheduled for ten," Jake Tyrone referred to the Mayor of Jefferson City.

"My agenda sounds just like it did down there," Hiram chuckled as he waved a thumb in the direction of Capitol Hill.

"I can jazz the schedule up a little if you want, Hiram," Jake said. He knew the talking heads were chatting about the acting president's casual approach to office with even their supporters beginning to speculate that he might be too old for the heavy responsibilities that came with the job.

"Don't over-react, Jake."

Hiram could still read his friend like a book, a little book with big print because Hiram wasn't a reader. "We can't be too concerned about what those northern intellectuals think."

"Maybe, just for appearances, I should release a schedule showing your morning briefings, meetings with your National Security Advisor, maybe the Secretary of State."

"Jake, Jake," Hiram laughed. "We both know I cancelled those damned briefings. They're boring, the same stuff over and over. A bombing in Baghdad, a demonstration in Manila, a one percent drop in the value of the dollar. And I don't even have a National Security Advisor."

"There are all kinds of advisors and assistants sitting over there in the West Wing scratching their heads and waiting to be told what to do," Jake said.

"Waiting to tell me what to do," Hiram corrected Jake. "But, they're not my advisors and assistants. They all belong to the beloved Harrison Tate."

"Why don't we rectify that? I have the first draft of a list of names and positions," Jake said

Jake, acting on an Adams request, had their Capitol Hill political staff in the Rayburn building working hard to refine the list of proposed White House assignments.

"All things in due course, Jake, in due course. We don't want the voters to think that we are stomping on Tate's grave before the dirt dries. Give that task force time to find the killer first."

"Or not find him," Jake said.

"Or not find him," Hiram agreed. "Care for a touch more?" Hiram asked as he topped off his coffee cup.

"Thank you, Mr. President, not this morning."

Hiram raised his cup in mock toast to Jake. "So we got ole Clark Kendall coming for a visit. Christ, Jake, my daddy must be turning over in his grave, me sitting here as president with that little pickaninny from down the road dropping in to pay his respects."

"The correct word today is African American," Jake corrected.

"I remember when Mr. African American Clark Kendall was a colored cutting daddy's lawn with a push mower," Hiram said. "Paid him fifteen cents and that was all he was worth."

"The mayor has been organizing the African American vote for you in Jefferson City for thirty years," Jake persisted.

"Oh stop it, Jake. You know I'm no racist. I'm just reminiscing about my daddy, and when I do I don't get the politically correct words right."

"I know, but we have at least one more election ahead of us," Jake cautioned, "the biggest one of all."

"I know. Walls have ears, Jake. You're the one who's always telling me that."

"Maybe we should think about moving over to that big house next door," Jake said. "At least there we can control who's doing the bugging."

"That's what Dick Nixon thought and look what happened to him," Hiram chuckled.

Before Jake could respond, the acting president's intercom buzzed. Hiram pushed the lever. "Yes Miss Mary." Hiram always treated the third member of their little Missouri team with respect. Mary Murphy had been with him for longer than even Jake.

"The acting vice president wishes to speak with you, sir," Miss Mary said.

"Oh put him on," Hiram answered.

"No sir, he's standing outside your door waiting for permission to enter."

"Tell him Jake and I are working on my schedule. I'll get back to him."

"The vice president says he has a major problem with Congress, and he needs to consult with you urgently," Miss Mary persisted.

"OK," Hiram said. He glanced at Jake. "You heard that? What's chewing on his ass?"

"Your acting vice president, Tate's secretary of the treasury, presented his famous plan to select committee chairmen yesterday afternoon," Jake said.

"I'll bet he enjoyed that," Hiram laughed as Acting Vice President and Secretary of the Treasury Alexander Hamilton Sperry entered the room.

"I apologize, sir, for disturbing your meeting with your chief of staff," the grim faced New Yorker glanced disapprovingly at Hiram's coffee cup. "But I need your advice and assistance."

"Will you have a cup?" Hiram ignored the humorless man's disapproval. He had selected Sperry to serve as his acting vice president, a calculated political act, and not a demonstration of confidence or admiration for the man. Besides, Hiram considered it only a short-term aberration.

"No thank you, Mr. President," Sperry answered coldly, clutching a book-sized sheath of papers in his hand as he waited to be invited to take a seat. Sperry did not like the acting president any more than Adams liked him.

Hiram thought about making Sperry stand but decided against it. He considered himself a gentleman and did not act out of spite, not over petty things like standing or sitting.

"Please sit down and join us, sir. Frankly, we were just chatting about my schedule, not plotting or deciding the fate of the world." Hiram said, practicing a line he intended to use with his ten o'clock visitor. "We have a few minutes before our next appointment," Hiram glanced at Jake for confirmation.

"Yes sir, just three to be precise," Jake reacted as expected.

"We've got a serious problem, sir," Sperry waved his papers. "This might take a lot longer than that."

Hiram smiled indulgently and waited.

"I thought our legislative liaison people had the skids greased," Sperry said. "But somebody or some group is working in the background." Sperry waited for Adams or Tyrone to comment. They were the congressional experts.

"The Congress has a way of doing that," Adams chuckled.

Sperry did not react; he waited for the ex-Speaker to at least ask a question about the critical legislation. The vital seconds allotted to him ticked past, and Sperry grew more anxious.

"I met jointly with the chairmen of the six key committees, all accompanied by the senior member of the opposition," Sperry decided to force the issue. "They've had my draft plan for a week, and I agreed to a conference to address any questions or concerns they might have." He paused, again, to give Adams a chance to display his expertise.

Adams nodded but said nothing.

"Not a single person from either party asked a question," Sperry declared. "We're talking about the welfare of our economy, the future of the damned country, and they asked not a question."

"I know that can be frustrating," Adams sympathized.

"It's more than frustrating, sir. It's stupid. Somebody's playing politics at a time of national crisis."

"Can you attach names to that accusation?" Jake asked, speaking for the first time.

"I was hoping that you or the president might help me."

"Certainly, somebody said something," Jake said.

"They told me they had my plan under advisement," Sperry raised his voice. "Who the hell is going to study my recommendations? Some damned fresh out of college staffer?"

"I would say more than one," Jake chuckled. "Six committees, two parties, I would say at least a hundred."

"A hundred what?" Sperry demanded, not the least interested in what the president's bourbon drinking, good old boy crony had to say.

"Staffers," Jake said.

"I suspect they don't like your plan," Adams said, stressing the "your."

"I think you can anticipate the Congress will submit its own plan," Jake spoke directly to Sperry. "You can expect a major rewrite of your proposal."

"It isn't a proposal," Sperry said as he waved the paper mass in the air. "This two thousand page plan authorizes hundreds of complicated, carefully integrated actions designed to get us out of this damned recession. If we don't act now, the recession could deteriorate into the worst depression that this country has ever suffered. Decades could pass before the economy recovers on its own, if ever."

"I'm sure that our congressional colleagues understand that," Adams displayed his most serious expression.

"They don't act like they do," Sperry said, his strident tone indicating that he was on the brink of losing his temper.

"Why don't we let Jake take a glance at your plan," Adams said. "And, depending on his findings, we'll see if there might be a few levers we could pull or whistles we could blow. We might even consider having our public affairs office release a position paper."

"We're well past that point, sir. The time has come for you to lean on your old colleagues, hard. You have to get engaged."

"I could have someone take a close look at the secretary's plan," Jake ignored Sperry's acting vice presidential rank, "and see what we can come up with."

"You've had the plan on your desk for a full week," Sperry glared at Tyrone.

"Jake, I'll leave this little matter in your hands," Adams decided. "Now, Mr. Vice President, you are going to have to excuse us. Jake and I have a few things to discuss before my ten o'clock."

Sperry's face turned bright red. "Mr. Speaker…Mr. President," he corrected himself. "That just is not sufficient."

"I will not need your copy, Mr. Secretary," Jake stood up and spoke before Sperry could finish his protest. "I'll put my assistant to work on locating that copy you say I have in my possession. I must have mislaid it somehow."

While Jake was distracting the angry vice president, Adams punched the intercom. "Miss Mary, please have my Secret Service fellow come in. Jake and I have a few things we need to coordinate with him.

An angry Sperry turned from Tyrone to glare at the president. The outer door opened abruptly, and an intense Secret Service agent entered the room.

"Sir?" The agent looked at the president.

"Oh thank you," Adams smiled. "The acting vice president is just leaving."

The puzzled agent stepped back and Sperry looked in disbelief at Adams and then Tyrone. Recognizing that he had been outmaneuvered, he decided he had two choices, to leave as ordered, or to be thrown out. Sperry thought about continuing his protest. Adams, Tyrone and the agent waited. Finally, Sperry capitulated. He turned towards the door and brushed past the waiting agent.

As soon as Sperry cleared the doorway, Adams nodded at the agent.

"Thank you, sir," Adams said. "You may close the door as you leave."

"I think that went well, Jake," Adams nodded at his friend. "Would you like a little nip before our next visitor?"

A chuckling Jake sat back down, shaking his head negatively as he did so.

"When will our friends in the House put our/their plan to a vote?" Adams asked.

"In time to catch the evening network newscasts," Jake answered.

"Do we have the votes?"

"We wouldn't let it reach the floor if we didn't. We had to give our Republican colleagues their small victories, but we've got a bill we can all live with."

"Politics is a little more than simple comprises honestly reached," the former Speaker laughed. "I'm sure it's going to cost us."

"Nothing we can't live with," Jake smiled.

"I don't know what I would do without you, Jake," Adams chuckled as he poured another small nip into his coffee cup before returning Jack

Daniels to his crib in the desk drawer. "It's too bad that old Andrew Johnson can't witness our little maneuvering to learn how easily we in today's Congress deal with the executive branch. Direct confrontations sometimes relieve all that emotional pressure, but they never solve the real problems.

"Remind me to never trade horses with you," Jake laughed. "You don't really expect me to read that damned plan. It would take me a month and I wouldn't understand a word of it."

"I don't think anyone else would either, Jake."

Gif parked his Prius in the visitor's slot behind the bowling alley and entered via the back door. He nodded at the security deputies and made his way to his old office. He waved at Kitty's replacement, who smiled but did not welcome him, and entered the sheriff's office to find Dick Simmons behind his big fancy desk.

"Gif," Simmons greeted him without offering his hand.

"Want to try sitting here? To see if it still feels the same," Simmons slapped his hand on the arm of his fancy executive chair.

Gif shook his head and sat down in one of the padded chairs that faced his and Harrison's old place of command. Even the drapes behind Simmons's chair had been changed.

"How are things going?" Simmons asked, his tone a trifle too forced to please Gif who remembered how it felt to sit with his back to those same windows.

"I wish I had never heard of the Redskins," Gif said.

"Anything you can share?" Simmons asked.

"How are your investigators doing?" Gif countered.

"They are not doing well. They've looked at the hazing, the violence on the practice field, the argument over the girls," Simmons said. "They've identified a couple players with potential motives, all weak, but they haven't developed any evidence that proves another team member fired the shotgun. They haven't come up with the name of another Redskin who owns a twelve gage."

"Neither have we," Gif agreed. "We looked at those things you mentioned. I'm having trouble with the killer's motive. If anyone on the team had a reason to retaliate, it was the two boys who were shot. They were the ones who were being treated unfairly. I'm not sure where to look next."

Simmons nodded, giving Gif the impression that Simmons was only feigning interest.

"We're depending on you, Gif," Simmons said.

"It could have been a disgruntled fan, a boy friend of one of the girls, or just an unhappy drunk," Gif ignored Simmons' comment.

"I wish you luck."

"All we can do is just keep asking questions," Gif said.

Something about Simmons' demeanor troubled Gif. His old protégé appeared to be just going through the motions. There was no fire in the man. Gif had the impression that Simmons really didn't care how the investigation was going. Gif had to admit, however, that his view could be colored by what he had learned about changes in Simmons life style and standard of living.

"Is Billie doing OK?" Simmons asked.

"Billie? He's fine. The problem is me," Gif said.

"Oh?"

"Yes," Gif did not elaborate.

"Would you like someone else assigned to assist your investigation?" Simmons asked.

"No, we'll struggle through. Sometimes, though, I wish I had Gizzie to back me up."

"Gizzie? I know how much you thought of her," Simmons said. He hesitated, waiting for Gif to react.

Gif did not.

"Have you talked with her lately?" Simmons asked.

Gif shrugged, noncommittally.

"I'm sorry to have to tell you that Gizzie reached that point we all ultimately reach, earlier than most I'm afraid."

Gif said nothing.

"Early burnout," Simmons said.

"This job eats on most of us," Gif agreed. "From the inside out."

"Exactly that's what happened to Gizzie. I understand that she is a real housewife, these days."

"I'm sorry to hear that," Gif said.

"Me, too," Simmons agreed. "Do you think you will be able to catch the Redskin shooter for us?"

"I don't know," Gif replied. "Maybe I'm suffering from the same thing as Gizzie. The Harrison thing hit me hard."

"I know," Simmons said. "I felt all hollow inside."

Gif was not sure he was sincere.

"Has your team developed anything that Billie and I missed?"

"I doubt that," Simmons said. "You state and federal guys have resources that we local guys lack."

"Brains and instinct are not limited to the state and federal levels," Gif said. "I stopped by and visited Gizzie," Gif admitted, testing Simmons for a reaction.

"I was really sorry to lose that girl," Simmons said.

"I think she misses the place too," Gif played the game.

"Did she say why she left?" Simmons asked. "She never gave me a reason. Burn out was just my guess."

"I think her feminine instincts kicked in," Gif lied. "I also paid a visit to Martha," Gif said, watching his former friend closely.

"How is she taking it?" Simmons feigned compassion.

"You wouldn't believe it, Dick. She ran off all of her Secret Service detail and fired the help. She said she's lived in the Leesburg house almost all her life, took care of it herself, and didn't need all the attention."

"You're right. I don't believe it. I hope she knows that if she needs any help whatsoever, all of her old friends are only a few blocks away."

"She knows it, Dick. I think she needs solitude in a familiar setting. Neither she nor Harrison felt comfortable on Pennsylvania Avenue."

"I wouldn't either," Simmons replied.

After having seen Simmons' new mansion in Waterford, Gif believed him. The White House would seem like too much of a come down.

"Well, Dick, I just wanted to touch base," Gif said. "I appreciate your loan of Willie's services."

"Good," Simmons said. "I hear that you've brought some of your OSI people in to help with your investigation. That surprised me. I know you like to do your own leg work."

Gif answered with a nod. "We all get older, Dick. I find the leg work puts a lot of strain on old joints."

Simmons smiled. "I also hear that you are covering old ground. It doesn't sound like your joints are slowing you down much."

Gif picked up on the innuendo in the 'old ground' remark. "I assume your source told you that Tracey and I have negotiated a truce?"

"I don't blame you, Gif. Tracey is still a damned sexy woman. A little tough on the edges for my taste. She intimidates me."

"You ought to try living with an orthopedic surgeon," Gif said.

"You've got more stamina than I have."

"I hear that you and Polly split." Gif smiled as he demonstrated that two could play the 'I hear' game.

"Yes," Simmons stared at Gif. "We ran into a patch of troubled water; I'm sorry to say. I've remarried, to a much younger lady. It takes a lot out of a fellow, just keeping up."

"Really, I'm sorry to hear that Dick," Gif left his response ambiguous, letting his former protégé wonder if Gif referred to his first marriage or paramour.

"I've got to get back to work, Dick," Gif said. "It has been interesting talking with you."

"Please don't forget about our Redskin problem," Simmons stood up from behind his ornate desk.

"No problem, Dick. Now that I have help, I'll push a little harder," Gif said. "Mind if I pass the time of day with a few old friends on my way out?"

"Of course not, Gif," Simmons said. "Please ask Billie to keep in touch. Remind him that we're still paying his salary."

Gif left Simmons office with an uneasy feeling in the pit of his stomach. The brief exchange with his former protégé had turned into a fencing match. He now understood why Gizzie and Billie felt as they did even though they were too considerate to speak frankly. Gif nodded at Kitty's replacement and departed with the strong sense that this could be his last visit to a place he had once considered a second home.

Gif turned right, looked back to see if he were being followed, took the stairs to the basement, and entered the drab office that housed the department's lifeline, the communications center. There, he found a familiar face.

"Sheriff Gifford," a matronly lady who had been serving as dispatcher when Gif first joined the department greeted him.

Gif struggled to remember her name. Before he could respond, the dispatcher's radio crackled.

"52, 52, mother, where in the hell are you?"

"Mother, 52, sorry about that. I was chatting with Sheriff Gifford."

"Oh," the deputy in Car 52 responded.

The man's reaction told Gif that the deputy didn't have a clue who Sheriff Gifford was, but the conversation gave him the name he was trying to recall. Mother was Faye Tucker's handle, the name she used on the airways.

"What can I do for you 52," Faye spoke into her microphone as she rolled her eyes at Gif. "Another new guy," she whispered.

"I need a check on Virginia plates, Wild Guy," the deputy laughed. "I know," the deputy continued, "but that's what they say, Wild Guy."

"Roger that 52, standby," Faye responded.

"Faye, I'm sorry to bother you," Gif said. "But I need to check your logs for the day of the Tate thing."

"Sure thing, Gif, help yourself," the friendly dispatcher pointed at the computer on a nearby desk. "Alice won't mind."

"Thanks," Gif smiled. "I won't be long."

"I have to warn you," Faye called to Gif's back. "Billie and half the federal government have already been here and done that. I don't think they found anything."

"You know me, Faye; I have to see it for myself before I believe it."

Faye chuckled dutifully and returned her attention to Car 52's request.

Gif sat down, moved the mouse to wake the sleeping computer, checked the program map, and selected vehicle logs. It took a few seconds to locate the right date. He quickly scanned the entries until he got to the right time frame. There, he found the names for the cars and deputies who had been dispatched to provide area support to the Harrison Tate's Secret Service detail at the river. Gif took out his notebook and jotted down the names. Nothing in the log stood out for him, not until the entries started flowing for the time of the shooting. At exactly 1608 hours, the report of the attack caused a major reaction; the dispatcher responded with an all points bulletin ordering patrols to set up roadblocks throughout the area at intersections within fifteen miles of the Tate riverfront home.

Gif leaned back and glanced at Faye who was still occupied with her radio. The information in the log told him nothing because he assumed that Billie was already interviewing the deputies who had manned the initial four vehicles assigned to support the protection team. Gif started to rise then had a sudden thought. He referred to the program map again and selected the log for unmarked vehicles. When he located the entry for the date and time of the shooting, he found that only one unmarked vehicle had been logged out. That posed no surprise, but the identity of the person who had taken the car gave him a start. Sheriff Richard Simmons had signed for a fifteen-year-old Toyota at 1405 and had not returned it until the next day. Gif leaned back in his chair and thought back to his days as sheriff. He could not recall ever having used an unmarked vehicle. His preference had run to a new Bronco or cruiser. The department, at least then, had few unmarked cars, all of which were clunkers whose virtue was their ability to pass unnoticed not their reliability.

Gif moved the computer mouse to another date, that of the Redskin shooting at Tiny's. Again, he found only one entry in the unmarked vehicle log, and again it was Sheriff Richard Simmons who had signed out the same old Toyota.

Gif put the computer back to sleep, paused to offer silent thanks to the still busy dispatcher, and closed the door behind him just as two young deputies were passing.

"You say the old lady uses mother as a handle?" One of them said as he stared at his companion.

"That's her choice?"

"So I'm told."

"Christ that's funny," the first deputy joined his companion in laughter. "A woman whose name is Tucker calls herself mother."

Gif at first had difficulty fathoming what was so funny about that. Everyone had always called Faye mother. Suddenly, a realization about what the deputies were laughing about struck him. He had worked with Faye for over twenty years, known her for over thirty, and no one had ever referred in his presence to the oddity of that nickname. Faye was a Mother Tucker. Gif left the department wondering if Faye did it deliberately to amuse or challenge the tough talking deputies or if she was really that oblivious to street talk.

An irate Acting Vice President/Secretary of the Treasury Alexander Hamilton Sperry slammed the door to the Andrew Johnson Suite behind him, not caring who might notice, and crossed the corridor to his own much grander offices.

"Get Clapp in here," he growled at his wide-eyed secretary.

"He's waiting inside," the secretary answered. Although she had served Sperry in Albany and New York, she could not remember seeing him this angry.

As soon as Sperry had disappeared into his own office, banging the door shut behind him, the secretary turned to her assistant who occupied a desk across the large room, shrugged her shoulders, shook her head in disapproval, and spoke softly.

"We're going to be walking on egg shells around here today."

The assistant moved her wrist with extended fingers in the universal sign of shaking off trouble and turned to face her computer screen.

The door to the corridor opened, and an attractive assistant secretary of the treasury entered, not one of Sperry's New York mafia but a political appointee engineered by an influential Ohio senator. Rumor had it that she was the senator's mistress who had been stashed in the Treasury Department in a senior position, a matter of financial accommodation and geographic convenience.

"I need to see the vice president immediately," the assistant secretary announced, waving a document in the air.

"The vice president is in conference," the lead secretary held up a restraining palm.

"He'll see me," the assistant secretary declared as she placed her hand on the doorknob leading to the inner office.

"Honey, enter at your own risk," the older secretary said as she exchanged anticipatory looks with her assistant who leaned even closer to her computer screen.

The assistant secretary opened the door. Before she could step inside or utter a single word, the acting vice president who was now seated about thirty yards away behind his massive desk shouted: "Get the hell out of here."

The ashen faced assistant secretary quickly retreated, carefully closing the door softly behind her. She turned on the vice president's executive secretary. "Why didn't you warn me?" She asked, unable to control the tremor in her voice.

"I think I did, honey. Next time, listen," the vice president's secretary replied with a smile.

The assistant secretary hurried to the door to the outer corridor. "The senator is going to hear about this," she huffed.

"I wouldn't be surprised," the acting vice president's secretary chuckled.

"This place is a loony bin," her assistant whispered.

In the inner office, Acting Vice President Sperry grabbed the huge report containing his economic plan and threw it at the window across the room. The heavy object hit the bulletproof glass, bounced off, landed on a table, struck a large antique lamp, and fell with the lamp to the floor.

Clete Clapp, the acting vice president's chief of staff, who was sitting comfortably on the large leather sofa with his crossed feet resting on the coffee table, leaned forward, appraised the tangle of wire and fragments of colored antique glass on the floor, and laughed.

"Nice shot. I understand that was made from a vase that was one of Andrew Johnson's prize possessions."

"He won't miss it," Sperry pushed himself out of his chair, circled his desk, and walked over to the debris. He kicked his economic plan, sending it in a shower of colored glass chips across the room where it slid unceremoniously into the open door of the suite's private john.

"I take it that the meeting with Adams went no better than our session last night with those congressional shits," Clapp said.

"It's not funny," Sperry said as he gave the dented lampshade a kick. As a demonstration of anger, the effort failed. The shade wrapped itself around Sperry's shoe and resisted his efforts to dislodge it.

Clapp stifled the urge to laugh.

Sperry stamped his foot until he liberated it from the damned shade and returned to his desk where he sat down and stared at his assistant.

"Don't sit there grinning like a goddamned monkey, do something," Sperry ordered.

Clapp, not the least bit intimidated, sat up straight, deliberately uncrossed his ankles, lifted his feet from the gleaming glass coffee table, and kicked the damned thing. It crashed against the two upholstered chairs that faced the sofa. The table, unbroken, landed on its side, spilling crystal bric-a-brac, gifts from affluent lobbyists, in all directions. Both Clapp and Sperry watched as a hand-blown Corning ware vase rolled half way to the massive desk.

"Shit," Sperry exclaimed.

Clapp, not sure if Sperry was passing judgment on the results of his kick or still complaining about his reception in the Andrew Johnson Suite, decided it best if he did not ask. Clapp knew that Sperry needed him to handle the heavy lifting, but he feared that thing with the coffee table might have been a little drastic.

Sperry leaned back in his chair and growled at his assistant. "Sometimes, Clapp, you push your luck."

Clapp in a show of independence, leaned his head back against the armrest, turned and arrogantly placed his legs, shoe clad feet and all, on the sofa. Now in a reclining position, he stared at the ceiling and tried to project an attitude of total indifference. He knew from experience that was the only way to cope with Sperry when he was having one of his tantrums.

The two sat that way in total silence until Sperry finally broke it about ten long minutes later.

"Clete, I suspect we may have underestimated that old man."

Clapp, who knew that when Sperry used his first name he was working his way back to earth from whatever orbit he might be in, nodded, but he did not reply. He waited for Adams to talk himself down.

"He set us up. The bastard has had an agenda from the very

beginning," Sperry said. "He's going to run for president on his own economic plan, the country be damned."

Clapp was tempted to point out that Sperry should not be surprised. Sperry was doing the same thing himself, but Clapp kept his mouth shut. His time for talking would come later.

"Adams and that Missouri jackass he calls his chief of staff just sit over there," Adams glared at the wall in the direction of the Andrew Johnson Suite, "laughing at us while they plot how they are going to use us."

"A damned abuse of your generous hospitality," Clapp agreed.

Sperry glared at his assistant, wondering if he were patronizing him.

"We should evict him," Clapp tried to recover. "A president belongs in the White House with his own people around him."

"He just sits here pretending he is standing like a Colossus with one foot on the Congress and the other on the White House," Sperry rather liked that metaphor.

Clapp was tempted to note that this modern day Colossus also had one fist grasped firmly around Sperry's neck and was dangling him in the air for all to see, but again he kept quiet and let Sperry have his rage.

"He's had me put all this work into trying to save the country, and it was all for nothing."

"But he appointed you acting vice president."

"He's simply using me to neutralize the Republican Party while he persuades the voters that he is the country's savior. That's why he kept Tate's cabinet and all his staff appointees in place, every single one a marionette, while he sits here pulling any string that he wishes. The bastard lied to me. The shit should remember that an earthquake broke Colossus's knee and the monster tumbled."

"You will have to come up with an earthquake, then. How are you going to do that?" Clapp asked, impressed that Sperry even knew who Colossus was, let alone what happened to him.

"How are we going to create an earthquake," Sperry corrected him. "What do you recommend?"

Clapp, who usually had no trouble coming up with underhanded solutions, didn't have a ready answer. "If you resign now, they will be able to say you quit in a huff because the Congress didn't buy your plan," Clapp improvised while he talked.

"And the damned politicians will steal our ideas, put them into their own patchwork plan, and take all the credit," Sperry picked up on the thought.

"Then, Adams will be free to move over to the White House, toss all the Republicans out on their collective ass, and claim they were just playing politics with the country's future," Clapp started to get interested in the discussion.

"And even though they lost the last presidential election, the damned Democrats will control the White House and Congress while they prepare for the next election with Adams running as an incumbent.

"The old guy's eighty years old, for Christ sake," Clapp said. "Maybe he will do us all a favor and die of natural causes before this comes to pass."

"We should be so lucky. Do you think ..."

'Walls have ears, even ours," Clapp cautioned.

Sperry laughed bitterly. "You should know."

Clapp on his instructions had arranged for microphones to be planted in the Andrew Johnson Suite. "Has there..."

Clapp waved a cautionary finger in the air. He pushed himself off the sofa and crossed the room to turn on CNN. He returned to a spot in front of Sperry's desk, leaned over and whispered: "Nothing we can use."

"What?" Sperry spoke loudly. "I can't hear you."

"Nothing," Clapp spoke in a low voice.

"Then do your God damn job better," Sperry ordered.

Clapp returned to his place on the sofa.

"We've got some planning to do," Sperry declared. "I am not going to let all of this work go for nothing."

Clapp nodded agreement.

"Now get out of here and go figure something out. We'll discuss it later," Sperry ordered.

Clapp obediently stood up and started for the door.

"And get someone in here to clean up this damned mess," Sperry ordered.

Before the door closed behind him, Sperry heard his secretary ask:

"What in the world…happened in there?"

Sperry glared at the door, stood up, and began to pace. He always did his best thinking while pacing.

Chapter 28

Joyce Tryon, not sure she had drawn the best investigative straw, started her morning at the FBI headquarters, or at least she tried.

Joyce, following Sarah's directions–Sarah seemed to be an expert in almost everything–waited until ten o'clock before embarking on her drive into the city from Loudoun. Ostensibly, she delayed in order to give the Virginia commuter traffic a chance to thin down. In reality, Joyce stalled because she found D.C. intimidating as well as overwhelming. Washington was a black city, the murder capitol of the United States, a festering cauldron of street crime. Although she had twice before visited the nation's capitol as a tourist with her parents, and despite the fact she was an African American, she was still apprehensive. She read the *Post* and watched the local television coverage like everyone else. Not a day passed without multiple murders, drug shootouts, muggings, gang fights, robberies, rapes, and assaults of all kinds.

Joyce concealed her worry with bravado as best she could. She followed I-95 across the 14th Street Bridge, turned right on Pennsylvania Avenue, and searched for the oddest building on the street, one that looked as if it were about to tip over backwards. Sarah told her she couldn't miss it, and to her surprise she did not. She turned left, found the parking lot where it was supposed to be, negotiated with the attendant and returned to Pennsylvania Avenue and the bureau's main entrance. It was there that her troubles began. Formalities ate up the better part of an hour, so it wasn't until almost eleven that she was escorted to the large room that served as the task force's base.

"Hi, I'm Reggie Crawford," the special agent that Tracey had recommended as Joyce's point of contact introduced herself.

"Detective Joyce Tryon," Joyce offered her hand. "I'm working with Inspector Gifford's team."

"My sympathies," Crawford smiled.

Not sure how to respond to that, Joyce ignored it. "I'm taking a look at the Walker case," Joyce said.

"Good, it'll be a relief to have someone around here who knows what they are doing." To emphasize her point, Crawford turned and looked at a group of males sitting at a table, coffee cups in hand, chatting.

Joyce did not know what to say about that either, so she said nothing.

"Don't get me wrong," Crawford said, reacting to her visitor's deadpan expression. "We've been working all this stuff twenty-four, seven, and we've reached a dead spot, so to speak. We don't have a clue who is shooting all these people, not the president, not Nan Starbright, not James Dexter, and we suspect that the Walker thing was coincidental."

"I understand," Joyce tried to establish a modicum of rapport with her escort. Except for the cynicism, Crawford appeared competent. At least she remembered the cases they were investigating. "I've had those kind of days myself."

"Good," Reggie smiled, recognizing she had come down rather hard on her visitor. "A fresh pair of experienced eyes frequently helps."

"I'm not sure," Joyce said. "I doubt that one person can do what hundreds have tried," she caught herself before she completed her sentence by saying "and failed."

"Have you worked for Gifford long?" Reggie asked.

"Two years. Do you know Inspector Gifford personally?"

Reggie laughed. "Two years can be a lifetime where Gifford is involved. I had the unfortunate task of serving as Gifford's point of contact on the Congressional Serial Killer investigation."

"That must have been interesting," Joyce tried to avoid criticizing her boss to an outsider.

"Yes, but not for me," Reggie said. "I spent most of my time trying to find Gifford, and when I did my primary function was as driver."

"Gif does tend to work alone."

"That's putting it mildly. My boss expected me to keep him

informed about Gifford's every thought, and Gifford didn't tell me duck shit. How is he as a full time supervisor?"

"He tends to let us sink or swim on our own," Joyce answered honestly.

"And that's why you are here all by your lonesome?" Reggie said. "Don't worry, we need all the help we can get. Let me set you up in your own cubbyhole and I'll show you where the case files are stored."

"Thank you."

"When you are ready to discuss things with some of the agents who have worked on the Walker investigation, I'll introduce you," Reggie said.

'Do you really think Walker screwed himself to death," Joyce asked bluntly.

"The cause of death is not in doubt," Reggie answered with equal candor. "We don't know if someone played more than a supportive role," she referred to Nan Starbright, "or why someone killed Starbright and Dexter."

"It sure looks like someone thought they had information they didn't want shared," Joyce said.

"It does, and the person who can best speculate on that is your boss. He's the one who interviewed each of them in depth while the death of Walker was fresh in their minds."

"What do Gifford's reports say?" Joyce asked seriously, making a mental note to start with them.

"Gifford's reports?" Reggie laughed. "If Inspector Gifford put his thoughts on paper, he hasn't shared them with the working members of the task force."

"Nor with me," Joyce admitted. "Gif requires everyone at OSI to put everything on paper, except for himself."

"Why does that not surprise me," Reggie said.

"I know he talks with Director Schultz," Joyce tried to defend Gif.

"Just talk?" Reggie laughed. Noting the expression on her visitor's face, Reggie patted her on the shoulder. "Forget I said that. Whether the old guys are cavorting or not is none of my business. At least they are generationally compatible."

"Our team is working out of Gifford's place in Loudoun," Joyce thought she was changing the subject.

"So is Director Schultz," Reggie smiled. "How do you like the mountains?"

"They're better than downtown Richmond," Joyce countered.

"I know. I've seen Gifford's place, and I spent my first tour as an agent in Richmond."

"Richmond? Really? When was that?"

"Six years ago."

"I was walking a beat then," Joyce said.

"We all have to start somewhere," Reggie said. "Even this is better."

Two hours later after a skipped lunch Joyce had scanned most of the pertinent reports on Walker and Nan Starbright. She had just finished one that indicated that Nan's sister from Miami was in town camping in Nan's apartment when Reggie came in.

"How are things going?" Reggie asked.

"I'm tired of this place already," Joyce admitted. "May I ask you a couple of questions?"

"Shoot!"

"Don't tempt me," Joyce laughed.

Reggie pulled up a straight chair and waited.

"You were the one who found Nan?"

"Yes," Reggie said.

"Why were you visiting her?"

"Just to let her know we knew she was back in town living under another name. Barby Dolle," Reggie said.

"I guess in her business any catchy name will do," Joyce said. "And you don't have any idea why someone shot her?"

"Not really."

"Who knew that Nan–I prefer that name—was the person who was with Walker at the time of her death?"

"Until her death, only seven people. The whole world knew that Walker died in bed with a mysterious female. Identifying her was one of the things those involved in the investigation were working on."

"Seven people?"

"All right, just between you and me."

"I can't promise to withhold information from Inspector Gifford," Joyce said.

"No problem. Gifford was the one who identified Nan. He tracked her down, questioned her, decided she was just what she claimed, a high priced call girl. Gifford briefed the two directors, Harrington and Schultz, and they in turn informed the acting president, acting vice president and their two assistants, Tyrone and Clapp."

"Oh shit," Joyce said.

"That's right, oh shit. If we take Harrington, Schultz, and Gifford out of the equation, we are left with four people who knew about Nan, the acting president, acting vice president and their two assistants. And you can just imagine what secrets those four have access to. We don't know who leaked."

"Christ, a political conspiracy," Joyce declared. "One or more of those four is responsible for Starbright's death."

"Are you sure?" Reggie asked.

Joyce nodded.

"I reacted just like you, but think about it."

"Walker's death sure paved the way for those four to get control of the top two offices in the country," Joyce said.

"Right, but if the cause of death was accidental?"

"Yes…but…" Joyce thought a few seconds before continuing. "What if Nan was the one who fed Walker those extra strength pills?"

"But she persuaded your boss that she didn't. No one could prove otherwise. Why kill her?"

"Maybe she could identify someone else, someone high ranking, who did not want to be identified."

"No one could have predicted that Walker would take those pills and climb in bed with Nan at exactly that particular moment in time. In fact, no one but the president knew he would be on the river that afternoon. He didn't even tell his protective detail his plans. How could a conspiracy coordinate Walker's death with that?"

"Christ I don't know."

"Then how can we investigate the acting president and vice president and their two primary assistants?"

"Nan can't tell us."

"And neither can Dexter, Walker's chief of staff."

"Are you telling me that we have a perfect crime?"

"I'm not telling you any such thing. I promise you if you find something we can investigate you won't be able to keep us out of it."

"And you are telling me that Gifford is square in the middle of all of this."

"No I'm not. I don't know where Gifford is standing. You are in a better position to know that than I am. Gifford doesn't tell me anything. He even excludes me and my boss from his meetings with Schultz and Harrington."

"Do you think that is why Schultz is sleeping in the mountains with Gifford?"

Reggie laughed. "This case is so loaded I'm particularly not going to speculate about why anybody is sleeping with anybody, not even Mickey Mouse and Minnie."

"Can we visit the crime scene?" Joyce asked, deciding to break out of the eternal circle of speculation. "I'm told that is where every investigation should start."

"Which crime scene?" Reggie asked.

"The one where the answer lies, or at least used to," Joyce said.

"Barby's place?"

"Let's go."

They tapped on the door to announce their presence to any law officials who might be inside and to their surprise, it opened.

"Oh," a Latina reacted.

""Benita," Reggie took the lead. "You remember me?"

"Yes, what?" Benita closed the door to a crack and peeked out at them.

"We need to talk," Reggie said.

"You do, me no do," Benita answered.

Reggie shoved her foot into the door. "The correct response is yes, ma'am," she said.

After an uncertain pause, Benita stepped back, and the two visitors entered.

"OK, assholes," Benita smiled as she lowered herself into a period piece chair that sported gold gilt and striped silk and waited. "I know nothing."

Reggie and Joyce crowded into a matching love seat facing the frowning Latina. Reggie looked at Joyce who got the message.

"Benita, Inspector Gifford asked me to stop by and ask you a few questions about your sister," Joyce took the lead.

"OK." Benita said.

"We're so sorry to hear about your sister," Joyce tried.

Benita did not react.

"Inspector Gifford asked me to tell you that we are going to punish the person responsible."

Benita did not move.

"The inspector wanted to be sure that you are comfortable," Joyce lied.

"Bullshit," Benita said.

"You have to help us," Joyce said.

Benita frowned.

"We are sure that Maria would want you to help."

"Me, too," Benita smiled as she rubbed her thumb and forefinger together.

"How much?" Joyce asked.

"One thousand," Benita answered.

Joyce shook her head negatively.

"Me know…me know…no thing," Maria again struggled to communicate in English or at least pretended to.

Joyce looked at Reggie for help.

"I know better than that," Reggie decided to play the heavy. "The Inspector told me that you were more than appropriately compensated."

"No understand," Benita said. "You go now."

"All we want to do is find the person who killed your sister. Do you understand?" Joyce added a little pressure of her own.

"Benita just working girl, you understand?" Benita played her own game.

"OK, Benita, how much?" Reggie asked.

"One thousand. Me go home," Benita smiled.

"You tell me, I'll pay you," Reggie said.

"OK."

"OK what?" Reggie demanded, tiring of the fencing.

"OK, you pay, me talk," Benita said.

"Oh, shit," Joyce joined the dialogue.

Reggie opened her purse, took out her weapon, laid it on the table, and then unfolded her wallet.

Benita waited, unimpressed.

Reggie counted out a few bills.

Benita did not react.

Reggie dropped two one hundred dollar bills on the pile and stared at Benita. Holding her empty wallet up for Benita to see she said: "That's all I have with me. Take it or leave it."

Benita, smiled, reached across the table, grabbed the money, and stood up. "Maria tell me john took pills, jumped her, grunted long time, and die."

"Oh shit," Reggie said, grabbing her money from Benita.

"You cheat Benita," Benita protested.

Reggie turned to Joyce. "I told you we were wasting our time."

Back on the street, Joyce turned to Reggie. "Sorry about that."

Reggie shrugged.

"Can you take me to Dexter's place?" Joyce asked.

"Why not," Reggie answered. "We'll pass it on the way back."

When they reached Dupont Circle, Reggie, who was driving, turned right on New Hampshire Avenue.

"Dexter lived in the big building on the left," Reggie announced as she pulled to the curb. She tossed the Police Business card on the dash and led her companion into the shabby building.

"The vice president's chief of staff lived in this building?" Joyce asked.

"It's not much," Reggie admitted. "But neither was Dexter. He was just a go-fer."

"I think I'll stay in Richmond," Joyce said as she glanced at the girls of color who were circling Dupont and 16th Street in their mini-skirts.

"If I remember correctly, Richmond has its share of working girls," Reggie who was tiring of this expedition said.

"Just show me Dexter's apartment," Joyce let her own irritation show.

"OK. Then I'll take you where they marinated the little jerk," Reggie replied.

"I'll save that experience for another day, partner," Joyce said.

A bored Reggie led the way to Dexter's shabby apartment. She ripped the police tape off the door, ignored the nosy neighbor who opened his door to check on the visitors, and unlocked the door.

"Don't worry about the fag across the hall," Reggie said as she closed the door behind her. "We've already interviewed him in detail. I'll show you the file when we get back to the playroom."

"What did you find here?" Joyce asked, now determined to cut short this trying phase of her investigation.

"Not much," Reggie answered. "Just the guy's clothes, wallet, keys, and whatever."

"He took nothing with him?" Joyce asked.

"Only what he needed to pay for his beers and transportation. I assume you read in the newspapers that we found an envelope stuffed with cash."

Joyce shook her head. "I usually don't read the Washington papers."

"Good for you," Reggie smiled. "We found an envelope with a stash, one hundred and four thousand dollars and twenty-five cents. Dexter had kept a running account on the envelope, just dates and amounts, no names. He apparently started with $500,000 and drew it out over time. Some of the recurring notations match the monthly rent for the Crystal City apartment. Others we suspect were payments to Nan Starbright. The rest, we don't know, probably the usual D.C. crap."

"I don't understand," Joyce played the rural innocent.

"Political payouts of some kind. Who knows? Probably money for booze, women, all the extra expenses that our nation's leaders like to keep from their wives, mistresses, supporters, the voters. We didn't release all the details to the media. We announced the finding of an envelope with $100,000 but nothing about the notations."

"The cash came under the table from the lobbyists and special interests," Joyce said.

"Presumably. Dexter kept a running account to cover himself. He probably showed it to Walker when he needed a replenishment."

"Only dates and amounts on the envelope?"

"Yes," Reggie confirmed. "Nothing incriminating, a list of money dispensed, a thousand here, five thousand there, no names, just numbers."

"Too bad," Joyce feigned disinterest.

"Yeah, too bad," Reggie agreed. "See anything here that tells you anything?"

"No, I just wanted to be able to tell the boss I visited the place."

"Gifford will like that," Reggie laughed. "You've done a good job of matching his footprints. They're all over this damned town. Too bad he doesn't share."

Joyce nodded but said nothing.

Chapter 29

Gif arrived home to find Jerry Quigley hunched over his computer in the otherwise silent house.

"Hi boss," Jerry greeted him.

"Do you have any e-mail addresses for me?" Gif asked.

"I'm not having much luck," Jerry said. "The government web site has addresses listed, but I don't think those are what you want. Any e-mail that goes there will be handled by clerks."

"That's not what I'm looking for, Jerry," Gif said. "What about the Andrew Johnson Suite?"

"I can't find any kind of e-mail going to the Andrew Johnson Suite, per se."

"What about the e-mail they might have sent and received from home computers, laptops, or desktops?

"Adams lives in a hotel. I don't think he has a computer."

"What about Sperry?" Gif asked.

"He lives in Georgetown, but again I don't think he or his wife is on the internet," Jerry replied.

"What about Tyrone and Clapp?"

"There are computers in both of their homes, and somebody in each place is on the internet. I haven't tried to read their e-mail."

"Do it," Gif ordered.

"You actually want me to try to read the e-mail of the president's and the vice president's chief of staff?" Jerry asked.

"Just their home e-mail. And I want to know everything you can learn about what their home computers do on-line."

"Do we have warrants or some kind of authorization?" Jerry asked.

"You do."

"May I ask who authorized this?"

"No, Jerry. You cannot. Just do what I order you to do."

"Yes sir. You want me to learn everything I can learn about Clapp's and Tyrone's home computers including reading their personal e-mail?"

"You got it," Gif said. "Just stay away from their office computers."

"Right. Who do you want me to share this with?"

"Me."

"Not Truman? The team?"

"Me, only. Just don't get caught."

"Jesus," Jerry reacted. "What about Adams and Sperry?"

"Jerry, just the two names I gave you. Don't get carried away. Keep away from their offices.

"Do we know if these guys have any kind of security protection on their home computers?"

"I don't know, but the kind of e-mail I'm looking for is the kind they wouldn't share with others."

"Then they have software protection and use encryption programs," Jerry mused.

"Will that be a problem?"

"Let me take a look and find out," Jerry said, obviously pleased at the chance to show off his skills.

"Just you and me, right?" Gif made Jerry confirm his instructions.

"Yes sir."

Sarah Whitestone who had been assigned responsibility for the Tate shooting enlisted Billie Williams to accompany her on her first visit to the crime site starting where every good investigator should.

"You know I was just out here with Gifford," Billie complained as he followed the almost hidden country lane to the Tate homestead. "I'm beginning to feel like a damned tour guide."

"You would think a president would spend some of his big bucks on fixing this place up," Sarah ignored Billie's whining.

Billie shrugged.

"How many times was Gifford out here?" Sarah asked.

Billie glanced at his companion, not quite sure what was behind her questions. Sarah made no secret of the fact that she was a lesbian, and that made Billie uncomfortable. He didn't care a damn about her sexual preferences, liking to think it was none of his business, but being alone with her was not something he enjoyed. He simply didn't know how to react to her outspoken act.

"I'm sure Gifford was out here many times when Tate was sheriff, but if you're asking if this was his first visit here since the shooting, the answer is yes. I think. You know Gifford."

"Why do you have such a stick up your ass, Billie?" Sarah challenged him. "You know exactly what I was asking."

Billie shrugged and did not respond. He didn't like women talking like cops.

"Well?" Sarah did not let Billie avoid answering her question.

"I simply was trying to give you a precise answer," Billie replied irritably.

"Good. Keep doing that, and we won't have any problems," Sarah said.

Billie stopped the Bronco abruptly and turned on Sarah. "Let's you and I get one thing straight, Whitestone. I don't give a damn what your sexual preferences are. Just keep them to yourself, and we'll get along just fine."

Sarah laughed. "Who said a damned thing about my sexual preferences, Billie? Relax; you really aren't my cup of tea."

"What does that mean?"

"I thought you didn't want to discuss my preferences," Sarah smiled.

Not sure how he had gotten himself in that bind, Billie replied simply: "Good, let's keep it that way." He took his foot off the brake and continued down the rocky road.

A few silent minutes later, Billie stopped between the barn and the back of the house.

"They've got the house pointed the wrong way," Sarah observed.

"You think they should have a view of the barn instead of the river?" Billie asked, rather pleased with that sally.

Sarah ignored him. She got out of the car and started around to the front of the house with Billie following along behind.

"Why isn't there a cop out here preserving the site?" Sarah asked. "I didn't even see any marking tape?"

"Maybe because this isn't where the shooting occurred," Billie replied.

Sarah stopped abruptly and turned on Billie. "Then what in the hell are we doing here."

"The shooting happened downriver. I doubt the Feds will have a guard standing on the water directing traffic," Billie chuckled. "Maybe, you should volunteer for the job."

Sarah responded with a simple smile.

"I would be delighted to drop you off," Billie pushed his luck. "We can use President Tate's old boat. I'm sure he wouldn't object."

"Did Gifford use the boat to get to the site?"

"Of course," Billie said.

"Good, we'll do the same. After you show me the site, I'll handle the boat, and you can walk back."

"Women," Billie grumbled as he turned toward the shore.

"Lesbians," Sarah imitated Billie's tone as she followed along behind.

Willie let that remark slide.

Forty-five minutes later, after a quick visit to the shooting site, they returned to the Bronco. As they were making their way back up the rocky trail that passed as a country lane, Sarah said:

"I'm sure you are supposed to be doing something useful today beyond acting as a tour guide. What was it?"

"Gifford wants all the residents re-interviewed," Billie admitted. It was an onerous chore he had been trying to postpone as long as possible.

"If I'm not mistaken, Gifford ordered you and Harold to handle that, and to make sure you asked the residents for the names of others they had seen in the area and if they had seen any strangers passing through," Sarah smiled as she referred to their recent team meeting. "Where is Harold now?"

"Harold also has the Redskin case. We're working as sort of a team, I guess. Harold wanted to start with Tiny's …"

"A bar. Why doesn't that surprise me," Sarah laughed.

"... and Redskin Park. Since I've already done both, I let Harold go on his own," Billie ignored the interruption. "I was getting ready to do some research at headquarters that Gifford also wants right now when you drafted me to play tour guide. Since you are uninformed about many things, including how to get here, that's what I'm doing. Shows how dumb one of us is."

"How many residents?" Sarah ignored Billie's little tirade. Firing sharp ripostes was her stock in trade, and she wasn't sure Billie understood.

"Thirty homes," Billie answered.

"Let's get at it."

"You're kidding?"

"We'll start at Route 15 and work our way west. "I didn't see that many houses on our way here."

"That's country living for you. Have you ever seen a farm?"

Sarah ignored Billie.

Encouraged, Billie pushed his luck. "Some farms even have barns. A barn is where they keep the animals."

"I know about animals, big fat dirty pigs…" Sarah smiled at Billie, checking to see if he was following where she was going.

"Some of the houses are even located on the river," Billie, oblivious to the fact that Sarah was preparing to launch a counterattack, continued. "This is the country, not a big city like Richmond with slums, public housing, and all that wonderful stuff."

"…and country bumpkins with cow shit for brains," Sarah said.

"Are you saying I have cow shit for brains," Billie finally picked up on what Sarah was saying.

"Richmond is a terrible place. Ever been there?" Sarah did not answer Billie's question.

Billie reluctantly shook his head negatively.

"You shouldn't shake your head so much," Sarah laughed. "Who knows what might fall out."

They visited ten residences, four of which had no occupants at home, interviewed six disinterested housewives and eight unhelpful kids before the found an elderly couple sitting on the front porch of an ancient farmhouse, smoking, watching the passage of an occasional car, and slapping mosquitoes.

Billie parked the Bronco in their narrow driveway and followed Sarah to the house, letting her take the lead in interviewing the old folks. Billie's notes indicated their name was Brewster and the original sheriff's department deputy who contacted them had found the couple unhelpful, difficult, alternately garrulous and non-responsive, attitudes he attributed to near senility.

"This is a complete waste of time," Billie grumbled, speaking softly so that only Sarah could hear.

Sarah ignored him.

"Mr. and Mrs. Brewster," Sarah greeted the old couple with a smile and a wave of her credentials. "I am Detective Whitestone from the Office of Special Investigations, and this is Deputy Williams from the Loudoun Sheriff's Department."

The old man moved his head slightly downward, once, in acknowledgement. The old lady said nothing. She continued to rock and stare toward the road as if the two visitors did not exist.

Sarah halted at the foot of the porch stairs. "We are investigating the President Tate shooting. Do you have time for a few questions."

"Time's all we got, and we ain't got much of that," the old man grunted.

Taking that as a positive response, Sarah climbed the steps and commandeered the single available rocker on the right of the door. Billie looked for another chair, found none, and like a good country boy sat down on the top step, turned sideways and leaned back against the post that supported the porch railing. The post gave slightly, creaked its protest, but held.

"Do you remember where you were on the day President Tate was shot?" Sarah asked with her ballpoint poised over her notebook. Sarah deliberately tried to create the impression that she was intensely interested in the answer to her question.

The old man's bloodshot eyes focused on Sarah, but he did not respond. Sarah wondered if he had understood.

"Same as always," the old lady spoke for the first time.

The response, vague as it was, at least confirmed that the old lady could hear and comprehend. Sarah, who was about to surrender, decided to keep trying, mainly because she did not want to admit that Billie had been right.

"Ma'am, I'm parched. Could I have a drink of water?" Sarah asked, coughing to reinforce her falsehood. Sarah was simply trying to get the woman off to one side where she could question her separately.

"Water's in the kitchen," the old man foiled that maneuver.

"May I get it myself?" Sarah asked.

The old man nodded.

"Deputy?" Sarah addressed Billie.

Billie, who had been patiently and with inner amusement watching Sarah struggle, looked at her.

Sarah tipped her head towards the front door, giving him an unspoken order.

Billie thought about telling her to get her own damned water but changed his mind. He stood up and entered the house where he found himself in a spotless country parlor furnished with seventy year old Sears and Roebuck, the kind whose condition let it pass as priceless antique in the eyes of unknowing tourists. Billie went on into the kitchen dominated by an aged fridge and an oilcloth covered pine table. He glanced at the stained sink, opened the nearest cupboard, found a shelf of gleaming jelly glasses, took out two, opened the fridge and was pleased to discover an old juice jar filled with water. He filled the two glasses, put the jar back in the fridge, took a sip of cold well water and returned to the front porch.

"Who's for a cold drink?" Billie played host.

The old man held out his hand, and Billie handed him the full glass.

The old lady did not react. Billie started for the front step. Sarah stopped him.

"You are a life saver, deputy," she opened her hand as she reached out.

Billie gave her the half-filled glass that he had already sampled and sat down with his back against the porch rail. Sarah glanced at her glass, looked at Billie, and to his delight smiled as she raised the glass to her lips. Billie watched as she drained the jar before setting it on the porch rail behind him.

She going to want me to take a piss for her next, Billie thought.

"Mr. Brewster," Sarah said. "I'd bet your family has lived here a long time."

"Two hundred and fifty-five years come November," the old man surprised Sarah with a specific answer.

"November?"

"Yep. Damned fools. Almost starved that first winter. Built the first cabin right on this spot. Time they finished got snowed in. Lived on squirrel stew for months."

"That's a Brewster for you," the old lady chuckled. "Squirrels are rats with bushy tails."

"Indians damned near got them too," the old man ignored her.

Sarah smiled, realizing that it wasn't the first time the old man had heard his wife badmouth the Brewsters.

"Damned Iroquois and Algonquin crossed down river a piece every fall. Thought this fine hunting land belonged to them."

"Brewsters ate nothing but rat stew," the old lady chortled.

"As a matter of fact," Billie said. "There's an old Indian trail a few miles up the mountain," he pointed with his thumb behind him.

"You from here, boy," the old man demanded.

"Born, raised and educated," Billie answered.

The old man nodded approval.

"My folks was here before the Tates," the old man said. "Great, great, great granddaddy helped Tates build their cabin over there," he inclined his head to the right.

"The old man," Mrs. Brewster glanced at her husband. "Showed young Tate where the best fish holes are."

"You knew Harrison Tate," Sarah said, pretending to write a note.

"Yep."

"Used to see him drive by in his sheriff's car," the old lady said. "He'd wave, and I'd wave."

"Never talked with him since he got important," the old man said.

Billie was surprised. Sarah seemed to have the incommunicative couple competing with their stories.

"We was sitting here that day," the old lady said.

"Didn't see nothin'," the old man said.

"Heard the shot," the old lady glared.

"Now Marsh, we talked about that," Brewster gave Billie the impression he was chastising her.

"No, you shut up," the old lady ordered. "I say what I want."

"Don't need any trouble," the old man said as he pushed himself out of the chair.

Without uttering another word he entered the house and let the screen door slam behind him.

"You heard the actual shot?" Sarah asked, sitting up straight.

"Deed I did. Sittin' right here."

"Do you know what time?"

The old lady nodded. "Bout four. Don't have a watch," she held up her wrinkled, slender wrist, exposing gnarled joints. "Jist after the school bus went by. Then all those police with the lights flashin' came rushin' past."

"How long after the shot?" Sarah asked.

"A piece."

"There was that little ole red car," the old man added from his position behind the screen.

That comment caught both Sarah and Billie's attention.

"We don't know nothin' about that," the old woman spoke firmly. "I tole him not to mention it."

"Why is that ma'am?" Billie asked.

The old lady glared at him.

"Cause she never talks about strangers," the old man said.

"What other people do ain't none of our durn business," the old woman frowned.

"Was the car going toward Lovettsville?" Billie asked.

"Nope," the old man said.

"I'm not sayin' another durn thing," the old woman pressed her thin lips shut and clasped her bony hands together on her lap.

Sarah assumed she was angry because the old man had interrupted her story.

"How soon after the sound of a gun?" Sarah asked.

"A piece," the old lady said.

The old man held up five fingers.

"Five minutes?" Sarah asked.

The old man nodded.

"Did you recognize the driver?" Sarah asked.

The old man shook his head negatively.

"Nobody from hereabouts," the old woman declared, apparently forgetting her anger.

"Was he driving fast?"

The old man nodded affirmatively.

"What make of car?"

"Little Japanese thing," the old man said.

"Why anybody drives those trashy things I don't know," the old lady declared. "Now you all go," she ordered. "And you shut up," she turned on her husband.

"Yes ma'am," Billie said obediently as he rose to his feet.

"Would you know the car if you saw it again?" Sarah asked as she stood up.

"Nope," the old woman said.

"Yep," the old man replied at the same time.

As they were leaving, the old man returned to his chair.

"I told you, old man, to keep your durn fool mouth shut. Now they'll be back botherin' us."

"I don't care. I liked young Tate," the old man said defiantly.

When they were back in the car, Billie turned on Sarah. "Give or take a half century, there goes you and I," he laughed.

"Not in your lifetime," Sarah chuckled.

Billie made a U-turn and headed back towards 15, waving at the Brewsters as they passed. Neither returned the wave. "I'm tired of this interviewing for today," Billie sighed.

"Durn fool, I told you to keep your durn mouth shut," Sarah gave a good imitation of the old lady.

When Billie and Sarah arrived at Gif's mountain home, they found the front yard filled with parked cars, the house empty, and all their teammates plus Gif and Tracey sitting on the back patio with cold Budweisers in their hands.

"Not everyone is working overtime, I see," Sarah said.

Joyce and Harold raised their bottles in salute.

Before anyone could respond, Sarah turned to Billie who was just exiting the house.

"Get me a chair and a beer, you durn fool," Sarah used her recently acquired accent.

To everyone's surprise, Billie nodded and disappeared in the house. Seconds later he returned carrying a single Budweiser.

"Git you own, old lady," Billie mimicked the old man.

They all waited for Sarah's tart response. Instead of speaking, she held out her hand. Billie reacted by raising the bottle to his lips, swallowed deeply, and then offered the bottle to Sarah who took it. Billie returned to the house followed by a call from Gif:

"There are more chairs in the back hall closet."

Everyone waited to see what Billie did next. He again surprised them by reappearing with a second beer in one hand and two folding chairs in the other. Sarah took the second beer, held it while Billie opened the chairs and set them side by side. Sarah returned the second beer to Billie, and the two of them sat down simultaneously in what looked like a choreographed action.

"Christ, what's that all about?" Joyce Tryon asked.

Sarah replied with a wink.

"We're practicing for our seventieth," Billie said.

"Let's compare notes, briefly," Gif took charge. He turned to Sarah. "Last come, first up."

Sarah who usually dominated meetings with her sharp tongue reacted with a shy smile. "Billie?" She deferred.

Billie took a deep drink of his Budweiser before setting it on the brick patio beside his chair. "We had an interesting day," he began. He then described their visit to the river filling his account with manufactured detail about the temperature, the speed of the current, the dried condition of the leaves on the trees and a description of the unmaintained Tate property.

Finally, Gif reacted as Billie intended. "Please gloss over the natural detail," Gif intervened.

"I was just setting the stage," Billie smiled. "Now for the tour de force." He hesitated to build up the anticipation before turning to Sarah.

"Ole man, I tole you not to say a durn thing," Sarah smiled.

Everybody waited.

"Sarah…" Gif cautioned.

"So spoke Mrs. Marsha Brewster, President Tate's neighbor," Sarah laughed. "I am pleased to report that Mr. and Mrs. Sam Brewster were sitting on their front porch on the day of the shooting, heard the sound of the shot at about 1600 hours just after the school bus went by. Approximately five minutes later a small, old, little red Japanese car driven by a stranger to the area raced past heading east on Lovettsville Road in the direction of Route 15. A short time later, a bevy of police cars with flashing lights descended on the area."

"How long after the red car passed was it before the cops arrived?" Gif asked, obviously trying to estimate how long the red car had to clear the area.

"I can tell you precisely what Mrs. Brewster estimated," Sarah paused for effect before continuing. "Mrs. Brewster said, and I quote, 'a piece.'"

"Can you be more precise?" Gif asked.

"Yes," Sarah smiled and held up five fingers. "According to Mr. Brewster."

"Minutes?"

Sarah nodded.

"Do you think it would help if we had a follow up debriefing?" Gif asked.

"No," Sarah answered, "but if someone would like to try, please be our guest."

Sarah looked at Billie who nodded in agreement.

"How in the hell did my people and the sheriff's men miss the Brewsters?" Tracey asked.

"The Brewsters are in their late eighties, have been neighbors of the Tates forever, and were reluctant to get involved," Billie interjected. "They are a nice old couple who remembered their neighbor fondly. It was only after Sarah got Mr. Brewster to start telling us how he used to show young Harrison where all the good fishing holes were that he admitted to hearing the shot. Mrs. Brewster banished him to the house for speaking out of turn, but Sarah got them to admit they saw the red car. I'm not sure either would admit to having told us what they heard and saw if we asked them again tomorrow."

"That was good work," Gif brought the discussion to an end. "Let's move on."

Gif did not share his thoughts about the little red Japanese car with the others.

"Joyce, how was your day?" Gif changed the subject by moving on to the Walker investigation.

"I had a great day," Joyce laughed. "I visited the task force office, met a friend of our boss, Reggie Crawford, who tried to smother me under effusive praise for Inspector Gifford, and read a mountain of files."

Joyce paused and smiled first at Gifford and then at Tracey. Only Tracey smiled back, acknowledging she knew the true nature of the Crawford/Gifford relationship.

"Please continue," Gif said, trying to short-circuit any further discussion of the petulant Crawford.

"After a couple of hours, the helpful Reggie took me out to murder scene one, Nan Starbright/Barby Dolle's place." Joyce reported. "There I met Nan's sister Benita who tried to shake us down for a thousand bucks. After a little bargaining Benita surrendered and gave us the hot poop. She said and I quote, Joyce picked up her notebook:

"Maria told me that her john took his pills, jumped her, grunted and died."

After a brief pause, the team erupted with laughter, applause and a few pointed remarks. Even Gif and Tracey laughed. Gif let the pandemonium linger for a couple of minutes before he intervened.

"Good work, Joyce. Is that all you have to report?"

Joyce glanced at Tracey before continuing.

"I also visited crime scene number two, the apartment of James Dexter. This is not news for Tracey, but it might be for the rest of the team. There, I learned that the envelope the investigators found contained one hundred thousand four dollars and twenty-five cents, not the flat one hundred thou reported by the media. It also had a brief accounting on the envelope. Nothing fancy, just dollar amounts and dates, starting with a five hundred thousand figure."

"That's right," Tracey said. "We deliberately held back information from the media for obvious reasons. Please respect that confidence."

"Reggie and I speculated," Joyce continued. "That the envelope probably contained the vice president's slush fund. Some of the figures on a monthly basis matched the rent of the Crystal City apartment while others were probably payments to Nan Starbright."

"We're not sure of the significance of that information," Tracey said. "I personally agree with Joyce. The envelope contained the vice president's petty cash."

"Thank you for sharing that, Tracey. Anything else, Joyce?" Gif again tried to move the meeting along.

"No, sir. It's not much, but it takes time," Joyce said.

"You're doing just fine," Gif reassured her. "Harold, do you have anything to report on the Redskin case?"

"I spent the day at Redskin Field irritating everybody, visited the crime scene at Tiny's, and introduced myself at the bowling alley," Harold Creighton said. "I can't say I learned anything of significance. I'm not sure that those working the case can say anything more. I have yet to find anyone who can even suggest a viable lead to the shooter. I don't know why the media has connected the case to the others. Maybe our leader has an idea why his buddy Mavis floated that nonsense."

All eyes turned to Gif, including Tracey's which had an amused twinkle in them.

"Mavis Davis is not my buddy," Gif let his irritation show. "She can allege I am the connection, but that's nonsense."

"Hey guys," Jerry Quigley who had been playing with his computers in the living room table called. "You might want to see this."

They all dutifully filed into the house where Jerry pointed at the television set. "Mavis baby is coming on with a Breaking News report."

"Her timing is flawless," Sarah Whitestone declared as the team aligned itself in a half circle facing Gif's television.

Gif stood behind his recliner, leaning on the back.

"That Mavis sure knows how to draw an audience," Sarah said, pointedly looking at the group around the recliner.

Gif ignored the comment.

The commercial ended. "Breaking News" scrolled across the screen. Suddenly, a full picture of Gif and Tracey standing in front of Gif's house looking into the camera emerged. Tracey was smiling and Gif sported a heavy frown. Underneath the picture in large words was a caption:

Investigators Investigate, Each Other?

"Mavis caught the real you, boss," Sarah set the tone for the team's response.

"I do believe Mavis lied to us," Tracey smiled. "Her cameraman obviously took that picture from the truck."

"This is not worth watching," Gif controlled his temper with difficulty.

"She has my attention, boss," Sarah said.

"Investors Investigate, that's almost repetitive," Joyce observed. "Alliterative, but not very good writing at all. I wonder what …"

"Don't even think it, let alone say it," Gif growled as he grabbed the remote and switched off the set. He tossed the remote onto the recliner and turned to his tech guru. "Harold, figure out some way to fix this damned thing so it won't show that channel."

Gif slammed the door behind him as he returned to the patio.

"Guys, I think the boss just terminated the meeting for today," Tracey said.

The others followed Gif outside, silently retrieved their files and notes, and returned to the house.

Tracey waited until the others departed before going into the kitchen where Gif joined her.

"I wonder what Mavis had to say," Tracey said.

"Nothing of value, I'm sure," Gif replied.

"I have to agree with Sarah. I thought that was a good picture of you. I wonder if we could get Mavis to print a copy for us," Tracey said.

Gif reacted by retreating to the patio. Tracey got two bottles of Budweiser from the fridge and sat down next to Gif in the patio swing, opened her bottle, and waited for him to calm down.

Finally, Gif turned to Tracey, lifted his bottle in toast, and asked:

"What do you think she reported? She nailed you, too, this time."

"Mavis is not worth thinking about," Tracey smiled. "She just hustles a little harder than most of her peers."

"Don't try to tell me that hustling is a woman's right."

"It is a man's world and…"

"A woman's got to do what a woman's got to do," Gif said. "Someday someone is going to sue the pants off that broad."

"I don't think it will take a law suit to accomplish that objective," Tracey laughed. "Inspector, do you have first hand evidence to the contrary?"

Gif's cell phone buzzed.

"I wish you would set that damned thing on chime. That buzzer irritates me," Tracey complained.

"I should just throw the damned thing away," Gif said as he reached for the offending technology.

Tracey grabbed his knee. "I don't recommend that you answer it," Tracey said. "The timing is quite ominous."

Gif picked up the phone, checked the identity of the caller, turned the phone off and put it back on the table.

"Richmond?" Tracey said.

"Richmond!" Gif announced at the same time.

They laughed together.

"She would just hang up on you, anyway." Tracey said.

"Only after you deliberately provoked her with another of your offline lover comments," Gif said. "I'm sure all she wants to do is let me know that my stuff is back in the hall," Gif said.

Tracey lifted her bottle in toast. "To Mavis, I'm sure Doctor Bliss caught the Breaking News report."

"That would have been a double blow, you and Mavis, again," Gif laughed before realizing that the joke was on him.

Chapter 30

Gif cooked a steak, two baked potatoes and two ears of corn on the barbecue. When they finished, Tracey leaned back and smiled.

"I didn't realize you had such domestic skills. I thought everything served here came out of a box labeled meat loaf."

To her surprise, Gif reacted irritably.

"Why don't you try cooking one of these nights."

"I don't cook," Tracey said, standing up and stacking the dishes. She posed: "What you see is what you get."

Gif laughed. "I'm not complaining. Leave those go," he indicated the dishes. "Come take a walk with me."

Gif took the dishes from Tracey, set them on the table and grabbed her hand. As he led her across the lawn toward his favorite forest path, Gif again surprised her.

"We have to talk."

"And walls have ears, even here?"

"This place has been bugged before," Gif said.

"I remember. And now, you're putting on a show for any potential listeners."

"Not just that."

"Do you want me to start performing at night?"

"You're doing just fine," Gif laughed. "What did you think of the reports?" Gif referred to his team's synopsis of their day's efforts.

"You want the truth?"

"It's time we talked frankly," Gif said.

"That will be a first," Tracey laughed. "OK, I didn't hear anything new except for that bit about the little red car."

Gif did not react, waiting for Tracey to continue.

"Now it's your turn, lover, that's the way conversations go," Tracey smiled. "Me talk, you talk."

"I know," Gif referred to his team's reports, "but to be honest I don't expect them to come up with anything your and Tom's troops haven't uncovered."

"And we don't have a clue who is killing all of these people," Tracey admitted. "In addition to putting on a show for potential listeners, why did you bring your team down here if you don't expect them to develop new evidence? If I'm not mistaken, I think I heard someone use words like take a fresh look, etcetera, etcetera. Was that all window dressing too?"

"I seem to find myself stuck in the middle of this thing despite my best effort to keep out of it," Gif admitted.

"Poor baby, mean old Tracey, Mavis, the grieving widow Martha, the Loudoun Sheriff's Department, the White House, and the media are all conspiring against you."

"I'm not paranoid," Gif snapped. "There is someone out there conspiring."

"Just teasing."

"I'm deadly serious," Gif said. "I brought the team down to help create the illusion that I'm actually doing something."

"And you are. I know you better than you think. While everyone is watching one hand, you've got the other in someone's pocket," Tracey laughed. "I'm not protesting. Just keep it out of mine."

"Tracey, we are caught in the middle of something big," Gif tried again.

"Tell me about it, big boy," Tracey pulled her hand out of his and stopped, making Gif turn to look at her.

"No nut is behind all of these killings," Gif said.

"I agree. If it had stopped with Harrison Tate, I might have bought the Secret Service's theories."

"But the killings didn't stop. Someone has deliberately eliminated all those involved who either knew or suspected who might have killed Harrison," Gif said.

"And I don't believe in coincidences. That Walker thing for example. Neither does Tom," Tracey referred to their mutual friend, the FBI director.

"So what does an investigator look for first?" Gif asked, leading Tracey in the direction he wanted her thoughts to go.

"Motive of course," Tracey said. "What is this Murder Investigation 101?"

"It's not money, jealousy, revenge or madness," Gif ignored the question.

"Of course not, it's unmitigated ambition. We have a conspiracy on our hands," Tracey said.

"I agree. And who are the conspirators?"

"You say it, lover. This is your game."

"It isn't, Tracey. It's ours, and it's no game."

"So tell me. Is the evil genius behind all these murders that nice old man or the ambitious newcomer from New York?"

"Adams or Sperry," Gif agreed.

"I can't picture either of those two putting on black Ninja outfits and sneaking around shooting people," Tracey laughed.

"Evil genuises don't do the heavy lifting," Gif said. "They hire others to do the dirty stuff."

"Or, they have others hire the bad guys. If they are geniuses, they are smart enough to insulate themselves from the evil deeds."

"We could debate that premise," Gif laughed. "If the geniuses plan the evil, they are evil."

"OK, we're throwing Tyrone and Clapp into the equation," Tracey said. "Which evil team are you betting on?"

"I don't see Tyrone and Clapp on the point, either," Gif said.

"I agree. They're both political hatchet men. I can visualize either one wielding a knife in the back, but I don't think either one is capable of all these shootings."

Gif chuckled at Tracey's imagery. "If you mean a political knife in the back, I agree, but actual physical assault is beyond either one."

Gif and Tracey resumed their walk in silence, each lost in thought. Finally, Gif restarted their discussion. "Either Adams or Sperry is the evil genius, either Tyrone or Clapp is the messenger who delivers the cash to the hired assassin, which team is it?"

"Tom has reached the same conclusion," Tracey said. "But we haven't discussed it. I think both of us are too scared to actually put our suspicions in words, and suspicions are all we have. Like you, we don't know which team is responsible, the acting president's or the acting vice president's. How do we investigate people on that level?"

"As soon as you and your investigators start asking questions all hell is going to break out. The media will learn of your suspicions and panic the public," Gif agreed.

"Panicking the public is easy to do. And we don't want to have that happen because the politicians will run for cover," Tracey said.

"And as they run they will blame the messengers," Gif said.

"We'll all be fired, and by that I mean you, me, and Tom, and the investigators; civil service or not, we all ultimately report to the politicians who will dispatch those of us they can't fire to some Siberian coal mine."

"All but you, baby. Your job is temporary anyway," Gif said.

"I will always have you, lover. How secure are you?" Tracey took his arm.

"You've got your retirement; they won't or can't touch that, and I've got the colonel. Unfortunately, he reports to the governor and the last time I looked he was a politician."

"We can always live here on our savings," Tracey squeezed Gif's arm. "All I need is a decent rocking chair and a television set."

"I'm not kidding, Tracey. I'm going to catch the bastard that killed Harrison," Gif stopped and turned to face her.

"We are, lover. We just have to figure out how to do that little thing," Tracey said.

"How are we going to do that?" Gif asked.

"I'm waiting for you to tell me. You always do, ultimately. Now," Tracey kissed Gif lightly, "let's go back to your chalet and see what other kind of show we can put on."

"This doesn't bother you, possibly performing for an audience?" Gif asked.

"I'm here, aren't I."

As they approached the house, Tracey returned to the subject: "I know you're working some angle. When you are ready to share, I'm all ears. Until then, I'm all…yours."

Gif did not reply.

Tracey poked him with an elbow. "At least giggle, lover."

In Georgetown five men, a substantial congregation of Republican power, all wearing dark, tailored suits and maroon ties, sat in Acting Vice President Alexander Hamilton Sperry's study sipping fifty year old Remy Martin brandy from crystal snifters.

"I don't know how you drink this stuff," Tracey H. Ripper, the House Minority Leader lifted his glass.

"What do you prefer, Rip?" Sperry, who presided from behind his glass desk, an innovation installed by his wife who considered herself an avant-garde decorator, asked. "Courvoisier?"

"None of that French piss, Ham." Ripper used a nickname he knew Sperry despised. "I've never outgrown good old American bourbon, preferably the cheap stuff."

"Some people never mature," Sperry smiled thinly.

"To mature is just a polite way of saying to rot," Ripper said.

Sperry and Ripper had disliked each other for almost forty years; each nurtured an enmity that had started during their Harvard days when they had belonged to the same fraternity. Then, now, and during all the intervening years, their New York and Alabama genes had clashed.

"May we dispense with the pleasantries, gentlemen," Senate Majority Leader Clarence T. Tipton said. Tipton, older than the others, considered himself the senior man present despite Sperry's grand titles. He glanced at his watch. "I promised my wife I would be home by eight."

"Clarence, I called this meeting to discuss the future of this great nation," Sperry tried to exercise the authority that he felt his positions afforded him.

Tipton, the senior senator from Ohio, frowned but did not reply. He simply tapped his watch for the benefit of his Republican colleagues from Capitol Hill. Tipton knew that the other three, Terrence A. Godfrey, the House Whip, and Jerry E. Toogood, the Senate Whip, and Ripper, considered their host arrogant and ambitious beyond his capabilities. Not one of the four was dedicated to assisting Sperry's effort to be the party's next presidential candidate.

"As you are all aware, the Congress has decided to ignore the administration's emergency economic plan and write its own," Sperry said.

"You shouldn't take that personally, Ham," Tracey Ripper interrupted before Sperry could continue his spiel. "What administration are you talking about, Tate's, Adams's, or yours? We don't have a bonafide administration; we don't even have a president who sits in the White House."

"You know what I mean," Sperry growled. "Adams and I together speak for both parties."

"Neither of you was elected to the positions you now hold; neither of you speak for a party," Ripper challenged. "You hold an elective office without a single vote to your name."

"Read the constitution," Sperry said.

"Adams, at least, was elected to represent the people of a Missouri district in the House for two years. Why are you surprised that the Congress chooses to believe that it is more qualified to speak for the people than a bastard administration that represents only itself? After you have been in this town a little longer, you will learn that the Congress passes the laws, and the executive branch administers them.

"If you had attended class more often, Rip, you might recall that you and I shared Political Science 1 as freshmen," Sperry snapped. "I'm not talking about a simple law, I refer to the Department of Treasury's plan to rescue our economy before the country falls into a depression like it has never seen before."

"I suggest you are overstating the case, Mr. Secretary," Senate Majority Leader Tipton deliberately used Sperry's secondary title.

"I beg to differ with you on that, sir," Sperry turned on Tipton.

"As a member of the president's cabinet, sir, that is your right," Tipton snapped back. May I ask you a simple question?"

Sperry nodded.

"Do you still consider yourself a member of the Republican Party or did you become an independent or something worse when you accepted the acting president's offer of the acting vice presidency?" Tipton deliberately put heavy emphasis on the "acting" in both titles.

Sperry flushed. "The purpose of this meeting is to discuss the emergency not minor political matters like my party affiliation."

"Sir, I for one do not consider party affiliation a minor matter," Jerry Toogood of Texas drawled.

"I'm a Republican damn it. I've been one since my father taught me about politics as a young man. As the Grand Old Party's highest ranking official…"

"Some of us question the validity of that assertion," Tipton challenged him.

While Sperry tried to control his temper and devise a suitable response, Tipton smiled at his three Hill colleagues who raised their glasses in approval.

"Please gentlemen, let us not quibble over mere words," Sperry tried again. "I need your support. The country needs your support."

"And the country will always have it," Tipton smiled, pleased with himself for ignoring Sperry's personal plea.

"We owe it to the American people not to make this a congressional/executive branch thing," Sperry insisted.

"You misunderstand the situation, sir," Toogood joined the fray. "I assure you that the Republican Party and its representatives on the Hill will write a bill that will guarantee that the economic doom you fear will not happen."

"Speaking for the House Republicans," Ripper, the Minority Leader, said. "We will draft a plan the Congress will accept and the people applaud."

"Can't we work out a compromise?" Sperry asked.

"Of course. All legislation is a compromise," Tipton agreed.

"I'm talking about support for my plan," Sperry said.

"Face it, Mr. Secretary," Tipton said. "Your plan is dead."

"I'll go public. We'll see," Sperry threatened. "This recession is real. People are hurting."

"And all the words in the world won't save them," Tipton replied. "Am I right or wrong?" He turned to his colleagues.

"Right," Toogood answered.

"Right," Godfrey answered.

"Sorry, Ham, right," Ripper made it unanimous.

A red-faced Sperry stood up. "I thank you gentlemen for your time and advice." Sperry dismissed them.

"You are making a mistake not taking it, Mr. Secretary," Tipton got in the final word.

Sperry, detecting a note of mockery in the way Tipton pronounced his title, glared but did not respond.

Sperry watched from the front door as the visitors made their way to their parked cars. He heard his old fraternity brother Ripper say: "He always was stubborn, dumb-mule stubborn."

Sperry turned and slammed his front door behind him.

"How did it go?" Clete Clapp emerged from the front room where he had been waiting while the party chieftains conferred.

Sperry answered by turning his back and marching into his study. Clapp followed.

"Close the damned door," Sperry ordered as he resumed his place behind the desk.

Knowing better than to challenge his boss when he was in this kind of mood, Clapp obediently shut the door and sat down on the couch, keeping space between him and his master. Sperry turned in his chair and stared out the window with unseeing eyes, trying to figure out what to do next. He had few viable options and knew it. Both parties in Congress had turned him down, and so had Adams. In the latter's case, he had not even tried to hide his amusement.

"Who do you want me to kill?" Clapp asked, trying to make light of their situation.

Sperry responded with a glare. "If I were you, I wouldn't say things like that. Someone might hear and think you are serious."

Clapp shrugged his indifference. "They sweep this place every day."

"Damned politicians. They've got us in a box." Suddenly, a realization struck him. Tate had been a better politician than Sperry had given him credit for. Tate had seen this problem coming. "We've been set up," Sperry admitted.

"What do you mean?" Clapp asked, suddenly wishing he had a stiff drink. He glanced at the Remy Martin bottle setting on the bar, thought about pouring himself a snifter full, but Sperry answered before Clapp could decide whether it would be worth provoking his boss even more.

"I shouldn't have taken this damned job!"

"Which one?"

"Either one. I should have stayed in New York. I should not have listened to you. This is all your fault."

"I'll take the blame if you want, but I insist you didn't make a mistake. Don't think that way. That is what your enemies want you to do," Clapp decided to chance speaking honestly. "You accomplished everything you could there. From governor it was either up to Washington or back to the bank. You can still beat them if you try." Clapp was not sure he believed his own words.

"The bastards actually had the nerve to ask what party I belong to," Sperry admitted.

"Oh no," Clapp reacted before he shut his mouth.

Sperry glared at his assistant. "They were laughing at me. Their minds were set before they came, and they showed up for one reason only, to ridicule me."

"I doubt that," Clapp said loyally. "They're afraid of you. They know you are in a position to seize the nomination, the highest ranking man in the party."

"That's my God damned point. If they succeed in labeling me an independent, a man with no party, then I'm dead."

"So resign the acting vice presidency and show that you are the Republican Party leader. Use your status against them."

"That is the stupidest…" Sperry started to attack his assistant but stopped, suddenly realizing that he was speaking the truth. Sperry had only one option: let the Democrats push their damned plan, resign in protest, stand strong and lead while the Hill Republicans picked at legislative nits in the opposition counterproposal. "That damned Adams planned this all along. He's going to run for president," Sperry said.

"That's always been an option," Clapp said, not wanting to have his boss get too far out in front of him. "But I think it is now clear. He tried to promote you out of contention, and you can't let him."

"Yes, quit before he fires me," Sperry said. "Can he actually fire me?"

"I don't know," Clapp admitted.

"I thought you were supposed to be my political advisor, the expert," Sperry decided to blame Clapp for his problems.

"I'll research the question, but I doubt anybody knows. The Constitution is terribly vague about the position of vice president, and there are no precedents for an acting vice president. You are setting new ones."

"What would happen if Adams asked the entire cabinet to submit their resignations?" Sperry asked.

"They of course would have to resign."

"And the White House staff left over from Tate?"

"Them too."

After a few seconds of thought," Sperry continued. "I would be out as Secretary of Treasury. What would keep Adams from making a clean sweep of it, asking me to resign the vice presidency too."

"He could ask."

"If I refused?"

"Without the support of the Democratic or Republican parties, I don't think public opinion would back you," Clapp answered honesty.

"Then you are saying I have to act first, resign in protest over the economic plan, make it a matter of principle," Sperry said.

"Right," Clapp agreed, seeing that he had no alternative.

"We'll use the turndown of my plan and the Republican leadership refusal to support me as the peg," Sperry decided. "When should we declare war?"

"The sooner the better," Clapp said.

"Set a press conference for nine tomorrow morning. Make sure we have CNN and the four networks live. Tell our public relations people we have an important announcement about the economic plan. Adams, the Democrats and those Republican jerks in Congress are going to think I'm just going to whine about the congressional refusal to support the plan. We'll drop an atomic bomb on them."

"Yes sir," Clapp leaped to his feet.

"And don't leak my intentions to another soul. If anything gets out before my conference, you're dead."

Clapp rushed from the room worried that he might already be a zombie, a walking dead man. He had visions of his career as a political expert dissipating before his very eyes.

Chapter 31

The next morning Gif and Tracey slept in. Gif let Tracey use the bathroom first and by the time he had showered and shaved, Tracey had departed. Gif heated his coffee in the microwave, burned his bagel, and wolfed it down at the dining room table where Jerry Quigley was already playing with his computer.

"Where's everybody? Gif asked.

"Off investigating," Jerry replied.

"Getting anywhere with my request?" Gif asked between bites, simply making conversation.

"I'm working on it," Quigley responded, obviously preoccupied.

"When will you have something?" Gif asked.

"Soon, maybe. I'm on to something interesting."

I'll wait," Gif said. "Be careful."

"Maybe this afternoon," Quigley stalled.

"OK," Gif said and retreated to the kitchen.

Gif devoted about half an hour to housework. He cleaned the dishes out of the sink and stacked them in the dishwasher. With the washer running, he scrubbed the counter tops, checked the fridge, made a list of items he needed, and ran the sweeper throughout the house. While he worked, he mentally reviewed the items on his investigative to-do list and decided to start with a visit to Nan Starbright's apartment. He had been surprised to hear Joyce report that Benita was still in town, and he had a few follow-up questions he wanted to ask her. Benita was the only one who had talked with Nan Starbright after Walker's death, and Gif suspected that Benita still knew more than she had revealed. He assumed that Benita either was bargaining for more cash or simply did not recognize the importance of Maria's sibling confidences.

❧

The trip to Silver Spring required a little more than an hour, not as long as he had anticipated. Gif decided that his stars were in alignment when a parking space opened a half block from Nan's apartment house just as Gif arrived. He easily maneuvered the Prius into the spot and was in a good mood when he knocked on Nan/Benita's door. He rapped twice and stood back so that Benita could easily identify him through the viewer.

"I no have the money, I spend it," Benita called through the closed door, misinterpreting the reason for his visit.

"Benita, I just want to talk," Gif smiled. "The money's yours to do with as you wish."

After an extended pause, the door opened and Benita with mussed hair and wearing a housecoat peered out.

"I no take money from those children," Benita declared.

"Children?" Gif laughed. "I know nothing about any children."

"Those little girls from your office who tried to cheat me," Benita accused.

"I don't know anything about that, Benita. May I come in?"

Reluctantly, Benita stepped back. Gif, once inside, closed the door behind him.

"May I sit down, Benita?" Gif asked.

Benita nodded. "I just woked and need coffee," she said as she turned towards the kitchen.

Gif checked his watch. Eleven o'clock. "You must have had a late night," Gif made small conversation.

Benita laughed. "Working girl hours. Competition very pretty. Benita must work harder."

Gif didn't comment on that. "Would you happen to have a second cup?" Gif asked, hoping to prolong the already limited conversation.

"Two dollars," Benita said.

"Agreed," Gif said, taking two dollars out of his wallet and placing them on the coffee table in front of him.

While he waited, Gif glanced around the apartment. Obviously, Benita had been conducting her own search. The apartment was littered with discarded Spanish newspapers, clothing, shoes, open drawers. He wondered what if she had been searching for something more than her sister's money.

Benita reappeared carrying a small tray with two cups of coffee and two pieces of buttered flat bread. Benita set one of the cups in front of Gif, grabbed the two dollars, and retreated to a chair with the tray. There, Benita sat, tray in her lap, and began to munch on the bread.

"Benita, did you find what you were looking for?" Gif decided the direct route was the best way to deal with the suspicious Hispanic.

Benita smiled, took another bite of bread, and ignored Gif's question.

"Benita, you are in a position to make a great deal of money," Gif said. This time he hoped to entice Benita to at least ask him a question.

"No like Benita's coffee?" Benita asked, glancing at Gif's untouched cup.

Gif picked up his cup and sipped. It was thick, hot, strong and full of sugar. Gif liked his black. He swallowed and smiled. "Just the way I like it," Gif said.

"Hispanic instant," Benita said, dismissing that subject.

Gif waited.

"How much?" Benita finally asked.

'How much?" Gif repeated.

"How much damn money?" Benita demanded.

"The task force has put out a reward for information on Vice President Walker's death," Gif lied. The task force had indeed announced a reward for information leading to the arrest of President Harrison Tate's killer, one million dollars, but nothing had been offered in the case of Walker. Gif was not about to tell Benita that.

"One thousand dollars," Gif said. Benita already had $1,000 of the taxpayer's money, and Gif was just haggling now as tactic, a diversion that Gif hoped would get the taciturn Benita talking.

"OK, ten thousand," Benita said.

"That's too much Benita," Gif shook his head. He pretended to push himself off the couch.

"OK," Benita smiled, giving Gif the impression that she knew something of value.

"I first must hear your information," Gif said. "If I agree it's useful, we'll decide how much."

"OK," Benita said.

Benita's sudden change in attitude confused Gif. He doubted that his charm had persuaded the street hardened Benita to suddenly cooperate on a cash and carry basis. He wasn't even sure what her OK meant. Gif waited for her next move, but Benita just chewed on her flat bread, smiling, apparently enjoying herself. Gif, for his part, despised bargaining of any kind, and dealing with Benita was frustrating.

Gif stood up.

Benita swallowed her bread and jumped up. "OK, Maria tell me something, just in case."

"Just in case what?" Gif sat back down, beginning to feel like a Jack in the Box.

"Just in case what happened, happened," Benita smiled, pleased with her answer.

"Speak," Gif ordered. Benita's sudden ability to speak passable English warned him that Benita the actress had turned serious.

"OK. Maria told me she screwed the vice president to death," Benita said before breaking out into laughter.

"You just made a big mistake, Benita," Gif said, standing up again.

Once on his feet, Gif hesitated. Instinct told him to wait her out; Benita's behavior troubled him. Not only was Benita playing with him as if she had the upper hand, the crazy Hispanic acted as if she had something that she knew was worth ten thousand dollars. Gif stared at Benita, pretending to be angry. That didn't work because she ignored Gif and toyed with her flat bread. Gif turned and started towards the door.

"I'll sell it to the media," Benita said. "How much do you think your friend Mavis will pay me?"

Gif stopped. "OK, Benita one last chance," Gif said.

"Maria sent me an envelope for you," Benita announced. "She didn't tell me any secrets, she just said that if anything happened to her I should come to Washington, give you the envelope and wait. She said after you read it you would give me a big reward, not two thousand dollars, not pennies. Big money."

"Why didn't you tell me this when I talked with you and gave you a thousand dollars?" Gif said, not sure if she was still playing games or not.

"The thousand dollars just got you into the bidding," Benita laughed. "Now, I'll see who makes the best offer."

"How do I know the envelope contains anything more than a thank you note?" Gif asked, aware that the clever Hispanic was still playing him like a carnival mark.

Gif continued on to the door and was reaching slowly for the knob when Benita called: "You don't want to see the envelope?"

Gif turned and saw that Benita was waving a small gray envelope in the air. He assumed she had had it in the pocket of her housedress the entire time.

Gif turned, approached Benita, and held out his hand. Benita stuffed the envelope down the front of her dress.

"How much?" She demanded.

"That's it," Gif declared as he again turned towards the door.

"Maria promised me the letter in the envelope would answer all of your questions and that you would give me a very big reward," Benita said. "Don't make a mistake you will always regret."

"Maria may have promised you a reward, Benita, but I didn't. Show me the envelope," Gif insisted.

Benita extracted the envelope from the top of her housedress. Gif returned and held out his hand. Benita held the envelope against her bosom. "Do I have your word you will not open it until we reach an agreement?"

"You have my word. Let me see the envelope." Gif was now ready to say anything.

To his surprise, Benita handed him the envelope. Gif grabbed it and looked at the front and read his name written in clear distinct letters.

Inspector Gifford

He turned over the envelope and studied the seal. It did not appear to have been opened; at least he saw no steam marks or glue where there should not be any.

"What does it say?" Gif demanded of Benita. "I know you opened it."

Benita shrugged. "I haven't opened it. I haven't read what's inside."

Benita held out her hand, waiting for Gif to return the envelope.

Gif took out his ball point pen.

Benita jumped up and grabbed the table lamp which she raised over her head.

"You gave me your word, inspector," Benita said.

Gif hesitated. He looked at Benita and her raised lamp and then at the envelope.

"All right, Benita," Gif capitulated. ""Put the lamp down. Let me open the envelope. If Maria's letter is what she told you, I will see that you get a fair reward."

"A big reward," Benita insisted.

"A big reward," Gif said.

"You promise?" She said.

"I promise," Gif answered.

Benita returned the lamp to the table and sat down.

Gif, not completely sure what he had agreed to, slid the pen into one corner of the envelope and carefully tore it open while preserving the seal for the lab techs to study. Inside, he found one folded page of notepaper. On it was a message in the same handwriting.

Inspector Gifford,
If you are reading this, I am dead. I assume you
are standing in my apartment and that my sister Benita
is with you. Go into the bathroom, stand on the toilet,
lift the ceiling tile over your head and you will
find a small box. Inside is a recorder. It will answer
all your questions. John Walker was a decent man and
did not deserve what they did to him or me for that matter.
Please reward Benita as I promised.
Nan Starbright

Gif read the message once, glanced at Benita in disbelief, and then read it a second time.

"Do you know what this says?" Gif demanded.

Benita coyly shook her head and held her hand out, palm up.

"I don't believe you," Gif said.

Benita, still smiling, again held her hand out, palm up.

Gif, holding the note tight, held it up for Benita to see. "Is this your sister's handing writing?"

Benita nodded. Gif pulled the note away before she could read it, folded it, and slid it back into the envelope which he put in his inside coat pocket.

"Wait here," Gif ordered and went into the bathroom where he closed the lid on the toilet and climbed up on it. The seat cracked under his weight but held him. He looked up and examined the ceiling tile overhead. It rested firmly in place and appeared unmarked. At least he could not detect any untoward fingerprints. Feeling a little silly, he placed a palm against the center of the tile and pushed upward. From his awkward position below, he saw nothing. Still holding the tile in an inclined position, he reached as far as he could into the open end. He felt nothing. He lifted the tile higher on the right and tried again. Nothing. He wondered if Nan was playing games with him from the grave. He reversed hands and tried the left side. This time the tips of his fingers touched an object. He reached in as far as he could, grabbed the end of a small box and pulled it to him. After lowering the tile back in place, Gif noticed Benita watching him from the bathroom doorway.

"I'll be damned," Gif said, showing astonishment, not cursing.

Benita smiled at him, and Gif smiled back.

"See," a triumphant Maria said as she held out both hands.

With difficulty, Gif leaned over and grasped the sink and tried to step down. He slipped and felt a sharp pain in his right knee when his foot hit the floor. Benita grabbed his arm and helped him regain his balance.

"You're an old man, Gifford," she laughed.

Despite the pain, Gif, still clutching the small box in his right hand, laughed too.

"Thank you, Benita," Gif said.

"Thank you is all right, but not enough. Now, give me my big reward."

"Benita, I must check this out. If it is what I think it is, you will have your big reward. I promise."

"OK," Benita said. "But give me some reward now. I'm hungry."

Gif opened his wallet, let Benita look inside, and pulled out every dollar bill he had. Before Gif could count it, Benita snatched the small bonanza from his hand. Gif had no idea how much money he had just lost; he noted tens and twenties but no hundreds, and he didn't care. If the box contained what he thought it might, the investment would be worth every penny.

"You promised!" Benita looked him in the eye.

"I promise. You will have your reward by tomorrow."

"This afternoon," Benita insisted. "I can't stay in this dump forever."

"This afternoon," Gif agreed as he headed for the door.

As the door shut behind him, Gif heard Benita call after him. "This afternoon, Gifford, or I will call your friend Mavis and sell my story."

Gif hurried back to his Prius, sat down, and ripped the brown wrapping off the small box. Inside, he found a miniature recorder. He pushed a button and was greeted by the sound of a male and female talking. Gif immediately recognized Nan Starbright by the slight accent. It took him a few seconds to realize that Senator George Ames was the male.

"George, I'm not sure," Nan Starbright said.

"I'm not asking you to be sure, honey," Ames said. "I'm telling you what to do. Take these damned pills, hide them somewhere, and add them to the bottle when I tell you to.

"How will you do that?"

"Every time Walker tells you to meet him here, call me on my cell."

"What will the pills do to him?" Nan asked.

Ames laughed. "Honey just do what I say. Believe me when I say you will have the time of your life."

"I'm not sure I want to do that," Nan said softly.

"Do you want that $50,000 or not?"

"Will the pills hurt him?"
"Do you think I would give my friend something that might hurt him?"
Nan did not answer.
"Walker will get a rise that he'll never forget,' Ames laughed.

At that point the tape appeared to end. Gif started to hit the stop button and rewind to hear the conversation again but hesitated. Just to make sure that there was nothing else on the recording he let it continue as he reviewed in his mind what he had heard. Clearly, Senator Ames had promised to pay Nan to add the stronger pills to Walker's bottle without his knowledge, but he had no proof that she had. Suddenly, Nan's voice spoke to him from the machine.

"This is Nan Starbright speaking from my apartment on August 20th. I just received a call from Vice President John F Walker directing me to meet him at his Crystal City apartment. Following previous instructions from Senator George Ames I am calling the senator to alert him to John's plans."

Gif sat up straight and listened closely to the haunting voice from the past. If Nan did as Gif anticipated, she would give him the connection he was seeking.

"George, Nan."
"Honey, tell me he called."

Gif grabbed the recorder and held it to his ear. He had trouble hearing Ames--it sounded as if Ames were speaking in a tunnel from some distance away--but Gif could make out the words. Gif assumed that Nan had made the recording by simply holding it near the phone earpiece.

"I'm to meet him at the apartment within the hour," Nan said.

"Make sure he takes the damned pills. If this works the checks in the mail," Ames said.

Gif heard the sound of Ames's cell phone clicking off.

"I don't want a damned check," Nan shouted. "Cash, cash, cash, shit, shit, shit."

Gif sympathized with the dead call girl's frustration.

"This is Nan Starbright. I have just alerted Senator George Ames to my session with Vice President John Walker. As instructed I will take the extra strength pills provided me by Ames and will add them to John's bottle without his knowledge. Senator Ames has assured me that they will not harm John. This tape will serve as evidence of my ...that I am only acting ...that I only do what Ames ordered as a trick."

Gif turned off the tape, started the Prius, made a U-turn and headed for the Hoover Building.

Forty-five minutes later Gif burst into the director's reception room, smiled at the frowning secretary, and entered Tom Harrington's office without knocking. He found his friend sitting at his conference table meeting with several of his subordinates, not one of whom Gif recognized.

"Gif," Harrington looked up in surprise.

The subordinates frowned at the intruder.

"Sorry, Tom, it's important," Gif smiled. "Do you think you and Tracey could spare me a few minutes."

"Audrey," Harrington called at the open door behind Gif. "Please call Director Schultz and ask if she could join Inspector Gifford and me in my office. If that's not convenient, we can come down to her office."

"Gentlemen and lady, please excuse us," Harrington smiled at his subordinates.

As one they pushed their chairs back, stood up, looked curiously at Gifford, and departed, closing the door behind them. It immediately opened again and Harrington's secretary appeared.

"Excuse me sir, Director Schultz is on her way."

"Coffee. Gif?" Harrington looked at his visitor.

Remembering the foul brew he had been forced to drink with Benita, Gif nodded affirmatively.

"Coffee, please Audrey," Harrington ordered. As she started to close the door, Harrington added: "The Inspector prefers his hot, black and strong."

After the door closed, Gif asked: "Tell me please. Why is it that some women think they have to act like robots to be efficient?"

"I don't think Audrey likes you, Gif," Harrison laughed. "She gets along fine with everyone else."

"I guess we got off to a bad start," Gif said.

"Maybe," Harrison smiled. "Either that or she thinks you don't appreciate her."

"She's right about that," Gif smiled back.

"What's up?" Harrington asked.

"I think we've got a crack in our conspiracy," Gif said, taking the small recorder and envelope with its note from Nan from his suit coat pocket and placing both on the table in front of him.

Harrington sat up straight.

"If you don't object, why don't we wait for Tracey," Gif said.

Before Harrington answered, the outer door opened and Audrey appeared carrying a tray. Behind her came Tracey carrying a cup of her own.

"What a surprise," Tracey greeted Gif. "I must admit that I feel like I've seen you somewhere else today."

Gif restrained the impulse to say: "Like four hours ago in bed."

After the robot known as Audrey withdrew, Tracey pointed at the envelope and recorder in front of Gif and asked: "What's that?"

"Read this first, and then I'll play an interesting tape for you," Gif replied, handing the note to Tracey who sat directly across the table from him.

Gif and Harrington waited in silence while Tracey quickly scanned the note. When finished, she handed it to Harrington on her right and looked at Gif. "Where in the hell did you find that?"

Gif waited politely until Tom Harrington read Nan's note, folded it and slid it back into the envelope.

"Obviously, Benita gave it to me," Gif answered Tracey's question. "She apparently has had it all the time, that's why she came to Washington, and she just waited a while to improve her bargaining position."

"Camping out in Nan's apartment," Tracey said.

"She could have gotten herself killed," Harrington said.

"That thought occurred to me too," Gif said. "I think Benita's streetwise and tough enough to take care of herself."

"Is she armed?" Tracey asked.

"I didn't ask," Gif said.

"Is that what you found in the ceiling?" Tracey pointed at the recorder.

Gif nodded.

"Oh boy," Tracey clapped.

"I think I better suggest some improvements in our search techniques," Harrington said.

"The ceiling in the john," Tracey laughed.

"As will be self evident, the speakers are Nan Starbright and Senator George Ames," Gif announced before pushing the play button on the recorder. When the tape finished, Tracey spoke first.

"I'll be damned. We have to find out what Ames did with that heads up. He knew where Walker would be that afternoon."

"If Ames was working with another person and he told that person about Walker's plans, and if that person also knew where the president was going to be that afternoon, we might not have a coincidence on our hands," Gif flatly stated what the other two were thinking.

"And Walker's death might not have been an accident, Tracey slapped the table.

"We've got to be damned careful with all this," Harrington said.

"What do you know?" Tracey said. "The damned media have been right all along. We've got a real political conspiracy."

"Real careful," Harrington said. He turned to Gif. "How do you suggest we handle this?"

"We've got to lean on Senator George Ames," Tracey declared.

Harrington, waiting for Gif to respond, did not comment.

'Let's find out what the phone records and computers tell us," Gif said.

"I'll have Jeff and Reggie handle it personally," Tracey said. "They can start with Senator George Ames's phones and computers."

"With warrants. Everything legal and by the book," Harrington said.

"Yes sir," Tracey saluted her former subordinate. "We'll treat it like a sting operation. Special search warrants and all that nice stuff."

"What will you tell the senator?" Harrington, now the man who had to deal with the media and the politicians, asked.

"As little as possible," Tracey said. "Don't worry, Tom, I know the routine. Let me get out in front on this."

"I'm with you guys every step of the way," Harrington said. "Just because I'm sitting in this office acting like a bureaucrat, it doesn't mean I've forgotten who put me here." He looked first at Tracey and then at Gif.

"I like a good corruption investigation cover story," Gif smiled.

"Why did I anticipate you might suggest that?" Tracey laughed.

"Do you think Ames will buy it?" Harrington asked.

"What politician wouldn't?" Tracey asked. "They all have their hands in somebody's till. Besides, it might help to let him worry a little."

"But we don't want to alert any members of a conspiracy, assuming there is one," Harrington cautioned.

"We don't want to give anybody a reason to start killing off any more potential witnesses," Gif surprised Tracey by siding with Harrington.

"Like Senator George Ames," Tracey laughed. "I guess we better put him under twenty-four seven protective surveillance."

"With a little more manpower than we had on poor Dexter," Harrington said. "And don't forget one other little thing. As of now, we three are the only ones aware of this new evidence," he nodded at the recorder. "I suggest we keep it that way and also remember that someone out there does not hesitate to eliminate anybody who gets in their way no how senior or junior they might be."

"I'm rather glad Tracey is boarding with me," Gif agreed. "And you should take a look at your own protective detail, Tom, particularly at home."

"I agree," Harrington said.

"I would like to be the one to discuss the situation with Senator Ames," Gif said.

"Agreed," Harrington spoke for the FBI.

"It's your wicket," Tracey, the leader of the task force, agreed.

"Good," Gif stood up. "I'll leave this stuff for your techs to work on, but I'll want it back for my conversation with Ames," Gif pointed at the recorder and envelope. "I'd like to get my personal mail back someday," he smiled, referring to Nan's note.

"I understand how you might feel nostalgic," Tracey laughed. "But I wouldn't hold my breath. If this thing breaks out like it should, all this stuff will be stored in the National Archives. They might send you a copy with a fancy letter of appreciation."

"I also have a suggestion," Gif said.

"We owe you."

"I recommend that we hold off on any high level briefings for now," Gif said.

Tracey and Harrington laughed.

"At least until we determine who might be left standing," Harrington agreed.

"I can't agree on anything so important until I discuss it with my significant other," Tracey declared.

Harrington stared at Tracey, and Gif studied the far wall, not quite sure where Tracey was heading. Tracey silently watched Gif until their eyes met. Gif blinked, and Tracey laughed. "OK, I think I just did. No briefing of anybody outside this room until the three of us meet and concur."

"On that high note," Gif stood up. "I'll withdraw and leave the grunt work to you two.

As he headed towards the door, Tracey called after him. "May I ask where you are going now? Do you have another bathroom ceiling to inspect?"

"I thought I might visit Redskin Park and see how practice is going. Since everything seems to be connected, I probably should figure out how that little case figures in."

"Right," Tracey said. "I forgot about the Redskins. It's strange how a political conspiracy can render insignificant the murder of two football players."

"I haven't forgotten them," Gif said.

'Neither have two million fans," Harrington said.

"Then do something about it, lover," Tracey said.

At the door, Gif remembered something important. "Oh yes, there is one more little thing."

"It figures," Tracey said.

"I owe Benita a little reward," Gif said.

"No problem," Harrington said.

"How much is little?" Tracey asked. She knew Gifford well enough to question his definitions.

"Am I correct in recalling that the task force announced a bounty of one million dollars for information leading to the arrest of the killer of President Harrison Tate?"

"You're kidding," Tracey blurted.

"We're still a long way from that point, Gif," Harrison said, glancing at Tracey.

"I know, but Nan promised Benita," Gif said.

"Ms. Starbright could have promised her sister a trip to Mars, but we're talking about a common streetwalker not K Street royalty," Tracey said.

"I rather like Benita at this point," Gif said. "Have Reggie deliver a bouquet of roses from me and accompany them with a box of hundred dollar bills. I'll pay for the roses."

"How many hundred dollar bills?"

" Five hundred of those suckers," Gif said as he opened the door.

Tracey turned and stared at Harrington. "Help me out," she appealed. "How much is that?"

"$50,000 I think," Harrington scratched his head.

"That'll do," Gif said. "I promised Benita she would have it this afternoon at the latest."

"Dinner is on me," Tracey called as Gif opened the door. "Expect Chinese. I won't be able to afford anything more than that."

As Gif passed through the outer office, he exchanged cold stares with the efficient robot and departed without another word.

"Arrogant shit," Gif heard Audrey declare as the door closed behind him.

That rather put a fine cap on his day. He collected his Prius and headed out I-66 towards home not Redskin Park.

Chapter 32

Acting President Hiram Alphonse Adams was sitting in an overstuffed leather chair in the Andrew Johnson Suite perusing the *Washington Post,* his favorite northern newspaper, which was not saying much for it, when the door burst open and Jake Tyrone rushed in.

"Slow down, Jake, you're too old for such haste. Remember your gentle southern upbringing," Adams cautioned his friend and aide.

Jake ignored the old man's advice and hurried to the television where he jabbed the on button. "You won't believe this," Jake announced as CNN appeared on the screen. "The damned fool is holding a press conference."

The monitor displayed a smiling Acting Vice President Alexander Hamilton Sperry standing at the podium.

"I guess he's announcing that the big bad Congress decided not to follow his New York City banker advice," Adams laughed.

"Listen," Jake ordered as he turned up the volume.

"…and it is for that reason that I am announcing my resignation as acting vice president and secretary of the treasury," Sperry declared.

"The damned fool," Adams parroted Jake's initial report.

"Has the acting president accepted your resignations?" A network reporter shouted.

"My letters of resignation are here in my hand." Sperry picked up two documents from the podium and waved them for all to see. "The moment I leave this room I will step across the hall and deliver them to the acting president myself. I assure you that my decision is final. As I said, like the American people, I am tired of all the political games, Republican and Democratic. It's time that we returned the government to the people."

"He's going to run as an independent," Adams declared.

"Which will split the conservative vote and make you a shoo-in. I wish we could hold the election tomorrow," Jake declared.

"Let's have a touch of morning coffee," Adams said as he pushed himself out of the chair. "Damned joints," he complained as he creaked erect.

Jake beat the acting president to his desk, opened the side drawer, and liberated Jack Daniels. He half filled two cups and topped them off with coffee from the decanter. Adams circled around behind Jake and lowered himself heavily into his padded chair. Jake handed him his presidential cup, lifted his own in toast, and drank deeply.

"For medicinal reasons only," Adams sipped as Jake put Jack Daniels back into his resting place.

"The asshole holds a press conference just across the hall and doesn't have the grace to tell us what he is doing," Jake said.

"Turn that thing off," Adams nodded at the television where Sperry was sparring with an excited media corps.

"I am looking forward to the challenge…" Sperry was saying when Jake hit the off button.

"Correct me if I'm wrong, which I seldom admit, Jake, but didn't that man just announce that he was on his way here to submit his resignations in person?" Adams said.

"Yes sir. Do you want me to have the Secret Service deny him entry?"

"Oh no, I am truly looking forward to this historic meeting. Please instruct the Secret Service to escort Mr. Sperry from the premises as soon as he hands me those glorious documents. I wouldn't want him to suffer an attack of second thought."

"Yes sir," Jake smiled as he downed his morning pick-me-up before turning and walking at a measured pace away from the man who now sat alone at the pinnacle.

In the outer office Jake relayed his master's instructions to Miss Mary who would in turn pass them on to the Secret Service. As soon as Jake finished speaking, Miss Mary who had been taking notes with her head bent forward leaned back and rewarded Jake with a full southern lady smile.

"Isn't life just full of wonderful surprises," Miss Mary said.

Jake astonished her by leaning over and kissing her on the cheek. "It sure is, Miss Mary."

As Jake was returning to the inner office, Miss Mary called after him:

"Jake, are you sure you want him removed forthwith?"

"That's what the president ordered."

"Without even a chance to return to his office to collect his personal pictures and papers?" Miss Mary smiled broadly.

"Forthwith, forthwith," Jake returned the smile. "Means throw the arrogant bastard out on his ass with only the clothes on his back," Jake declared. "Please excuse the vulgarity, Miss Mary, but I always get carried away on joyous occasions."

"Apology not needed. Sentiments shared. Forthwith it shall be," Miss Mary turned to her phone.

Jake returned inside to find Acting President Adams had used the remote to turn the television back on.

"The animals are crucifying him, Jake," Adams declared. "Come join me and watch the fun. I now understand the crowds at that Coliseum who so enjoyed watching those mangy lions eat the dirty Christians."

Jake took his customary seat in front of Andrew Johnson's desk and turned to the side so he could watch the television as ordered.

"Imagine how old Andrew Johnson would have felt if he could have sat here in this chair of his and watched the media consume those Radical Republicans who had tormented him so." Adams continued to exult as he turned off the television.

Jake sat quietly for a few minutes before speaking. "Sir, I imagine that Mr. Sperry will be here shortly. I have a suggestion."

Adams held up a fat forefinger before punching the intercom.

"Yes sir," Miss Mary answered.

"I'm having an important conference with Mr. Tyrone. Should Mr. Sperry arrive with two papers in his hand, have him take a seat until I am ready to receive him."

"Yes, sir," Miss Mary said before turning to the two stern Secret Service agents she had been briefing. "Please position yourselves before the door to the president's office and do not allow any one to enter until I personally authorize it," she ordered.

The two agents took their station with crossed arms. The smiles on their faces indicated their pleasure at the duty that waited ahead of them. Like most members of the protective details, they despised the arrogant, soon to be former acting vice president.

"You take his left arm and I'll take his right," the more muscular of the two whispered. "We'll give the SOB a proper escort from the building without letting his big feet touch the floor."

"What is it, Jake?" Adams asked his old friend.

"Wouldn't it be appropriate if we named a replacement before the damned fool leaves the building?" Jake asked.

"Excellent idea. I'm confident the media pack will follow him over here. Make sure the network boys and girls bring their cameras. Let the people witness history in the making. What did that Persian fellow say, something like the moving finger writes and having writ moves on. Something like that. As soon as he hands me his damned letters, he's history. That damned finger will have writ. I'll accept them and while he is on his way to the door, I'll announce his successor. The king is dead. Long live the king. Who should I name?"

"A Democrat, of course, not a southerner. We can't have two men of Dixie on the ticket," Jake smiled.

"Of course not. We need balance, a vote getter, a pretty young man, age and youth sells. What about that boy from Montana?"

"Ames?" Jake shook his head negatively. "He's got some things in his past."

"I know he likes the ladies, but we all do."

"Please take my word for it. Select Ames and we'll live to regret it," Jake persisted.

"OK, Jake," Adams smiled. "You know these kids better than I do. I don't want one of those Ivy League types. Too intellectual, too liberal, too dumb in a practical sense. They think they know everything while they know nothing. Wasn't that the name of a party, the Know Nothings. What about the Midwest or the left coast?"

Before Jake could answer, the intercom buzzed.

"Yes Miss Mary?" Adams answered the interruption cordially, speaking for posterity.

"The acting vice president would like to see you sir," Mary said. "I told him you were busy, but he said it was important."

"Please ask the acting vice president to wait. I'll see him shortly," Adams pretended he did not know what Sperry wanted.

"I wouldn't choose anyone from California. Their women are too pushy, too masculine, for my taste," Jake picked up on their conversation.

"OK, Washington State then. I rather like that young guy," Adams said.

"A Hispanic American, not a bad idea," Jake said, pretending that he had not been guiding the conversation in that direction. "He's ambitious, flexible, a good party man."

"They say he has a touch of the woodpile in him," Adams said, his tone indicating that was a negative.

"All the better," Jake tried to make it a positive.

"The only thing that's lacking is that he isn't gay. That would be better than having a woman. I'm not sure the country is ready for that," Adams smiled.

"Why don't I give Senator Hernandez a call? If he's willing, we could take him on as a trial and dump him before the convention if he doesn't work out."

"OK," Adams agreed.

"I would like to suggest one little thing, sir," Jake said.

Adams waited.

"I recommend that you do not quote that Persian fellow, the one who wrote the moving finger thing."

"And why is that?"

"I was talking with a former ambassador to Teheran a while back and that Persian fellow's name came up. I may have used cited your favorite quotation," Jake smiled.

"And?"

"The ambassador told me the Persian poet's name was Omar Khayyam."

"That's the guy."

"The ambassador recommended that I not mention the name in mixed company,"

"Jake, where is this leading?"

"Khayyam in Farsi it means my testicles."

"Oh my," Adams laughed. "I must remember that fellow's name."

"Khayyam," Jake repeated.

"Yes, Khayyam," Adams repeated.

The acting president was still laughing when Jake slipped out the side door that led to the hall and the closet he used as an office.

Adams added a little Jack Daniels to his cup, topped it off with coffee from the carafe, and picked up the remote and turned on the television. To his delight, he found CNN broadcasting live from his outer office. Pandemonium raged. The cameraman panned the entire office starting with a close-up of the acting vice president's back. Sperry was pretending to look out the window. Next, the screen showed two burly Secret Service agents with crossed arms blocking the entrance to the Andrew Johnson's Suite. Finally, the camera focused on Miss Mary sitting patiently, smiling at the circus that was disturbing the normal tranquility of her office. Adams stifled the urge to call Miss Mary and congratulate her on her composure; he didn't want the media to misinterpret the gesture.

Jake in his office checked his rolodex, found Hernandez's office number, and dialed.

"Senator Hernandez's office," a perky voice answered.

"This here's Jake Tyrone, I work in President Adam's office," Jake said. "May I speak with the senator please?"

"Yes sir," the voice replied without hesitation.

Ten seconds later, the senator came on line. "Yes, sir, what can I do for you?"

Jake was pleased to note that he did not detect the slightest accent. "Senator, Jake Tyrone."

"Yes sir."

"I assume you have been watching the nonsense taking place at this end of Pennsylvania Avenue?"

"Yes sir."

"What do you think of it?" Jake put the young man on the spot.

After only a slight hesitation, Hernandez responded. "I think it is disgusting, sir. That man is putting his personal ambition ahead of country."

"I agree with you," Jake said. "Where do you stand on this economic plan business?

"I firmly agree with President Adams," Hernandez replied.

The response made Jake smile. Nobody knew what the acting president thought on that issue, not even Jake. The old man wanted the House to rewrite Sperry's masterpiece, but Jake doubted he had a clue what it should contain.

"We need a good Democratic plan, not some warmed over Republican banker's idea to save the rich and to hell with the common man," Hernandez continued with clichés.

"And the budget?" Jake asked.

"This is no time to worry about nickels and dimes. We should spend what we must and raise taxes on the rich if we have to."

"And national defense?" Jake asked. He knew that at a minimum he had to pretend to probe the Senator's views."

"We need a strong military?"

"Terrorism?"

"Kick the shit out of the rag heads."

"What do you feel about the vice presidency?" Jake dropped his bombshell.

"Sir?"

"The vice presidency?" Jake repeated.

Hernandez hesitated, obviously uncertain what Jake was asking him. Jake said nothing, interested in how the boy handled a little pressure.

"We need a good, loyal Democratic vice president who supports President Adams to the fullest," Hernandez said.

"Would you be interested?" Jake asked.

"In the vice presidency?"

"In the acting vice presidency," Jake said.

"Well, I should discuss it with my wife," Hernandez said hesitantly.

"We need an answer right now?" Jake pressed.

"Yes sir, I'm interested," Hernandez's voice broke as he spoke.

"Good. Stay tuned to CNN and drop by and see me later today," Jake said and hung up.

Jake returned to the Andrew Johnson Suite where he found Adams watching television again.

"Look at that, Jake. That mob is just outside our door," Adams laughed as he pointed first at the television set and then the door.

"We've got an acting vice president," Jake said.

"Good," Adams nodded, reaching for his pen. "What's his name?"

"Senator Joseph Hernandez, junior senator from the grand state of Washington," Jake imitated a speaker at a political convention.

Adams wrote down the name on his pad. "I hope his accent is American, Jake."

"Close your eyes and you wouldn't know he was Hispanic," Jake said.

"We'll have to limit his television exposure at first, at least until we clean him up a bit," Adams said.

He put his pen down, emptied his cup and dropped it into the drawer beside Jack Daniels, picked up the remote and turned off the television. He straightened his tie and looked at Jake. "How do I look?"

"Like a real president, sir," Jake answered.

"Bring in the circus," Adams ordered.

As Jake walked towards the door, Adams called after him. "I think we ought to give a little thought to moving across the way," he looked in the direction of the White House. "I'm getting a little tired of the ambiance in this place. Old Andrew let too many people push him around."

When Gif emerged from the bedroom, he found Jerry Quigley hunched over his computer screen.

"Hey boss, I'm glad to see you," Jerry announced.

"Good morning Jerry, where is everyone?" Gif asked.

Gif was still feeling the euphoria of the previous day's developments. All he needed in a case was a small crack, and he had one. It was now up to him to figure out how to lever the opening wide enough to drive his posse through. Although that thought mixed its metaphors, it did not trouble him.

"Director Schultz got up early. She grabbed her coffee and took off for D.C. All of the others are out doing their thing. Look at this," Jerry pointed at a web site page.

Gif stood behind Jerry's chair and stared at the screen. It didn't look like much to him. "Explain what I'm looking at," Gif said.

"This is http://www.urperiscope.com/pirouetting," Jerry said.

"And what the hell is that?" Gif asked.

Jerry, amused, smiled indulgently at Gif.

"It's a point of interest to your investigation, Jerry said. "This is an internet bulletin board where people can post messages for people with like interests to read. Each sub-interest has its own page and / pirouetting is one, though not a very popular one I admit."

"And what is pirouetting?"

"It's whirling madly around on one foot," Jerry laughed.

"You're wasting time, Jerry. What is your point?" Gif, who considered a preoccupation with the internet juvenile, did not find Jerry's attitude amusing.

"You take things too personal, boss. This is an important bulletin board that gets thousands of hits a day."

"And why is that important?"

"I found this page stored in the contact list on the personal computer of one of those names you gave me. Want to guess which one?"

"No, tell me," Gif ordered.

"The acting president's chief of staff."

"Jake Tyrone?"

"Yes."

"He's interested in ballet?"

"No, pirouetting."

"You're reaching, Jerry."

"Somebody using his computer is interested in that bulletin board," Jerry said.

"Then he or his wife or a grandkid likes ballet. What else can you tell me?"

"Right now? Nothing. I just found the entry in the contact list and was checking it out when you came in."

Irritated, Gif turned towards the kitchen but stopped abruptly when a thought struck him. "You found that on Tyrone's computer?"

"Yes."

"Great. That means…."

"Yep," Jerry smiled.

"Without getting caught?"

"I hope," Jerry said.

"Keep working, Jerry. Don't waste too much time worrying about that pirouetting thing."

"Right, boss," Jerry said.

Tired of talking about computer web pages, Gif turned toward the kitchen just as his cell phone buzzed. He checked the Caller ID, saw that it was Tracey, and picked up.

"What?"

"Did I wake you?" Tracey greeted him.

"No," Gif laughed. "I've been up for hours."

"Forget your coffee and toast," Tracey let him know she did not believe him. "Turn on CNN now," Tracey ordered and hung up.

Gif returned to his study, sat in his recliner, and used the remote to tune in to Channel 29.

"…viewing the reception room of the Andrew Johnson Suite in the Treasury Department," Gif caught the CNN reporter in mid sentence.

Gif stared at his monitor. The room was filled with jostling men and women. The camera focused on two husky men in suits blocking a closed door.

"The door to Acting President Adam's office is closed, and two Secret Service agents are denying entry," the CNN reporter gratuitously explained.

The camera then shifted to a smiling, mature woman sitting at her desk.

"Miss Mary Murphy, the acting president's secretary, sits patiently at her desk ignoring the chaos all around her, waiting for the president to instruct her to admit the waiting acting vice president," the reporter continued.

The camera shifted from Miss Mary to the back of a man looking out of the window. Gif had the impression that he was trying to ignore the raging tumult behind him.

The CNN reporter continued his monologue:

"Meanwhile, Acting Vice President Alexander Hamilton Sperry stands at the window with his letters of resignation in hand while he waits for Acting President Adams to admit him to his office. Ladies and gentlemen, we are witnessing history being made. Acting Vice President Sperry has been kept waiting for thirty minutes in full view of the world. As Sperry just announced on national television, he plans to resign both of his offices, the acting vice presidency, and his post as secretary of the treasury.

"Never before in this nation's history has a vice president announced in advance his intention to relinquish his post. In fact, to this reporter's knowledge this is the first time the nation has had an acting vice president representing a party different from that of his president. Given today's shocking events, this reporter doubts that it will ever happen again. The president's secretary has informed us that the acting president is aware that his vice president is out here but is seriously engaged in an important consultation. Frankly, this correspondent cannot imagine what is more important at this historical juncture than his meeting with Vice President Sperry."

At that moment, the door to the suite opened and Jake Tyrone whispered something to the Secret Service guards. Sperry turned; Tyrone stepped back, and Sperry entered. Gif expected the door to shut, but it remained open. The media mob hesitated, watched the open door, expecting the Secret Service to block their way. When neither guard moved, the mob shoved forward in an undignified rush. The CNN cameraman used his equipment to force his way in with the first mass. The picture on Gif's screen bounced, but the camera stayed on, allowing the viewer to sense what the media was feeling.

The CNN reporter continued his spiel:

"The door to the Andrew Johnson Suite has opened. Acting Vice President Sperry still clutching his letters of resignation has entered the Oval Office to meet with President Adams."

The reporter grunted as he joined the jostling crowd.

"We are being allowed to witness this historic occasion. I assume that you are still…still…excuse me, excuse me CNN…" the reporter shouted. "This is very difficult ladies and gentlemen. There, I am now inside the room. President Adams remains seated at his desk with his chief of staff, Jake Tyrone, standing at his side. Acting Vice President Sperry is speaking to President Adams, but the president seems to be ignoring him."

The picture that appeared on Gif's television confirmed the reporter's words. Gif like most of the watching world saw Sperry standing in front of the president's desk but Adams was looking at his chief of staff ignoring Sperry. Sperry appeared to speak to Adams who continued to ignore him. Gif could not hear Sperry's words but assumed they were not friendly. Sperry glared at the indifferent president and threw his letters of resignation onto the desk. Adams ignored them. Adams turned to smile directly at the camera. Sperry whirled about and the camera followed him. Sperry pushed through the jostling media.

"Mr. Vice President," the CNN reporter called.

The camera turned towards the reporter who was pointing his microphone at Sperry. The angry acting vice president brushed it aside, and then he stopped. He reached for the microphone, but the CNN reporter refused to surrender it.

"We have finally reunited with our cameraman," the reporter gasped, breathing heavily. "Acting Vice President Sperry has dropped his letters of resignation on the president's desk and now has a few words for the American people."

The reporter held the microphone so that Sperry could speak into it.

"Ladies and gentlemen of America, you have just seen your acting president at work. What you witnessed is what you get when trying to deal reasonably with this president. I tried to explain the reason for my presence here today, but our non-elected leader refused to listen. I placed my letters of resignation on his desk, but he did not deign to read them. This is how he reacts every day to advice from his cabinet, which was appointed by a duly elected president. He treated his government's plan for combating the recession we now suffer with the same indifference. He cavalierly refused to read or support it. Faced with such incompetence, I resigned as your acting vice president and as secretary of the treasury. I now leave this madhouse with a solemn promise. I will continue to fight."

The reporter pulled his microphone back and announced dramatically:

"There you have it ladies and gentlemen. You have just witnessed one of the most bizarre resignations in our country's history."

The camera followed as Sperry pushed his way through the struggling media and out the door. Others shouted questions at him and held their microphones up for comment, but Sperry brushed them aside as he made his escape.

"Holy shit," Jerry Quigley exclaimed from his position behind Gif's recliner.

Gif ignored him and concentrated on the unbelievable drama that was still unfolding. The camera turned from Sperry's retreat back to the president.

Adams stood up. "If I may," he smiled at the camera.

All microphones and cameras were aimed at him.

"That was really something, wasn't it?" Adams said, looking directly at the CNN camera. "I've seen a lot of circus clown acts in my eighty years, but this beats them all. Now, let me interpret for you the amazing event you have just witnessed," Adams paused for effect.

The media stood transfixed. Not a single reporter interrupted with a shouted question.

Adams waited for several dramatic, silent seconds before continuing.

"Former Acting Vice President Alexander Hamilton Sperry has just resigned with a heartfelt tantrum. I was rather worried for the poor man; he seemed so excited and out of control. Now you understand why I had to fire him. These," Adams picked up the two letters of resignation and dropped them in his wastebasket. "They are literally not worth the paper they are written upon. I fired Mr. Sperry last night as my chief of staff, Mr. Tyrone who now stands by my side, will attest."

Adams looked at Jake who nodded back.

"Mr. Sperry returned from a conference on Capitol Hill yesterday in a monumental rage. Your nation's elected representatives had the audacity to inform Mr. Sperry that they preferred to write their own economic recovery plan. That's the way the system works. Propose, negotiate, compromise, agree. Mr. Sperry is so new to Washington that he had difficulty adjusting. He seems to think that his millionaire background entitles him to special consideration. I tried to reason with Mr. Sperry, but he was so out of control that I had to ask for his resignation. He declined, so I fired him. Those," Adams leaned over and peered into his wastepaper basket, "represent Mr. Sperry's attempt to delude the American people. Shame, I say, shame on you, Mr. Sperry.

"You have seen me put that dreadful episode exactly where it belongs."

Again, Adams peered into his wastepaper basket.

"With that behind us, I have a few announcements to make. I hereby request that every cabinet secretary, every policy level appointee, and all key White House staffers submit their resignations effective immediately. I simultaneously ask that those individuals remain and work in place until their replacements have been identified, cleared and announce themselves ready to assume work. I have nothing but the highest respect for those of you appointed by President Tate whose commanding presence I, too, miss, and I say, I know, he would ask you to do as I request."

Before the media could react with a barrage of questions, Adams held both hands high in the air and continued.

"I have one more important item to share with you. I here and now reveal my selection of Senator Joseph Hernandez of the most beautiful state of Washington to serve as my acting vice president, replacing the now departed and most volatile Mr. Sperry."

That announcement momentarily stilled the media including the CNN reporter.

"I regret to say, ladies and gentlemen of the media, I cannot take your questions at this time," Adams said. "To the people of America still watching, I give you my solemn promise. Your government is in firm and temperate hands. Thank you."

Gif muted the sound and leaned back in his chair. Like everyone else in the country, he was having difficulty digesting what he had just witnessed.

"Damn, it's like the bloody French Revolution," Jerry Quigley observed. "The heads are rolling."

Gif silently nodded his agreement. Privately, he tried to assess what it all meant to his conspiracy theory. Gif assumed that if Sperry had been the Machiavelli behind it all he had just lost despite the rash of murders.

After spending an inconsequential day, Gif was seated on the patio wrestling with his myriad thoughts and waiting for Tracey to arrive with a report on the meeting with the special judge when he heard the crunch of gravel announcing the arrival of a car. Assuming that it was just another team member, Gif ignored it as he pondered. He heard a knock on the front door and a familiar male voice ask.

"Is Sheriff Gifford home?"

"On the patio," Jerry answered.

Gif turned to find Sheriff Dick Simmons standing at the rear door smiling at him.

"You look comfortable, Gif, mind if I join you?"

"Come on out, Dick," Gif greeted his former protégé.

"I was in the neighborhood and thought I'd drop in and see how things are going," Simmons said.

"Have a seat. I'm just enjoying the fresh mountain air," Gif said as he wondered what Simmons really wanted. Social visits were not what he and his old subordinate ever exchanged, not even when they were working together.

"I don't blame you," Dick said as he sat in the chair opposite Gif. "Did you by chance catch the breaking news?"

"I watched it on television," Gif said, shaking his head. "I've never seen anything like it."

"I heard it on the radio. It sounded like Sperry needs a straitjacket," Simmons said.

"Maybe they all do," Gif said. "There must be a better way to run a government than this."

"It tells us small time politicians," Simmons referred to his own elective office, "that there are better ways to earn a living. I wasn't sure I agreed with you about politics and politicians before, but today changed my mind."

Gif did not reply. Instead, he stood up. "I'm going to have a coffee, Dick, want to join me?"

Simmons pretended to consider the question.

"I've got coffee, beer, coke, whatever."

"Help yourself, I'm fine," Simmons decided.

Gif entered the house and fixed himself a microwave coffee. While the coffee was heating, Gif coughed to get Jerry's attention. When Jerry looked up from his computer, Gif silently mouthed four words.

"Shut down the computer."

When he returned to the patio, Gif sat down and looked at his visitor.

"So, what can I do for you, Dick?" Gif asked. Gif wanted to get rid of Simmons before any more of the team arrived for the staff meeting.

"I not prying, Gif, but I'm starting to get a little pressure from the council on the Redskin thing. You know how our local politicians feel about the Redskins."

"I understand, Dick, and I know I should have gotten back to you with a status report," Gif said. "But the problem is, I 'm ashamed to say, I don't have a single suspect. We've taken a look at everything I can think of and come up empty. If your boys have any leads and are ready to share them, we're here to help."

"I think I've already had this conversation, Gif," Simmons smiled and took a drink of his beer. "Brian," Simmons referred to his chief investigator Brian Sadler, an ex MP that Simmons had brought in from the outside, "reports the same problem. Do you think there could be a connection with all those other shootings?"

Gif laughed. "You're referring to that stupid Mavis Davis television report."

Simmons nodded. "That and the fact you've brought a team in from Richmond," he nodded towards the house where Jerry was working.

"That's all for show," Gif said. "The television report was an outright fabrication. I don't see any connection. I'm not working the other shootings," Gif lied. "And my team is here trying to come up with something I missed. We're all getting older, you know."

"I know, Gif. In fact, between you and me, I'm thinking of turning in my shield myself. I'm tired of all the bullshit, and I'm ready to retire. We've got a small place at the shore, and it's looking more attractive every day."

Gif let that comment slide. He figured that Simmons was no more than forty-five, well below the retirement age.

"Do you think we will ever find out who shot Sheriff Tate?" Simmons used the title all of Harrison's old friends employed when speaking fondly of their friend who had climbed to the pinnacle.

Gif's first impulse was to correct Simmons by using Harrison's most recent title but resisted. "Killers always make mistakes, you know that Dick," Gif replied instead.

"Where would you and I be if they didn't?" Simmons said. "What does Director Schultz say?"

."We don't discuss the investigation," Gif lied. "I find it difficult talking about Harrison," he tried to end any discussion of that topic.

"I know. We all do."

At that moment, the crunch of gravel signaled the arrival of another car.

"I think you have guests arriving," Simmons stood up. "And I have to get back to work.

"Any time, Dick," Gif waved noncommittally.

Simmons departed by cutting back through the house.

"How's it going, son?" Simmons asked Jerry as he circled the table stopping behind Jerry's chair.

Jerry smiled as he looked up from the blank screen. "I was just putting some of Mr. Gifford's notes on the computer. He's not computer literate, you know."

Simmons frowned as he patted Jerry on the shoulder. "It's a generational thing," Simmons said before departing through the front door

Just as the front door screen banged behind Simmons, Tracey came around the side of the house and joined Gif on the patio. She looked around, puzzled. "I saw the Bronco out front. I thought you had company."

"Sheriff Simmons," Gif said, rising and kissing Tracey on the cheek. "He just left that away." Gif pointed at the back door.

"Christ, did you see that near riot on television?" Tracey asked.

"I turned it on as soon as you hung up. What does it mean?"

"Half of our conspiracy suspects just got fired," Tracey said.

"I know."

"It might make part of our job a little easier," Tracey said as she sat down.

"Or harder. Want a beer?" Gif asked.

"Of course," Tracey smiled.

When Gif returned, Tracey greeted him with a frown. "Good news and bad."

Gif laughed. "That doesn't surprise me. What's up?"

"The special judge declined to authorize a tap on Ames's office phone. He went along with a tap on his cell phone and home phones but wouldn't touch anything official."

"I can't say I'm surprised," Gif said. "Putting a tap on the Congress doesn't happen every day."

"No shit," Tracey chuckled mirthlessly. "He couldn't possibly conceive that we might find a corrupt politician."

"What do you think the special judge would say if we asked for a warrant authorizing taps on the former acting vice president, the guy the acting president just fired?" Gif asked.

"Tom and I just discussed that. We decided to hold off for a couple of days and see how things develop," Tracey said.

"That will give us time to see how the Ames thing works out," Gif said. "I hope the special judge can keep his mouth shut."

"About Ames? I don't think that is a problem. Our request focused on the Walker death. The problem would arise when and if we start talking about warrants in support of a conspiracy investigation possibly involving the president."

"You have doubts about this special judge?"

"He's only human. Investigating a senator is one thing. Investigating a conspiracy involving the office of the presidency is another."

"It's an unprecedented situation," Gif said.

"We'll cross that bridge when the time comes. What do we do now?"

"With Ames? I'll ring his bell."

"I mean with Sperry out of the picture. How do you read that?"

"How do you? You're the one with the political antennae."

Gif held two fingers in a V from his forehead.

Tracey responded by waving a forefinger at Gif. "What do you think?"

"I'm not sure that Sperry and his gang getting fired means he didn't start the whole thing."

"It sure means that it blew up in his face if he did," Tracey said.

They both silently thought about that for a few seconds.

"Anybody who tries to pull off something this big knows the risks and takes chances. Christ, shooting a president, killing a vice president, and anyone else who might know something," Gif said.

"OK," Tracey nodded. "We'll continue to look at Sperry and Adams." As soon as the words were out of her mouth, she laughed nervously. "Listen to me. Do I sound like I've lost it?"

"Tracey, why don't you and Tom back off? Leave the burden on me," Gif said. "Tom can cover himself and the bureau, and you pull in your horns. They can only accuse you of incompetence."

Tracey rubbed the top of her head. "Are they showing that badly?"

Gif smiled. "I mean it. Back off."

"No," Tracey declared. "And Tom feels the same way. You're not the only one who is determined to catch the bastards."

"Why don't you concentrate on Sperry and let me worry about Adams," Gif suggested.

"You want me to hustle off to New York and let you stay here and have all the fun. I don't trust you. As soon as I am out of sight, you and Mavis and/or the bone doctor are going to start playing house."

Tracey," Gif started to protest but did not know what to say.

Tracey laughed. "Just kidding, lover. You go to New York, investigate Sperry, and leave Washington to me. As you said, I'm the expert when it comes to this political nonsense."

"I'm not going to New York. The answer is here," Gif said firmly.

"Where are you going to start now?"

"Tomorrow morning I am going to make a call on Senator George Ames, and I'm going to need that little recorder that I loaned you. The senator should find it interesting hearing his conversation with a dead person replayed."

"It's at the lab, Gif. I'll pick it up tomorrow morning, and we can visit Senator Ames together."

"I'm not sure," Gif reacted.

"I am. If you want the damned recorder, you get what comes with it. Me," Tracey declared.

"Double teaming might be a good idea," Gif capitulated. He thought about reminding Tracey that the recorder belonged to him but did not.

"Damned right. Do you think he'll fold?"

"He struck me as soft. We've got him on tape forcing Nan to feed Walker the pills."

"And giving him advance warning. The good senator knew that a rendezvous was going down, so to speak."

"And he is going to tell us who he alerted. If it was someone who knew that Harrison was taking the afternoon off…"

"That someone could have triggered the hit on Harrison. It meant that he had to act within a tight time frame…"

"But if it had been planned in advance, all that someone had to do was send the activate signal," Gif finished the thought.

"It's worth a try," Tracey said, her words indicating skepticism.

"Assuming that Ames stonewalls us, he will contact his principals. He's not the kind to take the heat on his own."

"We've got the taps and the 24/7 surveillance."

"And we keep knowledge about my little recorder and what's on it limited to you, me and Tom," Gif cautioned.

"Do you have any more eggs handy?" Tracey asked.

"Eggs?"

"Yes, sir. Now that you have told me how to suck an egg, maybe it would be best if I started with a fresh one."

"OK, I apologize," Gif said. "We have a plan. If…when Ames reports our approach, there's going to be a strong reaction from the top, whoever."

"And you understand that reaction will probably provoke another attack," Tracey said.

"On Ames."

"That's why we have a 24/7 watch on him," Tracey said.

"And you should keep your eyes wide open."

"If two investigators approach Ames, they should both keep their eyes open," Tracey said.

"Maybe it would be best if only one of us leans on Ames."

"No, lover. Both of us go, or neither of us go. I've got the evidence."

"And it belongs to me," Gif said.

"Not now," Tracey smiled.

Gif did not argue the point.

"One piece of good news," Tracey said. "Reggie reports that she met your deadline with Benita. She arrived yesterday afternoon a little after six and found Benita expecting her."

Gif waited.

"The lovely Benita appreciated your generosity."

"Fifty thousand?"

"Five hundred one hundreds," Reggie smiled.

"And a big bouquet of roses?"

"And a big bouquet of red roses. Benita was waiting at the door with bags packed. She should be safely back in Miami Beach by now."

"Good," Gif said. "At least that is one bystander safely out of the line of fire. I hope she took the roses with her."

"I don't know about the roses," Tracey said. "Benita didn't strike me as the kind of girl who would be impressed with flowers."

"When they are accompanied by five hundred big ones she is," Gif laughed.

"What did your Sheriff Simmons want?" Tracey changed the subject.

"I'm not so sure he is my Sheriff Simmons," Gif said.

Tracey waited for Gif to explain.

"He wanted to know what was happening with the Redskin case."

"Oh?"

"He's the one who got me involved in the first place, remember?"

"It's so hard to recall ancient history at my age," Tracey smiled. "What did you tell him?"

"That I wasn't making much progress."

"Is that true?"

"That seems to be the case in all my investigations these days," Gif said wryly. 'Maybe it's my age too."

"It is showing," Tracey smiled.

"He was also curious about the Tate investigation," Gif ignored Tracey's gibe.

"Really?"

"Yes, he worked for Harrison when he was sheriff, too."

"What did you tell him?"

"I told him I wasn't involved. He asked what you had to say about it."

"What did you say?"

"That we didn't discuss it."

"Did he buy that?"

"I doubt it, but you showed up just in time. Simmons took off through the house while you came around it."

"I have that effect on men," Tracey laughed.

"What's for dinner?" Gif asked.

"Dinner?"

"I think you promised that dinner was on you."

"That was yesterday. Sorry, it seems to have slipped my mind. Give me a couple of minutes to freshen up, and I'll see what's in the freezer."

"Freshen up and we'll set a precedent tonight," Gif said.

"Right," Tracey pushed out of her chair.

"We'll dine out at your expense," Gif called after her.

Gif sat on the patio for a few minutes before joining Tracey in the bedroom. To his surprise, she had changed clothes and was standing before the mirror applying fresh lipstick. He washed his hands, changed his shirt, and led Tracey towards the front door.

"Tell the guys to go ahead without us," Gif spoke to Jerry who sat at the dining room table fiddling with his computers.

"Got a sec, boss, there's something here you might want to see," Jerry said.

Gif walked over to the table, stood behind Jerry's chair and looked at the television screen. It was still focused on that damned web page that Jerry had shown him that morning.

"Looks interesting, Jerry," Gif patted him on the shoulder and turned for the door.

"Let me…" Jerry called after him.

"Sorry, Jerry, later. Duty calls," Gif smiled as he followed Tracey out the door.

Chapter 33

Following his impromptu press conference, Acting President Hiram Alphonse Adams patiently sat at his desk and ignored the shouted questions as the reinforced Secret Service detail herded the unruly media mob out of the Andrew Johnson Suite. As soon as the door closed behind them, Adams turned to Jake Tyrone and asked:

"How do you think that went, Jake?"

"We couldn't have programmed it better," Jake chuckled.

"Then we better have a little celebratory nip," Adams said as he opened his desk door and took out the ever present Jack Daniels.

"Let me do the honors, sir," Jake said as he took the bottle and carefully poured a small portion in each of their cups. He then filled the cups with coffee from the decanter.

"Don't worry, Jake. I'm carefully controlling my small vices," Adams let his watchful assistant know that he was watching.

"I know sir," Jake said as he twisted the cap on Jack and placed him back in the president's desk drawer.

Adams pushed out of his chair and lifted his cup to Jake. Jake responded in kind. Adams then led the way to his favorite overstuffed chair where he sat down, still smiling.

"Want to see how the media is handling the news?" Jake glanced at the television.

"No," Adams answered. "We know what they are saying."

"I'm not sure," Jake said. "You gave them a real shock."

"We did," Adams smiled. "I hope you didn't make a mistake with that Hernandez thing."

Jake, accustomed to shouldering the responsibility when things went wrong, ignored Adam's finger pointing. "If he doesn't work out, no problem. We'll drop him before the convention. In the meantime, we'll just find some funerals for him to attend."

Adams chuckled at that adroit comment. "You remember what that feller said about the vice presidency?"

"I do. It's not worth a cup of warm piss," Jake smiled.

"We'll let things quiet down a little over there this afternoon," Adams glanced in the direction of the White House. "Then have them move my things over to the Oval Office this evening. I'll start work there tomorrow morning."

Jake, accustomed to Adams' arbitrary management style, nodded. Many years earlier, he had learned that Adams would sit docilely in his office letting the world swirl around him while projecting the image of complete disinterest. Then, suddenly, he would sit up, take charge, and hurl orders like a drill sergeant, driving all around him to distraction. Jake suspected that the martinet was about to start his march.

"Would you like to have me arrange to have your things moved into the residency while you are in the office?" Jake asked. Adams was a widower who currently resided in a suite at the nearby Willard Intercontinental.

"Has Mrs. Tate moved out?" Adams asked. "I don't want anyone to think I am pushing her."

"Oh no, sir," Jake answered. "No one could possibly think that. Mrs. Tate now resides in Leesburg. The staff and the residential quarters anxiously await your presence."

Until now, Adams had been completely disinterested in what was happening at the White House, and he had changed the subject every time Jake had tried to discuss it. Mrs. Tate was at the Leesburg residence the day of the shooting, and she had never returned to the White House. Her staff moved all the Tate possessions to Leesburg the day after the state funeral."

"Still, I don't want to appear unseemly. I will remain at the Willard for now, but we can schedule future affairs of state over there."

"Over there?"

"The people's house, Jake. That's what they used to call it."

"We're going to have to devote some time to staffing," Jake referred to the fact that the acting president had just asked for everyone's resignations.

"You work on the White House staff, all those advisors, lawyers, counselors, and I will take care of the cabinet," Adams said. "We can worry about the independent agencies later."

"Are you sure you don't want me to prepare some lists for you, like I always do?" Jake asked.

"I've had Harry working on that Jake," Adams referred to Harold Wilson.

Jake looked sharply at Adams. As the chief of Adam's congressional staff and currently the acting president's chief of staff, Jake had always considered himself the top staffer. Wilson managed Adam's Speaker's staff, thus they were natural competitors. This was the first time since they had moved to the Andrew Johnson Suite that Jake had learned that Adams had been separately consulting any assistants from his two legislative staffs.

"Don't worry, Jake," Adams smiled. "You are still my main man."

Jake, who always handled all of Adams' more delicate matters, campaign funds, under-the-table donations, political skullduggery and everything that went with it, was not so certain. He knew for a fact that the old man was so devious that Jake doubted that the left side of his brain knew what the right side was plotting.

"I'm not worried, just surprised," Jake admitted.

"Don't allow yourself to be surprised, Jake," Adams admonished. "We're top dog now, and we all have to stay on our toes."

"When do you want to announce your new White House appointments?" Jake asked. Privately, he seethed. There was no way he was going to let the old man move him out. Jake had enough information on the illegal stuff to take Adams with him if he tried something like that.

"I think I'll introduce the new Cabinet tomorrow morning," Adams said, surprising Jake again. "Please have Johnnie talk with Harry and set something for the Oval Office at eleven." Adams referred to Johnie Jefferson, his Director of Communications, the only office in the White House whose staff Adams had appointed and whose existence he had acknowledged.

"Yes, sir," Jake said. That simple order told him that he had lost control of Adams.

"From now on, Jake, as White House chief of staff, you will manage the office and that includes Johnnie. You are going to be one busy fellow. I recognize that means I'm going to have to meet personally with a lot of these other people and that you may not have time to sit and hold my hand constantly.

"I understand," Jake answered obediently. "Do you mind if I take a little time to go over to the West Wing to make sure everybody understands?"

"Of course," Adams agreed. "And take the time to select whatever office you want for yourself and to work on that staff list."

Recognizing that he had been subtly dismissed Jake departed. In the outer office, he stopped to speak with Miss Mary.

"Brace yourself, Miss Mary," Jake whispered. "I think we have a hurricane heading our way."

"Good, it's about time the old man put away the bottle and got to work," Miss Mary said.

The next morning Gif was burning the toast and Tracey was heating the coffee in the microwave when Tracey decided to check the morning news.

"Do you mind if I turn on the television?" She asked while Gif was searching the mess in the fridge for the butter.

"Must you?" Gif asked.

"If you had a morning newspaper delivered like everyone else, I wouldn't have to disturb you while you go about your chores," Tracey replied as she hit the remote.

Seconds later the television burst into life with a CNN Breaking News report.

"Christ, Gif look at that," She declared.

He strolled into the den and heard the CNN newsreader chattering. "Yesterday, the United States of America experienced its second revolution, and the White House figuratively is waist deep in blood."

Gif stared at the screen. The words "Second American Revolution" were rolling repeated across the top of the screen which featured a picture of the White House with the flag flying at half-mast.

"This morning," the newsreader with the peroxided hair, altered eyebrows, thick mascara, and Botox lips, smiled at the viewer while she continued: "an almost alien force, at least one composed of strangers, has taken over the executive branch of government. Yesterday's occupants are gone, lock, stock, and barrel. Or as a member of the modern generation might observe: cell phones, blackberries, and laptops. Our previously passive, some say supine, acting president this morning abandoned his previous resting place in the Andrew Johnson Suite in the nearby Treasury Building"–the camera featured the back of the Treasury Building–"and moved to the Oval Office, the symbolic command post normally occupied by this nation's leader, a location he had previously shunned. Yesterday, he fired every single staff member who had been appointed by the duly elected Republican Administration of President Harrison Tate and ordered them to evacuate the building forthwith. The unwitting staffers were forced from their desks by the Secret Service and were not allowed to take a single piece of paper with them. Those that protested were told that their personal items would be sent to them in due course by Federal Express.

"Today, strangers, all affiliated to the rival Democratic Party, are sitting at those very desks leafing through the flotsam and jetsam of the departed rivals. Nobody can explain what triggered this sudden revolution. Yesterday, Acting President Hiram Alphonse Adams sacked his vice president, the holdover secretary of the treasury of the Tate administration. Why? Who knows? Many of you may have witnessed that odd press conference held by Acting Vice President Alexander Hamilton Sperry during which he announced his intention to resign forthwith. Accompanied by the media, Mr. Sperry marched across the hall to the Andrew Johnson Suite where after a lengthy and embarrassing wait he was granted admittance to the president's presence only to be told he could not resign because he had already been fired. Sources tell this correspondent that a difficult meeting between the then acting vice president with prominent Republican leaders precipitated the crisis. These sources speculate that Mr. Sperry over-reacted to the news that neither party in the Congress intended to support his economic plan.

"Americans woke up yesterday morning secure in the knowledge that their government was in the hands of a virtual coalition of the two major parties. They went to bed with a new monolithic regime in command. Acting President Adams, the former Speaker of the

House, and a brigade of bureaucrats and politically faithful from his Democratic Party now control the executive and legislative branches of government, leaving only a divided Supreme Court as a balance. Informed observers have even speculated that the octogenarian who now leads us plans to suspend all future elections."

"Those people are going crazy, Gif," Tracey laughed.

"Turn it off, it's just bullshit," Gif declared as he returned to the kitchen.

"I wonder if Tom submitted his resignation." Tracey said.

"I wonder if Adams accepted it if he did," Gif said. "What about you?"

"What about me?"

"Are you going to submit yours?"

"He didn't say task force chairman, did he?"

Gif shrugged.

"I'll wait," Tracey said, "until someone knocks on my door."

"I wouldn't spend a lot of time in the office if I were you," Gif advised.

Gif and Tracey drove directly to the Hart Office Building from the Hoover Building where Tracey had retrieved Nan Starbright's note and recorder. They cleared security with ease and took the elevator to the 6th floor.

"Have you ever met the senator?" Gif asked.

"I've seen his picture on television and in the papers, but I've never had the honor of shaking his hand," Tracey replied.

"You might shake more than his hand, today," Gif said.

'That might be interesting," Tracey chuckled. "I understand he has a lot of experience shaking things."

"He's a pretty boy, but don't let that Kennedy charm overwhelm you," Gif cautioned.

"The so-called Kennedy charm never overwhelmed me, not even Jack's," Tracey said.

"I didn't know you had met Jack," Gif needled. "Were you intimate friends?"

"You don't know everything about me, buster," Tracey replied.

Gif was not sure if he had won or lost that exchange.

"Here we are," Gif said as they approached the door to Ames's reception room. "Don't be surprised if they don't stand up and applaud our appearance. We don't have an appointment."

"I'm accustomed to that kind of reception," Tracey said as she entered first.

Inside, they were met by surprised looks from the two secretaries and the young man Ames had initially introduced to Gif as "Clifford" his chief of staff and legal advisor. Clifford was standing next to the lead secretary's desk.

"Oh, shit," Clifford muttered as he immediately rounded the desk and rushed into the inner office without knocking.

"Senator Ames, please," Gifford addressed the executive secretary.

"If you will have a seat, sir," the secretary frowned. "I will ..."

Before she completed the sentence, Gif opened the inner door and entered to find Senator George Ames with his hand on the knob of a second door that led to the corridor. Clifford stood halfway between the desk and Ames.

"Senator, please don't," Gif spoke firmly.

Ames hesitated.

"This is Director Schultz," Gif glanced at Tracey. "I believe you know her by reputation."

"Director Schultz," Ames stammered. "You both will have to excuse me. I have a vote call on the floor."

"No, stay," Tracey ordered. "I have a warrant in my purse and will restrain you if I must," she bluffed.

"Close the damned door, senator," Gif ordered. He turned on Clifford. "Get the hell out of here before I charge you as an accessory assisting a felon to flee."

Clifford blanched, but to his credit he challenged Tracey. "Let me see the warrant, please."

Tracey pulled a folded paper from her purse and waved it in the air.

"Sit down," Gif ordered the senator. "If you think you had problems following my last visit, you had better have Clifford call in the best legal defense team he can find."

"Maybe you had better wait outside, Clifford," Ames said, returning to his desk where he apparently felt more secure.

"Are you sure, senator?" Clifford asked weakly.

"I'll call if I need legal advice," Ames stood firm.

Clifford departed. After the door shut behind him, Gif pointed at the conference table. "Over here," he ordered as he sat down at the head of the table.

Tracey shoved the paper back into her pocketbook and joined Gif at the table. Gif took the small recorder and the blue envelope containing Nan's note from his inside jacket pocket and placed them in front of him.

"I don't agree to your recording this meeting," Ames said as he walked around the table and took the chair on Gif's left facing Tracey.

"What is this about, Director Schultz?" Ames spoke directly to Tracey as he stared at the envelope and recorder.

"The task force has a few questions to ask you about your relationship with Ms. Starbright and Vice President John F. Walker," Tracey replied formally.

"I've already answered Inspector Gifford's questions to the best of my ability," Ames blustered.

"And you will answer them again, senator," Gif played the heavy.

"I have nothing more to say," Ames declared, making a show of pursing his lips and clutching his hands together on the table in front of him.

"First, read this note," Gif said pointing at the blue envelope.

Ames leaned forward, turned the envelope towards himself with one finger, and read it. "It's addressed to Inspector Gifford, so what?"

"Do you recognize the handwriting, senator?" Gif asked.

"Why should I? This is not addressed to me and this is the first time I have ever seen it."

"Inspector, I think we should advise the senator of his rights," Tracey interrupted.

Gif nodded.

"You have the right to remain silent." Tracey began.

"Wait what am I being charged with?" Ames blustered.

"Anything you say can be used against you in a court of law." Tracey continued.

"All right," Ames declared. "That looks like Nan's handwriting. I can't be sure."

"Open the envelope," Gif ordered.

Ames carefully opened the envelope and read Nan Starbright's note to Gif. When he finished, he folded the blue paper and put it back in the envelope, which he dropped on the table next to the recorder. Gif waited for Ames to comment.

"Nan wrote that," Ames admitted.

Gif calmly reached across the table, pulled the miniature recorder towards him, and pressed the on and play buttons. A clear woman's voice said:

"George, I'm not sure."

"I'm not asking you to be sure, honey; I'm telling you what to do. Take these damned pills, hide them somewhere, and add them to the bottle when I tell you to."

Gif hit the stop button on the recorder. "Do you recognize the female's voice, senator?" Gif demanded harshly.

Ames nodded affirmatively.

"Who is it?" Gif asked.

"That's Nan."

"Nan who?"

"Nan Starbright," Ames said.

"And the man?" Gif asked.

"It sounds like me but I can't be sure," Ames said.

"Please answer carefully. Take all the time you need and consider your response," Tracey cautioned.

"Senator, we have had voice experts examine this tape. They confirm the speaker is you. Are you really saying you don't remember this conversation?"

"I told you I gave some pills to John to try, as a friend," Ames said.

"You didn't say you paid Ms. Starbright money to give the pills to the vice president," Gif said.

"I may have misspoke," Ames said.

"That's funny, senator," Gif smiled. "Listen to the rest of this tape" Gif pressed the play button.

"How will you do that?"

"Every time Walker tells you to meet him here, call me on my cell."

"What will the pills do to him?"

"Honey, just do what I say. Believe me when I say you will have the time of your life."

"I'm not sure I want to do that.

"Do you want that $50,000 or not?"

"Will the pills hurt him?"

"Do you think I would give my friend something that might hurt him?"

"Walker will get a rise that he'll never forget."

Gif hit the stop button and waited for Ames to comment. The pale faced senator said nothing, just sat there with his hands clasped while he stared at the recorder. Gif pressed the play button again. After a pause the recorder continued:

"This is Nan Starbright speaking from my apartment on August 20th. I just received a call from Vice President John F Walker directing me to meet him at his Crystal City apartment. Following previous instructions from Senator George Ames I am calling the Senator to alert him to John's plans."

"George, Nan".

"Honey, tell me he called."

"I'm to meet him at the apartment within the hour."

"Make sure he takes the damned pills. "If this works, the check's in the mail."

"I don't want a damned check," Nan shouted. "Cash, cash, cash, shit, shit, shit."

After another pause during which none of the three people sitting at the table spoke, the tape continued:

"This is Nan Starbright. I have just alerted Senator George Ames to my session with Vice President John Walker. As instructed

I will take the extra strength pills provided me by Ames and will add them to John's bottle without his knowledge. The senator has assured me that they will not harm John.

This tape will serve as evidence of my …that I am only acting … that I only do what Ames ordered as a trick."

Gif turned off the recorder and turned to stare at the shaken senator. "Now, do you recognize the female's voice, senator?" Gif demanded harshly.

Ames nodded affirmatively.

"Who is it?" Gif asked.

"That's Nan."

"Nan who?"

"Nan Starbright," Ames said.

"And the man?" Gif asked.

"It's me," Ames said weakly.

"Ms. Starbright made that crystal clear, senator. Now let's discuss what happened to Vice President Walker again," Gif said.

"Senator, do you now recall that conversation in its entirety?" Tracey took over the questioning.

""Now that you have refreshed my memory," Ames answered.

"Did you pay Ms. Starbright $50,000 to secretly add those pills to the vice president's medications in his bathroom cabinet?"

Ames hesitated.

"Did you senator?" Tracey pressed. "Do you want Mr. Gifford to replay the tape?"

"I paid her $50,000 Ames admitted."

"Just to play a trick on the vice president, your mutual friend?" Tracey said. "That was a very expensive trick. Was the $50,000 from your personal funds?"

"Not just to pay for the joke," Ames said.

"For what other reason?"

"Ms. Starbright was a very expensive call girl that the vice president and I shared," Ames said.

"You are saying that you paid for the vice president's vices?" Tracey pressed. "Fifty thousand dollars? A man of the opposing political party?"

Ames swallowed deeply, crossed and uncrossed his arms, unclenched and clenched his hands. “Yes,” he spoke softly.

“Were any of your Democratic colleagues aware of this illicit activity?” Tracey asked.

Ames shook his head negatively.

“This was completely your own idea?”

Ames nodded yes.

“Please answer the questions, senator,” Tracey ordered.

“I resent this inquisition,” Ames protested.

“We can do it here, or we can do it in a public venue where the media will certainly learn of our interview,” Tracey said.

“This was my idea,” Ames admitted.

“Where did you get the $50,000?”

“From private funds.”

“Your private funds?” Tracey pressed.

“Yes, damn it,” Ames answered.

“Did you give Ms. Starbright a check or cash?” Tracey asked.

“I don’t remember.”

“Come on senator. You really don’t expect Inspector Gifford or me to believe you can’t recall where you got the $50,000?” Tracey laughed.

“It was cash.”

“From which account?” Tracey demanded, opening her notebook to give Ames the impression she had a list of his personal accounts.

“I don’t remember.”

“Don’t or won’t?”

“I think I should consult my lawyer.”

“Fine,” Gif said. “Call Clifford in. We will play this tape for him and for the media and make sure these questions are raised.”

“You can’t do that.”

“Of course I can. The note makes it perfectly clear that Ms. Starbright intended that we find the tape. All legal and above board. No warrants required,” Tracey resumed the attack.

“Where did you get the money?”

“From a friend,” Ames replied.

“Which friend?”

“I can’t say. He wishes his identity to remain private.”

"We can take you before a grand jury and force you to answer," Tracey said. "This is now a murder investigation."

"A murder investigation?" Ames hands began to tremble.

"And you are the prime suspect," Tracey said. "Where did you get the money?"

"I can't tell you."

"That must be some friend you are protecting," Tracey laughed.

"Where did you get the pills?" Tracey asked.

"I don't remember," Ames answered.

"Why did you order Ms. Starbright to inform you as soon as the vice president scheduled a rendezvous?" Gif took over the questioning.

"I…I…" Ames stuttered. "I wanted to enjoy the trick."

"Why not wait until afterwards to discuss it in detail with Ms. Starbright and the vice president?"

"I don't know," Ames said.

Gif laughed, looked at Tracey, and mimicked Ames. "I don't know."

"Who wanted advance information about the vice president's rendezvous?" Gif demanded.

"Why? Is it important?" Ames challenged.

"It sure is," Gif smiled. "It indicates that you were part of a much larger conspiracy. You needed to know exactly when the vice president would be given those pills so that your fellow conspirators could coordinate the attack on President Tate. That way you could eliminate both the president and vice president at one time in a most unbelievable coincidence."

"That's ridiculous," a shaken Ames blurted.

"No it isn't, Senator Ames," Tracey jumped in. "It is what happened. We've got the evidence and it places you right in the middle. This is your opportunity to tell the truth. If you don't, you are going to need a staff of attorneys."

Ames pushed his chair back from the table and began to pace.

"Tell us now who you called to report the vice president's rendezvous," Gif demanded.

Gif's order prompted Ames to pause in mid-stride. He surprised both Tracey and Gif by smiling. He walked to the door to his outer officer, opened it, and pointed: "Get out right now. Both of you and don't come back. If you do I'll have the Congressional Police throw you out."

After issuing that dramatic challenge, Ames strode into his outer office. He spoke to his aide/legal counsel: "Come, Clifford, I have a floor vote to make," and marched out the door.

A surprised Gifford looked at Tracey and shrugged. "I guess it was something I said."

Tracey smiled, gave him a thumbs up, and led the way to the elevator.

Once they were back out on the street Gif turned to Tracey: "What?"

"Senator Ames just told us that someone who wanted to keep track of the vice president gave him the money for Starbright, that he is not as scared of us as he is of that person, meaning it is someone who can reward or punish him, and that he did not call, I repeat call, that person to report. You asked who he called, and he picked up on that."

"I screwed up?" Gif asked.

"No you got us the lead we needed. The bastard didn't call anyone. He either met them or sent them an e-mail. That's why his damned phone logs didn't tell us anything," Tracey smiled.

"What now, boss," Gif smiled.

"Drop me off at the Hoover Building, right now. I have to get some of Tom's people over to that damned Hart Building office and to Ames' home to make sure he doesn't dump any computer hard drives before I have time to get the necessary warrants. That interview plus your handy mini-recorder will be all I need."

"Want me to hang around for a while?" Gif asked.

"Nope. You'll just be in the way. Go investigate the Redskins, and I'll make my own way home."

"Maybe I'll just drop by the White House on my way and check on the revolution," Gif smiled.

"You keep away from there," Tracey ordered.

"One of us has to do some interviews in the West Wing," Gif countered.

"Not today, lover. Let me grab Ames' computers, find out who he informed, and then we can handle those interviews together. I rather thought we made a good team, today."

"I enjoyed it," Gif said, making no commitments.

Acting President Hiram Alphonse Adams had a broad smile on his face as he lowered his substantial behind into the chair behind the Resolute desk in the Oval Office for the very first time. Miss Mary Murphy stood at the door, the only witness to this historical event.

"I always wondered what it would be like to sit in this chair, Miss Mary," Adams declared.

"You look like it was made for you," Miss Mary shared her superior's exuberance. They both had labored for forty years to get to this moment.

"Oh Miss Mary," Adams said as he rubbed the palms of his hands on the shiny surfaces of the chair arms. "I can't tell you what this means to me." Suddenly, Adams lifted his hands into the air and studied them carefully, a frown on his face.

"Sir?" A concerned Miss Mary asked. "Are you all right?"

Adams, an odd expression still on his face, shook his head negatively. "I'm fine. I just had a terrible thought, but I'm too much a southern gentleman to share it with you."

Mary smiled as realization struck her. "It's all right sir. I thoroughly disinfected your desk and chair."

"I should have known," Adams leaned back in the chair. "Thank you Miss Mary."

They both had remembered how President Bill Clinton had abused that very chair and desk.

"Well, Miss Mary, now that we are here, what shall we do first?"

"Should I call Mr. Tyrone?"

"No," Adams said after a brief pause. "Jake is holding his own staff meeting so you and I are going to make do on our own."

Miss Mary nodded. She had privately always considered the chief of staff to be a bad influence on Adams. Obediently, she waited for instructions.

"I think I would like to confer with Johnie," Adams decided.

"Yes sir," Miss Mary shut the door behind her as she hurried to summon the president's special assistant for public affairs.

As he waited, Adams admired his new office and thought about how the nation would react when they learned that his first act in the Oval Office was to confer with a man of color.

"Sir?" Johnie Jefferson paused in the doorway, apprehensive about interrupting the president on this busy day.

"Johnie, come in. I wanted to share this glorious moment. You are my first visitor in this grand place."

"Sir, I'm honored," Jefferson said. He closed the door behind him and did not know what he should do next. Dealing with Adams in his Capitol Hill office was one thing, but now he was sitting in the Oval Office with the entire world at his knees, or so Johnie thought.

"Sit down, Johnie, I need your advice," Adams pointed at a chair facing his desk.

Obediently, Johnie sat where the president ordered.

"Johnie, I think it would be appropriate for me as a first act to speak to the American people. How do I do that?"

Johnie sat up straight in his chair. "Sir, I could inform the networks and schedule a national address. When would you like to do it?"

"What do you recommend?"

"Tonight in prime time," Johnie said.

Adams frowned. "I was thinking more like right now."

"Now, sir?" Johnie leaped to his feet.

"Yes. Should we do it right here? I rather like the setting. It looks rather…presidential." Adams smiled.

"There's a CNN crew in the newsroom," Johnie said. "I don't know how long it will take the networks to get their anchors and crews here. Would an hour be too long?"

"Just fetch the CNN boys, now, Johnie," Adams ordered. "I'm in the mood and don't know how long it will last."

"Yes sir," Johnie turned and hurried from the room.

Adams was still sitting at his desk ten minutes later when the door opened and Johnie entered followed by a single CNN cameraman, the CNN White House correspondent, and four members of the Secret Service protective detail who had been lounging in their ready room located directly below the Oval Office.

"Set up right there," Adams pointed at a spot directly in front of his desk.

"I have a few words for the American people, but I don't intend to answer any questions so keep your mouth shut," Adams spoke to the White House correspondent whose name he couldn't remember.

"Sir, do you want to broadcast live?" The correspondent, a fortyish female with too much makeup and lacquered hair, asked.

"Of course," Adams glowered. The damned woman couldn't keep her mouth shut for ten seconds.

"If you forgive me," she held up her cell phone. "I'll inform Atlanta that we are going live from the Oval Office. They will alert our network. When the red light on the camera comes on, I will tell our viewers what is happening and defer to you."

"Be quick, be brief," Adams ordered.

The correspondent turned her back on the president, hit a button, whispered into her phone, and waited. She turned to face the cameraman and nodded. He aimed his equipment at her and waited. Thirty seconds later, the red light flashed on. The correspondent smiled and said:

"This is Andrea Marshall speaking to you from the Oval Office. Acting President Hiram Alphonse Adams has a message for the American people."

The cameraman turned his lens towards the president who was waiting with a scowl on his face. As soon as the camera focused on him, Adams burst into a huge smile:

"Good morning America, here I am sitting at this fine desk in the Oval Office for the very first time. The moment I walked into this magnificent room, I decided the first thing I would do is report to the American people who are responsible for my being here. First, let me tell you about this fine desk. It was built with timbers from the H.M.S. Resolute, an English ship that an American whaler rescued from the icy waters of the Arctic and returned to her rightful owner. Years later, a grateful Queen Victoria had a desk built from the Resolute's timbers and presented it to President Rutherford B. Hayes. This desk has been used in the White House by almost every American president since that time. You can imagine, therefore, how awed I am to be sitting here for the very first time."

The CNN correspondent who stood with her microphone pointed at the president glanced at Johnie with a look of confusion on her face.

She had been summoned to the Oval Office for an exclusive newsbreak, and the president was rambling on about his damned desk. Johnie, fearing the president might be watching, ignored the correspondent's silent plea. Adams did not miss the exchange, however.

"Please forgive me for rambling," Adams immediately dropped his folksy introduction.

He was speaking extemporaneously and was angered that the correspondent did not recognize that. He made a mental note to have Johnie withdraw her White House credentials.

"Despite the terrific pressure that I am feeling, the critical decisions that I must make despite an awareness of my own inadequacies, I realize I am the one that fate and the odd coincidence of perverse events has thrust into this position of supreme responsibility. The media has described recent developments as a revolution, a Second American Revolution. While I am loathe to subscribe to the media's sensational labeling, I frankly admit that the terrible situation that fate has imposed on us indeed resembles a revolution, a violent, sudden change in our country's leadership. Although I am a simple southern boy, as you all know, I have served in this nation's capitol for over forty years. Some call me stubborn, and I admit it. I am stubborn in the defense of this country, its people, its government, and its future. If it is a revolution we now face, I am willing to take on the challenge. Past presidents have had their labels, the New Deal, the Square Deal, the New Frontier, so if the media insist, call this administration the New American Revolution. Some consider revolutions a bad thing. I do not agree that the First American Revolution was bad. We fought for our freedom and established a government and built a country that is the envy of the world. In this our New American Revolution, I promise you we will emerge stronger and more admired than we ever were. We now have a new leadership which will solve our economic problems and bring to justice those responsible for the murder of a president and a vice president and at least two of our loyal citizens. That is my promise to you, the American people, and that is why I have imposed myself on you this morning. Thank you."

As soon as he stopped speaking, the cameraman turned his lens on the correspondent who ended the surprising newsbreak with a single sentence: "We now return you to our network headquarters in Atlanta, Andrea Marshall, CNN News."

Adams waved his hand in Johnie's direction.

"Johnie, please escort our visitors back to the press room and then come right back," Adams ordered.

A few minutes later Johnie returned to the Oval Office. "I hope that was satisfactory, sir."

"Not completely, Johnie. I don't like that Andrea Marshall. Return to the press room, withdraw her White House pass, and ask her to leave."

"May I give a reason, sir?" A shaken Johnie asked.

"Yes. Tell her I did not like her demeanor."

Chapter 34

Gif and Tracey began their day with a team meeting around Gif's dining room table. Without going into details, Gif told them that he and Tracey had met with Senator Ames and that the task force was taking a closer look at Ames's involvement with the Walker incident.

"We are beginning to suspect that Walker's death was not an accident," Gif said.

"Great," Joyce Tryon who had team responsibility for the Walker death said. "I assume you learned something more from Benita."

Gif who had told Joyce that he would be paying Benita a visit nodded. "I'll brief you later on that Joyce. I don't have anything of interest to the whole team at this time."

"She was holding back, wasn't she? I knew she was negotiating for more money."

Gif nodded, trying to shut Joyce off.

"She told you something that took you back to Ames. Walker gave Nan the pills," Joyce said.

"Are you saying that you think there might be something to this big conspiracy theory thing?" Sarah asked, inadvertently giving Gif a chance to recover from Joyce's pursuit.

The exchange woke the entire team from its near lethargy. All looked at Gif and waited for his answer.

"That might prove to be the case," Gif admitted, without making it clear whether he was replying to Joyce or Sarah.

"What do you know that you are not sharing?" The always outspoken Sarah demanded.

Gif smiled and ignored the question. "Do you have anything you can share with us?" He deferred to Tracey who had just gotten off the phone with the task force's lead investigator Jeff Cohena."

"I agree with Gif. We need to take a closer look at Senator Ames's involvement with Vice President Walker," Tracey said. "Just for those in this room, following our meeting yesterday with Ames, the task force obtained warrants to search Ames' office and home."

"You had to have something stronger than suspicions and conjecture to get warrants for that," Sarah said. "A US senator draws a lot of water."

Tracey glanced at Gif. "Yesterday afternoon we seized a lot of files at Ames office and home, his personal laptop, his office computer, and a home desktop," Tracey said. "Jeff Cohena, the task force lead investigator, just gave me the bad news."

"Bad news?" Sarah said.

"Yes. We were particularly interested in any phone calls or e-mail messages the senator sent and received on the day of Walker's death. Our initial readout is negative. All messages had been erased on the phones and the logs contained nothing of great interest. All of his e-mail had also been deleted. Our techs are working on his hard disks to see what they can recover."

"Would it be possible for me to work with them?" Jerry Quigley asked. "I've been doing some internet research of my own," he patted his computer.

Tracey glanced at Gif who nodded affirmatively.

"Certainly," Tracey replied. "When we break up here, I'll introduce you to the bureau techs who are working on the disks."

"Enough of Ames for now," Gif said. "Why don't you guys let us know what you have been doing? Joyce, were you able to come up with anything more on the red car that the old couple remembered."

"The Brewsters," Sarah reluctantly let Gif lead her away from Joyce and their inquisition.

"Billie arranged for us to interview the deputies who were deployed to the river to supplement President Tate's protection detail," Sarah said. "Billie," Sarah surprised Gif by deferring to Billie Williams. Usually, Sarah dominated team meetings with her sharp tongue and over-sensitive ego.

"We had to tread softly," Billie said. "We didn't want to get the guys in trouble with the sheriff or his boy Sadler. Fortunately, the four deputies in question are older guys who came on board when Gif was sheriff." Billie turned to Gif. "You might remember Butch Adams, Byron Shutts, Arnie Kaufman and Angelo Biancho?"

Gif nodded despite the fact the names meant nothing to him. The department had expanded by three hundred deputies during his tenure.

"Unfortunately, none of them saw anything out of the ordinary during their deployment. Butch was parked at the Route 15 and Lovettsville Road intersection, Byron at the road that leads to the Tate property, Arnie in Lovettsville, and Angelo was cruising the area. Maybe thirty cars came up Lovettsville Road. None stopped in the area near where the shooting occurred, which was just below the farm restaurant. Angelo said he checked out the lot at the restaurant, and nobody was there but two cooks preparing for the evening meal. Two school buses came through, one with high school kids, and one from the intermediate school. They stopped long enough to unload a couple of the area kids but that's all."

"We haven't questioned the kids yet. Maybe they saw something," Sarah contributed. "We'll check with the schools and get their names tomorrow."

"So no one saw the little red car," Gif said.

Both Billie and Sarah smiled.

"We were just getting to that," Billie said. "Butch saw a car that answered that description" Billie paused for effect.

Gif waited, anticipating the coup de grace. Sarah and Billie were obvious playing him.

"Sheriff Simmons was also in the area driving a red unmarked Toyota from the motor pool, one of the cars used by the narcotics guys. He also responded to the alert that the president's detail sent to the department."

"That must have been the car the Brewster saw race by," Sarah said. "Apologize for getting your hopes up."

"Dick mentioned he had been in the area," Gif said. "He didn't say what car he had been driving."

Billie turned to Gif. "I did find out something of possible interest in the Redskin investigation. Want to hear it now or later?"

"Now's fine, Billie."

"On the way home last night, I stopped off at Billie's to check the place out. It was almost deserted, but a couple of locals were there. I had a couple of beers and worked the talk around to the Redskins. We chatted a while and the locals described the fight. Nothing new, but they made it sound a lot bigger thing than the bartender and Redskins did. The locals were probably three sheets in the wind by the time it all happened. I got the impression that a couple of them practically live at Billie's. Anyway, to make a long story short, one of them remembered seeing a small car in the parking lot that didn't belong to the usual crowd. No one else saw it, and nobody remembered a stranger in the bar that night, just the locals, and the Skins."

"Could he describe the car?" Gif asked.

"Sorry. It was old, that was all he remembered."

"Did he see anyone in it?"

Billie shook his head. "The guy was loaded when I talked with him, so he was probably well past it the night of the shooting. I wouldn't be surprised if the car was a figment of his imagination."

Gif turned back to the table. "Anybody else got anything?"

"Last night I checked out the bar where they nailed Dexter," Joyce said, bringing up the shooting that Gif had virtually ignored.

"You and Harold make a great team," Sarah laughed.

Both Harold and Joyce waited for Sarah to explain.

"Beers and bars, beers and bars," Sarah chanted as she slapped the table with her open palm.

"I'd like to be on that team," Truman Johnson who was feeling like the odd man out in this team effort said.

"You're on," Joyce said. "Got any plans for tonight?"

"I'm ready," Billie chimed in.

"It's a threesome," Truman agreed.

"Count me out," Sarah said.

"You're not invited anyway," Joyce smiled.

"Children," Gif called them to order.

"I got lucky," Joyce said.

"A boy or a girl?" Sarah asked waspishly.

The others ignored Sarah and waited for Joyce to elaborate.

"The place is a college kid hangout, mainly Georgetown and Catholic Universities," Joyce said. "Three of the kids from Georgetown were there the night Dexter got shot. They even remembered Dexter.

He was standing next to them at the bar where they were discussing Emerson and Thoreau and this guy seemed to be listening to their debate. He started to contribute a thought when another guy on his left said something to him. Dexter, they didn't know his name then, turned away, answered the new guy and then went to the john. The new guy waited a few seconds then followed Dexter in the john. The kids never saw either of the two again and left the bar soon thereafter. They didn't learn what had happened until they read the papers the next day."

"Do you have the kids' names?" Tracey asked.

Joyce answered by holding up her notebook.

"Mind if I pass them along to the task force?" Tracey asked.

Joyce jotted the names and addresses on a piece of notepaper and handed it to Tracey. "I don't think they know much more than they gave me," Joyce said. "They didn't exchange more than a few words with Dexter or the new guy."

"It's the first we've heard of the new guy. The bartender never mentioned him," Tracey said. "Did the kids describe the new guy?"

Joyce smiled. "Early to mid forties, about five foot ten, wore a dark shirt much like the one Dexter was wearing, and had a Redskin hat pulled low over his face."

'White, African American, Hispanic?"

"White. The kids said he look like a blue collar tough."

"I guess that means he needed a shave and was muscular in build," Tracey smiled.

"Right," Joyce smiled back.

"Anything else?" Tracey asked.

"No, but I think I might give that bar another try tonight," Joyce said.

"With company," Truman said.

"Agreed," Willie said.

"Good work, Joyce," Gif said as he copied the description into his notebook.

⁂

Former vice president/former secretary of the treasury Alexander

Hamilton Sperry was sitting in the library of his Georgetown home when the front door bell chimed.

"Will you get that please," his wife called from the kitchen.

"Get it yourself, I'm busy," Sperry answered, making no attempt to moderate the irritation he felt.

His Secret Service protection had withdrawn along with the domestic staff who had been on the public payroll. Only Sperry and his wife remained behind. Sperry had his bags backed and was waiting to catch a taxi to the airport where he planned to board the shuttle for New York City. Sperry was moving back to his Fifth Avenue penthouse while his spouse remained in Georgetown to manage the packing out of their personal effects and the sale of the house. Sperry did not plan to return to D.C. until he moved into the White House.

"He's in the library," Sperry heard his wife say.

"I'm not home," Sperry shouted rudely, hoping to have his spouse turn away any visitor. There was not a single person in the District of Columbia that Sperry was interested in meeting today. Yesterday had been that painful.

"Good morning, sir," Clete Clapp, Sperry's former chief of staff, greeted him.

Like Sperry, Clapp was now unemployed. Sperry glared at his former subordinate.

"Do you have a few minutes?" Clapp asked. "There are several issues we should discuss."

"Issues?" Sperry laughed. "Those are my suitcases stacked near the door, and I'm on my way to the airport. If you haven't heard, I've been sacked."

"Sir," Clapp hesitated. "This is very important."

"Speak!" Sperry ordered, much as he would command a dog.

"I need to know where you want me to set up shop," Clapp said.

"What shop?"

"For the run for the White House," Clapp answered. "We'll show…"

"Clapp, you don't understand," Sperry spoke rudely. "I hold you responsible for what has happened."

Clapp blanched. "Me…responsible for what, sir?"

"If you had done your job right, we would be sitting in the Oval Office, not that fat old man."

"We must discuss how I handle certain other…matters, sir," Clapp decided to avoid Sperry's self-serving accusation.

"I wash my hands of anything you might be involved with, Clapp," Sperry stood up and moved past Clapp towards the hallway.

"That's not possible," Clapp followed.

To their right, a smiling Mrs. Sperry watched from the kitchen doorway with a cup of coffee in her hand.

"It's not? Don't hold your breath." Sperry announced and waved to the limousine driver who had just pulled into his driveway.

Clapp turned and cast an unspoken appeal in her direction. She simply shook her head negatively.

The limousine driver appeared in the open doorway. Sperry pointed at the bags, and the driver picked them up and returned to his car.

Sperry turned, nodded at his wife, and said: "Let me know when you plan to join me, and I'll have somebody meet you at the airport."

Sperry looked at his former assistant. "Clapp, find a job," he ordered and departed slamming the door behind him.

Senator George Ames paced the floor of his office, ignoring the two white haired men in the tailor made pin striped suits who patiently waited for their client to return from orbit.

"I'm really in a bind," Ames spoke to the far wall just before he reversed directions.

"Senator, we're you're attorneys," the older man smiled. "Just tell us what the problem is, and we'll advise you."

"I open my mouth, and I'm a dead man," Ames declared.

"Whatever you tell us in confidence stays with us," the older man said.

"Believe me, you don't want to hear my problem," Ames said.

"Sir, we cannot help you if we can't evaluate the legality of the situation you are facing," the younger man said. He looked at his superior who responded with wiggle of his hand, palm down, a signal to relax.

"I told Clifford this would be a waste of time. They've seized my computers, all of them, personal and official. They've tapped my phones, and they have twenty men watching me day and night. You've seen them; they are sitting in my outer office and standing in the hall outside that door." Ames pointed at his private exit."

"How do you know this?" The older man asked. He was the senior partner of Seymour, Seymour & Cartridge, a K Street law firm renown for defending bureaucrats and politicians who had run afoul of the law.

"I've got eyes. I'm not naïve. I know how they do things," Ames said.

"They being the Federal Bureau of Investigation?" Seymour Jr. asked.

Ames answered with a stare.

"What are the charges?" Seymour Sr. asked.

"They haven't charged me, yet."

"Corruption?" Seymour Jr. joined his father in double-teaming their nervous client.

"Don't I wish?" Ames said as he resumed his pacing.

"What kind of evidence do you think they have, senator?" Seymour Sr. began to lose his patience.

"They have a damned tape for starters," Ames admitted.

"Audio or video?" Seymour Jr. asked.

"What's the difference?" Ames asked.

"A lot. If it's just audio that gives us latitude to bring in experts to dispute the voice identification."

"It's audio, but court proceedings are not what worries me."

The two Seymours exchanged troubled looks.

"What worries you?" Seymour Sr. asked.

"If I tell anyone my story, even you two, I'm a dead man," Ames said.

"Who is going to kill you? Seymour Jr. asked.

"The God damned trouble is I don't know. If I did, I could tell the FBI everything, and they would protect me."

"I don't understand," Seymour Sr. said.

"I'll tell you in language you can understand. The FBI has me by the balls. If I tell them my story, they probably won't believe me. Even if they did, I'm a dead man. By the time they identify the ...this other person, he would have me killed. I'm just a link, probably the last one in this dreadful tragedy, and if I am removed, this other person is safe."

"Then why hasn't he removed you before now?" Seymour Jr. asked.

"He probably thought I was harmless. Then, the damned FBI shows up with that damned tape."

"Sounds like you have a problem, senator," Seymour Sr. stood up. "I don't think this is our kind of case."

"What in the hell do you think I've been trying to tell you," Ames shouted. "I'll kill that damned Clifford."

"I'm not sure that solution will work for you, senator," Seymour Sr. said as he led his son and junior partner to the door.

It was eleven o'clock when Tracey and Gif climbed into the Prius for their journey to the District.

"I know where I'm going," Tracey said. "But I'm not so sure about you."

Gif did not immediately respond, not because he didn't know where he was going, but because he was not sure he wanted Tracey to know. They rode in silence until they passed through Leesburg and were racing the traffic down Route 7 towards Route 28 with its connection to the Dulles Access Road.

Finally, Tracey broke the quiet. "I'm not getting out of this toy car until you tell me where you are going." She crossed her legs and turned on the radio in time to hear 103.5, the all news station, report a repeat of the acting president's first media conference from the Oval Office. Both listened in rapt silence. When the acting president finished, Gif reached over and turned off the radio.

"The New American Revolution," he repeated. "Do you think the old guy has slipped a few gears?" He asked.

"It sounds like it. How could he have masterminded this conspiracy, if that is what we have?" Tracey asked.

"If he did, he had to have had a lot of help. I can't picture him slipping into a Ninja costume and gunning down all these people including Har…his predecessor as president of the United States."

"Help would have been easy for him to come by," Tracey said.

"Who? Tyrone? He's almost as old as Adams."

"Tyrone is in his sixties," Tracey confirmed. "But he has legs. I'm not sure that Adams is mobile."

"Maybe they both are suffering from Alzheimer's," Gif said.

"So what do we do?" Tracey asked.

"Continue to lean on our only link, Ames," Gif answered as he turned off 28 on to the Dulles access road.

"That guy has a great big target painted on his back," Tracey said.

"And we put it there," Gif said.

Tracey smiled. "You think someone might have noticed that we raided his home and office, and we've got him under surveillance?"

"And we harassed him in his office."

"That was your doing," Tracey said.

"I didn't say it wasn't," Gif responded.

"So what do we do now?"

"Find out who is gunning for Ames."

"How do we do that?"

"By talking with our prime suspects," Gif smiled as he moved the Prius into the center lane and pressed his foot on the accelerator.

"I knew it. You are going to interrogate the damned acting president and his chief of staff," Tracey said as she slapped the dashboard.

"Do you have any objections, Madame Task Force Commander?"

"Hell no, I'm going with you," Tracey said. "Besides," she smiled sweetly. "You need me to get into the Oval Office."

"I was wondering about that. Do you think you can help?" Gif asked.

"Watch me," Tracey laughed.

⁂

Tracey used her old FBI Director credentials plus her title to get them past the White House initial line of protection, the uniformed Secret Service. When the detail at the entrance to the West Wing hesitated, Tracey leaned on the senior officer present, a sergeant.

"Look Buster, I command the presidential task force, and I have an urgent meeting with your new boss, the acting president of these United States. If you want to keep your job here, get out of my way, or you're going to be out on the street with all those stuffed shirts in white collars who got thrown out on their asses yesterday."

"Give them blue badges and let them through," the sergeant capitulated.

Tracey led the way past the West Wing offices that were in the throes of intense confusion. Some boxes were being packed, and other boxes were being unpacked; workers were moving furniture, arguing over desks, struggling to open locked safes, and rushing from room to room. Pictures of Harrison Tate were being removed from the walls, and pictures of Hiram Alphonse Adams were being hung in their place.

"Nothing like a good revolution to shake things up," Tracey observed.

"It won't be long until they ask each other the key question," Gif said.

"What is that?" Tracey asked, knowing she was playing Abbott to Gif's Costello.

"Are you a New Revolutionist?"

Tracey laughed, recognizing that Gif referred to the trite 1962 question of the Kennedy administration: "Are you a New Frontiersman?" A negative response could get you sent to New Mexico for paramilitary training.

"Good morning, Director Schultz," Miss Mary greeted them in the anteroom to the Oval Office. "Is the acting president expecting you?"

"I'm not sure, Miss Mary," Tracey replied. "But Inspector Gifford and myself have an urgent need to meet with the president."

"Things have been rather hectic around here this morning," Miss Mary spoke honestly.

"I know. We heard the president's first conference," Tracey said.

"That was really something. I didn't even know that the president was going to do that," Miss Mary confided. She glanced at the closed door and whispered. "He's been in there by himself all morning, ever since he threw the media out. He has a one o'clock with his new cabinet, and I don't even know their names. I'll see if he will see you," Miss Mary said.

Still standing, Gif and Tracey waited as Miss Mary tapped on the door to the inner sanctum before opening it and disappearing inside. Seconds later she opened the door wide and with a broad smile announced: "The president will see you now, Director Schultz and Inspector Gifford."

Not knowing what to expect Gif winked at Miss Mary and followed Tracey into the Oval Office. As the door closed behind him, he glanced at the big desk and was surprised to find the chair behind it empty and the surface of the desk completely devoid of paper. Tracey stopped abruptly in front of him, and Gif, still staring at the desk, bumped into her.

"Over here," Acting President Hiram Alphonse Adams called to them from a chair that he had moved to a position where he could rest his feet on the windowsill and peer out at the Potomac River in the distance.

Tracey thrust an elbow at Gif as punishment for the careless bump in her rear.

"Mr. President," Tracey recovered and crossed the room to the chair where Adams sat.

"Thank you very much for this visit, Director Schultz," Adams greeted Tracey with a smile.

"I think you have met…" Tracey started to remind the old man who her companion was.

"Oh, I remember Inspector Gifford very well," Adams waved at his second visitor. "Inspector Gifford caused me considerable worry and discomfort a few years back when he and his task force pursued that serial killer, the one who was killing all those gay congressmen. Inspector Gifford, I never properly thanked you for that. At the time I was so discomfited that I would have preferred you had been a little less efficient."

Gif was surprised that Adams remembered him and was quite unsure how to reply to the president's impolitic reference to gay congressmen.

Before Gif could respond, Adams continued to play the host. "Please, pull up two chairs and join me. I just can't get enough of this magnificent view. That office over there," Adams pointed at the Treasury Department, "was quite confining, too dark, and too damp. I'm sure it wasn't damp, but the air conditioning was set too low. I had to stay there for a while to keep an eye on that boy Sperry. I never felt I could trust him, and, of course, he was a Republican."

Adams was so garrulous that Gif was not sure either he or Tracey would be able to get a word in around the rambling let alone ask the pointed questions he had in mind. Tracey, reading his mind, nodded towards two chairs, indicating that Gif should move them to the window as Adams suggested.

Gif grabbed the back of a second large upholster brown leather chair and pushed it to a position on Adams' right. Then, he grabbed a simple hardback chair, slid it to the left, and turned it so he could face Adams and Tracey.

As soon as Tracey and Gif were seated, Adams changed directions again.

"All right, director, tell me the bad news."

The sudden question caught Tracey by surprise, pleasing Gif because he had never seen that particular expression of bewilderment cross her face.

"Sir…"Tracey began then hesitated.

"I assume you have identified the bastard who killed my predecessor," Adams declared. "Who was it?"

"We haven't quite reached that point, yet, sir," Tracey said before punting. "I think it best if I let Inspector Gifford brief you. Like he did during the Capitol Hill investigation that you referred to, Inspector Gifford has been riding point for our current task force."

"So I heard," Adams said, surprising Gif and Tracey again. They both wondered where he could have heard that.

"Mr. President," Gif said, deliberately dropping the acting from Adams' title. It made addressing the man awkward, almost conveying the impression that the speaker was reminding the old man of the tenuousness of his position. "We have the proverbial good and bad news."

"Son, don't mince words. Hit me with the bad news first," Adams continued to control the discussion in a way that Gif had not anticipated.

"We suspect that you have risen to the position you now hold as the result of a conspiracy," Gif said bluntly.

Adams surprised Gif by laughing at that statement.

"You call that bad news," Adams said. "I didn't think I would enjoy this place, but creeping up on it the way I did makes it almost bearable. At least today, I'm having a grand time. How I got here is a different matter, but here I am."

"A criminal conspiracy, sir," Gif did not back down.

"As far as I'm concerned, all conspiracies are criminal," Adams declared. "You aren't accusing me of something, are you?"

At this point, Gif was not sure what he was doing. Before he got here, his approach had seemed quite simple. Lean on the president and see how he reacted. The problem, he was learning, was to get Adams to stand still long enough for Gif to lean on him. Gif decided to take a more candid, a more pointed approach.

"Sir, we have solid evidence that indicates that Vice President Walker's death was not an accident," Gif began.

"Really," Adams interrupted. "I never thought it was."

Gif ignored that comment for the moment. "That evidence when combined with the fact that President Tate was shot militates against the assumption that the sudden demise of our nation's two leaders was coincidental."

"And that leads you to conclude that there had to be a conspiracy," Adams pursed his lips and nodded his head in agreement. "That follows. And…"

"And, lacking information concerning the identity of the conspirators, any professional investigator must start by focusing on those who gained from the commission of the violent acts," Gif interrupted the president.

"Of course," Adams agreed. "And that is why you are here since you conclude that I am the one who gained the most." Adams suddenly started chuckling, surprising both Tracey and Gif. They exchanged looks and waited for the old man to elaborate.

"Son, let me tell you one thing. Being lifted from that comfortable chair down the street that I earned with over forty years of hard labor and being shoved into this grand office is not something I would conspire to attain. When you reach my age, all you truly want is to return home, sit down, and nod off to sleep in front of the television, as bad as it is."

"Do you deny having participated in a conspiracy?" Gif asked bluntly.

"I just did in my good ole boy manner," Adams answered. "I also frankly admitted I'm beginning to enjoy myself again, and I confess, just between the three of us, that I am tempted to do whatever it takes to stay here. Excessive pride is a dangerous thing, but I am proud of what I have accomplished in my life."

"Do you have knowledge of others who might have conspired to raise you to this position," Gif asked despite the fact that he was beginning to believe the old man and rather liked the person behind the good ole boy persona.

"If I did, I would have called you and this lovely lady and reported it," Adams said.

"Do you have supporters who might have conspired to elevate you to this office without your knowledge for reasons of their own?" Gif asked.

"The only person who can answer that question is Jake, Jake Tyrone, my chief of staff. I haven't troubled myself with minor details like campaign financing and wooing supporters since I hired young Jake over thirty years ago."

"Have you any reason to suspect that Jake may have decided to participate in a conspiracy without your knowledge for reasons of his own?" Gif asked.

"You mean like finally collecting money he might need for his own retirement?" Adams smiled. "Although Jake is still a young man in my eyes, he is sixty-three."

"Yes. An excessive desire for money or recognition can lead a person to do things he or she might normally avoid," Gif said, sounding like a naïve preacher even to himself.

"Not Jake," Adams said with emphasis. "Talk to him yourself."

"Is there anyone else among your staff or supporters you suggest we talk to, sir," Gif asked.

"Of course not. As I indicated, time, age, and circumstances have conspired, if I may use that word without negative implications, to isolate me. My world today is largely circumscribed. Jake and Miss

Mary effectively control my actions. You can't possibly be suggesting that Miss Mary would be involved in some kind of innovative plotting."

"No, sir. Not Miss Mary," Gif smiled.

"Do you have any more questions, inspector? I anticipate one of my keepers will soon open that door," he glanced in the direction of Miss Mary's office, "to remind me that I have to meet our new cabinet."

"No, sir," Gif answered.

"And what about you Madam Director?" Adams turned on Tracey. "You have been remarkably quiet. You wouldn't happen to be a southern gal, would you?"

"No sir, California born and raised," Tracey, who had been captivated by Adams' adroit performance, answered.

"Too bad," Adams smiled.

"Inspector Gifford spoke for me," Tracey responded to Adams' indirect challenge. "He leads our task force team investigating the conspiracy."

"And you share his views that one truly exists?"

"Yes, sir, I do."

"And I do also. As your president, acting though I may be, I charge you two, together and separately, with bringing the bastards who killed President Tate, Vice President Walker, Ms. Starbright, and Mr. Dexter to justice."

"Yes, sir," Tracey and Gif answered in unison as they started for the door.

"Oh, one more thing, inspector," Adams called after them.

Gif and Tracey stopped and turned.

"How does the murder of those two football players fit into this conspiracy business?" Adams asked. "I hear that you, inspector, are also charged with that investigation."

"Sir, no matter what the media might think," Gif answered honestly. "I frankly don't know."

"Let me know, inspector, when you find out," Adams dismissed them with a wave of the hand.

When Gif and Tracey were back in the hallway, Tracey turned to Gifford.

"Christ, he's some act," she smiled. "What do you think?"

"I think we better drop in on Jake," Gif said. "Do you mind asking the questions?"

"Afraid you are in over your head?"

"You handled the senator a lot better than I did the president," Gif answered honestly.

"I had the leverage, then. Here, we're just bluffing," Tracey said.

"And if Jake is anything like Adams, we're overmatched," Gif said.

"We'll see," Tracey said. "Follow me."

Assuming that Jake Tyrone had moved into his predecessor's office, Tracey opened the door just as a group of smiling men and women in their thirties and forties filed out of the inner office. Tracey and Gif stepped to the side and watched while the group continued out into the corridor.

"Our new staff. Mr. Tyrone just held his first meeting. May I assist you, director?" The matronly executive secretary who guarded the inner office greeted them. Tracey recognized her from visits to the Speaker's Office at an earlier time but did not remember her name.

"We don't have an appointment, but the president whose office we just left, suggested that we have a chat with Mr. Tyrone," Tracey replied.

"If President Adams suggested it, I'm sure that Jake will see you," the secretary replied.

She stood up, entered the inner office, and closed the door behind her.

"I'm glad I brought you with me," Gif smiled at Tracey.

"You are so sweet, inspector," Tracey said as she winked at the second secretary who was watching them with unconcealed curiosity.

"It's nice to see you again, director," the younger assistant smiled.

"The same," Tracey answered as she shook the girl's hand. "Half of Capitol Hill must have moved in here this morning."

"Just the Speaker's Office," the girl laughed. "We've been waiting like forever to get here."

The door to Tyrone's office opened and the executive secretary held the door for Tracey and Gif. "Mr. Tyrone will see you now, director."

They entered to find the new chief of staff still sitting at the head of a long conference table.

"Director, it's good to see you again," Jake stood up to shake Tracey's extended hand.

"May I introduce Inspector Gifford," Tracey said.

"Ahh, Inspector Gifford. I've heard much about you," Jake said. "You're now working with Director Schultz on the task force." It was a statement not a question. "If you don't mind, we'll just sit here," Tyrone waved a hand at the table. "Please excuse the mess," he glanced at the stacks of paper that surrounded him. "Our predecessors moved out only yesterday, rather abruptly, as I suspect you've heard." Tyrone chuckled, pretending he was enjoying a good joke.

"We promise not to take up too much of your time," Tracey said as soon as she was seated.

"I understand that you just met with the president," Jake said. "Would you mind telling me what that was about? Since I'm supposed to be in charge of his scheduling, I would appreciate it if you would give me a heads up on any future briefings."

Neither Tracey nor Gif reacted.

"I assume you discussed your investigation," Jake continued, ignoring their non-responses.

"We'll tell you exactly what we told the president, Mr. Tyrone," Tracey said.

"Good, but please start by calling me Jake."

"Yes, Jake," Tracey said. "I should tell you that Inspector Gifford is in charge of the investigation into the deaths of President Tate and Vice President Walker."

"So I've heard," Tyrone said as he nodded at Gifford before turning his attention back to Tracey.

"Inspector Gifford recently acquired solid evidence indicating that Vice President Walker's death was not accidental," Trace said.

Tyrone stared at Gif, expecting him to elaborate. Instead, Tracey continued.

"We now conclude that the deaths of President Tate and Vice President Walker at virtually the same moment in time were not accidental. As a consequence we also conclude that they died as the result of a conspiracy." Tracey paused to give Tyrone a chance to react.

"I must admit I am not surprised," Tyrone said.

"Really?" Tracey said.

"Yes, I am not a great believer in coincidences, and I have also read the articles written by informed observers who tabled the conspiracy theory. Some of their views struck me as rather absurd, but at the same time, they make one wonder. Have you identified the conspirators?"

"We are in the process," Tracey answered.

"And does your new evidence point you in a particular direction?" Tyrone looked again at Gifford.

"Yes, we are now looking closely at those who stood to benefit from the deaths of my good friend and former colleague Harrison Tate and his vice president," Gif answered, determined to make his position perfectly clear.

"And that is why you are here today," Tyrone observed matter-of-factly.

"Yes," Tracey said.

"And this is what you told the president?"

'Exactly."

"And that is why you approached him directly without forewarning," Tyrone smiled. "How did President Adams react to your brash accusation?"

"With aplomb," Tracey laughed.

"I'm not surprised," Tyrone said. "He immediately denied it of course."

"Yes. He stated that at his age he would prefer to be home watching television," Tracey smiled.

""But…"

"But he admitted that he was beginning to like the Oval Office."

"I've noticed the same thing myself," Jake laughed. "When we were over there," Jake glanced in the direction of the Treasury Department building, "the acting president and myself spent our days just about the way we did in the Speaker's office. We would have a dash of Jack

Daniels in our coffee and chat about everything but governance. I must admit it troubled me a little when he arbitrarily selected a Republican as his acting vice president."

"Why do you think he chose Sperry?" Tracey asked.

"I don't know. Maybe because he thought that our current economic situation required it."

"I sense you didn't approve of Mr. Sperry?" Tracey pushed.

"I think you've probably noticed the way that worked out. Not very well. If the acting president had asked for my advice, I would have recommended against Mr. Sperry."

"And now?

"I think that Acting Vice President Hernandez will prove to be a good choice. May I ask what all this has to do with your visit here today?"

"Yes," Tracey said. "After President Adams denied having any knowledge whatsoever about a conspiracy to elevate him to high office—he stressed that given his age and unstated incapacities he remained quite isolated in his position--we asked him who in his office might be better informed since we were starting our inquiries with those who had benefitted the most from the recent revolution."

Tyrone laughed. "I see you picked up on that slogan very quickly. The New Revolution."

"Was that your suggestion?" Tracey asked.

"No, that was completely the president's idea. I suspect we are going to have more of that coming from the Oval Office these days. I'm the chief of staff, here, but the president has made it perfectly clear that my role now will be less that of confidant and friend and more of office manager. So, you see, I'm not really the one who has gained from the revolution."

"And that troubles you?"

"Of course not. As much as I enjoyed my previous relationship with the acting president, the current situation requires it. I will manage the staff, the executive branch if you will, and the president will focus on policy and his primary role as the public face of his administration. That alone is a full time job for him. Did the president actually suggest that you talk with me about this alleged conspiracy?"

"He said that you would know better than anyone else if any of his supporters acted in a misguided way to elevate him to higher office, without his cognizance or connivance," Tracey said, closely watching Tyrone's reaction to that virtual accusation.

"I'm flattered, but I must admit the president's confidence in me was misplaced. I have no personal knowledge of any conspiracy whatsoever."

"Do you have secondary knowledge?"

"Secondary knowledge? Whatever that means, the answer is no. I have no knowledge of a conspiracy period."

After a few seconds of silence, Tyrone continued. "Let me make something clear. Mr. Adams likes to refer to his age, and that is perfectly understandable. He's eighty and that's old, probably too old for the pressures he is going to face in this new job. That being said, I must add that if anyone his age can handle it, Hiram Alphonse Adams can. In fact, I suspect that if he survives he might even contemplate running in the next election. He might talk about retiring to his chair and watching television, but don't believe it for a second."

Tyrone hesitated, giving Gif the impression that he might be feeling he had said too much. However, Tyrone surprised him by continuing in the same vein.

"I am old too, you know. Too old for this damned job. I'm sixty-three and thinking about the pleasures of retirement myself, seriously. I'm never going to be president. I'm probably proof of that notional law that one is always promoted one step beyond one's ability. The highest I'm going to climb is here, and as I admitted, I doubt that I should be sitting in this chair with these stacks of papers piled high in front of me."President Adams showed as Speaker what he thinks of staff. He ignores staff, but here I am, the keeper of the staff. I will work my way into a heart attack while he sits down the hall playing George Washington. You know your history, I'm sure. Washington had his Thomas Jefferson and his Alexander Hamilton who created and ran his government while Washington presided over the country from Mount Vernon where he lived grandly and graciously. Hamilton and Jefferson fought and connived, and Washington let them, probably encouraged them in their constant plotting. I don't know who the president has decided to put into his cabinet, but I assure you, he will have his Hamilton and Jefferson, competitors who want to be king. If you think I managed a conspiracy to put Hiram Alphonse Adams in this position, you are insane. I'll support him to the grave, but God, that's where this job will take him. He's too old to handle the pressures of the presidency, but I must admit that if any man his age can cope with the challenge, Hiram Alphonse Adams can."

The president's chief of staff took a deep breath, sighed, and then declared:

"But Christ, I love him and will kill myself with all this damned paper for him," he shoved a paper column and sent it scattering across the table, "in order to give him what he wants."

Tracey glanced at Gif who answered with a shrug. After that tirade, neither could think of another question to ask.

"Forgive me," Jake Tyrone smiled. "Forget what I just said and remember. President Adams and I are products of decades on Capitol Hill. Don't pay any attention to all the fancy speeches of politicians. In our Congress, right policies emerge from all of the conflict and scheming. Every law results from compromise, the eternal congressional art form. Some laws are good, and some are bad. Fortunately, most of the time bad law eventually is changed, just like the politicians who advocated them. I'm not sure I answered all of your questions, but I have already said more than I should. That was the old man in me talking. I assure you that no one in President Adams' entourage fomented a disgusting conspiracy just to get him to the Oval Office."

Jake Tyrone stood up. "Please remember I am always here to answer your questions," he said as he dismissed them.

Again, when they were back in the hall, Tracey turned to Gif. "Anyone else you want to interrogate?" She asked.

Gif shrugged. "Sometimes in this business you get in over your head. Those two are master dissemblers, far over my head, but I believe them both. I guess I better broaden my investigation."

Tracey grabbed him by the arm. "I agree about those two; maybe we both are wrong, but I trust them," she referred to Tyrone and Adams. "I know one thing for sure. We still have a conspiracy to unravel."

"And we will," Gif agreed. "I promised Martha I'm going to catch the bastard that killed Harrison."

"But what about the Redskins?" Tracey smiled.

"And that's not funny either," Gif grumbled. "Somebody murdered those two young men."

"Where do we go now?"

"To ask questions of those who may have participated in a despicable and possibly unsuccessful conspiracy," Gif answered.

When they were back in the Prius, Gif turned to Tracey: "You know, I'm getting awful tired of that place," he looked at the entrance to the White House.

"I'm surprised that Adams didn't fire us," Tracey said. "He could have, you know. I wonder why he didn't. We accused him of conspiring to commit four murders."

"He didn't insist on knowing about our evidence," Gif said thoughtfully.

"Neither did his buddy Jake."

"You know what has happened to everyone who had knowledge about this damned case," Gif said. "Do you have a weapon with you?"

Tracey patted her oversized handbag. "Do you?"

Gif reached behind him and checked his belt under his suit coat.

"Why didn't the metal detector go off?" Tracey asked.

"Because you so intimidated that poor sergeant, he didn't protest when we walked around it," Gif smiled.

"OK, cowboy, where are we going now?"

"Check that notebook of yours and get me to our former vice president/secretary of the treasury's abode."

Chapter 35

Gif circled the block that contained former Acting Vice President Alexander Hamilton Sperry's house three times before he decided to park illegally beside a hydrant located a few hundred yards away.

"This should be another forgettable experience," Tracey cautioned as they approached the black lacquered door with a fancy bronze knocker. "Do you want to play the heavy this time?"

"I'll take Sperry with pleasure," Gif answered. "He has a reputation for being an arrogant pig."

"Just your kind," Tracey laughed.

Gif banged the knocker several times and waited.

"I assume you noticed that our former vice leader has no protection," Tracey said.

"I noticed. I guess that the Secret Service does not recognize acting vice presidents who have been fired."

"Do you think they provided a protective detail to Agnew in prison?"

"Did he actually serve time?"

"Who knows, who cares," Tracey shrugged. "Maybe they gave him some kind of amnesty for taking his bribes in his West Wing office."

Gif banged the knocker again, and the door opened suddenly as he was in the process.

"We're not interested," a stylishly dressed woman in her forties said as she started to close the door.

"Wait," Gif said, blocking the moving door with the palm of his hand.

"Go away," the woman ordered. "Or I'll call the cops."

"We are the cops," Gif said as he displayed his credentials.

The woman glanced at them. "So what? Go away. We gave last month at the office. When we had an office," she laughed.

"Mrs. Sperry?" Gif asked.

The woman stared but did not answer.

"I'm Inspector Gifford and this is Director Schultz. We are from the Tate Task Force, and we have some questions for your husband."

"I'm sure you're not alone," the woman laughed. "What do you want from me?"

"Is your husband home?" Tracey tried.

The woman looked at Tracey. "Yes."

"May we speak with him please, Mrs. Sperry?" Gif asked while maintaining his pressure on the partially closed door.

"How would I know?"

"Please ask him to come to the door?"

"I can't do that."

"May I ask why not?"

"I already told you. He's at home."

"Mrs. Sperry," Tracey said. "Are you saying that this is not Mr. Sperry's home?"

"That's right, honey."

"May I ask where that might be," Tracey asked, smiling at Gif's frown.

"New York City."

"Is that where Mr. Sperry is now?" Gif asked, now thoroughly exasperated.

"I assume so. That's where he said he was going when he caught the shuttle. Now go away."

Gif pulled his hand from the door, and it slammed in his face.

"New York?" Tracey asked, checking her watch.

"Let's visit Mr. Clapp first," Gif said.

Twenty minutes later Gif turned the Prius into the parking lot of a Crystal City apartment building located a short block from Vice President Walker's hideaway.

"Do you think it an odd coincidence that Clapp lived this close to Walker's playpen?" Tracey asked.

"I'm skeptical about everything connected with this investigation," Gif answered.

"How do you want to handle this?" Tracey asked.

"Why do you keep asking that?" Gif said, still irritated by Sperry's spouse's cavalier attitude. "Let's just play this one by ear. What do you know about Clapp?"

"One or two p's?" Tracey asked.

"The man not the disease," Gif said.

"The man is a disease," Tracey replied. "He's connected."

"The Mafia? Why didn't you share that little item before this?"

"No, not the Mafia. I'm told he has a reputation in New York. He's not one of Sperry's banking buddies; he's a New York hustler from the tough side of city politics. He latched on to Sperry when he was running for mayor. That worked out well and Sperry hired Clapp for his gubernatorial campaign. The bureau's New York office reports that Clapp made himself so useful to the governor that he brought Clapp with him to D.C. as a political consultant. Somewhere along the way, Clete got himself the fancy title of chief of staff. Nobody at the Treasury Department knows what he really did for the secretary because he doesn't know squat about economics or how to print money."

"I wonder if Clapp is preparing for a move back to New York," Gif said.

"We'll have to ask him," Tracey said.

They took the elevator to the fifth floor, located 503 without difficulty, and Gif rapped on the door with his knuckles.

"Go away," a male voice ordered.

"This is beginning to look like it is going to be one of those days. Nobody wants to talk with us. Do you think it's me or is it you," Gif said as he slapped his palm on the door.

"What the hell?" A male in his forties, dressed in slacks, a black T shirt and wearing sandals, opened the door. He stared at Gif and then Tracey before stepping back. "I'm busy, make an appointment." He tried to shut the door, but Gif quickly pushed inside with Tracey following.

"Mr. Clapp, we have a few questions," Gif said. Gif took out his credentials.

"I know who both of you are," Clapp said. "I've nothing to say without my lawyer present. Leave! Or I'll charge you with forcible entry."

Tracey smiled as she glanced at the moderate sized apartment. "Nice place, but a bit cluttered," she said. "How many rooms?"

"If you want to rent it, speak to the super," Clapp said. "It's available. Now leave."

"Soon?" Gif asked as he tossed some newspapers to the floor and settled down on the sofa.

"I'm trying to pack," Clapp snarled.

"Had your fill of Washington?" Gif asked.

Clapp did not answer. He stood near the open door and waited for his unwanted visitors to depart.

"I'm sure Mr. Clapp is job hunting," Tracey spoke to Gif.

"Did the acting president also terminate your employment?" Gif asked.

"Oh, excuse me a minute," Tracey spoke before Clapp could answer.

Gif and Clapp watched as Tracey crossed the room and left the apartment, closing the door behind her. Gif was as surprised at Tracey's odd behavior as Clapp was, but he said nothing.

"What is she up to?" Clapp asked.

"You know women," Gif shrugged. Tracey's abrupt departure had at least caught Clapp's attention. "She probably left her handcuffs in the car. Do you know how I can reach Secretary Sperry?" Gif decided to stall.

"I don't know and don't care. The asshole canned me," Clapp declared.

Gif waited for Clapp to explain.

"The government stopped paying my salary when the old fart fired us," Clapp said sourly. "And Sperry told me to take a walk. He's an asshole," Sperry repeated his epithet.

"The president or Sperry?" Gif tried to keep Clapp talking until Tracey returned.

"Cut the crap, Gifford. I'm busy. Go join your friend and take your questions with you," Sperry pointed at the door.

I assume your parting was not amicable," Gif said, amused by Clapp's anal fixation.

"You assume right," Clapp said. "I'm a political advisor, and Sperry has no future."

"What happened?"

"That should be obvious. When the dumb shit signed on with Adams, he killed any future he had with the Republican Party. Then, Adams and Tyrone set him up. They let him present his damned plan to Congress, which was programmed to reject it. Predictably, Sperry blew a fuse, and Adams, who arranged everything, used Sperry's reaction as the opportunity to dump him. Sperry's damaged goods. He talks about running as an independent, and he's too dumb to see that is exactly what the Democrats want. Sperry will drain off enough Republican votes to give Adams a cakewalk to victory."

"That sounds pretty obvious to me," Gif said.

At that moment, a smiling Tracey returned. "Excuse me," she said, turning to Gif. "What have I missed?"

"Mr. Clapp just told me an interesting story about how Adams and Tyrone manipulated Sperry out of office setting up a Democratic victory in the next election."

"Sounds like a real conspiracy to me," Tracey picked up on Gif's lead.

"Adams is an old shit, but he's cunning. Sperry was setting himself up to be the next Republican presidential candidate, and in my opinion he had a real shot at winning," Clapp said.

"Why did Sperry let Adams outsmart him?" Tracey asked.

"He's an arrogant asshole," Clapp declared. "He thought he had a chance to have everything now."

"Why would he think that?" Gif asked.

"When Adams offered him the vice presidency, Sperry took one look at the old man and decided he didn't have to wait. He even encouraged Adams to move into that damned Andrew Johnson Suite where he could control him."

"Why did Adams accept the offer?" Gif asked.

"In order to set up Sperry and put a lock on the next election, that's why."

"If you saw this coming, why didn't you warn Sperry?" Tracey asked.

"I had everything set up for him, but he stopped listening to me," Clapp said.

"How did you have everything set up for him?" Gif asked quickly.

Clapp reacted strongly to that question. He stared at Gif, frowned, and crossed his arms and legs. A bodily reaction that told Gif that Clapp was girding to resist them again.

"I've already said too much," Clapp said. "I've nothing to tell you two about anything. You want to learn more about Sperry, ask him yourself."

"What are you going to do now Mr. Clapp?" Tracey asked.

"I'm getting out of this hick town and returning to New York City where I have friends and contacts."

"Back to politics?" Gif asked.

"That's what I do?" Clapp declared.

"Good," Gif said. "I need your expert opinion on something."

Clapp squinted, a sign that he didn't trust Gifford.

"Informed observers," Gif said, "have speculated that Vice President Walker's death was not accidental, that it was not coincidental, and that Walker and President Tate died as a consequence of a major conspiracy. What do you think about that?"

"You tell me," Clapp laughed. "You think I was involved somehow in a conspiracy? That's nonsense. I'll assure you of one thing before you take your fat ass off my couch and haul it out of here. If I planned something to get Sperry and myself in the White House, I wouldn't be here packing my bags for New York."

"Sometimes conspirators make mistakes, Mr. Clapp," Tracey said.

"Not this guy," Clapp said. "I don't know a thing about any conspiracy. Go over to Pennsylvania Avenue and ask those guys sitting in the White House these questions."

Clapp stood up and waited for Tracey and Gif to leave.

Neither moved.

"I said leave," Clapp ordered. "Do I have to call my attorney?"

"Mr. Clapp," Gif did not move. "Sit down. I'll let you in on a secret. Sensitive information has just come into our hands that confirms that indeed there was a conspiracy."

"I don't believe you."

"Start believing, Mr. Clapp," Tracey said. "We have information from an absolutely impeachable source that Vice President Walker's death was not accidental."

"What do you mean not accidental? He overdosed on pills, right?"

"How do you know what caused Walker's death?" Gif demanded.

"That's what I read in the papers."

"How do you think the conspirators coordinated the president and the vice president's murders?" Gif asked.

"I don't know if anybody coordinated anything," Clapp answered loudly. He turned and dramatically marched to the door. "Now get out."

Just as he was reaching for the knob, someone rapped hard on the door. Clapp opened it to find two smiling men in dark suits waiting. One held a piece of paper in his hands.

"Mr. Clapp?" The man with the paper asked.

"Who the hell are you?" Clapp challenged.

"Come in," Tracey called. "Mr. Clapp," she continued. "That piece of paper is a warrant authorizing these agents of the Federal Bureau of Investigation to search your house."

"You shits set me up," Clapp turned on Gif and Tracey.

"Please take that into custody," Tracey ignored Clapp and spoke to the second agent. She pointed at the laptop setting on the cluttered desk near the window.

Tracey turned to Gif.

Gif nodded and followed Tracey out the open door, leaving the agents to deal with a sputtering Clapp.

In the elevator, Gif turned to Tracey. "I wondered what got into you."

"I saw the laptop and decided we needed it."

"We'll probably get more out of it than we would have out of Mr. Clapp," Gif laughed.

Tracey, pleased with herself, smiled. "I gave Tom a call and fortunately Jeff Cohena had had the prescience to have a warrant for searching Clapp's place in hand. Now what?"

"Do you really think that I have a fat ass?" Gif asked, pivoting so that Tracey could make an informed opinion.

"Why do you ask that?"

"Something Mr. Clapp said."

"Turn again."

Gif made another full pivot."

"Yes," Tracey said as the elevator door opened.

"Yes what?" Gif asked.

"It's really fat," Tracey said.

"How would you like to take in a New York City play tonight?" Gif changed the subject.

"Really?"

"No, but we should hop up to the big city and have a talk with Mr. Sperry before he has a chance to coordinate with Mr. Clapp," Gif smiled.

"That apartment won't take more than a couple of hours," Tracey referred to the search going on behind them.

"I doubt that Mr. Clapp and Mr. Sperry will want to discuss our interest on the telephone," Gif said.

"And we have Mr. Clapp's laptop," Tracey smiled. "I'm beginning to feel a lot better about this investigation."

"I'm not," Gif said. "Harrison and the others are still dead."

"But at least we've got some movement," Tracey said as they climbed into the Prius. "I guess I won't have time to pick up a change of clothes," Tracey looked at Gif who shook his head negatively.

"Not unless they have a dress shop on the shuttle," he said.

Chapter 36

Gif's watch said seven PM when they got out of the taxi in front of Sperry's 5th Avenue apartment. After flashing their badges at the doorman and warning him against phoning an alert to Sperry, they boarded the elevator for the penthouse.

"Who's turn?" Gif asked as they ascended.

"I applaud your job on Clapp," Tracey smiled, obviously amused at her word play.

"The good fairy can be scary with Sperry if she wishes," Gif smiled back.

"Oh, sir, this fairy fears she might fail fairly with Sperry," Tracey fired back.

The elevator door opened and they found themselves in an opulently furnished lobby.

"I'm impressed," Gif said. "Look at all the gilt, gold and glimmering glass."

"I'm giddy," Tracey said.

"Then I'd best fire the first gun," Gif said as he rapped with the polished brass doorknocker.

They waited but got no response.

"Do you by chance have an appointment?" Tracey asked.

Gif laughed and rapped harder.

Still, they waited in silence without response.

Gif reached a third time and was wielding the knocker as hard as he could when the door opened suddenly.

"What?" An irate Sperry glared at them.

"How in the hell did you get up here?" Sperry challenged after recognizing Tracey. "I'll have that damned doorman fired."

"Good evening, Mr. Sperry," Gif ignored Sperry's rudeness while deliberately not using either of the boorish man's former titles. "I am Inspector Gifford, and I believe you know Director Schultz."

Sperry did not respond.

"We need a few minutes of your time," Gif said politely.

"Make an appointment," Sperry growled as he started to close the door.

Gif caught the door with his left hand as he put his credentials back into his suit coat pocket with his right.

Sperry and Gif locked eyes.

"This is not a social visit, Mr. Sperry," Tracey spoke for the first time.

"So talk with my lawyer," Sperry said.

"We can do this the easy way or the hard way," Gif used the old cop show cliché.

Tracey glanced at her companion with scarcely concealed amusement.

"I'll give you exactly five minutes," Sperry capitulated by stepping back.

Gif followed Tracey into a hallway featuring a worn Persian runner and lined with gold gilt period furniture.

Sperry led them into a room on the right that was as big as Gif's study, dining room/parlor, and kitchen combined. The obligatory brown leather sofa and chairs flanked an oversized walnut desk. Filled bookcases lined three walls, and an immense window framed by dark green drapes looked out on Central Park. Sperry sat himself behind the desk, presumably to establish his control of the meeting, while Gif and Tracey seated themselves some twenty feet away on the sofa.

"We should have brought our megaphones," Gif smiled at Tracey.

Sperry ignored his unwanted visitor's irreverence.

"You now have exactly four minutes," Sperry said as he ostentatiously examined his thick, gold wristwatch.

"Mr. Sperry," Gif said as Tracey took her notebook and ballpoint pen from her purse. "Your former chief of staff sends his regards."

Sperry's thin lips curled up at the corners in what Gif assumed was an attempt at a sneer, but Sperry did not reply.

"As we were leaving, representatives of the task force armed with a search warrant were assisting Mr. Clapp in his unpacking," Gif said.

Again, Sperry did not react.

"They seemed particularly interested in Mr. Clapp's phone messages, office diary and his laptop, of course," Gif continued.

Sperry again made a show of consulting his watch.

"Mr. Sperry," Tracey joined the one sided conversation. "We can have a team of agents join us in the time it takes you to consult your lovely watch once more."

Tracey pulled a folded paper from her purse and placed it beside her on the couch.

"Is that a warrant you are trying to threaten me with?" Sperry demanded as he reached for the phone. "Maybe I should call my attorney."

"As you wish," Tracey said, not answering Sperry's question.

"We really would not like to have the media learn of this visit," Gif said.

Sperry took his hand off the phone.

"I should warn you both," Sperry frowned. "That I have an appointment with some very influential members of the political establishment this evening."

Neither Gif nor Tracey reacted.

"To discuss my pending campaign for the presidency," Sperry flashed what he presumably considered a threatening smile.

"If they should arrive before we conclude our conversation," Tracey smiled back. "We will be obligated to inform them that on behalf of the Tate Task Force we are investigating your involvement in a conspiracy responsible for the commission of a series of homicides."

"That's ridiculous," Sperry blustered as he folded his arms and glared at visitors.

His reaction, however, told Gif and Tracey that they now had his full attention.

"We will tell you exactly what we explained to Mr. Clapp," Gif said.

"Your discussion with Clapp interests me not in the least," Sperry said. "Clapp is a former, I repeat, former employee whose views I have learned are completely unreliable."

"Mr. Clapp had nothing but good things to say about you," Gif said.

"I'll bet," Sperry laughed. "I suggest that you treat Mr. Clapp's testimony with extreme caution."

"Mr. Clapp related an interesting account about how Adams and Tyrone manipulated you out of office setting up a Democratic victory in the next election."

"Nonsense."

"Clapp seems to think it was all part of a much larger conspiracy," Gif said.

Sperry shook his head but did not deign to comment.

"He believes you accepted the acting vice presidency because you thought you saw an opportunity to speed up your timetable for moving into the Oval Office."

"And how did Clapp think I was going to do that in this little dream of his?"

"The acting president is indeed an older man on the edge of retirement," Gif said, not quite answering Sperry's question. "However, Mr. Clapp said that you invited the acting president to use the Andrew Johnson Suite where you could control him."

Sperry unfolded his arms and clasped his hands together on his desk. "Adams moved into the suite because it suited him. Located between the White House and Adams's real home on Capitol Hill, it let Adams stand like a Colossus between the two power centers."

"Clapp thinks that Adams accepted because he saw it as an opportunity to use you to attain his own objectives," Gif said.

"How astute of Clapp. How does Clapp think Adams planned to do this?"

"He says Adams played to your weakness. He dangled the acting vice presidency in front of you, knowing you would see it as an opportunity to move your own plan forward. After you took the bait, he used your belief in the efficacy of your economic plan against you. He sandbagged you in the Congress, and as he anticipated, your ego got in your way. You over-reacted, and he fired you, thus putting an end to your presidential aspirations. Clapp suggests you sealed your own doom when you grasped the acting vice presidency, the poisoned fruit so to speak. That single act turned the Republican leadership against you."

Sperry's face flushed bright red, and he visibly struggled to temper his response.

"And," Gif smiled. "Clapp says that he had everything set up for you, but when Adams dangled the vice presidency in front of you, you stopped listening to him."

"That stupid little shit. I should never have listened to him in the first place." As soon as the words were out of his mouth, Sperry hesitated. He relaxed, then smiled. "You quote Clapp as saying he had everything set up for me. What did he mean by that?"

The question delighted Gif, but he hid his reaction. His entire approach had been focused on getting Sperry to reach this point. "Mr. Sperry, I believe you just asked the wrong question."

"What in the hell do you mean by that?"

"You should have asked why we questioned Mr. Clapp in the first place," Gif said.

"Very well, why did you?"

"As we quite candidly told Mr. Clapp, our investigation has recently acquired reliable information that indicates that Vice President Walker's death was not accidental."

"Walker died as the result of an overdose of pills," Sperry declared with a frown.

"That's the very same reaction that Mr. Clapp had," Gif said. "Have you by chance coordinated your responses?"

"And what did you say to that?" Sperry ignored Gif's question.

"I asked him how he knew what caused Walker's death."

"And Clapp said that's what he read in the newspapers," Sperry chuckled. "So do I." Sperry challenged Gif to repeat his question about coordinating responses.

"And then I asked him how he thought the conspirators coordinated the president's and the vice president's murders," Gif said.

"What conspirators?" Sperry asked.

"We're going in circles, Mr. Sperry," Gif smiled. "How did they coordinate the killing of the president and the vice president at virtually the same time? That must have been very difficult."

"How would I know?" Sperry blurted.

Gif did not respond.

"Are you making an accusation?"

"As they say on TV, Mr. Sperry, we are just trying to collect the facts," Gif said.

"Director, are you going to sit there and let this mere subordinate ask insulting questions?" Sperry turned on Tracey. "I was the one who recommended that you head this investigation."

"Acting President Adams appointed me," Tracey replied.

"I don't know anything about any conspiracy," Sperry raised his voice. "And if there was one, I …." He stopped, glared at his inquisitors, and suddenly got himself under control.

"If there was one…" Gif repeated Sperry's words back to him.

"Then I answer with a question. Who gained? Isn't that what you always look for? The motive. Who profited? Certainly not me. Ask the damned acting president that question," Sperry said coldly. He stood up. "That's all I have to say without my lawyers present. If that's really a warrant," he pointed at the folded paper lying between Tracey and Gif on the sofa. "Then call in your damned agents and use it. Otherwise, get out."

Tracey and Gif exchanged looks. Neither spoke. Tracey picked up the folded paper and put it back in her pocketbook, and they both stood up.

"Thank you, Mr. Sperry for sharing your valuable time with us," Tracey said.

"Good evening, Mr. Sperry. We will be talking again. Have a nice meeting," Gif said as he turned to follow Tracey to the elevator.

Sperry did not bother to escort them to the door.

As they waited for the elevator, Tracey said: "That was interesting. What do you think?"

"I think we have to find out for ourselves how the conspirators communicated," Gif smiled. "No one seems to want to answer the question for us."

"The computers," Tracey said.

"What is that paper you have in your purse?" Gif asked.

"My utility bill," Tracey said. "Please remind me to send in a check. Do you think we should collect Mr. Sperry's computers?' She asked as the elevator door opened.

Gif answered with a shake of his head. "I didn't see any lap top in there, did you?"

"No," Tracey answered. "I doubt that our host would deign to use a computer for himself."

"I agree. Let's see what Mr. Clapp's lap top has to tell us."

When they reached the street, Tracey turned to Gif. "What now?"

"Are you hungry?"

"Are you?" Tracey asked.

"Do you really want to go to that damned play?"

"I would rather grab a bite at the airport and get to D.C. to check on the computers."

Gif hailed a taxi.

They arrived at the airport just in time to catch the last shuttle.

As they waited, Gif turned to Tracey. "What do you think about our conspiracy now?"

"Me?" Tracey feigned surprised. "You are actually asking for my opinion?"

Gif waited.

"What do you think?" Tracey deferred.

"You first."

"Tomorrow morning, one of us is going to have to lean on Mr. Clapp real hard," Tracey said.

"We'll double team him," Gif agreed.

"What are we going to do about dinner?"

"Quarter-pounders for two."

"Beats meat loaf."

They arrived at Gif's retreat a little after midnight to find one car parked in front. Inside, Jerry Quigley was sound asleep in Gif's recliner. Gif used the remote to silence the television before joining Tracey in the bedroom.

Chapter 37

Tracey and Gif found their uninvited houseguest sitting in front of his computer screen when they opened the bedroom door.

"Gif, Tracey you've got to see this," Jerry Quigley greeted them.

"Give me a chance to wake up," Gif protested.

"You're really going to like it," Jerry insisted.

Tracey and Gif stood behind Jerry's screen. As soon as he saw it was focused on http://www.urperiscope.com/pirouetting, Gif groaned and started for the kitchen.

"Wait, let me show you," Jerry said.

"I'm looking," Tracey said.

"I've seen it," Gif said as he grabbed a clean cup and spooned in the coffee.

"Fix one for me, too," Tracey ordered.

Gif filled the first cup with water, shoved it into the microwave, and while the machine did its zapping, Gif prepared a second cup. He took a bagel from the fridge, sliced it, and put it in the toaster. Meanwhile, the excited tech fidgeted.

"Well show me something," Tracey prodded him in the back.

"Wait," Jerry said. "I have to explain it all, and Gif has to pay attention. It's important."

Finally, Gif handed Tracey her coffee. He returned to the kitchen, buttered his burnt bagel, and with coffee and breakfast in hand rejoined Tracey.

"As I told you before," Jerry pointed at the monitor. "This is a bulletin board."

"I know," Gif said as he took a bite of his bagel. "Please explain again in simple terms so Tracey can understand."

Tracey hit Gif with an elbow, spilling coffee on the floor."

"Look what you did," Gif complained.

"Don't worry, I'll clean it up," Tracey said as she headed for the kitchen. "Go ahead," she spoke to Jerry. "I'm listening."

"She's all ears," Gif laughed.

"A bulletin board is just that," Jerry said patiently. "It's a place where people can post messages to other people of like interests. Each sub-interest has its own page and the /pirouetting is one."

"OK, I got that," Tracey said as she leaned down and swabbed the coffee spots with a paper towel.

"Last night the bureau techs broke down Clapp's laptop."

Gif stopped chewing his bagel and started paying closer attention to Jerry's chatter.

"You'll be interested in the messages he sent during the past couple of weeks to his page on urperiscope."

"That urperiscope.com/pirouetting page?" Gif said, exhausting his expertise".

"No, /pirouetting was not his page," Jerry said. "I think Clapp had it listed in his contact page as a reminder."

"A reminder?"

"Yes," Jerry said. "Clapp was trying to be clever. He deleted all the messages he sent to his page, which was urperiscope.com/scooter, and I don't blame him. Want to read them?"

"If he deleted them, how can we read them?" Gif asked.

"We retrieved the web page address and messages from his hard drive. When you delete anything on your computer, it stays on the hard drive until another message is stored in that same place or you use a special program to erase the hard drive."

"And we were lucky?"

"Yes, but since we now know he had a web page, it doesn't matter if he deleted the messages from his computer," Jerry smiled. "We recovered them from his hard drive, but all we have to do is go to urperiscope.com/scooter. The messages are all stored there. The wonder of the internet is that all this crap floats out there forever."

"You're confusing me, Jerry," Gif admitted.

"Take my word for it. Clapp had a web page and we can read the messages that he posted."

"What do they say?" Gif asked.

"Read them for yourself." Quigley hit a few keys and a new web page appeared. www.urperiscope,com/scooter. It consisted of five cryptic lines:

Msg. 1. Meet you at the fishing hole.
Msg. 2. The trout and the bass are biting.
Msg. 3. Good luck. Nail that big fellow.
Msg. 4. We gotta clean a little fish. Meet me
At the usual place tonight.
Msg. 5, One more little one. Meet me
at the usual place tonight."

"Clapp posted these messages on his bulletin board page?" Tracey asked.

"Yes," Jerry answered.

"Are you sure?" Gif demanded.

"They were sent from Clapp's laptop," Jerry said.

"Can you tell when they were sent?" Tracey asked.

"Could Henry Ford build a horseless carriage?" The tech smiled as he checked his notes.

"The first message was sent August 14th at 1431 hours, Messages 2 on August 20th at 1415 hours and Message 3 on August 20th at 1500 hours," Jerry said.

"But who received the messages?" Gif asked.

"Anyone who checked that billboard page," Jerry answered.

"How do we determine who that was?" Gif asked.

"By checking their computers," Jerry answered. "Can you suggest where I might look?"

"Shit," Gif said as he sat down at the table opposite Jerry. "Are you sure you can't tell me who logged on to that page?"

"Just teasing, boss. Only one person logged on to that page between 1400 hours and 1600 hours on August 20, several times I might add." Jerry held up his notebook. "Are you sure you want to read this name. It'll shock you."

Gif held out his hand for the notebook, but Jerry waved it in the air. "I'm overdue for a promotion," Jerry smiled.

Gif grabbed the notebook and looked at the name. He wasn't

as shocked as Jerry had anticipated he might be, but he did not like reading it nonetheless. Gif handed the notebook without comment to Tracey, not bothering to repeat what he was thinking.

Tracey took the notebook from Gif. As she studied it, her eyes widened. She looked at Gif. "Do you believe this?"

Gif nodded. Jerry had printed out the name:

Richard Simmons

"What in the hell was he doing checking this web page?" Tracey asked.

Gif shook his head, treating the question as rhetorical.

"I'll be damned. That little red car was an unmarked vehicle?"

"Jerry, were these messages only from Clapp to his web site. One way?" Gif asked.

"There's more," Jerry declared.

"I'm not sure I want to hear it," Gif said. If this information checked out, his good friend Dick Simmons, Gif's protégé who he had personally selected to replace him as sheriff, had killed Gif's mentor, President Harrison Tate who had preceded Gif as sheriff. "Shit," Gif swore.

"After we figured this stuff out we checked the other pages and discovered that Sheriff Simmons had his own urperiscope web page." Jerry moved his mouse, tapped the keyboard a couple of times, and leaned back: "Have a look." This time the web page carried a different address: www.urperiscope.com/whizzer.

Msg. 1. Big fellow nailed.
Msg.2. Little fish cleaned.
Msg.3. Second little fish cleaned.

"Let me get this straight, Jerry," Gif said. "This whizzer web page belongs to Simmons. Who sent these messages to that web page?"

"Simmons," Jerry answered.

"You're sure?"

"They came from Simmons's computer. You get the computer. You got the sender."

"Msg. 1 was sent when?" Gif asked.

"It was posted at 1640 hours," Jerry replied.

"Can you tell me who checked this second page?" Gif asked.

"I can. Clapp was the only one who logged on to read the sheriff's messages.

"Those bastards brazenly used the internet to communicate," Gif said.

"If they had used different bulletin boards, it would have been a lot harder to link them," Jerry said.

"One more question," Gif said. "This one may be more difficult. You originally found urperiscope on Tyrone's computer."

Jerry nodded affirmatively.

"Is there any record of Tyrone's laptop ever logging on to the /scooter and /whizzer pages?"

"Good question," Jerry said. "I can find no record that Tyrone's computer ever logged on to those specific pages. The web site urperiscope.com/pirouetting but not the /scooter and /whizzer pages."

"What does that tell us?" Gif asked.

"Only that someone using Tyrone's computer once visited the web site. Nothing more. I could find no record of e-mails between Tyrone and either Clapp or Simmons."

"Jerry, congratulations," Tracey patted the beaming tech on the shoulder.

"You guys deserve the credit. You found the laptop," Jerry smiled.

"What about the times for messages four and five?" Gif asked.

"Four and five on Scooter and two and three on Whizzer match up with the hits on Starbright and Dexter," Jerry said.

"I think I better ask Tom to send a team to round up Mr. Clapp," Tracey said.

Gif nodded and Tracey rushed in the bedroom to her cell phone. When she returned, she gave Gif a thumbs up.

"I think you and I need to have another extensive conversation with Mr. Clapp before we visit Sheriff Simmons," Gif said.

Tracey replied with a wave of her purse.

The ride to D.C. was a quiet one with Gif's mind silently churning over Dick Simmons's betrayal.

After reaching the Hoover Building, Gif parked in Tracey's reserved slot and accompanied Tracey directly to the 7th floor and Tom Harrington's office.

"Good morning, Director Schultz," a smiling secretary, the robot, greeted Tracey. She ignored Gif.

Tracey led the way into Harrington's office where they found Tom Harrington sitting behind his desk signing papers. He looked up when the door opened, and greeted them with a broad grin.

"Congratulations, you two. I hear you've been busy."

After Tracey and Gif were seated in the two subordinate chairs facing Harrington, Tracey began:

"Tom I don't know what you've been briefed on and what not, but things are breaking open."

"I think I'm up to date, but pretend I don't know anything," Harrington said. "I'll butt in to save time if I've already been briefed on a particular subject."

Tracey looked at Gif who waved a hand to indicate she should proceed.

"We started with Clapp, didn't like what we heard, and stalled until your boys showed up with a warrant. We didn't want him to have a chance to monkey with that laptop."

"I know about that," Harrington said. "I assume you heard the techs worked on it most of the night." Harrington glanced at Gif. "If that tech of yours ever needs a job, let me know."

"Jerry briefed us this morning on what they found," Gif said. "Those bastards used web pages on an internet bulletin board to communicate."

"I'm glad they did," Tom said. "We've got them cold."

"We also know who the bastard who shot Harrison was," Gif said. "I still have difficulty believing it."

"I know. That's something we're going to have to discuss. I gave the go ahead on Clapp as soon as Tracey called. I assume you want us to pick up Ames, Simmons, and Sperry. I've got Jeff and several teams standing by as we speak. I didn't want to move until I was sure you two were ready."

"We want to lean on Clapp now that we have the computer evidence and get him talking before we bring in the others," Gif said.

."We anticipate that Clapp will fold fast, so you should have a New York team standing by to arrest Sperry as soon as he does," Tracey said.

"And make sure Sperry doesn't slip away before then," Gif said. "He's the one behind the whole damn thing."

"We've got Ames, Simmons, and Sperry under surveillance now. How do you want to handle Simmons and Ames?" Harrington looked at Gif.

"I would like to take care of Simmons myself," Gif said.

"I thought you might say that," Harrington said. "I took it on myself to have my people collect the necessary warrants and to have a team keep a discreet watch on him too. I'll pull them off if you want."

"No, that's fine, Tom," Gif said. "Just make sure they remain discreet but don't let him run."

"Right, and I'll have a team standby to bring in Ames." Harrington made a quick note. "What did you learn in New York?"

"Not much," Tracey answered for Gif. "Sperry confirmed that he and Clapp are no longer associates. He tried to intimidate us with his plan to run for the presidency as an independent. We let him know we had reliable information that indicated Walker's death was not an accident, that it was contrived to coincide with the attack on President Tate. He denied knowledge of a conspiracy and alleged that in the unlikely event such a thing happened it was either Adams and Tyrone's plot or his former aide Clapp acting without his knowledge."

"Why did Clapp and Sperry part company?" Harrington asked.

"We'll know more after we lean on Clapp," Tracey said. "But it appears to me that Sperry used Clapp to set up the attacks on Tate and Walker, as part of a complicated plan to win the elections, but Adams outmaneuvered him. The old man used the acting vice presidency to lure Sperry into his web, outmaneuvered him in Congress, and then dumped him, destroying any chances of an electoral victory. When that happened, Sperry cut his losses by unloading Clapp who was so deeply involved in setting up the murders that he could not retaliate against Sperry."

"So Sperry planned the whole thing and presumably bankrolled it," Harrington said.

"Yes," Tracey said. "Sperry carefully kept his hands off the actual implementation, using Clapp as a cutout."

"I assume we will be able to track the money," Harrington made another note.

"Definitely," Tracey smiled. "Always follow the money trail."

"And thanks to your tech, Gif, we know how Clapp and Simmons communicated," Harrington said.

"We'll need to get our hands on Simmons's computer to complete the circuit," Gif said. "We know how they communicated, but we don't know how they initially hooked up. We're told that Clapp grew up in New York City politics, and it's possible one of his dubious contacts there put him on to Simmons. That's something we're going to explore in due course with Clapp and Simmons. I'm afraid we're going to learn that Simmons has been working professionally as a hired killer for some time now. That makes me feel terribly, terribly stupid. I put the bastard in his current job."

Neither Tracey nor Tom pursued that subject.

"God, it's funny how these damn cases break down," Tom mused. "We run into a seemingly impenetrable wall. We butt our heads against it again and again, can find no way around it, and then we find a small crack and before we know it the wall comes crumbling down."

Harrington's private line rang before he could continue.

"Yes?" Harrington listened before breaking out in a broad smile. "Good, bring him in, but nobody says a word to him until Director Schultz and Inspector Gifford have their go."

Harrington hung up and looked at his visitors. "We've got Clapp. Jeff Cohena will personally escort him until you two take over."

Gif and Tracey exchanged glances before standing up.

"You two make a devastating team," Harrington stood up with them. "If you ever …"

"Don't say it, Tom," Tracey laughed. "I'm not sure how long I will be able to tolerate the sight of the inspector."

"We're taking it minute by minute, Tom," Gif chuckled.

"More like second by second," Tracey corrected.

Gif turned and headed for the door with Tracey barely a step behind him. Tracey turned her head and cast a look at Tom that said: "See what I have to put up with."

Gif did not say a word.

Chapter 38

Gif and Stacey were sitting in a bare room with pale green walls and a scarred table and metal folding chairs when the door opened and a stern faced agent entered followed by Clete Clapp wearing handcuffs, a smiling Jeffry Cohena, Reggie Crawford and a phalanx of special agents.

"Thank you, Special Agent Cohena, gentlemen, and lady," Tracey greeted them. Tracey nodded at the accompanying team before glaring at Clapp. Before she could speak again, Gifford spoke for her.

"Take the cuffs off this piece of shit," he ordered gruffly.

SAC Jeffrey Cohena watched carefully as one of his agents removed the cuffs as ordered. "We'll stand by outside, inspector, director," he said before leading his team out of the room and closing the door behind him

"Sit down," Gif ordered an apprehensive Clapp.

Gif and Tracey sat side by side facing Clapp who had his back to the door. Clapp rubbed his wrists before speaking.

"What is this all about?" His words were challenging but his quavering voice revealed his worry.

Gif and Tracey sat quietly, each deliberately letting their silence feed Clapp's anxiety.

"What did Sperry tell you?" Clapp finally demanded.

Neither Gifford nor Tracey responded.

After another two minutes of silence, Gif looked at Tracey then back at Clapp.

"We found some interesting items on your computer, Clapp," Gif said.

Clapp shifted nervously in his seat.

"What can you tell us about that most interesting web site, urperiscope.com/scooter?" Tracey asked.

The words urperiscope.com/scooter hit Clapp like a slap in the face. His pale face turned several shades whiter, and he seemed to collapse inwardly. Beads of sweat gathered on his upper lip. For a few seconds, Gif thought Clapp was going to faint.

"Talk or we'll dispense with this opportunity for you to explain your role and simply charge you with four counts of murder," Tracey said. "Maybe, you would like that, to be remembered in history just like John Wilkes Booth."

"Could I have a glass of water?" Clapp pleaded.

Tracey stood up, opened the door, spoke a few words, and waited. When she turned, she had a small paper cup half filled with water. She handed the cup to Clapp and sat back down.

"We found urperiscope.com/whizzer, also most interesting," Tracey said while Clapp sipped his water. "Who selected those childish names, scooter, whizzer? Was that you, Clapp? Surely you could have been more imaginative than that."

When Clapp did not respond, Gif stood up and turned toward the door.

"Wait," Clapp pleaded, spilling his water on his shirtfront.

Gif stopped, turned, and stared at Clapp.

"Please sit down. I'll tell you everything."

Tracey took a portable recorder from her bag, hit the record button, and waited.

"I was just a go between," Clapp blurted. "I sent those messages to my web page. Scooter, that was mine."

"And Whizzer?"

"I monitored that page. That's all."

Gif laughed. "And you didn't know what the messages meant," Gif said.

Clapp hesitated as he searched for a good response.

"Just tell us the truth, Clapp," Tracey ordered softly.

"Start at the beginning. Who originated the plan to kill the president and vice president of the United States?" Gif demanded harshly.

"Sperry, it was all Sperry's idea. He gave me the money to pay the others. He told me how much. Everything."

"We know that, Clapp," Tracey said. "We just want to hear you say it so we can determine how much Sperry told us was the truth and how much was lies."

"He blamed it all on me, didn't he?" Clapp showed a flash of bravado.

Neither Tracey nor Gif responded.

"All right," Clapp said as he pressed the fingers of his right hand against a throbbing temple. "It started last June. Sperry called me into his office and told me the time had come for us to act. The economy was in decline, rapidly descending into recession. Unemployment was rampant, almost 9.7%. Home foreclosures were nearing record levels, reserves in even the major banks were falling precipitously, and Sperry said we had to act before the country fell into a depression even worse than that of 1929. I believed him. What did I know? I was a political advisor."

"Just tell us what you did, Clapp, and forget the window dressing," Gif ordered.

"Sperry said he was the only one who could save the country. His plan had to be implemented, and Tate didn't understand the dangers that lay ahead."

Gif began tapping the table with the fingers of his right hand.

"Sperry said that anybody who was bright enough to recognize the importance of his plan could be president. He said that left Walker out. Both had to be replaced. If they would not resign, somebody had to help them leave office, and Sperry decided to be the one to do it."

"Tell us about your involvement," Gif ordered.

"One day in July Sperry called me into his office. That wasn't unusual. I was his political advisor, and I assumed he wanted to have a survey conducted or have me contact an ally or contributor. Instead, he handed me an envelope and told me to deliver it to Senator Ames. I didn't know Ames well, but I had met him at Georgetown cocktails. We traveled normally on different levels. I felt the envelope and realized it was too thick to be just a note, so I asked Sperry what was in it. He told me to mind my own business and to take the envelope to Ames's office and to give it to him personally.

"As soon as I got back to my office, I opened the envelope and found it stuffed with hundred dollar bills. Not wanting to keep it lying around, I took it immediately to the Hart Building where I found Ames waiting for it. I didn't ask what it was for, and Ames didn't say. He asked me for my cell phone number, and I gave it to him.

"Two weeks later Sperry gave me another envelope and a small box and ordered me to deliver both to Ames. The box was taped shut, but I opened it anyway and found a large bottle of pills. I don't know what kind of pills because the bottle didn't have a label on it."

`"And the envelope?" Tracey asked.

"I opened it too. It contained more hundred-dollar bills just like the first envelope. I didn't count them. I didn't want to touch them. I delivered the box and envelope to Ames, and this time Ames said he would keep in touch. Sperry kept asking me every couple days if Ames had called, and all I could say was no. Then, the day that Walker died, Ames called me on my cell phone and told me to tell the boss that an appointment was scheduled."

"Appointment with whom?" Gif asked.

"Ames did not say."

"What time did Ames call?" Tracey asked.

"Around two. I immediately told Sperry. He seemed excited by the news and told me to keep him informed. I asked about what, and he said to keep my cell phone on and tell him right away if Ames called again. Ames did. About four, and this time he seemed real nervous. He just said, it's done, and hung up. I went to Sperry's office and told him that Ames called and said it was done. That's all I know about that. I was just a messenger between Sperry and Ames."

"What about the messages to urperiscope.com that we found on your computer?" Tracey asked.

"Again, I didn't know what they were all about. Sperry told me to get a web page there with the user name scooter. After I did that he ordered me to post that first message: 'Meet you at the fishing hole.' I asked him what the hell that meant, and Sperry said it meant I was to meet a man that night at nine on Haines Point at the bench near the first hole on the golf course. I asked for the man's name, and Sperry laughed. He told me not to be stupid. The man would be dressed all in black and wear a Redskin hat. He would ask for my name, and I would say Chris Columbus. Sperry gave me a locked briefcase to hand to the man. That's all."

"When did this happen?" Tracey asked.

"About a week before the shooting."

"Did you ever see this man again?" Tracey asked.

Clapp swallowed hard before answering.

"Just twice. About a week after the shooting, I don't remember the exact day, Sperry called me in and ordered me to send that crazy message about cleaning a little fish. He gave me a locked gym bag and told me to meet the same guy that night at nine on Haines Point. By this time I suspected what was happening, particularly after I read those other messages from whizzer, but I was in too deep to back out. I did what I was told, and the guy grabbed the bag and took off."

"And the third time?" Tracey asked.

"Same thing. A couple days later Sperry had me send the message about one more fish. I delivered another bag that night to the guy. I was really afraid I might be the little one that time, but I didn't have a choice. I was in too deep to back out. All I did was send e-mails and deliver bags."

"Your story is that all you did was follow Sperry's orders," Gif said.

"That's right. I was just a message boy."

"Tell me about Message number 2, the one that you posted on scooter that says the trout and bass are biting," Tracey said.

Clapp hesitated. "I sent it."

"When?"

"A little after two o'clock on the day of the shooting," Clapp said. "I had just returned from lunch and Sperry called me to his office. He said: 'post this on scooter immediately.' He handed me a piece of paper with the words: 'The trout and the bass are biting' on it. I did what I was told, that's all."

"Do you still have that piece of paper?" Tracey asked.

"No, I never had it. As soon as I read it, Sperry took it back."

"Do you know what that message meant?" Gif demanded.

Clapp hesitated. He looked around the room.

"Answer my question," Gif insisted.

"I didn't at the time," Clapp said. "I just did what I was told. I sent the message."

"But now you know what it meant." Gif said.

Clapp nodded.

"Say it," Gif ordered.

"It told someone that the president was going fishing that afternoon, but I don't know who."

"The man you met on Haines Point," Gif said.

"Maybe."

"When did you send message number 3?" Tracey asked, "the one that said: Good luck. Nail that big fellow."

Clapp swallowed hard before answering. "Could I have some more water?" He held up the paper cup.

"No," Gif said gruffly.. "Answer the question. When did you send message number 3?"

"About a hour after the first one. Probably around three o'clock Sperry called me up to his office and told me to send it. I did what I was told."

"And you know what that means," Gif said.

Clapp nodded.

"It means you ordered your friend in the Redskin hat to kill the president," Gif said. "Say it!"

"I didn't know that is what it meant," Clapp whined. "I was just a messenger doing what Sperry ordered."

"You ordered a man who you personally paid to kill President Tate," Gif said.

Clapp leaned against the table and hid his face in his folded arms.

"But after the president was shot you realized what had happened, what you had done," Gif said.

"Yes," Clapp admitted.

"And when you sent message number 4 saying that a little fish had to be cleaned you knew that Sperry and this other guy were getting ready to kill somebody else," Gif said.

Clapp hesitated before answering. He looked at Gif and then Tracey before answering. "Maybe I should talk with a lawyer."

"Do you really think a lawyer can help you now?" Gif laughed.

"Probably, I suspected," Clapp blurted.

"What does that mean?" Gif demanded.

"Probably I suspected that is what another fish meant. Then after that call girl got killed I figured she was the little fish."

"And the fifth message, the one that said that another little fish had to be cleaned?"

"I thought maybe it was me or maybe Ames. Sperry was eliminating everyone who knew anything about Walker and Tate. I didn't know that guy Dexter was even involved."

"Do you have anything that can corroborate your story?"

"You've got the messages on my computer."

"All they tell us is that you sent those messages," Gif said.

"I didn't send all of them," Clapp whined. "I just read those on the whizzer page because Sperry ordered me to."

"You didn't tell me anything about the Redskin killings," Gif said. "Did Sperry order you to arrange those also?"

"I didn't arrange any of that. I was just the messenger, and I don't know anything about those Redskins. Did Sperry do that too?"

Gif turned to Tracey. "Any more questions you want to ask Mr. Clapp?"

"Not right now," Tracey said.

"I have one more question," Gif said as he took an envelope from his pocket. Gif opened the envelope and extracted a newspaper clipping. It had a picture of a man in a Loudoun County Sheriff's uniform.

"Do you recognize this man?" Gif demanded.

Clapp looked at the picture, swallowed hard, looked at Gif and then Tracey, and said: "That's the man in the Redskin hat. Is he really a cop?"

"That's the man you met at Haines Point?" Gif asked.

"Yes," Clapp answered weakly.

"Are you sure?" Gif insisted.

"Yes."

Gif took the picture back, put it in the envelope, and placed the envelope back in his pocket.

"All right, Clapp," Gif said. "Special Agent Cohena and several others are going to continue this debriefing. First, though, I want you to write down everything you told me and everything else you might remember about all of this," Gif ordered.

After they left Clapp, Gif and Tracey met with Jeff Cohena.

"What did you think of that?" Tracey asked Gif.

"The same as you," Gif said grimly. "Clapp had two things on his mind. Getting even with Sperry for dumping him, and covering himself. I think he did a pretty good job of involving Sperry, at least that is what I wanted to hear, truth or not. But he did not even come close to covering himself."

"You don't think he's an exploited subordinate who only did what his boss wanted?" Tracey smiled.

"I think that Clapp is the one who came up with all the stupid solutions to Sperry's problems. Clapp considers himself the political operative, the guy with all the right connections in the New York underworld. You can bet Clapp is the one who came up with the shooter, not Sperry who doesn't really travel in the right circles for that. And all of that computer spy communications stuff was Clapp's idea too. We didn't see a computer in Sperry home or office, so the odds are that he is not computer literate. Further, I imagine that Jeff's boys will find that Clapp has a lot of unexplained cash stashed somewhere, probably in brand new hundred dollar bills.

"I agree, Tracey said. "But that doesn't make Sperry innocent either. He's the one that approved Clapp's solutions to his problems, and he is the one who financed it all, probably from hidden campaign funds. It was a real conspiracy with no innocents involved."

"And that includes the shooter and the playboy senator," Gif agreed. "We don't know what Sperry promised Ames.'

"Either the vice presidency or cash," Jeff Cohena who had listened to the debriefing from the next room with members of his staff said. "Or, Sperry had something on Ames. That picture that you showed him. Was that Simmons?"

Gif took the envelope from his pocket and handed it to Cohena who immediately opened it. As soon as he saw the caption under the picture, he smiled."

"You can keep the picture. We're on our way to Leesburg," Gif said.

"Clapp's all yours, Jeff," Tracey said. "Lean on him after he finishes his creative essay. Inspector Gifford and I have another arrest to make."

"I've got two teams standing by with warrants," Jeff smiled. "One for Simmons's office and the other for his home. Our surveillance reports that the sheriff is now in his office."

A sour faced Gifford shook his head, but he did not comment.

As Gif directed the Prius towards Leesburg, Gif turned to Tracey. "I really am not looking forward to this. All I really want to do is shoot the bastard."

Behind them, four cars filled with FBI agents followed.

Chapter 39

Gif parked the Prius directly in front of the back entrance to the former bowling alley. Two black sedans parked directly behind Gif, and two more stopped in front.

"What's this, sheriff? A raid?" The older deputy ending his career as a back door security guard greeted Gif.

"Something like that," Gif answered.

"Two agents in their black quick reaction outfits deployed to each side of the now baffled deputy.

Gif led the way to the sheriff's suite with Tracey at his side and four more agents following closely behind them.

"Don't let anyone enter or leave until I give the word," Tracey ordered as she and Gif entered the sheriff's outer office.

"Sheriff Gifford," Gloria who had replaced Gif's faithful Kitty, greeted him.

"I don't think you've met Director Schultz," Gif politely introduced his companion.

"Gloria," Tracey said.

"I've read so much about you, director," Gloria responded. "You are a role model for all us working girls."

"I'm a senior citizen, now," Tracey laughed. "Besides, we girls don't need role models any more. Just go for it."

"Is he in?" Gif interrupted the chat.

"Yes, sir, go right in," Gloria said.

Gif opened the closed door to his old office and entered to find Sheriff Richard Simmons sitting behind his grand desk.

"Gif, I was just thinking about you," Simmons greeted Gif with a smile. "And Director Schultz. This is indeed an honor. How can we assist you?"

Gif sat down in the chair directly facing Simmons while Tracey selected a leather padded straight chair on Simmons's right, putting as much distance between herself and Gif as she could.

"Please, sit next to Gif," Simmons said, playing the genial host. "That's not a very comfortable chair where you are."

Tracey answered with a shrug and stayed where she was.

"Dick where is your laptop?" Gif asked, showing he had no interest in playing Simmons' game.

The question surprised Simmons. His eyes narrowed, and he stared at Gif. "Why do you ask, Gif?"

"I see the office work station on that table behind you, Simmons, but I don't see your laptop." Gif deliberately used his former friend and protégé's last name.

"Is this an official visit, Gifford?" Simmons replied in kind.

"Yes where is your laptop?" Gif insisted.

"In my study at home," Simmons replied coldly. "What business is that of yours?

"We didn't think you would be using the office computer to communicate with urperiscope.com/whizzer," Tracey said.

That comment appeared to stun Simmons. He stared at Tracey and then at Gifford. "What is that?" Simmons asked softly, his voice almost a whisper.

"It's the web page that you used to communicate with urperiscope.com/scooter," Tracey replied.

"Communicate? I don't know what you are talking about, director," Simmons said.

"We have arrested your colleague Clapp," Gif said. "Teams of agents are debriefing him as we speak, and he is singing his heart out."

"I don't know anyone named Clapp," Simmons replied, a little more forcefully this time.

"Mr. Clapp is the former chief of staff to former Acting Vice President Alexander Hamilton Sperry. I'm sure that you are familiar with Mr. Sperry."

This time Simmons took a deep breath, placed his elbows on the arms of his chair, and formed a pyramid with his fingers. He rested his chin against the fingertips.

"Of course I know who he is," Simmons finally replied.

"The scooter web page belongs to Mr. Clap, and the whizzer page belongs to you," Tracey said. "I don't have to tell you that, however. There are five interesting messages on Mr. Clap's page, and your laptop, only yours, visited that site exactly five times."

"That's nonsense," Simmons declared forcefully as he dropped his hands to the arms of his chair.

Gif watched the movement carefully, making sure that the hands stopped there and did not move on to Simmons' holstered weapon. Gif turned his chair and let his coat drop away from his own weapon, which he had holstered on the side today. Tracey also opened her purse, which she held on her lap.

Simmons, reacting to Gif and Tracey's obvious movements, lifted his hands and clasped them in front of him on the desk.

"There are three interesting messages on your web page," Tracey continued. "And Mr. Clapp, only Mr. Clapp, who you claim not to know despite your nocturnal meetings on Haines Point, visited your site three times."

Simmons shook his head negatively. "What can I say? Nonsense is nonsense. Somebody's playing games with you."

"Do you have the briefcase and two gym bags also stored at your home? Are they in your study with the laptop?" Gif asked.

Simmons did not respond.

"The case and bags are filled with mint condition one hundred dollar bills," Gif said. "That will make them easy to trace."

"I don't know anything about a briefcase and gym bags," Simmons said, his voice less certain.

"Director would you please ask the agents at Simmons' house to now serve the warrants and conduct their search," Gif said.

"My pleasure, Inspector Gifford," Tracey smiled at Gif as she stood up and moved to the outer office, opening the door wide enough for Simmons to see the black quick reaction uniforms of the waiting special agents. She left the door only half closed.

Gif watched Simmons closely as he stared at the door. "This is all a big misunderstanding, Gif," Simmons tried again.

Gif detected a pleading tone in his former friend's voice.

"Where did you get the money to buy that huge mansion?" Gif

asked. "They must be paying sheriffs better now than they did during my days in this office.

Simmons did not answer.

"And how did you pay for that new place at the beach?" Gif asked. "Cash, I'll bet."

Simmons did not answer.

"And those fancy foreign cars are impressive," Gif continued. "We both know how much it costs to maintain the younger editions of the modern spouse."

Tracey re-entered and sat back down in the chair along the wall.

"I was just asking Simmons where he got the money to pay for all his new toys," Gif spoke to Tracey.

"I'll bet he didn't answer," Tracey smiled at Gif. "Not to worry, I'm sure we'll soon find that nice little safe. It won't take long to tear down every wall, and in that safe there will be lots of cash and bank account numbers. I hope we don't frighten the sheriff's new toy girl too badly."

"These hit men are so unprofessional," Gif said.

"Especially, bad police officers who think they are too clever to get caught," Tracey said.

"They even use unmarked little red cars," Gif said.

Suddenly, Gif leaped to his feet and leaned across the fancy desk and shouted in Simmons' face: "How could you shoot Harrison Tate, the good man who once sat in this very room, who hired you and me, and promoted us until we took turns sitting here?"

Gif pulled his Glock from his holster and aimed it directly at Simmons forehead.

"Answer me, you bastard."

Simmons' only response was to lean back in his chair trying to distance his head as far from the menacing weapon as he could.

"That's not going to do you one bit of good," Gif said. "You didn't know, did you, that Harrison suspected the conspiracy and wrote me a note asking me to investigate. You left Martha to suffer a lonely widowhood. Do you know what she asked me?"

Simmons wiggled his head negatively.

"She said: "Kill that bastard who shot a wonderful man for no reason that a decent person can comprehend."

Gif stepped around the desk and approached Simmons who now cowered in his chair.

Gif again raised his weapon and pressed it against Simmons forehead.

Tracey watched calmly.

Gif glared at the trembling Simmons.

"Gif, no," Simmons pleaded.

Gif took a deep breath and stepped back. "I'm not going to shoot you, Dick. That would be too easy for you."

Simmons waited.

"But I'm going to be there when they stick that needle in you. You can expect excruciating pain," Gif said. "I will make sure it is slow acting."

Gif reached down and took Simmons weapon from his holster. "Is this the gun you used to kill poor Dexter? And Nan Starbright? Did you enjoy yourself?"

Simmons began to shake uncontrollably.

Gif glanced at Tracey. "Look at that Tracey. That's our professional for hire killer." Gif turned back to Simmons. "Why did you kill the two Redskins? Just for the fun of it?"

Simmons did not respond.

"Answer me, you stupid bastard," Gif shouted, raising his weapon again.

"I needed a diversion. I didn't want you focusing on…the other thing," Simmons mumbled.

Gif turned to Tracey. "He killed two young men with bright futures ahead of them just because he didn't want me to focus on the fact that he killed my best friend. Not only is he pathetic, he's stupid. Martha will have to forgive me. He's dirt, not worth killing."

Gif walked over to the door, opened it, and calmly said to the waiting agents: "He's all yours. Don't treat the sick bastard gently."

"Gif," Tracey said. "I'm going to ride back in with the team. I should be there when they debrief this bastard," she nodded in the direction of Simmons who the agents were handcuffing. And I want to hear what Sperry has to say."

"I've got a chore to handle myself," Gif said.

"Don't wait up for me," Tracey got in the last word. "I'm sure I'll be late."

After Tracey and the agents departed, Gif lingered in his old office for one last look. He frowned at the fancy desk and furniture, shook his head, and left for what he thought would be the final time, hopefully leaving all his memories of the place behind him.

He ignored the curious and sometimes apprehensive stares of the department employees, deputies and staff alike, and returned to his car. He drove around the shabby building and was pleased to discover that the inevitable informant had not yet alerted the media. Within hours, he anticipated, the leaderless department would be under siege. At least this time, he hoped, he would not be involved because he considered his obligations to the investigation were behind him.

Gif turned right, drove a few blocks to the Route 7 Business intersection, turned left and proceeded directly to the old Victorian home, which served as the primary Tate residence. Once again, Gif found the driveway unguarded. He parked near the steps to the front porch. After climbing out of the Prius, he noted the solitary figure sitting in the rocker calmly watching him.

"Gif, so nice of you to visit," Martha Tate, Harrison's widow, greeted him.

Despite her friendly greeting, Martha exuded sadness and grief. At least, that was the way her lonely presence on the front porch struck Gifford.

"Martha," Gif answered then paused. He didn't know how to begin. To say "we just arrested your husband's killer. It was an old friend and protégé, the county sheriff," just did not seem adequate.

"Come and sit a while," Martha said, giving Gif the sense that she was reading his every thought.

Silently, Gif sat down on the porch swing on Martha's immediate left.

"I so enjoy sitting out here watching the cars drive past. Everyone is rushing home to loved ones after a busy day," Martha said. "Harrison so enjoyed this porch."

"I know," Gif said. "I remember sitting out here with him. It was so…peaceful and relaxing."

"Would you like a coffee or a drink?" Martha offered.

"No thank you," Gif replied. "I can't stay," he lied. "I have much to do."

Martha nodded and kept rocking. Finally, she broke the silence. "Tell me what you came to tell me, Gif."

Still, Gif did not know how to start.

"Did you do what I asked?" Martha asked.

"There was a conspiracy," Gif said bluntly, deciding there was no delicate way he could tell her. "They killed Harrison because they wanted his job."

"I knew it had to be that," Martha said, still rocking.

Gif stared at her, admiring her stolid composure, dry-eyed, calmly waiting for Gif to explain the story of her husband's death. Martha at that moment appeared to Gif to be a reincarnation of the tough frontier women who had braved the wilderness and Indian menace to be with their husbands on the edge of civilization.

"Alexander Hamilton Sperry planned it all. He hired and dispatched the man who shot Harrison, Nan Starbright, James Dexter and those two Redskin players."

"Harrison and all those poor, innocent people," Martha said. "Just because he wanted that damned job. Harrison probably would have given it to him if he had asked nicely. He hated it."

"And Sperry arranged the death of Vice President Walker," Gif continued. "That was no coincidental accident either."

"I never thought it was. Not for a moment," Martha continued to rock.

Gif sighed, still holding more bad news for last.

"Was it someone we knew?" Martha asked, striking Gif with her prescience.

Gif did not reply. He had difficulty putting Dick Simmons' treachery into words.

Martha waited. "Did you kill the bastard?" Martha finally asked.

"It was Dick Simmons," Gif said softly, almost hoping that Martha Tate did not hear him and would let her question go unanswered.

"Dick Simmons," Martha said. "Dick Simmons," she repeated. "Harrison thought so highly of him. Was it for money?"

Gif nodded his head, unable to admit that betrayal cost a mere million dollars in hundred dollar bills.

"We all wondered where the money was coming from," Martha said. "We knew first hand he could not afford all those cars, the mansion and that ..." Martha hesitated. "That new, young bride. Harrison worried that Dick was taking bribes. That was something else he planned to talk with you about."

Gif nodded as the sad old lady reminded Gif of another thing he had been too busy to let his friend discuss with him.

"Did you kill him?" Martha asked again.

Gif shook his head negatively. "No, but I thought about it," Gif admitted frankly. "I think I would have if Tracey hadn't been there. But I decided I wanted him to have time to regret what he had done. I'm sorry."

"I'm glad, Gif. I should not have put that burden on you. It was just grief talking. I now realize that Harrison would be angry with me if you had broken the law because of something I had said. Thank Tracey for me."

"Simmons deserves killing, Martha. It wasn't something Tracey said. I just knew she didn't want me to do it, for my sake not hers. I just couldn't do it."

"I know, Gif, but I will enjoy watching him rot in jail for a while. I thank you for giving me that, and I thank God that Virginia has capital punishment," Martha said. "Now, tell me what are you and that lovely Tracey going to do next."

Martha's remarkable resilience relaxed Gif. "Right now I'm going to stop at the Giant, buy two large steaks, some salad, and a bottle of wine, and then I'm going to cook those steaks and drink a toast to Harrison. Will you join me?"

"Thank you, no, Gif. You've already given me a wonderful present. I'm going to sit here in my rocker on this lovely porch and think about the awful future that bastard Simmons has in front of him."

As Gif started for the steps, he had a sudden thought. "Martha," he said as he turned.

"Yes Gif," she answered.

The expression on Martha's face gave Gif pause. She looked like she had already given up on her day.

"Do you maintain contact with any of Harrison's old friends still involved in Loudoun politics?"

The question made Martha smile. "A few."

Gif sat back down. "It occurs to me that the county is going to need a new sheriff."

"Are you interested?" Martha sat up straight.

"Yes, but not for me," Gif replied. "Do you remember Gizzie Kane?"

"I certainly do. Harrison was disappointed when she retired prematurely," Martha said.

"Many of us were. She was an outstanding investigator who I thought one day would be Loudoun's first female sheriff."

"You're right." Martha immediately grasped where Gif was heading. "Have you talked with Gizzie lately?"

"Yes, a few days ago. I rather got the impression that Gizzie was bored with her retirement."

"Do you think she would be interested?"

"I am sure of it," Gif said with a certainty he could not guarantee.

"Leave it to me, Gif," Martha said as she stood up. "I think Harrison would want me to make a few calls right now."

As Gif was approaching the Prius, Martha Tate called to him one last time:

"Gif, Harrison never trusted Sperry."

Chapter 40

Gif did exactly what he told Martha Tate he was going to do. He stopped at the Giant, selected two thick rib eye steaks, filled a plastic container with little of everything in the salad bar, and grabbed a bottle of ten-dollar white wine. He debated with himself over the wine, knowing that connoisseurs preferred red with meat, but he went with his own preference. If he had to drink wine, Gif preferred his cold and white. If Tracey didn't like going against the better set, she could drink beer.

Gif arrived home to find the front door open, and the house empty. Even Jerry Quigley's intrusive machines had been carried away. Gif, who had not been looking forward to sharing the story with his team, was relieved. It was too soon for him to discuss it with others because of the pain he still felt at Simmons's betrayal. With Tracey, he could sit back, eat his steak, sip his wine, and talk about the future.

Two hours later, Gif was still alone. The steak, salad, and wine were in the fridge, and Gif sat on the patio drinking his fourth beer. Gif finally decided that Tracey was too busy to worry about something as mundane as dinner. He lit the charcoal and was in the kitchen pouring blue cheese dressing on the salad when his cell phone buzzed.

"What?" Gif answered, hoping the call was not from Richmond.

"Hi, it's me," Tracey greeted him. "Where are you?"

"Home. The charcoal is lit. Where are you?"

"Here," Tracey laughed. "Everybody's talking and pointing fingers. It's too good to leave. We found the money and the guns at Simmons' place."

"The rifle?" Gif asked the question that worried him the most.

"Yes. The dumb bastard had a full arsenal. Ballistics is working on a match with the slug they found behind Harrison's Kevlar jacket as we speak."

"Good," Gif relaxed. "Let me know."

"Don't wait for me, but save me some steak. I'll be late, real late."

"I wasn't sure about your plans," Gif said.

Tracey did not comment.

"I'm sitting here all alone," Gif said as a realization struck him. His mountain sanctuary was where he had always gone to be alone. Now, he sat in his rural paradise and worried why he had no company."

"Poor baby," Tracey said. See you later. I've got to run."

Gif stared at the salad, at the two steaks waiting side by side on the counter, and the unopened bottle of wine. He turned, looked at the silent television set in the other room.

"Shit," Gif declared.

He grabbed one of the steaks and shoved it back in the fridge. He opened the wine. With the steak and wine and a glass grasped precariously in one hand and the salad and silverware in the other, he retreated to the patio. He left his cell phone on the kitchen counter.

Six hours later Gif was sound asleep in his bed when a hand grabbed his shoulder and started shaking him. He woke to find a smiling Tracey standing by his bed.

"Christ, my head hurts," Gif complained.

"That happens when you drink a whole bottle of wine by yourself," Tracey said. "Where's my steak?"

"What time is it?" Gif asked.

"Three."

"Three what?" Gif carefully rubbed his throbbing temples.

"What three do you prefer?" Tracey asked as she started throwing clothes. "Christ, I'm filthy. I need a shower. You light the charcoal."

"You're kidding," Gif protested as he rolled on to his side. "Turn off the light."

"I'm starved. Fix dinner," Tracey ordered as she retreated into the bathroom.

"Didn't you have dinner?" Gif asked.

"A dry baloney sandwich doesn't do it," Tracey called.

Gif heard the shower running.

"There's no wine," Gif said as he sat up, suddenly realizing that he was still fully dressed.

"Nobody drinks white wine with red meat anyway," Tracey responded.

"I do. How did it go?"

"It's all wrapped up. I've got to brief the acting president in exactly six hours," Tracey said. "Want to join me?"

"Now or in the morning?" Gif asked.

"That's up to you," Tracey called. "Come wash my back."

"I'll light the coals," Gif said.

"Bring me a beer first. You never answered my question."

"What question?" Gif called over his shoulder as he headed for the kitchen.

"Do you want to join me?"

"Yes and no," Gif answered as he opened the fridge.

He took out the steak, the left over salad, now soggy from soaking in too much dressing, and two beers."

He opened one and started for the patio just as a naked Tracey with a towel in her hands appeared in the kitchen doorway.

"Are you sure?" She asked.

"About what?"

"Joining me." Tracey smiled as she grabbed the bottle from Gif.

"I'm not going to chat with another president for the rest of my life," Gif said as he returned to the kitchen and opened the second Budweiser.

"Put that back in the fridge," Tracey ordered.

"Put what?"

"That steak, and throw out that damned salad," Tracey ordered.

Gif did as he was told. "I thought you said you were hungry."

"I'm too strung out to eat," Tracey said.

"I guess we'll have to see what we can do to unstrung you," Gif said as he followed Tracey into his bedroom.

Tracey climbed into the bed. With pillows propped behind her, she sipped her beer as she watched Gif undress. Just as he started to climb into bed with her, Tracey held up her hand.

"Take a shower first. You stink," she smiled.

❧

The next morning Tracey was gone when Gif woke. He showered again and shaved and when he went into the kitchen he found a brief note.

"See you tonight. We have to talk. Clean up this damned pig sty."

Gif spent the day doing exactly what Tracey had ordered. He scrubbed the kitchen, ran the dishwasher, filled three plastic garbage bags with debris and carried them down the driveway to the road, and ran the sweeper throughout the house. He even cleaned the bathroom, changed the sheets, and put his and Tracey clothes, separately, through the washer and dryer. By two PM, he tired of his housewifely chores and retreated to the patio to contemplate his future. He had just sat down in his most comfortable chair when the sound of approaching motorcycles announced the arrival of unwanted guests. Gif hurried around the house in time to witness the arrival of a four-car caravan of three sedans and a huge limousine, which Gif immediately recognized. It was that damned armored monster that Harrison called the Beast.

The sight immediately brought unwanted memories to mind. Gif repressed those thoughts and waited. The two cyclists, both dressed in the uniform of the Loudoun Sheriff's Department, led the caravan into a tight circle that ended on Gif's lawn. The limousine stopped a few feet from the front door. A man in a dark suit leaped out of the front of the limousine and opened the rear door while others deployed on each side of Gif's house.

Gif was tempted to order them to turn their damned caravan around, get it off his grass, and leave. Instead, he just watched. As he feared, a smiling Acting President of the United States of America Hiram Alphonse Adams climbed out of the rear door.

"As they say," Adams greeted Gif. "If the mountains won't come to the White House, the White House has to come to the mountains."

Gif replied with the requisite, forced smile. Gif expected Tracey to emerge from the limousine next, but she did not. Adams, except for his armed escort, appeared to be alone.

"Mr. President," Gif said.

"Inspector Gifford," Adams replied. "May I address you as Gif, sir?"

"Yes sir," Gif answered.

"May I join you?"

"Yes sir." Gif replied.

Gif led the way around the house to the patio.

"Please sit there, sir," Gif indicated his favorite chair.

"I don't want to displace you, Gif," Adams said as he sat down.

Gif then sat in another chair and waited for Adams to explain the purpose of the visit. Members of the president's protective detail deployed in his back yard.

"I apologize for my rudeness in dropping in on you without invitation, Gif," Adams said.

"I'm flattered, sir," Gif gave the obligatory response.

"Please, Gif. My friends still call me Hiram," Adams smiled. "I imagine you know what my enemies say."

Gif chuckled without meaning it.

"I won't pretend that I happened to be in the area and just dropped in to be social," Adams said. "Director Harrington and Director Schultz briefed me this morning. They informed me that you personally are responsible for identifying the persons involved in that tragic plot."

"The directors were too kind," Gif deferred.

"Nonetheless, we aren't by chance in West Virginia are we?" Adams asked.

"Almost," Gif replied. "We're on the eastern slope of the Blue Ridge Mountains, and the Eastern Panhandle of West Virginia is just over the ridge."

"Interesting," Adams said. "It took so long to get here that I was sure we were in West Virginia. I was about to say, Gif, before I lost my train of thought—old age tends to do that to you—that I wanted to personally thank you. I know that President Tate was an old friend and colleague of yours. Did he visit you often?"

"Not often, but he chanced to visit here on that terrible day," Gif admitted. "He even invited me to go fishing with him. If I had…"

"Don't say it, Gif, because it wouldn't be true. Some think that our destinies are already written. I guess today's generation might say programmed. Between you and me, I don't believe that, but what happens, happens, and those of us who are waiting for our own futures to ravel, or unravel, have to recognize that. Like that Persian fellow wrote: the moving finger writes, and having writ, moves on." That's what you and I have to do."

"Mr. President, Harrison Tate was a close personal friend. He rescued me from a career that was wrong for me, and gave me one that fits perfectly. Unfortunately, I failed him. I will live with that for the rest of my life."

"Gif, let an old man differ with you. President Tate was your friend, and you served him well. You brought his killer to justice."

"Sir, I wish I had given that bastard what he deserved," Gif said coldly.

"But you didn't do that. Instead, you gave him exactly what Harrison Tate would have wanted, hard, unforgiving justice."

Gif nodded but did not agree.

"I have talked with Ms. Hanson several times. I believe you know her."

Gif nodded. Adams referred to Grace, Harrison's long time secretary. Gif felt guilty that he had not seen Grace since the day of the funeral and made a mental note to do so promptly now that he had the time.

"Ms. Hanson told me how close you and President Tate were. She even confided that the president several times invited you to join his administration, and you politely declined." Adams paused to give Gif an opportunity to comment.

Gif said nothing. What he and Harrison discussed was none of Adams's business.

"Mrs. Tate told me the same thing," Adams said.

Gif wished that Martha and Grace had not confided in the old man. Still, out of respect for the office that Adams held, Gif did not comment.

"And I come here hat in hand, so to speak," Adams continued. "On a similar mission. I need you. And your country needs you. I would like you to serve on my personal staff with any title you desire to advise me on all matters that interest you, particularly in the realms of national security and law enforcement."

Gif shook his head negatively but could not bring himself to speak.

"Would you like to be Director of the Federal Bureau of Investigation?"

"No sir. You have an outstanding director already in place."

"Please hear me out, Gif. I understand how you feel about bureaucracy, bureaucrats, politicians, but I believe recent events argue that the country needs someone of your vast experience in a position of influence. I'm told that you even have a perspective on the terrorist menace we are now facing. I've got enough theorists and intellectuals advising me. I now need a man with practical experience."

"Sir, please excuse me if I appear rude," Gif finally replied. "I'm an investigator not an advisor. I will speak honestly with you as I did, to my regret, to Harrison. I don't have the patience to deal with bureaucracies. By nature, I am a loner. I have a friend who good naturedly refers to me as the Lone Ranger. As my superior in the Virginia State Police, Colonel Townsend, and my subordinates in the Office of Special Investigation will tell you, I just don't work well with others."

"What you say doesn't surprise me, Gif, and it certainly doesn't deter me. I'm not asking you for a decision right now, today. Think about my offer. Now that's all I'm going to say about the matter."

"If you replace Tom Harrington, you are making a big mistake."

Adams stood up. "See, that's the kind of advice this tired old man needs. Gif, I'll leave you now with just one thought. They say the American people usually get the kind of the presidents they deserve. I say that in Harrison Tate's case that was true. The people deserve the best man available, and that is what Harrison Tate was, the best man. Now, in my instance, I'm old enough to recognize my shortcomings. I'm an accidental president. I need help. I need yours."

Adams shook Gif's hand and made his way to his waiting limousine. His protective detail hurried to their assigned places, the engines started and the caravan departed with Adams saluting Gif with a brief wave of his hand.

Two hours later, Tracey returned home, driving Gif's Prius. Gif hadn't noticed that it was missing.

"Did you get that mess cleaned up?" Tracey asked.

"Do you want to conduct an inspection?"

"No, I'm exhausted," Tracey said as she led the way to the patio.

"You must have had a late night," Gif smiled. "I understand that the president was underwhelmed by your morning briefing."

Tracey looked sharply at Gif. "Get me a beer and then tell me why you think that."

"I had an interesting visitor drop by," Gif said as he headed for the kitchen.

"Who?"

"Someone who attended the briefing," Gif called from inside the house.

Gif grabbed two Budweisers and returned to the patio. He handed one to Tracey and watched as she took her first drink from the bottle.

"The only people at the briefing were the president, Harrington, and myself. Since I just left Tom at the bureau, I assume you are trying to tell me that Adams just visited you."

Gif raised his bottle in toast.

"Are you kidding me? What did he want? Did he offer you a job?" Tracey asked in one breath.

"No, to talk, yes," Gif answered the questions seriatim.

"What job? What did you say?"

"Tracey, didn't you learn anything in Interrogation 101? Ask your questions one at a time. You give your subject the option of choosing which to answer when you stack your questions like that."

"I reject your schoolboy advice. Answer my questions in order asked," Tracey said.

"Re what job, the answer is nothing in particular. Re what did I say, I said no."

"No what?"

"No to the job offer."

"What are we going to do next?" Tracey smiled sweetly.

"Next, I'm going to light the coals and get ready for our dinner party," Gif smiled back.

"My ass, we are," Tracey blurted. "I'm in no condition for a dinner party."

"Stand up and let me check," Gif said.

"Check what?"

"Your ass. I want to check its condition because we've got guests on the way."

"What guests?"

"Guests from Richmond. They are all packed and leave in the morning."

"OK. I guess we owe them," Tracey said.

"I told them you would brief them on your investigation's dramatic finale."

"That won't be necessary. Tom is holding a press conference as we speak."

"Don't you want to watch it?" Gif asked.

"No. But I do have one more question."

"What's that?"

"What are we going to do with that damned green recliner when we get to Richmond?" Tracey asked.

"Have you been talking with Marjorie?"

"No," Tracey smiled. "But I notice you haven't either."

"Right, so I guess that settles everything," Gif smiled.

"Not quite," Tracey said.

"What on earth do we have to discuss now?" Gif said.

"We don't have anything we have to discuss now," Tracey said. "But we do have one more issue to settle before we go looking for that nice little country house with a view of the James River."

"What's that?"

"Later."

"Now."

"OK. An old broad named Mavis Davis."

"I doubt that that we'll ever see Mavis again. Now tell me what you really think of our acting president."

"Based on a couple of briefings?"

"That will have to do."

"I think..." Tracey stalled. "I think I agree with that old cliché. The American people get the kind of president they deserve."

"You mean like the baby boomers deserved Bill Clinton?"

"Exactly."

"Adams was born eighty years ago. That makes him a product of the depression generation."

"Does that qualify him to deal with our economic problems?"

Gif shrugged.

"What do you really think?"

"Politicians are all the same."

About the Author

A graduate of Potomac State College, West Virginia University and a teaching assistant at the University of Wisconsin where he worked on his doctorate in American History, Robert L Skidmore spent thirty-five years in the foreign service of the United States whose assignments took him to tours in Iran, Greece, New Zealand, Laos, Malaysia, and Portugal. The author of twenty novels and now, long retired, Mr. Skidmore indulges in two lifelong passions, researching history and writing, both of which enable him to play with his computers and avoid travel at all cost.